The Inn at Argenteuil

by

Stephen John Walker

ISBN 978-0-9856293-8-0

This is a work of fiction. Names, characters, places,
and incidents either are the product of the author's
imagination or are used fictitiously. Any resemblance
to actual persons, living or dead, events, or locales is
entirely coincidental.

BJW Publications Salem, Oregon USA

Dedication

To Barbara—there are no words . . .

A special thanks to the Rarotonga Grumpy Old Men's Club. The members warmly welcomed me into their ranks, and the stories they told about life in the South Pacific were invaluable.

In memory of Captain Don Silk, Harbormaster, Avarua, the Cook Islands, a friend and inspiration.

Paris, 1937

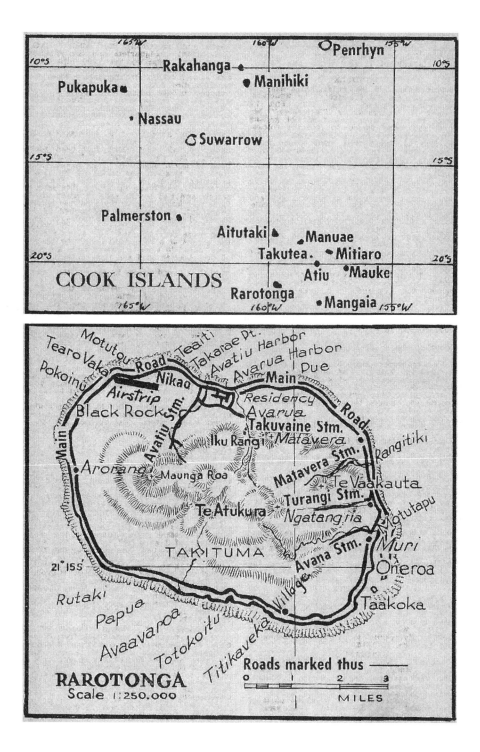

COOK ISLANDS

RAROTONGA
Scale 1:250,000

Roads marked thus ――――
0   1   2   3
MILES

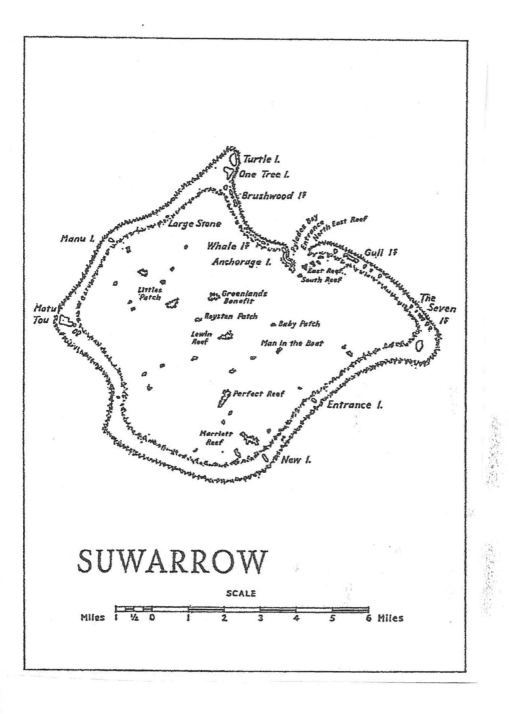

Turtle I.
One Tree I.
Brushwood I?
Gull I?
Pylades Bay
Entrance
North East Reef
Large Stone
Manu I.
Whale I?
Anchorage I.
East Reef
South Reef
Little Patch
Greenlands Benefit
Motu Tou
Royston Patch
Baby Patch
Lewin Reef
Man in the Boat
The Seven I?
Perfect Reef
Entrance I.
Marlott Reef
Naw I.

SUWARROW

SCALE

Miles 1 ½ 0   1   2   3   4   5   6 Miles

The Inn at Argenteuil

(Prologue)

"When this War's over," he said, "nobody is going to worry six months afterwards what you did or didn't do in the course of it. One month after it's ended, it will be forgotten. Everybody will want to forget it—it will be bad form to mention it. Within a year 'disbanded hero' will be selling matches in the gutter. No one likes an ex-soldier—if you've lost a leg, the more fool you!" *Ford Maddox Ford*

Gare de Lyon train station, Paris, December 2, 1922.
Six o'clock. Six more hours. Must find a mark! That Corsican bastard won't give me any more time. Must get the 10,000 francs before midnight.

Marcel Derouin, fond of his kneecaps, didn't relish the idea of them smashed by Carlo's thugs. Too fond of the horses, the money borrowed from Carlo he'd placed down on a sure thing at the race track in Auteuil—a sure thing that fell at the gate.

Marcel, a pickpocket and sneak thief by trade, sipped his *Pernod* at the station bar. He usually made a few francs panhandling, but Paris was full of veterans missing body parts, and his army pension didn't cover his debts. Sometimes he wished he had a whore for a girlfriend instead of a part-time waitress and Sorbonne student. But Constance loved him and pleased him. Pleased him and never asked what he did with his time, especially at night when he worked the boulevard St. Germain looking for drunk Americans. *Les Amis* seemed to be everywhere that year. While the French economy struggled to recover from the war, the American dollar was strong. Most *Amis* didn't have much money, but they could live cheaply. They filled the outdoor tables at the cafes along with other foreign artists and writers. This evening, wet, cold rain mixed with snow pushed the crowds inside. Marcel wished he'd worn his raincoat.

Marcel knew Paris. After his discharge from the army, with medals but minus an arm, he returned to the city. He worked for his father—a night bartender and pimp—at a bistro doing menial tasks: busing tables, cleaning toilets, and washing windows. With one exception, no one in the bistro staff helped Marcel when two hands were necessary. Many were immigrant Poles or Russians, always on the lookout for job opportunities for their friends and family members. Constance was that exception.

A student at the Sorbonne, Constance Gaultier aspired to be a teacher or maybe even a doctor. She made little money as a waitress. Competent, honest and efficient, she still didn't bring in the big tips. Tall, quite thin, and plain looking, she radiated little sex appeal. And she wouldn't sleep with the customers. Once, when Marcel spilled a tray of empty glasses and everyone in the bistro laughed at him, she helped him clean up the mess.

They became friends.

On her days off, they took long walks around the city. He'd show her his secret places—places he'd found when he lived on the streets before the war. She told him about her life at Argenteuil, a suburb of Paris on the Seine, where her parents ran a small inn.

Marcel told her about losing his arm, and how he'd been offered a job by the Corsican gangster, Carlo Pioletti, to pimp for him. Too much rough stuff for a man with one arm, so he worked at odd jobs in restaurants, hotels, cafes, and bistros, but always got fired because he couldn't handle luggage as a doorman or bellhop or mix drinks or wash dishes as a *plongeur*. Too many able-bodied veterans and refugees competed for the same menial jobs. French businessmen were only so patriotic.

They walked, they talked, they had sex. First in the apartment she shared with another waitress, later in a cheap apartment they rented on the rue Dragon. She was a virgin; he'd been seduced by one of his father's whores at fourteen. Sex with Constance he enjoyed. She never refused him. His dead arm made the missionary position uncomfortable, so a rear entry was normal. Constance didn't complain. She thought that was natural, since all the animals her parents raised at the inn did it that way. Sometimes they did it on a chair or the edge of their bed with Constance bouncing up and down on his lap. She liked that because she could see his face and his pleasure.

Fired after his father was killed in a knife fight with another pimp, Marcel went back to working the street.

He took daily long, brisk walks along the Seine and other parts of the city. That saved money from bus and Métro fares and kept him fit to sprint away from a hit on a mark gone bad. He knew the Métro and bus system intimately. And the train stations. He preferred to target tourists who hurried to catch a train—easier to escape that way. Once, he jumped on a train leaving the *Gare de Nord* to escape a pursuit and jumped off as the train slowly wound its way through the switching yards.

He knew the Métro before the war, but now he studied it—schedules, routes, stations, everything. And above at street level, in any station in the city or the suburbs, he knew where to hide or escape. When in doubt, he had his *médaille militaire* and *Croix de Guerre* in his pocket. Acting the war hero, he'd pin the medals on his coat and produce his disabled pension card. Most police were veterans and gave him a pass.

Marcel finished his drink and decided to go to the far end of Quay 4. The train from Strasbourg would arrive in five minutes. Travelers were boarding the 6:18 to Basel on Quay 5, and the crowds from both trains would jostle each other on the narrow platform. Good place to score, he thought. The week before, he'd lifted a wallet from an English tourist—five hundred francs, some English pounds, and a British passport. Goldbark, the Jew who ran a print shop on the rue Saint Marthe, paid good money for a British or American passport. Paris became a Mecca for Russian émigrés fleeing the Bolsheviks, and many needed papers to go to America or some part of the British Empire.

Marcel left the bar and headed for the quay, walking past the vendors who sold apples, cheese, Evian water, warm-wrapped sandwiches, and little flasks of brandy. Stopping halfway along the platform, he took a *Gauloise* from the pack in his shirt pocket and struck a match on a lamp post. He watched the crowd.

A red jacketed porter with a suitcase in each hand and a smaller green leather valise under one arm walked toward him, followed by a young woman. They passed and stopped at a second-class carriage. The porter set one suitcase down and opened the compartment door for the woman. Marcel watched the porter follow the woman into the compartment and place the suitcases on the overhead rack. He slid the valise under the seat. The woman tipped the porter and sat down.

* * *

Hadley Hemingway looked forward to getting out of Paris. She missed her husband. The weather was cold and wet. She'd just gotten over a rotten cold and wanted to enjoy some sun and snow in Switzerland. Living alone in a foreign city, even though her school-girl French served her well, was never comfortable. Her husband, Ernest, had been in Lausanne for almost two weeks covering an oil conference for the Hearst newspaper syndicate. He'd sent her a telegram telling her to join him there before they headed off to Chamby for the Christmas holidays. She knew he'd be pleased that she'd thought to bring his notebooks and manuscripts. He could write when the weather was no good for skiing or bobsledding. I'm thirsty, she thought. Better get something before the train leaves. Another train arrived on the next track as she opened the outside door and walked back toward the kiosks in the main part of the station.

Marcel watched the woman's back disappear into the press of passengers on the platform. He tossed his cigarette under the carriage, opened the compartment door and grabbed the leather valise from under the seat. Turning, and a dozen quick steps across the platform, he was in an empty compartment on the Strasbourg train. He elbowed his way along the corridor through several carriages before he stepped down into the crowd heading toward the Métro. Going down the steps to the subway station he forced himself not to run. A familiar rumbling beneath his feet told him the train was arriving. No shouting behind him. *Bon!* He jumped through the train doors before they were closed, took a seat next to a fat woman, and shoved the valise behind his legs. That was too easy, he thought. The valise wasn't fancy—old cracked leather with two straps and brass buckles. Heavy though. Must be something of value in it.

Marcel changed trains at Les Halles, got off at Saint Placide, walked the three blocks to rue Dragon, and turned into the courtyard. He slipped past the concierge without being seen; she'd hassle him about the rent again. He ran up the twelve flights of stairs to the fifth floor. In front of the door to their apartment he sat the valise down and knocked. No answer. Good, he thought. She's gone to work early or she's at the market. He searched for his key, found it, and opened the door. A rush of cold wind hit him in the face. *Merde!* She must have left the window open for the cat. *Where is the damn thing?* He hated the cat, a stray, but Constance fed it when it came in through the window, and that made her happy. He laid the valise on the kitchen table—their only table—and worked at the leather straps and buckles. He flipped open the lid.

Paper! Nothing but paper. Nothing! He turned the valise over and dumped the contents out on the table. *Just fucking paper!* That's why it was heavy— notebooks full of writing in English it looked like to him. Large envelopes full of typed papers. *Nothing. Nothing of value. Nothing here. Merde!* Marcel swept the valise and papers off the table.

Out on the street, he walked back toward the Métro station when he remembered his raincoat. *Merde!* Now he'd have to sneak past the concierge a third time. He turned around, froze, and then side-stepped into a doorway. A black Renault sedan had stopped in front of the apartment building. Marcel recognized this car—Carlo's. Two men got out of the car and entered the courtyard. The driver remained at the wheel, the engine running. Marcel peered around the corner of the doorway, his back up against the wet brick wall. The rain turned to snow. The two men came out of the building and stood for a moment looking up and down the street. One lit a cigarette while the second walked over to the car and talked to the driver. The Renault drove away. The two men crossed over to the other side of the street and waited under an awning in front of a bakery.

Snow piled up on Marcel's beret and the shoulders of his coat. His back was wet; he shivered from the cold. He stomped one foot and then the other. *Have to get somewhere, or go back for my raincoat. But if I move, they'll see me. This is just like the trenches.* His mind wandered back to that night in the bunker near Verdun, five years earlier. He'd been scrounging behind the lines in a nearby village and returned with three bottles of Vouvray, a block of goat cheese, and some chocolate. He presented these to his adjutant—it was the anniversary of the officer's marriage.

Marcel had always been good at scrounging. Raised by his pimp father and prostitute aunt, he left school at age twelve and lived on the streets of Paris. He panhandled the Avenue des Champs d'Elysees, picked pockets, and stole unwatched luggage in the train and Métro stations and food from the street market stalls. Caught by the police in 1914, he was given the choice of prison or the army.

Marcel enjoyed being a soldier—regular meals, clean clothes, boots that fit, a few francs in his pocket, and a warm, dry place to sleep. Resourceful and hard working, he was promoted to corporal in 1915. The battalion adjutant, impressed by Marcel's abilities and generosity, showed him the recommendation for promotion to sergeant he'd just written for the young Parisian.

A German barrage put an end to the celebration. A direct hit on the bunker killed six of Marcel's comrades. Unscathed, but buried in the rubble, Marcel dug his way out. He heard the adjutant crying out in pain and pulled him from the debris. He lifted the wounded officer in his arms and staggered down the trench toward the aid station. A German artillery shell exploded behind them, throwing both men down into the mud. A saucer-sized piece of shrapnel sliced off the top of the adjutant's head. Another severed Marcel's right arm above the elbow. He received the *médaille militaire* for bravery.

Marcel didn't see Constance come down the street from the other direction and enter the building.

"Mademoiselle, a moment, *s'il vous plait*," the concierge said from the little window of her office in the courtyard entrance.

"*Qui*, Madame Benoit. *Ca va?*"

"*Bien*. It is the matter of the rent, Mademoiselle."

"The rent, Madame? My friend said he paid it."

"I'm sorry, Mademoiselle, but that is not true. I've been watching for him today."

"He's not at home?"

"No, Mademoiselle. Two men went up to see him. They just came down and asked about him."

"Two men? What two men?"

"Two very rude men, Mademoiselle. They came in a big black car."

"I must go, Madame. I'll be late for work. Marcel will bring you the rent, I promise."

"Soon, Mademoiselle. Soon."

Constance climbed the stairs, her text books in a leather satchel in one hand, a cloth bag with bread, cheese, a bottle of cheap red wine, and fish heads—for the cat—in the other. At the door she put the bags down and took the key from her purse. She heard the cat calling from inside. She opened the door and stood there in surprise. There were papers scattered all over the floor. Snow blew in through the open window. The cat rubbed against her legs.

Marcel, what have you done now? I don't have time for this. She placed the groceries on the kitchen counter, walked across the room, and closed the window. In the kitchen she stripped the flesh from the fish heads and put them on a plate. Constance smiled as the cat attacked the morsels. She hung her coat on the back of the door and gathered up the papers, notebooks and folders off the floor. *What is all this? It's all in English.* She stuffed them in the leather valise on the table. In the bedroom Constance changed into a simple black dress. She put on her coat, locked the door to the apartment, and hurried down the stairs. She was late for work.

* * *

Something blocked the traffic on rue Dragon, and a large van stopped in front of the bakery. Marcel dashed out of the doorway and slipped around the corner. He ran down an alley and stopped under a fire escape at the back of his apartment building. He pushed some metal trash cans out of the way with his foot. He looked up. Not too far, he thought. He jumped up and grabbed the bottom rung of the sliding ladder. The ladder gave an inch or two. Damn thing must be rusted solid, he thought. The crusty bits on the rung tore the skin on his palm. He jumped up again, and this time the ladder came loose with a screech. He pulled it down far enough to get a foot on the bottom rung. The iron ladder was cold and wet. He stood there for a moment catching his breath. One rung at a time, he thought. Not too fast. He wrapped his arm around the ladder, reached up as far as he could and started to climb. Only a couple of meters to the bottom step of the fire escape. Half way up he cut his hand on a jagged edge of rust and lost his grip. Marcel fell backwards off the ladder and broke his neck on the edge of a trash can.

* * *

11:50—ten minutes to go, she thought. But where's Marcel? He's usually here by now to walk home with me. Constance looked out through the bistro's open door as the last customers left. Still snowing. She wished she had better shoes. Her feet would be wet and cold by the time she got home. She cleared off the tables and wiped out ashtrays; the empty wine bottles she dropped in a bin behind the bar. Where *is* Marcel? He'd never been late before. He didn't like her walking home alone that time of night.

"Where's your young man, Constance?" said Pascal, the bartender.

"I don't know." She put on her coat and pocketed her portion of the tips. She hesitated, and then said, "Pascal, could I get my weekly wages tonight? There's a problem with the rent, and I can't wait until Saturday night."

"Bad luck at the track?" Pascal knew about Marcel's habit; he scoured the racing forms while waiting at the bar before Constance finished her shift. Pascal slid the cashbox from under the bar and counted out some bills. He handed them to Constance. "A pretty young thing like you could make some extra money if you wanted to. Several of our regulars have asked me if you were available, if you know what I mean."

"I'm not that desperate, Pascal. We'll get by." She stuffed the francs in her purse and went out into the snow.

Constance wasn't surprised or shocked by his comment. She'd learned this was normal for women who worked late at the bars and bistros in this district. Her friend, Marla, who worked there during the day and evenings on weekends, warned her about it. It wasn't really a warning, but more like a suggestion about being careful. Constance knew Marla sometimes met customers after work and slept with them.

She wasn't a prude—Constance liked sex, enjoyed it, but only with Marcel, her first. Someday she wanted to marry and have children. She hoped that when she finished at the university she could find a position as a teacher—somewhere away from the city. But what would Marcel do? She hadn't thought that far ahead.

* * *

An ambulance pulled away from the curb and drove past as she neared the apartment building. A police car was parked in front. Constance turned into the courtyard and saw two policemen talking to the concierge. The old woman saw her and pointed.

"That's her," she said. "His girlfriend." The policemen turned to face Constance.

"Mademoiselle, you live with Marcel Deroin?" the older policeman asked. She nodded.

"We're sorry, Mademoiselle, but there's been an accident. We're afraid your friend is dead. A fall. His body was discovered in the alley."

"The alley? A fall? What do you mean? He can't be dead. There must be a mistake."

"No mistake, Mademoiselle. We have his papers."

Constance's stomach cramped, and she tasted bile rising in her throat. "Where is he? I must see him! Not Marcel. He can't be dead."

"I'm sorry, Mademoiselle, but he's been taken to the morgue."

Constance's vision blurred, her legs weakened. The older policemen had seen this reaction many times before; he took hold of her arm.

"Madame," he said to the concierge. "Let the young lady sit in your office for a minute, *s'il vous plait.*"

"Yes, of course. Come inside, Mademoiselle, and sit."

Constance sat at a table in the concierge's office. Her mind raced— *Marcel dead.*

"Here, Mademoiselle, drink this." The concierge handed her a glass of red wine. Constance's hand shook; as she raised the glass to her lips, a little wine spilled on her coat.

"Mademoiselle, we have some questions, and there are some forms to fill out," the policeman said. "Perhaps you can come around to the precinct in the morning." After a pause, Constance nodded. She sipped the wine. The policeman closed his notebook, and the cops left.

The concierge sat down at the table opposite Constance. "Now, Mademoiselle, I don't mean to be crass, and it is a difficult time for you, I know, but there is the matter of the rent."

"The what?" *You old bitch.* She knew she couldn't afford the apartment by herself. Marcel's pension helped with the rent and the food, when he didn't blow it on the horses. She'd have to quit school and hope to get more hours at the bistro. But without Marcel and school, why stay in Paris? She opened her purse and laid her wages on the table. The concierge picked up the notes and counted them.

"This is not enough, Mademoiselle. You *are* two weeks behind. Your key, *s'il vous plait.*"

"My key? Why do you want my key?"

"I can't let you back in your flat until the rent is complete. The owner is firm on that."

"What are you saying? What about my things: my clothes, my books?" Constance felt an urge to twist off the old woman's head like she'd done to chickens back home in Argenteuil.

"I'm sorry, Mademoiselle, but that's the way things are. No rent, no apartment. I'll call the police back."

"But where will I go? Where will I stay?" She stood, knocking over the chair.

"That's no concern of mine. I have my superiors to answer to." Madame Benoit held out her hand.

Constance reached into the pocket of her coat, took out the key and flung it at the old woman. "May you rot in hell, you old crone!"

Out on the sidewalk, Constance looked up and down the street. *Marla.* She lives just a few blocks away. She'll let me stay with her. I hope.

Constance had to beat on the door several times before her friend opened it a crack and peered out at her.

"Constance, *chérie*, what are you doing here?" Marla said. She opened the door wide. "Come in. Come in. You must be freezing. What has happened? Did that bum of a boyfriend kick you out?"

Constance wrapped both arms around her friend, laid her head on her neck and sobbed, "He's dead. Marcel's dead."

"*Merde!* Come, *chérie*. Come in and get warm. Your skin is like ice." Her friend led her into the small sitting room. Constance collapsed on the ratty sofa. Marla knelt in front of her and removed her wet shoes. She went into the bathroom and returned with a towel and bathrobe.

"Take off your wet things and put this on. Let me dry your feet."

Constance couldn't stop crying. Between sobs, she told Marla what had happened.

"That old bitch. Someone should cut her throat." Marla said. She stood. "I'll make some coffee. Or do you want something stronger?" Constance shook her head and lay down on the sofa. When Marla returned with the coffee, Constance was asleep.

* * *

Constance waited more than an hour at the police station before someone took her statement. There were many questions about Marcel she couldn't answer. She didn't realize until that moment how little she knew about her lover. He was a war hero who'd lost an arm and received a small pension from the government, but couldn't keep a job. His father had been killed in a fight with another pimp—Marcel had told her almost nothing about his past or his family. When they had a little extra money to spend, he said he'd won it at the race track.

A disabled veteran and a *Croix de Guerre* holder, the Ministry of Defense would arrange for Marcel's funeral. She'd be notified of the place and time. She gave Marla's address as her residence. Her friend said she could stay with her a while, but there would be times when Marla would want the flat to herself for an hour or two. Constance understood and would find a bistro where she could study.

* * *

The midday crowd at the bistro had thinned when Constance arrived. Word of Marcel's death was probably common knowledge on the street, she thought. Pascal caught her eye and pointed to the end of the bar. Carlo Pioletti stood there smoking a thin cigar and penciling in a racing form. Constance knew him to be a gangster, a pimp, and a loan shark. She sat on the stool next to him. He laid the paper on the bar and turned to look at her.

"*C'est bien.* We've never formally met," he said and extended his hand. "I'm Carlo. And you're Constance, Marcel's girlfriend. Sorry about your friend. I liked Marcel. He fought in the war. A hero of France. But that's all in the past. We must live in the present. Times are hard and money is tight. Marcel owed me money. I'm sure he spent some of that on you: gifts, meals at nicer places than this, some clothes, perhaps? Or even the rent on your apartment—I own that building, by the way. The point is, *ma chère*, I want my money. 15,000 francs. How are we going to solve this problem?"

"I have no money," she said. She knew where this conversation was heading.

"Perhaps we could find some more hours for you here, and some other activities. You're young and fresh. I have some associates who would enjoy spending time with you. Is that of interest?"

Constance knew immediately what she must do. "I have no clothes or my own place to live, Monsieur Pioletti."

"That is not a problem, Mademoiselle." Carlo put his hand inside his coat and brought out a wallet. He handed her 500 francs. "For some clothes. I'll provide you with a flat tomorrow. We'll meet here at ten in the morning to discuss the financial details."

"*Merci beaucoup,* Monsieur Pioletti. You are my savior." She leaned over and gave him a kiss on the cheek. *I'll have to leave Paris!*

* * *

Quite sure she wasn't followed when she got on the Métro the next morning, Constance changed trains twice and arrived in Argenteuil before noon. She walked along the river bank in a driving rain to her parents' hotel. Constance returned home a failure. She didn't care. Her parents had opposed her desire to get more education. They'd hoped she would stay on the north Seine, marry a solid local boy, and raise a large family. They didn't know about Marcel, and never would.

* * *

The concierge removed all of Constance's and Marcel's belongings to a hidden storage room. The door to the room was behind the tall armoire in her bedroom. A small room—she didn't know why it was there—barely large enough to stand up in, with no window, about three meters in length and two meters wide. But it was a good hiding place. Madame Benoit had evictees return before and try to steal back their belongings.

Part One: 1934-1943

1

"If you are lucky enough to have lived in Paris as a young man, then wherever you go for the rest of your life it stays with you for Paris is a moveable feast." *Ernest Hemingway*

Eisenstadt, Austria, June, 1934.
The young man sat at a table outside the café across from the *Domplatz*—his coffee cold, his sketch of Saint Martin's Cathedral almost finished. Drawings of buildings, store fronts, parks, and palaces of Eisenstadt—most in pencil, newer ones in charcoal—filled the notebook on the table. Today was market day in this eastern Austro-Hungarian city. Stalls offering fruits, vegetables, and baked goods lined the perimeter of the square. A military band, under a large gazebo in the center, played marches and Strauss waltzes. The aroma of grilled bratwurst made him hungry.

Klaus-Maria von Reichenhall wanted to be an artist. His father wanted him to be a lawyer or, at least, a teacher. The school year had ended, and he had passed the exams at the top of his class and would enter the university at Linz in the fall. His parents were so proud of him, and since he agreed to read law and literature, they acquiesced and would give him the money to spend time in Paris that summer. "A fine opportunity for him to practice his French and maybe some English also," said Siegfried, his father.

Siegfried von Reichenhall was a professor of foreign languages at the Eisenstadt *collegium* and a decorated veteran of the Austro-Hungarian Army. He served with the Esterházy regiment on the Italian front during the Great War. There he met and married Klaus's mother in 1915. Italian was a second language to Maria von Reichenhall, so Klaus and his siblings grew up speaking both it and German, and others. In the Reichenhall household, each day's activities were conducted in a different language: Monday French, Tuesday English, Wednesday Latin, Thursday Italian, Friday Greek, and Saturday Magyar, which was important, because this part of Austria had been Hungarian until 1925, and Magyar was still the *lingua franca* of the markets in Eisenstadt. Sunday was the only day when German was allowed, but even on that day the von Reichenhall children were encouraged to interject other languages into the conversation whenever they liked. Latin was a prerequisite for entry into the university, but languages came easily to Klaus, and he enjoyed trying out the ancient Roman tongue with *Pfarrer* Benedict, their priest and family confessor.

Fit and healthy from a regimen of cross-country skiing during the winter months, and hiking and mountain climbing the rest of the year, the eighteen-year-old—a bit over six feet tall with short, curly blond hair, and remarkably handsome and mature looking—turned the heads of not a few passing *fräuleins* and the occasional *hausfrau*.

Klaus laid his charcoal pencil down and took a sip of coffee. Cold. He frowned. Waited too long. He sensed someone behind him. The waiter, he thought, wants me to order another coffee. A slight hint of lavender changed his mind.

"*Grüss Gott,* Mattie."

"How did you know it was me?" She pulled out a chair and sat close to him.

"*L'eau de Provence.*"

"What's that?"

"An area in France where they grow the lavender scent you're wearing. How are you, *liebchen?*"

"*Gut. Vielen dank.* But I'll miss you."

"It's only for the summer, Mattie."

"Will you sleep with other women while you're in Paris?"

That surprised him. "*Never.* I am yours only."

"But three months *is* a long time, and some men need it. And you *are* an attractive man. I've heard those French girls are very aggressive."

"They could never compare to you, *liebchen.*"

"I will miss you *so much.*" She leaned closer and rubbed a breast against his arm.

"*That much?* What a wonderful idea. Perhaps a going away present is in order. Anyone home this afternoon?"

"No. Just my empty bed. We should go fill it."

* * *

Klaus always enjoyed watching Mattie undress. It first happened, almost by accident, after the summer fest the previous year. They drank more wine than usual. It gave him the courage to tell her that he loved her and wanted to marry her. They walked back to her home; her parents were still at the celebration and wouldn't return for some time. Neither said anything—they kissed, they touched, they were naked in her bedroom. Since then it had been a regular event whenever they could be alone for an hour or two. This would be the last time for months.

The afternoon sunlight streamed through the wall-to-ceiling windows of Mattie's bedroom, bathing the naked lovers on her bed.

"Those French girls would like this. I don't think they will let you be." She rolled over onto her side and ran a soft finger down into his blond pubic hairs.

"Don't be silly. Don't think about. I'm yours. And I don't want anyone else. Why would I?" He fondled her breasts.

"Good." She gently stroked his limp manhood and felt it stiffen. "Again?"

2

Paris.
Klaus enjoyed the overnight train ride to Paris. Comfortable in his first
class compartment, he dozed and daydreamed most of the time. Visions of
Mattie's breasts appeared often in his thoughts and kept his mind off of the
firm bottom of the young Swiss woman who pushed the concession trolley
along the train car's corridor.

* * *

Klaus fell in love with Paris. The city was alive and vibrant, not like staid
old Eisenstadt. His home town had one claim to fame—Franz Joseph
Haydn had been the *kapellmeister* at *Schloss Esterházy* for thirty years. Before
becoming the administrative capital of the *Burgenland,* the city had been in
the Hungarian part of the dual Austria-Hungary monarchy since 1867.
After its defeat in 1918, Austria-Hungary had been divided, and the eastern
Burgenland provinces, including Eisenstadt, became part of Austria.

* * *

His first night Klaus stayed in a hotel on rue de Rennes. During the taxi
ride from the train station, he asked the driver to give him a tour: the Tour
Eiffel, Notre Dame, Arc de Triomphe, Champ-Elysées, and the Louvre.
After a light dinner in the hotel dining room, Klaus exchanged a few
Austrian shillings for francs—tomorrow he would open an account with
Credit Suisse and deposit the draft from his family's bank in Eisenstadt. He
asked the desk clerk for directions to *La Coupole* on Boulevard du
Montparnasse. Klaus knew this Parisian landmark, noted for its literary
and artist clientele, from his studies of the city. He then went out into the
streets of Paris. The sky was clear—perfect for his first excursion into the
City of Light.

Following the clerk's instructions, Klaus walked down rue de Rennes
until it intersected with Boulevard du Montparnasse and turned left.
Traffic on the tree-lined boulevard—taxis, street cars, and open-topped
omnibuses—was heavier than he expected, and the sidewalks crowded;
hard to believe that Europe was suffering from a world-wide depression. It
seemed like all of Paris was out enjoying the warm summer evening. He
passed *Le Select,* another famous café before arriving at *La Coupole.* The
café's street tables were full, so he pushed his way through the standing-
room-only crowd into the bar and ordered a glass of *vin ordinare.* Observing
the packed tables and the passing multitudes, Klaus noticed that most of
the young people—two or three with sketch books might be artists, he
thought—were not dressed as well as he. He decided to do something
about that.

He finished his wine and headed down the boulevard. I want to go over
to Boulevard Saint Germain, he reminded himself. The hotel clerk told
him to continue along the Boulevard Montparness until he came to *La*

Closerie des Lilas. At that corner turn left again, follow Boulevard Saint Michel until it crossed Saint Germain. The clerk had provided him with a small map of Paris—he even marked out the route, but Klaus didn't want to pull it out of his pocket and look the tourist. If he got confused, he'd use his French. He stopped on the sidewalk outside *Café La Rotonde,* almost next door to *La Coupole,* and looked back up the Boulevard Montparnasse in amazement. *This is paradise. It's going to be wonderful summer.*

La Closerie des Lilas, easily recognizable by the lights and music, was as crowded as the other cafés. Klaus considered stopping for another glass of wine but decided against it. I have to pace myself this first night, he thought. I have all summer. He walked up Boulevard Saint Michel past the *Jardin du Luxembourg* and its palace. Klaus paused and stared at the well-lit structure. It's much like the Esterházy palace back home, he thought, and promised himself to sketch it soon.

Along Boulevard Saint Germain, he passed two other famous cafés—*Les Deux Magots* and *Café de Flore*—until he came to rue de Rennes again. Returning to his hotel, Klaus saw a number of women, some alone, some in pairs, standing outside the entrances of small hotels and *pensions.* The infamous Paris prostitutes, he thought. One pair stepped away from the building and blocked his way.

"My, aren't you the pretty fellow. Care for a little fun, Monsieur?"

"*Es tut mir leid, Fräulein.* Sorry, Mademoiselle, I'm too tired and have no money," he lied.

"No money? You are foreign, *n'est-ce pas?* German, no?"

Out of the corner of his eye, Klaus saw a man wearing a fedora and dark grey raincoat standing in the shadow of a doorway. *I must get away from here.*

"*Ja. Ich bin Berliner. Mais* I spent my last *sou* at the *Deux Magots.*"

"Nicely dressed German tourists like yourself always have money. We'll give you a special price for two at the same time."

Klaus looked past the two whores and saw his rescue approaching—two *gendarmes* walked toward them. The man in the doorway whistled softy. The women turned, saw the policemen, and stepped away. Klaus greeted the officers and continued on. He wondered if the hotel bar would still be open—he needed a drink. The hotel's doors were locked, so Klaus rang the bell for the night porter. A white-haired man in the hotel's livery opened a door and greeted him.

"*Bonsoir,* Monsieur Reichenhall. *C'est bien passé votre soirée?*"

"*Oui, Monsieur.* Very enjoyable. And educational. Any chance of getting a drink?"

"I'm sorry, Monsieur, but the bar is finished for the evening," he said as he handed Klaus his room key. "But I have a bottle of brandy under the counter, which I'd be pleased to share with you."

"*Bien, Grand-père.* That would be perfect." As the porter filled two small glasses, Klaus related his encounter with the ladies of the night.

"You were very fortunate, Monsieur. Those animals prey on foreign tourists, especially during these hard times. Many have received injuries."

"*Merci beaucoup* for the brandy," Klaus said and placed a five franc piece on the counter.

Up in his room, he mused while he undressed. *Won't sleep much tonight—too excited. I'm really in Paris.* But he was fast asleep as soon as his head hit the pillow.

* * *

The next morning, after a coffee and croissant breakfast in his room, and before looking for an apartment, Klaus stopped at the *Crédit Suisse* bank, completed his business, and withdrew 500 francs. He walked to the street market on rue du Buci. There, he bought from a pushcart vendor some used, but clean clothing, a tattered black beret, and a pair of scruffy Wellingtons. Klaus wanted to blend in with the artist community and knew his new traveling clothes would make him stand out. In a secondhand shop, he bought a worn cardboard suitcase. Later, the hotel desk clerk had a surprised look on his face when Klaus went out again wearing his new wardrobe.

He found an inexpensive studio apartment at *Pension Benoit* on rue Dragon.

"You are a foreigner, *n'est-ce pas,* Monsieur?" Madame Benoit, the concierge, said after showing Klaus the apartment.

"*Oui*, Madame. Austrian. From Eisenstadt."

Madame Benoit, hard of hearing, didn't catch the "from" and said, "So, Monsieur Eisenstadt, how long will you stay?"

Klaus thought to correct her but didn't. Von Reichenhall may seem a fancy name to her and others, so he would be known simply as Klaus Eisenstadt. "To the end of the summer, Madame."

"Fifty francs a week, meals, not lunch, included. Two weeks in advance, *s'il vous plaît.*"

Klaus took a new hundred franc note from his wallet and handed it to her. She raised it to the light and felt its crispness.

"Don't see one of these that often, from the usual occupants, that is," she said.

"I just made it this morning," he said smiling and wondering if she had a sense of humor.

"That's not funny, Monsieur. I've had bad money tried on me before. And your passport, *s'il vous plaît.* I'll return it in the morning after the police visit."

"The police, Madame?" He handed her his passport. She didn't look inside it. *Perhaps she can't read,* he thought. *Or doesn't care.* "Why the police?"

"They show up each evening and write down the names of those who have come and gone."

* * *

Some years ago, Carlo Pioletti, the owner, instructed Paulette Benoit, the aging concierge, to convert one of the courtyard apartments into a lounge and dining room for the occupants. Also, he told her to reserve the other ground floor apartments for use by his prostitutes and their pimps. He kept the rents low to attract an artistic clientele—profit came from the ready availability of drugs and other services.

Filled with students, other artists, and writers—most didn't have much money—the *pension* met all of Klaus's needs: two meals a day, close to Métro stations and bus routes, and a wonderful view of the city's rooftops from his fifth floor window. The room was bare bones: a lumpy single bed, night stand, and lamp with a very weak bulb—which he replaced—a sink, mirror, wardrobe, table, and two chairs. The bomb-site toilet was in a closet at the end of the hall, and he had to go down four flights to bathe in a communal facility. Fortunately, the bath was adjacent to the common room, so he could chat with other occupants while waiting his turn for the sometimes-hot water. All this was a bit more primitive than Klaus was accustomed to at home, but he wasn't put off by any of it. He knew an artist's life in Paris would be Spartan, and he wanted to absorb as much of it as he could.

That afternoon, Klaus checked out of his hotel room. When he paid his bill, he reserved a room for the night before his departure back to Eisenstadt. He also asked the elderly desk clerk to store his leather suitcase filled with travel clothes and return train ticket in the hotel's luggage room. The clerk shook his head in disbelief as he watched the young Austrian leave the hotel dressed in what *he* considered to be one step above rags.

Klaus decided to never let on that he had a substantial allowance— better to blend in if they thought he was as poor as they were. His change of wardrobe was a start, and he stopped shaving.

His first evening at the *pension*, Klaus met two fellow artists at dinner: Antoine, a Dadaist, and Estéban, a disciple of Picasso.

"Klaus . . . Klaus Eisenstadt," he said in answer to their query.

"German?" Antoine asked. "You're not a Nazi, are you?" He was about to pour some red wine from a carafe into Klaus's glass.

"No, Austrian." He nodded toward his empty glass. Antoine filled it. "*Merci.*"

"Well, Klaus, the Austrian, what do you think about Hitler?" Antoine said.

"I don't think about him at all. Why should I?" *Father thinks Hitler can bring the German people back to their rightful place in Europe. I don't agree.*

"He's a pig. A short funny-looking pig," Estéban said.

"All of Europe should be thinking about Hitler *and* that Italian Fascist Mussolini," Antoine said.

"Back home in *España* we have no *Fascistas*. Not yet anyways," Estéban said.

After dinner they invited him to join them for a drink at the Bistro Bénaud, around the corner and down the street from the *pension*.

"*Bonsoir*, Pascal. *Ça va?*," Antoine greeted the man behind the bar. "A bottle of your cheapest, *s'il vous plaît.*"

Another man came out from a hallway next to the bar, and brought the wine and three glasses to the table. "Something to eat this evening, gentlemen?"

"No, Monsieur Schlein. Just the plonk," Estéban said. "Meet our new friend. A fellow artist. Klaus . . . Klaus . . . What was it? Oh, right. Eisenstadt."

Klaus stood and shook hands with the owner. "Schlein? Are you German, Monsieur?"

"No. The family is originally from Alsace. We've been here since before the turn of the century. But your name . . . Eisenstadt was it? German?"

"Also no, Monsieur Schlein. Austrian from the *Burgenland.*"

"Another starving artist staying around the corner at the house of ill repute," Antoine said.

"Will you be in Paris long, Monsieur Eisenstadt?" Schlein asked.

"Just for the summer, I'm afraid. And please call me Klaus, Monsieur Schlein."

"Well, enjoy your visit, Klaus. Come for a meal. Francine, Pascal's wife," he nodded toward the bartender, "is an excellent cook."

"*Merci beaucoup,* Monsieur Schlein. Perhaps I will." Klaus looked around the interior of the bistro and saw several paintings. He got up from his chair and took a close look at the paintings. "Béraud . . . Béraud. Wasn't he a famous artist from before the war?" he asked his friends.

"*Oui,* but not that one," Antoine said and pointed to a painting of a bridge. "That's a Monet. A copy, *bien sûr.*"

Klaus returned to the table as three young people joined them—two girls and a man.

"Another bottle, Pascal. Champagne. We're celebrating," the man said.

"Why the celebration, Jean-Pierre?" Estéban asked.

"Why else, peasants? I've sold a painting."

"Who this stranger?" asked one of the girls. She was petit, dark-skinned with short black hair under a purple beret.

"*Pardon moi, mes amis,*" said Antoine. "This Klaus from Austria. Klaus, this is Isabelle, Charlotte, and Jean-Pierre, a not-so-starving artist, at the moment, *n'est-ce pas.*"

"Welcome to Paris, Klaus," Isabelle said. "On holiday?"

"*Oui et non.* I came to paint, but just for the summer. *Pardon,* Mademoiselle, but I hear a trace of accent . . . Spanish?"

"No, Monsieur, I am from Lisbon."

"*Ah oui.* Visiting?"

"No, I'm a student at the Sorbonne."

"*Tres bien.* What discipline?"

"Literature, especially the writers of what Gertrude Stein calls 'The Lost Generation'."

"I'm not familiar with that term . . . 'The Lost Generation'?"

"Those writers who came to Paris after the war: Joyce, Hemingway, Pound, Fitzgerald, William Carlos Williams, and many others."

"I would like to read some of these authors. Can you recommend a good bookshop?"

Jean-Pierre fidgeted in his chair and kept looking at the clock behind the bar. Not being the center of attention seemed to bother him.

"Paris is full of good bookshops, Klaus, *mon chérie,*" said Isabelle. "If you want English editions . . . you do read English?" Klaus nodded. "Then you must visit Shakespeare and Company on the rue de l'Odéon. An American, Sylvia Beach, is the proprietor. It specializes in books in English."

"Isn't she the one who published Joyce's *Ulysses?*" Estéban asked.

"*Oui, mon ami.* She is a wonderful woman for an American." She smiled at Klaus. "Would you like to go there tomorrow? I'd be happy to show you the way. It's a short walk from here."

"*Oui,* Isabelle, I would like that very much, if it's not too much trouble."

"No trouble, *mon chérie.* Say after luncheon at 1:00, here?" She reached across the table and touched his hand.

Jean-Pierre knocked over his chair when he stood. "Come. Let's go to *Les Deux Magots.* I need to be with people . . . lots of people. Join us, *amis?*"

"*Jamais,* too rich for me," Antoine said. Estéban agreed.

"Klaus?" Isabelle asked with a tilt to her head and raised eyebrows.

"Another time, perhaps." He didn't want to abandon his new friends.

She frowned and shrugged. Jean-Pierre and his entourage left the bistro.

"That painting." He pointed. "Do you know where it was done?" Klaus asked.

"The Monet? *Oui,* at Argenteuil," Antoine said.

"Which is where?"

"North of the city on the Seine."

"I think I'll go visit this Argenteuil."

"If you like Monet's work the Louvre is full of them. Too impressionistic for me . . . too old fashioned for my tastes."

"I think Isabelle fancies you, Klaus," Estéban said.

"Why is that?"

"We've both tried to get it on with her . . . with no success."

"Careful, Klaus, she's real man eater," Antoine said, and they both laughed.

3

Klaus ate lunch at the Bistro Béraud while waiting for Isabelle. Once again he looked closely at the Monet. Wish I could paint like that, he thought. It was past 1:00 when Isabelle joined him.

"*Bonjour,* Klaus. *Ça va?*"

"*Bonjour,* Isabelle, I was beginning to think you had forgotten."

"*Ah oui,* I am a bit late, but this is Paris. We're not as punctual as you Germans."

"I'm not German. I'm Austrian."

"Is there much difference?"

"I truly hope so. Would you like something to drink . . . some lunch?"

"Not now. Maybe later. I have eaten."

As they strolled toward the bookshop, Klaus was surprised when she took his arm and walked close enough for hip-to-hip contact. He remembered Antoine's warning.

"Is there someone waiting for you back in Austria?"

"Perhaps. Why do you ask?"

She pulled him closer. "Just curious. I would find it hard to believe that a handsome man like you wouldn't have."

They turned a corner into the rue l'Odéon. "Sylvia Beach's shop is just there." She pointed. "That's Adrienne Monnier's shop across the street . . . another fine bookshop."

A bird-like woman with wavy brown hair stood outside Shakespeare and Company smoking a cigarette and enjoying the afternoon sunshine. She smiled as they approached.

"*Bonjour,* Mademoiselle Beach.," Isabelle said.

"*Bonjour,* Isabelle. Who's your friend?"

"Klaus, ah . . . ."

"*Bonjour,* Mademoiselle. Klaus Eisenstadt." He offered his hand.

"Klaus is *Austrian,*" Isabelle said. "Don't call him a German." She laughed.

Sylvia put out her cigarette and took his hand. "*Bonjour,* Klaus. First time in Paris?"

"*Oui,* Mademoiselle Beach. Just for the summer."

"Sylvia, please. Do come inside." She led them into the shop. Klaus was most impressed by what he saw—book shelves lined the walls, but the central room of the shop was like a parlor with good light from the windows. Heavy old armchairs were scattered around the room. Autographed photos of what he assumed were authors adorned one wall. A small stove could provide heat. Not at all like the staid, well organized, and boring bookshops he frequented back home.

"Do you read English, Klaus?"

"Oh *oui,* Madam . . . Sylvia."

"What may I offer you?"

"I'm not sure. I've never read anything by an American author. What would you recommend?"

Sylvia pulled a book off the shelf. "Start with this," she said, and handed him a copy of *Farewell to Arms*. "It's brilliant. His work has changed the way fiction is written. He's also a good friend."

"Does he," he looked at the cover, "Hemingway, live in Paris?"

"No, in Key West . . . Florida. In the States."

"What's it about?" Klaus asked.

"It's a novel, as you can see. A love story . . . a tragic love story. It's about a young American in the Red Cross ambulance service in Italy during the last war."

Klaus considered mentioning that his father has served in the Italian Alps during the war but decided not to. "How much is it, Sylvia?"

"Would you like to join our Company?"

"Company? I don't understand."

"Shakespeare and Company is also a lending library." She looked at his clothes. "Books are expensive. For a small subscription, you may borrow one or two books . . . returning them after a fortnight or when you're finished with them, *bien sûr*."

"*Oui*, I would like to join your 'Company'."

"I'll get your cards." She went to a desk and returned with two cards. On the larger of the two he wrote his name, address, date, and amount of the subscription. She wrote his name on the smaller card and handed it to him.

"For your second book I recommend something by Joseph Conrad." She went to a shelf and returned with a volume. "He was a Polish seaman who travelled the world. Even though not his native tongue, he wrote in English. His works brought him great fame before the war."

"Why would I want to read him?"

"To compare the two, and see how fiction has changed in the past decades. Some say Hemingway is the father of modern fiction."

"What do you think, Isabelle?" She had been browsing the shelves and looked at the Conrad.

"*Victory*. I haven't read that, but I have read Hemingway. Trust Sylvia. She knows her authors."

"*Merci beaucoup*, Isabelle. Anything for you today?"

"Not today. I'm up to my knickers in D.H. Lawrence. Maybe next time." She took his arm. "Let's go to the Luxembourg and watch the regatta." Sylvia laughed.

"Regatta?" he asked.

"Come on. You'll see. *A bientôt*, Sylvia."

"Nice to meet you, Klaus. Hope to see you often."

They left Shakespeare and Company and went along rue l'Odéon to the *Jardin du Luxembourg*.

"I live just back there on rue de Condé." She said nodding to the right as they crossed the street into the park. "I love this part of Paris."

"I know this park. I passed by here the other night." He looked up at the Palace. "Wish I'd brought my sketchbook. Now, what's this about a regatta?"

"There . . . the Luxembourg regatta." She pointed to the *Grand Bassin* in front of the palace. Dozens of children cavorted around its perimeter watching their miniature sailboats tack back and forth across its surface. "They rent the sailboats from a man for a few francs and let the wind do the rest." The vendor with his cart of sailboats was on the edge of the pond.

"This is magical," he said. "I must come back . . . must, to paint this. Thank you for showing me the Luxembourg regatta." They watched the boats come to the edge of the pond, where the children pushed them off again with a short stick.

"What happens if the wind stops?"

She thought for a moment. "I have no idea. I've never seen that happen. Perhaps they wade out and rescue them. Don't think it's very deep."

"Next time I'll bring my paints and sketchbook. I must remember to keep them with me as I explore the city."

"Let's sit here." She pulled him to an empty bench. "What do you paint, Klaus?"

"I hope to follow the impressionists like Monet, Manet, Pissarro, and Renoir."

"That's not very modern, is it?"

"No, it isn't. I don't care for most of the modern works . . . too abstract, too radical. Even Piccaso. I prefer his early watercolors. Call me old fashioned, but I like to know what I'm looking at. And I love their use of color, light, and shadows." He gestured with his arm. "This would be a wonderful subject . . . the park I mean."

"What will be your first attempt?"

"Do you know Argenteuil?"

"No. Is it in the city?"

"No, but close. On the Seine just outside."

She placed a hand on his knee. "I think I'd like a glass of wine. You?"

"*Mais oui.* Where shall we go?"

"*La Closerie des Lilas.* It's near the other side of the park."

They walked along a tree-lined path through the park. To their left children flew kites. Women pushed their urchins in prams, and couples walked hand-in-hand, often exchanging kisses. Older men, with shouts of glee or dismay, played *pétanque.*

The outside tables at the bistro were not filled, so they sat in the last of the afternoon sun.

"Don't you have lectures to attend?" Klaus asked.

"Not unless I want to."

"How can you be a student at the Sorbonne and not go to lectures?"

"The lectures are not mandatory, *mon chérie.* We're given a reading list and a schedule for the exams."

"Strange system, it seems to me."

"Many students have to work just to survive."

"And you?"

"My father provides me with an adequate allowance, so I can spend my time reading and enjoying the delights of this wonderful city. He was a student here before the last war."

Dark clouds began to appear over the rooftops from the west. The temperature dropped a few degrees. "It's going to rain," he said. "Shall we go inside?"

She touched his knee. "I'd rather go to my flat. I'll cook you a fine supper, and you can look at my . . . books."

They hurried through the Luxembourg, and the rain came as they arrived at her apartment building. When they entered her flat, she turned and kissed him, her tongue exploring every corner of his mouth.

The next morning before he left, Isabelle dressed only in a man's shirt—not his—brought him a tray with coffee and croissants.

"I've never had breakfast in bed before."

"This is just the first course." She sat on the edge of the bed and removed the shirt.

* * *

On the train to Argenteuil he reflected on the previous night's experience. Sex with Mattie had always been wonderful, but with Isabelle it was like running a marathon. She was very experienced and demanding; he didn't get much sleep.

Klaus shouldered his artist's bag as he left the train station and walked along the boulevard Saint-Denis to the river. He stopped on the promenade between the highway and railroad bridges. This is perfect, he thought. West of the highway bridge he watched boats sailing on the boat basin and a barge in the main channel. *Just like I imagined. The light is wonderful here. I must catch both the morning and evening contrasts. Maybe there's a hotel when I can do that.*

East of the railroad bridge he found an ideal place on the rue Pierre Guienne—Hotel Gaultier. A bell over the door announced his arrival. The main room had two large tables with chairs around each. A short bar with stools occupied one corner. Paintings and photographs of the river and local scenes adorned the walls. A tall wide wooden cabinet with glass doors and filled with china, glassware, and porcelain figures rested against the wall. There was an open window at the back of the room. Klaus heard the clucking of chickens and the snort from a pig outside the window. A staircase to the left led to the upper floors. Through a doorway at the base of the stairs came a middle-aged woman. She wiped her hands on her apron.

"*Bonjour,* Monsieur. How may I be of service?"

"*Bonjour,* Madame. You have rooms for guests?"

"*Bien sûr,* Monsieur. That is our business."

"Of course. Stupid of me to ask."

She tilted her head. "You are not French, Monsieur?"

"No, Austrian."

"On holiday?"

"I'm an artist. I came here to paint."

"Many do." She told him the cost of a room and looked at his clothes. "In advance."

"*Bien sûr*, Madame. And meals?" *My poor artist façade is working.*

"Breakfast is included. A bit extra for the evening meal."

A tall, thin, plain-looking younger woman entered from a door leading to the back. She carried a package wrapped in butcher paper. "*Bonjour*, Mama. *Bonjour*, Monsieur," she said and went into the other room.

"Our daughter, Constance," the woman said. "Now, Monsieur, would you like a room tonight?"

"Not tonight, Madame. I need to go back to the city and get some things. I'll return tomorrow. I'd like a room and dinner for at least two nights, perhaps more." He paid for the two nights. Klaus spent the remainder of the day sketching various scenes along the river.

The following day, with his cardboard suitcase packed with a change of clothes and toiletries, he returned to the inn at Argenteuil. He informed Madame Benoit he would be away for a day or two, maybe more.

4

Paris, 1937.

Klaus and Mattie arrived at *Gare de l'est* after an overnight trip from Vienna. He hailed a taxi. The newlyweds went to a posh hotel on the boulevard Saint Germaine within walking distance to Shakespeare and Company and the Bistro Bénaud.

"But the expense, Klaus?" she said.

"It's our honeymoon, *liebchen*, and it's Paris." Klaus wasn't about to take his bride to *Pension Benoit*. Hard rain drenched the streets of Paris. They spent the day in bed. Their love making planted the seed of a first child. Hungry and thirsty, they dressed and left the hotel. The rain had stopped.

"First, I want to show you the Luxembourg regatta." They walked along rue Touron to the park, but the rain had chased away the sailors. "We'll come back tomorrow. Now, we must visit a bookshop, and then to my favorite bistro. We may meet some of my old friends." He hoped Isabelle wouldn't be there. "Madame Culon . . . Francine . . . makes the world's best *cassoulet*."

"What's a *cassoulet?*"

"It's a Parisian stew made with duck, sausage, herbs, and lots of beans. You'll love it."

"Sounds wonderful."

"Before we eat I want to introduce you to Sylvia Beach. She's an American who runs my favorite bookshop."

Near Shakespeare and Company, Klaus noticed a crowd gathered on the sidewalk. He wondered what was happening. Sylvia Beach stood outside welcoming people as they entered her shop.

"*Bonsoir*, Madame Beach . . . Sylvia," Klaus said. The bookshop owner raised an eyebrow and looked like she was trying to match the face with a voice. She grinned.

"Klaus? Yes, it is you. *Bonsoir*. I didn't recognize you without the beard. Thank you for the postcards from Austria. What a beautiful country. And this must be Mattie. *Willkommen* to Paris, Mattie." She gave both a kiss on each cheek. "When did you arrive?"

Before Klaus could answer or translate for Mattie, Sylvia looked over his shoulder and her smile increased.

"*Pardon*, Klaus, a moment, please," she said.

Klaus stepped aside as Sylvia reached out to hug a big man with a bushy mustache. They kissed.

"I've never done a public reading before, Sylvia," he said in English.

"You'll do fine, Hem." She escorted him through the crowd. The newlyweds followed.

Sylvia led him to a small table. On the wall behind was a photo of the man, but much younger. Klaus and Mattie stood at the back of the crowded, smoke-filled room.

"That's Ernest Hemingway," Klaus said. "I read his books and short stories when I was here during the summers. He's a very famous American author."

Hemingway sat at the table and pulled printed papers from his coat pocket. He began reading, slowly at first, laying each page face down on the table as he finished it. After three or four chapters, he stopped, laid the remaining papers down, looked up. The crowd's applause filled the room.

"Was it good?" Mattie asked.

"Wonderful, *Wunderbar!*"

"I wish I understood English."

Hemingway was swamped by people shaking his hand and offering copies of his books to autograph.

"Klaus, I'm starving," she said. They slipped through the crowd and out the door.

The Bistro Bénaud wasn't crowded. Two of Klaus' friends sat a table nursing glasses of wine. He and Mattie went to the table. Antoine and Estéban, with questions on their faces, looked up at them.

"Monsieur?" Antoine asked.

"Don't you recognize me, Antoine . . . Estéban?"

"It's Klaus, the good German!" Antoine jumped up and greeted Klaus with a peck on his cheeks. "Your beard, *mon ami,* you shaved it off." Estéban stood and Klaus shook hands with both.

"*Mais oui,* Antoine." He ran a hand over his chin. "A new look for my bride."

His friends looked at Mattie. "Bride? You're married?" Estéban asked.

"*Oui, mes amis.* This is Mattie. She doesn't speak French." She shook hands with the two artists.

"When was the big event, Klaus?" asked Antoine.

"Last week. We're in Paris for our honeymoon." He translated for Mattie.

The bartender came to the table. "Something to drink, Monsieur?"

"*Bonsoir et bien sûr,* Monsieur Culon. Do you recognize me?"

Pascal Culon looked at him sideways. "*Oui.* Klaus Eisenstadt." He noticed Klaus's fine clothes. "Not the starving artist now, are you?"

"*Non,* Monsieur Culon. I'm a student at the university in Linz." He turned to Mattie. "We're on our honeymoon."

"You must celebrate then. How about some champagne?"

"*Oui,* Monsieur, and fresh glasses for my friends. And one for yourself. You must join us."

Pascal returned with the wine and glasses.

"Is Madame Culon's *cassoulet* on the menu this evening?"

"*Bien sûr,* Monsieur Klaus."

"Have you eaten, *mes amis? Non?* We'll have four, Monsieur." He translated all this for Mattie.

"*Tout de suite, mais* first we must have a toast to the newlyweds."

When Madame Culon brought their meals, Klaus stood and introduced Mattie, who was a bit taken back when the cook kissed her.

"I'm not sure I care for all this kissing from strangers," she said to her husband in German.

"Enjoy it, *liebchen*. The French only do it if they like you."

"Your painting is still in its place of honor, Klaus," Francine Culon said and pointed to the far wall. His rendering of the bridge at Argenteuil hung next to a Monet print of the same scene.

"What did she say?" Mattie asked.

"I'll show you after we finish." Klaus ordered more champagne and coffee for all.

"Estéban, how have you been? Missed you last summer. Antoine told me you had gone back to Spain. Were you involved in the fighting?"

"*Non, mon ami.* I'm an artist . . . a man of peace. Unfortunately, I fear my homeland will fall to the Fascists, no thanks to the help from your German friends."

"They are not *my* friends, Estéban. I have no love for Hitler and his Nazis."

"What'd he say, Klaus?" Mattie could tell by his facial expression and tone of voice that something was wrong. He translated.

"Remember Isabelle, Klaus?" Antoine asked trying to change the subject. "She ran off to the south of France with that dreadful landscape painter, Jean-Pierre."

With a sense of relief he translated for Mattie and added they were fellow artist friends of his.

"Come, *liebchen*, I want to show you my painting." They stood and went to the far wall.

"This is the work I told you about," he said. "I gave it to the Schleins last summer. Wonder why they're not here this evening. Anyway, they were most friendly to me during my time here."

"It's beautiful, Klaus. Didn't you paint another?"

"Yes. Father has it in his office back home."

"Where did you paint this?"

"At Argenteuil, just north of here. I've told you about the inn where I stayed."

"Yes, I remember."

"Tomorrow, we'll take the train out there for a visit. I want to show you off to my friends there."

"You made many friends in Paris, haven't you, dear?"

"Of course. Paris loves artists." *Especially one man-eating student from Portugal.*

When they returned to the table Estéban had left.

"I must apologize for Estéban's comments, Klaus. Ever since he returned from Spain he's been a very angry man."

"That's unfortunate, Antoine, but what about you?"

"I get by. Sell a few sketches of my work to foreign tourists at a kiosk on the left bank." He drank some champagne. "I'm living with a woman who teaches French to rich foreigners at the Berlitz school. It keeps me in cheap wine and a warm bed. And you two, how long will you be in Paris?"

"Just a week, and then we're going to Italy to do some hiking in the Dolomites. My mother is originally from that area . . . the Austrian side, *bien sûr*. After that, back to Linz for my final year at the university." He translated for Mattie.

"What are you reading?" Antoine asked.

"Law."

"What? Not art history or something creative?"

"No, my friend. It's what my father wanted and he pays the bills."

"Like every summer painting in Paris dressed in rags? You had us fooled, Klaus."

"I am truly sorry, *mon ami*, but I wanted to blend in and be part of this life."

"You're forgiven, Klaus. Certainly after the champagne and this meal." He raised his glass in salute.

"The Schleins, Antoine. I'm surprised they're not here this evening."

"They're leaving, Klaus. Sold the bistro to Pascal and Francine."

"Leaving? What? Retirement?"

"Oh no. They fear Hitler. Think there will be another war and the Nazis will win. They're emigrating to America."

"But why leave France?"

"They're Jews, Klaus. Don't you know what's going on in Germany?"

"No, not really. I don't do politics."

"A lawyer who doesn't do politics? That's a first. To change the subject, will you come back to Paris someday?"

"We certainly hope so. It's my favorite city." Mattie caressed his thigh. "We must go, *mon ami*. Wonderful seeing you again. *A bientot.*"

As they walked back to the hotel, Mattie asked, "Why did that man call you Klaus Eisenstadt?"

"That's a long story, *liebchen*. Eisenstadt was the name I used during my summers here. I'll explain later."

* * *

The next morning after watching the Luxembourg regatta, they rode the train to Argenteuil. The weather was perfect—not a cloud in the sky. The newlyweds walked along the promenade by the river. Klaus showed Mattie where he'd set up his easel and worked on his paintings of the bridge and the boat basin. At the hotel, Madame Gaultier was thrilled to meet Mattie.

"You look much better without the beard, Monsieur Eisenstadt. You're quite a handsome young man."

"Is Constance about?" he asked.

"No. Unfortunately she's away visiting cousins in Normandy."

"That's a shame, Madame. I so wanted her to meet Mattie." He translated for his wife.

"To be honest, Madame, my name is not Eisenstadt. That was the name I used while pretending to be the poor artist. I'm Klaus von Reichenhall . . . *from* Eisenstadt."

The landlady looked at his clothes and said, "I noticed an improvement in your wardrobe, Monsieur." They laughed and he translated.

"Will you be wanting a room, Monsieur *von Reichenhall?*"

"Not this time, Madame. I brought Mattie here to show her the scenes that I painted."

"I'm sure my daughter will be sorry she missed you. Will you be in Paris long?"

"Just a few more days. Please give our regards to Constance."

From the hotel they strolled along the Seine and watched the sailboats in the basin.

"This is truly a beautiful place, Klaus. I see why you wanted to capture it in your paintings."

"Tomorrow we'll go to the Louvre, where you'll see the original Monets. They were my inspiration."

"Perhaps, when you are a famous attorney, we can return someday."

"Yes, *liebchen,* we'll definitely do that."

5

"There is in the nature of every man, I firmly believe, a longing to see and know the strange places of the world. Life imprisons us all in its coil of circumstances, and the dreams of romance that color boyhood are forgotten, but they do not die. They stir at the sight of a white-sailed ship beating out to the wide sea, the smell of tarred rope on a blackened wharf, or the touch of the cool breeze that rises when the stars come out will waken them again. Somewhere over the rim of the world lies romance, and every heart yearns to go and find it." *Julian (Dashwood) Hillas*

North Island, New Zealand, 1938.
Reginald Malcolm Pobjoy lived on a sheep farm overlooking Parua Bay on the north edge of Whangarei Harbour. The harbor, a ten-mile deep gash in North Island's east coast, extended inland to the mouth of the Hatea River. Reggie, as he was called, spent many hours on the hill above the farm watching ships work their way up and down the Whangarei Roadstead: wooden-hulled coastal steamers, flat-bottomed ketch-rigged scows and, upon rare occasion, a two-or three-masted schooner. He dreamt of going to sea. It was all Uncle Clyde's fault.

Clyde, his father's younger brother and a purser on the *Queen of Adelaide*, arrived for a visit every year or so when his ship was in Auckland. He'd travel by train north to Whangarei, and then by bus, taxi, or thumb to the Parua Bay Hotel. From the hotel he'd walk up the hill to the farm. The hotel did have a telephone, and sometimes he'd call from Whangarei hoping someone might be going up that way and send word of his arrival. Reggie's father often sent one of the Maori farm boys with the wagon down to the hotel to collect him.

Oh, the stories Uncle Clyde told—stories about Hong Kong, Manila, Calcutta, Batavia, and especially Pape'ete and other ports-of-call in the South Pacific. It all sounded so grand and exciting to Reggie.

Malcolm Pobjoy, Reggie's father, considered his brother a bad influence on his oldest son—put strange ideas in his head. The other Pobjoy children were too young to understand and just enjoyed the presents their uncle brought.

Reggie rode a bus to high school in Whangarei. During the lunch period, he'd stroll along the quayside on the Hatea River to see what kind of ships were moored there, unloading or taking on cargo. Not often, and a special treat to his eyes, a sailing ship, usually a copra schooner from Samoa, Fiji, or other islands, would be tied up alongside River Street. The crews were islanders for the most part. Once, while standing at the quayside admiring a white-hulled two-master, a man came down the gangplank and asked Reggie if he wanted a berth. Before he could answer, the man laughed and walked away. Reggie was fifteen, but the hook was set.

In the school library, Reggie discovered and devoured Melville: *Typee, Ooma, Moby Dick*, and Jack London's *South Sea Tales*. He enjoyed reading but thought it was something you did when you couldn't be doing anything else. Not a waste of time, just other things were more important. Reading was for the end of the day or when the weather was too rough for work outside. He also found two strange but exciting volumes by *Asterix*, the pseudonym for an Englishman, Robert Fletcher. Here was a man who'd actually lived among the islanders for seven years, not just some missionary or trader, but who'd held various positions in the European communities and administrations. Reggie didn't understand most of Fletcher's second book, *Gone Native*. Written from the viewpoint and in the voice of a Melanesian girl, it did show him that islanders look at life differently than the white man. Especially about time. But what really got his heart pumping and his dreams flowing were the books by Louis Becke and Frederick O'Brien. These men had worked and settled in the islands of the South Pacific in the last forty years. Reggie fantasized about becoming a supercargo, or even the skipper or owner, of a copra schooner sailing between Rarotonga and Tahiti. In his daydreams he would deal fairly with the islanders, maybe set up his own stores—run by ex-crew members—on some of the atolls. He didn't want to be a sheep farmer for the rest of his life.

Reggie learned to keep his dreams to himself. When he'd mentioned to his parents the possibility of finding work on a ship after graduation, his father said he didn't need to go anywhere.

Malcolm Pobjoy served in Palestine during the war and had seen many of those exotic places. He said they were filthy and full of thieving *kanakas*. Calcutta, Aden, Suez, Cairo, Jerusalem, and Damascus—he'd seen them all. You couldn't trust a one of them, he said many times.

"They'd slit your throat for a tuppence. And steal anything that wasn't under guard by white troops. Stay here, my son. Our Maoris are good decent people for the most part and know their place. This will be all yours someday."

* * *

One morning at the end of the month—late spring in the antipods—after a fierce storm, Reggie went up on the headland to check on the lambing. Dark clouds, heavy with rain, flowed over the Whangarei Heads to the east, but the wind had shifted to the northwest, and the storm front was sliding away from the harbor. He turned to look south across the water and saw a two-masted schooner aground on the mudflats in Parua Bay.

He fell twice on the wet grass running to the house to tell his father.

Malcolm and Reggie hitched up the two-horse team to the farm's wagon and drove down to the coast track just east of the hotel. Other rigs were parked along the edge of the road. A crowd of locals had gathered on the beach near the hotel to gawk at the schooner. The Pobjoys joined them. They learned that the ship's captain and supercargo had waded ashore, asked for the location of the nearest telephone, and were directed to the hotel. The captain wanted to hire a tug from Whangarei to tow the schooner up river for engine repairs.

A police constable arrived in his black Model A Ford, and accompanied the captain and supercargo when they went down to the beach to talk with the farmers. Reggie stood at the fringe of this group while they discussed the possibility of kedging the schooner off the flats into deeper water using their teams of horses. A tug was on its way from Whangarei, but it would save the captain—and the company, the supercargo emphasized—a fair bit of brass if the ship was afloat when the tug arrived. An offer of free whiskey at the hotel bar closed the deal.

Reggie waded out to the stranded ship. He read the faded name on the bow—*Wallaroo*. The peeling white paint on the hull was worn off in places. Barnacles and sea grass encrusted the exposed parts below the waterline. A tall, muscular Maori crew member wearing a sleeveless red shirt stood on the end of the bowsprit.

"G'day, *kia ora*," Reggie said, "What happened?"

The islander looked down at him and smiled. "*Kia orāna*. Engine quit. Storm blew us here."

"I'm Reggie. What's your name?"

"Tooks," the islander said.

"Where're you from?"

"Cooks . . . Rarotonga."

"Our farmhand, Ioapa, is from the Cooks . . . Penrhyn Island. But he calls it Tongareva."

"Penrhyn is English name," Tooks said.

"What's your cargo?"

"Copra."

"Where are you going? Auckland? How long have you been sailing on the schooner? Where'd you get the copra? What's copra?"

The Maori frowned. "You have many questions for a young man."

"Sorry, Tooks. I want to go to sea and want to know everything." A shout from the captain ended their conversation.

"Must work now," Tooks said. "Good to meet you, Reggie. *Kia manuia*."

Another crew member came forward; he and Tooks carried one of the ship's anchors to the stern.

During the flood tide, Reggie stood on the beach road and watched as the farmers and the ship's crew kedged the schooner off the mudflats. The *Wallaroo* anchored in deeper water and waited for the tug. Reggie could have stood there all day staring at the two-master, but his father said it was time to go back to the farm.

That evening up on the headland at dusk, Reggie watched the tug, belching volumes of black smoke from its stack, tow the schooner across the bay toward Whangarei.

* * *

A week after the *Wallaroo* went up river, Reggie and Ioapa drove the wagon the ten miles to Whangarei to buy supplies. They tied off the team in front of Harbittle's Mercantile on River Street. Reggie gave his shopping list to Mr. Harbittle while Ioapa walked to an open air market by the river to buy fresh fish, fruit, and vegetables. Reggie was relieved that Rosie wasn't behind the counter. A tryst with Rosie, the owner's daughter, was Reggie's first attempt at sex and a total disaster—he went limp as soon as he entered her. She'd laughed at him but said they could try again sometime.

Reggie stood in front of a metal rack filled with magazines. One health and bodybuilding journal was full of tall, blond, muscle-bound men. Well, I'll never look like that, he thought. Below average height, but well-built and strong from mending fences and wrestling sheep all his life, Reggie still felt intimidated by taller men—and women. His father was tall, as was his uncle Clyde. Must follow my Mom's side, he thought. She was short and stocky. He looked out the window at the river. His back was to the counter. He didn't see Rosie enter from a room in back of the shop.

"Reggie?"

Startled, he almost jumped. "Oh, hello, Rosie. How are you?" She wore a calico print dress that was too small for her short plump figure. Rosie walked from behind the counter and stood close to him. Reggie thought her perfume a bit overdone.

"Not good, Reggie. I need to have a word." She looked over her shoulder at her father. "Let's go outside."

Reggie followed her out the door. She sat on a wooden bench and patted the slats next to her. Reggie sat but left a gap between them.

"I'm in trouble, Reggie." She looked like she was going to cry.

"What sort of trouble?" He had no idea what she meant.

"You know . . . woman trouble."

"I don't understand." He was confused.

"My time of the month. It's passed. I'm two weeks late." She wiped a tear from her cheek.

"Late for what?"

"Oh, Reggie. You're so thick sometimes. I'm pregnant. I'm sure of it. I've never been late before."

He didn't know what to say. *Why was she telling me this?*

"I'm going to have to tell my dad soon," she said.

"That won't be easy. But who's the father?"

"You, Reggie. You're the father. Remember after the RSA dance?"

He didn't know whether he was angry or afraid. "Can't be. We didn't do anything."

"We did enough, Reggie dear. It's yours. I know it."

He knew she'd been with other guys in Whangarei before his failed attempt. And he probably wasn't the last. His mates joked about Harbittle's *merchandise* being readily available. What would his parents say?

"You'll have to marry me, Reggie dear." She wasn't crying anymore. She brushed a lock of red hair from her forehead. Her voice sounded stern and positive. "I've always wanted to live on a sheep farm. And I'm not raising a bastard by myself." She stood and faced him. "I'm going to tell my dad this evening. I know he'll come to talk to your folks. You'd best tell them yourself before then." She stood, turned, and walked into the shop.

Reggie sat on the bench—angry and confused. And afraid. Afraid of what his parents would say and do. Would they believe him? Would they force him to marry her? He and his father never talked much about sex.

On the farm one learned about that by watching the animals. He learned more from his mates at school than from his father. They boasted and described in great detail their conquests with the available local girls like Rosie. *And* this would lock him into a life he didn't want.

Reggie watched Ioapa return from the market with two full baskets and place them in the wagon.

He's not limping so much, Reggie thought. Father did a good job setting his broken leg. Ioapa had fallen off the back of the wagon some months ago and broken his leg. Reggie's father, a medical orderly in the Anzac Brigade, set the leg before taking the farmhand to meet the doctor at the Parua Bay Hotel. Reggie had assisted when more hands were needed. And had watched everything.

The Maori farmhand joined Reggie on the bench. He lit a cigarette and offered one to Reggie. The boy shook his head.

"Someday we will have a smoke together, Reggie."

"Get the goods from Mister Harbittle, Ioapa. I'm going for a stroll."

"Fancy fish'n chips, Reggie?" He pointed to the open-fronted shop just down the quay.

"Maybe before we go home. Get some now, if you like. I'm not hungry."

Reggie stood and walked along the riverfront. *What do I do now?*

Nearby, a fishing boat off loaded its catch to the waiting knives of the crew's wives. Squadrons of raucous gulls awaited the offal feast as the fish were cleaned, cut into steaks, or filleted on the quayside. Children wrapped the fish in newsprint, threw it into wicker baskets, and, with an urchin on each handle, scampered up the quay to the market.

Reggie walked past the fish cutters and stopped at the edge of the quay. The Hatea was as still as a lake—nothing moved on its surface. Why is that, he wondered. The smell of hot oil from the fish'n chips shop flowed around him, but he wasn't hungry. His stomach was unsettled. *I can't marry Rosie Harbittle and be stuck here forever.*

Reggie looked down river and saw the stern of the *Wallaroo*. Opposite the schooner and across the quay was a pub. A man slouched in the doorway, leaning against the wall. Reggie recognized him from the day on the mud flats—the captain. About the same height as Reggie but stouter, the seaman shielded his eyes with a hand from the afternoon sun's glare off the river. Lurching forward, he staggered toward the schooner's gangway. He must have a snoot full, Reggie thought. That's how Uncle Clyde described drunks.

The captain tripped on the edge of the gangplank, reached out for the railing but missed, and fell to his knees. Afraid the man might fall into the water between the ship and the quay, Reggie ran over and grabbed him under the arms with both hands to help him to his feet.

"Thanks, me boy. Bloody ship won't stop moving." His speech was fat-tongued—another of Uncle Clyde's expressions.

"What's this all about then?" said a loud voice from onboard.

It was the supercargo. He'd come out on deck from the cabin between the masts, followed by Tooks. "Pissed again is he?" The two men came down the gangplank and took the captain from Reggie.

"Put 'im in his berth, Tooks. We'll let 'im have some kip before we get underway." The supercargo, a tall, thin, red-headed man, turned to Reggie, "Thanks for the help, laddie." He thrust his right hand into a pocket of his trousers. "Here's a half-a-crown for your trouble."

"You're leaving?" Reggie didn't take the coin.

"Aye, right you are."

"Where're you going? Remember me? I helped you off the mudflats in Parua Bay. I talked to Tooks."

"Right, laddie. Thought I'd seen you before. Auckland . . . after Captain Harry has some kip." He put the coin back in his pocket and turned away.

"Will you be sailing to the islands again?" Reggie started up the gangplank. The seaman turned.

"Aye, laddie. When we be gettin' a cargo."

"Can I come along? I'm strong and a hard worker. I want to see the islands."

The supercargo took his pipe from a coat pocket and tapped it against the gangplank railing. "Show me your hands."

Reggie held out his hands, palms down.

"No. The other side, you silly git." He laughed. "I want to be seein' if you've ever done any work." Reggie turned his hands. "Aye, you've been on the rough side of it I can see. So, laddie, what's this all in need of? Some kinda trouble is it?" The supercargo filled his pipe and lit it. "You haven't debauched and murdered the local school mistress, have you now?"

"No, sir!" Reggie wasn't sure what debauched meant. "I want to see other places. I don't want to be a sheep farmer."

"Be havin' the necessary seaman's papers and passport, do you?" The supercargo leaned against the railing and drew on his pipe.

Reggie thought he was going to be sick. He didn't know he would need all this. *Now what do I do? I can't go home and face my father. I wish Uncle Clyde was here. He'd know all about these things.*

The red-haired man chuckled and said, "Not to worry, laddie. We'll sign you on for the haul down to Auckland. No papers needed for that. Give you a taste of the sea and the ship. You'll be the captain's boy, learn about the ship and all that. Bring your teethbrush, did you?"

Reggie shook his head.

"No worries there, laddie. Lots of kit in the trade room. Come aboard and we'll sign some papers." The supercargo stopped and turned. "How old are you?"

"Eighteen . . . two weeks ago," Reggie lied.

"That'll do. Come along."

"Wait! Please, Mister . . . I don't know your name. I have to go tell Ioapa, our Maori, I won't be going back to the farm."

"Davie McCombs—Mister McCombs or *sir* to you, laddie. I be supercargo of the good ship, *Wallaroo*. And a finer piece of the S.L.

Livingston Company driftwood never sailed the southern ocean. Do what you have to get done, laddie. We won't sail for an hour or more—the tide's just starting to ebb."

Reggie ran back to Harbittle's store to find Ioapa loading the supplies into the wagon.

"What is wrong, young Reggie? You're out of breath."

"I'm not going back home, Ioapa." He looked around. "I need a piece of paper and a pencil." He dreaded going back into the store, but he had no other choice. Mr. Harbittle was at the counter—Rosie nowhere in sight.

"A scrap of paper, please sir, and a pencil."

Harbittle placed both on the counter. "You seem a bit worked up, son. Is a there a problem? Anything to do with our goods?"

"No, sir. It's a personal matter." *If he only knew.*

6

Rivers of fog rolled over Whangarei Head when the *Wallaroo* motored down the Hatea River. As the schooner passed the opening to Parua Bay off its port side, Reggie stood at the rail and looked up toward the hills above the bay. He could make out the red roof of their house and sheep in the fields beyond. Smoke curled up from the chimney. Mom must be cooking dinner, he thought. Ioapa may not be back to the farm yet. What would his father think when he read my note? I told him I was going to sea and wasn't to blame for Rosie's condition. Maybe I'll write again from Auckland.

Reggie couldn't tell if Captain Houchins was pleased or not when the supercargo introduced him. He looked Reggie up and down and said, "Hrumph. So be it. Mister Marsten, give the boy a tour of the ship. Find out what he be knowin'."

The *Wallaroo* was a one hundred and ten foot long, husky, German-built ship, devoid of brightwork, unknown to varnish, the timbers and decks scarred by thirty years of weather and hard knocks. She had twenty-three feet of beam and drew close to two fathoms. The sails were stout oatmeal-colored canvas, the hull below the waterline a rusty black, the upper hull and the deckhouses a non-descript white.

There were two cargo hatches and two deckhouses. The hatches sat forward of each mast, the houses aft. In the forward house were the crew's quarters and the galley. The Chinese cook had a berth in the galley. The after house, about twenty feet long and four steps down from the wheel deck, had a tiny semi-private room for Captain Houchins and four berths arranged about a table. Reggie, as cabin boy, would sleep in one of those berths. If there were paying passengers to fill the berths, he would sleep in a hammock in the trade room or on a mattress on deck, weather permitting. Tooks introduced Reggie to the cook, Y Ling, Cachero, the engineer, and the rest of the crew, all Maoris from the Cook Islands.

Reggie returned to the wheel deck. The captain had one hand on the wheel and drank from a white porcelain cup.

"Be knowin' how to sort some tea, lad?" he asked.

"Yes, sir." *Hope I'll be doing more than make tea.*

"Good. Been to sea before? Get seasick do you?'

"No, sir. I don't think so."

"Well, we'll be knowin' for sure once we clear Busby Head." He pointed to a headland at the end of a peninsula off the port bow. "You'll get your sea legs by the time we make Auckland."

"Sir, may I ask you a question?"

"Haul away, lad."

"What? I don't understand."

"Ask your question, lad."

"When will we get to Auckland?" Reggie thought the captain was iritated by his question.

"Should drop anchor after first light, if'n there's a fair wind outside." Houchins set aside his cup and lit a cigar. "Go below, lad, and be learnin' some about trade from Davie . . . Mister McCombs."

"Yes, sir." As Reggie turned to go, the captain said, "Lad, on this ship it's 'Aye, sir' or 'Aye, aye, sir.'"

"Aye, sir."

The trade room, which opened from the aft cabin, was a surprise to Reggie. He'd read about them and supercargoes in Louis Becke's stories. He expected it to smell of rum and gunpowder, and filled with racks of rifles to repel pesky natives from coming over the ship's sides.

The *Wallaroo's* trade room had two small portholes on each bulkhead, and when he opened the door all was obscure at first. Rank odors of stick tobacco, cheap cotton prints, scented soaps, and what smelled like perfume competed for supremacy. Gradually his eyes discovered shelves, bins, and goods heaped from floor to ceiling: block and tackle, anchors, harpoons, fishing lures, pens, crackers, cheap jewelry, cloth, shoes, cases of Spam, medicine, hatchets, hats, and writing paper. And sewing machines. No guns and alcohol in view. The supercargo sat at a table, a hurricane lantern above his head.

"Come aboard, laddie." McCombs motioned to a bunk along the port bulkhead. "Sit yourself." He waved his hand about. "What do you think of our little emporium?"

Reggie saw a shelf of books—two by Becke next to a ship in a bottle. "I've read Becke's books." He pointed toward the shelf. "But I expected more—"

"Guns and booze, right, laddie?"

Reggie nodded.

"Well, laddie, some things haven't changed much since Becke's day. The captain runs the ship, and I do the trade. We all belong to Mister Vernon A. Rupp on Raro . . . Rarotonga . . . and his superiors at S. L. Livingston and Company in Auckland." He waved his hand about.

"At one time, a ship like this would carry guns—mostly old, worthless ones, of course—booze, mostly cheap rum and Chinese gin, and lots of trinkets for the ladies. But that's all changed."

The captain entered the room. "I'll have a few of your brown turds, Davie, me lad." The supercargo took a box off a shelf and handed him a half-dozen cigars. "Been hearin' what you're tellin' the boy." He lit a cigar. "Booze is still boss. I've better than six thousand quid in the bank in Perth, all made by sellin' liquor to the natives. It's against the law in the Frog islands, and banned by most missionaries in the others, to sell or trade or even give 'em a drop, but we all do it. If you don't have it, you can't get cargo." The captain went up on deck.

"Trade business is not what it was," McCombs continued. "Time was when cautious men dared not go ashore without being armed against aggressive natives. But now almost every inhabited island has its little store with a white man or half-caste as the trader."

"What's that ship in the bottle, Mister McCombs?"

The supercargo reached over and brought the square, pale blue bottle down to eye level. He gently placed it on his desk.

"She's a beauty, isn't she, laddie? Laid down by them master ship builders in Nova Scotia in '19. Did a turn as a collier across the Atlantic until spied by that Yankee cowboy writer, Zane Grey. He turned her into a posh yacht to chase after big fish down here in southern waters. Got his book about that tucked away here somewhere. Anyways, when they arrived in Tahiti in '25, or maybe it was '26, they were looking for a mate. I was on the beach at Pape'ete at the time and signed on as second." He paused to refill his pipe.

"What were you doin' on the beach, Mister McCombs? Lookin' for shells?" Reggie asked.

The supercargo stared at the boy for a moment, and then laughed and lit his pipe. "'On the beach,' laddie, means you don't have a berth. No job. No employment, as they say now.

"Anyways, we fished the Society and other Frenchie islands. Dropped anchor in Pape'ete and the like for a time, and to the Cooks and back. But there were some money troubles, and Grey had to offload her. She was bought by that outlaw priest, Father Rougier, in '28. He wanted to keep me on, but after I learned what he planned to do to her—strip out all the guts, the beautiful wood work and fittings—to haul copra, I gave my notice and went back on the beach."

"What happened to it?"

"*It?* Never *it*, laddie. Ships are like women and referred to as such—she or her."

"I'm sorry, Mister McCombs, I didn't know."

"No worries. You've plenty to learn. But what happened to her, you ask? She died a South Pacific island death." He tapped his pipe clean in an ashtray, refilled, and lit it.

"She hauled copra from the rogue priest's plantations on Christmas Island for a time, and then ran booze to the West Coast—California—during their Prohibition. Albert Freshour—'Alberti' they call him—crewed on her during that time. You'll meet him. He's the trader on Pukapuka. But she broke her back on a reef in the Australs in '34. A real shame that was. She *was* a beauty." McCombs gently placed the bottle back on the shelf.

"Why two names?"

"Ah, good question, laddie. She was launched as *Maréchal Foch*, after that Frenchie general during the Great War, I expect. But Mister Grey renamed her *Fisherman*. Some folks think that's bad luck—renamin' a ship."

"Did you make that?" Reggie pointed to the ship in the bottle. "How'd you get it in the bottle?"

McCombs turned, smiled, and brought the bottle back to the table.

"It's all about patience. And time. You have to think hard about each bit before you do it."

"I'd like to learn how."

"Well, Reggie, me boy, time we've loads of, but the patience's a bit harder. Plenty of frustration at times. I'd be pleased to show you how it's done."

"What's copra? Do the natives grow it?"

"Copra? It's the life blood of trade, laddie. Gold dust it be." The supercargo took a book from the shelf and opened it to a drawing of the coconut palm. "It's made from the dried meat of the coconut. The palms grow wild on all the islands. The natives use them for everything, and the white man has found even more uses for it: oil, milk, soap, shampoo, and even cattle feed. Easy pickin's it is. For a few baubles and such, one can make a fortune haulin' copra. The only problem be the bugs. Damn copra bugs infest any ship in the trade. Some folks aren't bothered by them, but I don't fancy them little buggers crawlin' over me self at night. That be why I sleep in a hammock. " He returned the book to the shelf. "But pearl shell be the crown jewel—the diamonds of the atolls. A hull full of pearl shell could set a man up for life. But like diamonds, it's hard to come by. Especially these days when folks be after it for a century or more."

The schooner's engine stopped, and the ship started to roll. McCombs glanced toward a porthole. Tooks opened the door to the trade room and said, "Come topside, Reggie. We're makin' sail."

"Go, laddie," McCombs said. "Lots to be learnin' now."

Reggie followed Tooks to the mainmast. The ship's foresails had been raised, and the crew was removing the canvas straps from the mainsail.

"Help Toa raise the main," Tooks told Reggie.

Reggie and Toa hoisted the big sail and secured the line around wooden belaying pins mounted in a bracket at the base of the mast. The schooner heeled to starboard as a fresh wind filled the canvas. The bow rose and fell in the ocean swells; Reggie hoped he wouldn't get seasick.

He went to the stern and watched Busby Head and the Whangarei headlands recede in the distance. *I've done it. I've gone to sea.*

7

A week later, the *Wallaroo*, loaded down with cargo and passengers, sailed north out of Auckland's harbor bound for the Kermadec Islands and the Cooks. Three of the passengers, two young men and a woman, were university naturalists going to the research station on Raoul Island to replace other scientists whose tour at the station was ending. The fourth, an older man, perhaps thirty, was the representative of the Auckland bank which handled the finances for the station. These four occupied the berths in the main cabin. Reggie slept in a hammock in the trade room.

The hatches were now covered with deck passengers and their belongings. The ship was loaded to the water's edge with cargo for the islands. Lumber lay in the narrow lanes between the cabin houses and the rails; even the long boat and dinghy were piled with cargo. There was barely room to move about on the deck of the *Wallaroo*—the only open area abaft the wheel.

The New Zealanders, the supercargo, and the captain took their meals on a gimbaled table in the long room they referred to as the salon. Reggie brought their meals from the galley.

After dinner one evening out of Auckland, the older man stood at the fantail smoking a pipe. Reggie joined him.

"Good evening, sir," Reggie said. The man nodded. "I heard the others say you're a banker."

The man tapped his pipe on the rail. "Yes and no, son. And I'm Declan Deerlove, but my friends call me 'Dee-Dee.'" He extended his hand. "And your name is Reggie, is it not?"

"Aye, sir. Reggie Pobjoy." They shook hands.

"A banker you asked." Deerlove refilled his pipe. "My father and two uncles own the North Island Merchants Bank in Auckland. I hope to join them in the business when I finish my service." He lit his pipe. "Our bank handles the government financing for the research station, and they asked me to go and take a look at how the monies are being spent. Bit of a boondoggle as far as I'm concerned, but an enjoyable way to pass my home leave before I rejoin my squadron in England."

"England? Why so far away from New Zealand?"

"Proper question, Reggie. You're most certainly not an enemy agent, so I'll tell you. I'm a flying officer—pilot—in 75 Squadron. We're based at RAF Elvington in Yorkshire awaiting our new aircraft—Wellington bombers. Once the planes and crews are sorted, we'll fly them home . . . if, of course, war doesn't break out in Europe."

"War? Will there be another war? My father was with the Anzacs in Palestine."

"As was my father and one of my uncles. Will there be another war? Hitler's already taken the Sudentenland and Austria. I don't think he'll be satisfied until he gets revenge for Germany's defeat in the last one."

"Will I have to fight?"

"That'll be up to you, Reggie. If you do get called up, or if you decide to sign up, try for the air force. We can always use smart young lads."

Over the next days, when finished with his chores, Reggie chatted with Dee-Dee when they were by themselves. The Royal New Zealand Air Force officer asked him how long he'd been on the ship. Reggie, a bit embarrassed, admitted it only had been a fortnight. The boy felt he could trust this man and told him the circumstances at home, his confrontation with Rosie Harbittle, and his desire to go the sea. Deerlove listened and voiced no judgment.

Three days out from North Island, a shout of "Whale!" brought everyone up on deck. When close to the ship's starboard side, one of the naturalists said, "That's a shark, not a whale." The fish passed close, near the surface. Yellow and green in color, it had a square head, immense pectoral fins, and a few white spots. It was thirty-five to forty feet long; the after third of its body and tail lean compared with the bulk of the head and shoulders. The female scientist, a marine biologist said, "Not a harmless whale-shark—*Rhinodon typus*. It's one of those man-eating monsters of the South Pacific." It passed astern, and then disappeared into the depths.

The *Wallaroo* dropped anchor under the cliffs of Raoul Island, the largest in the Kermadecs and off loaded the passengers and supplies. Before Dee-Dee left the schooner, he gave Reggie his address in Auckland. "Write to me. I'd enjoy hearing about your adventures . . . and if you ever need any advice about money."

Ahead was a thousand nautical mile sail northeast to Rarotonga, the principal island of the Cook Islands. Reggie, under Davie's guidance, worked on his first ship in a bottle. The barefooted, unshaven, and unwashed crew lived in pajamas. Fresh water was limited, as it would be impossible to replenish the casks for many days. When the schooner pushed through a windless calm by motor power for long hours, squalls would pass over. Then they bathed on deck and refreshed themselves with buckets of rain water. Reggie slept on deck because it was cooler, and no bugs.

A little after daybreak Reggie was awakened by Tooks, who said Rarotonga was in sight. From a distance the island looked like a cone-shaped green mass rising to several high sharp-toothed peaks. In the colorful sunrise, the beautiful mountain rose out of the violet sea. The island was surrounded by a barrier reef, against which the sea burst in white breakers. Schools of flying fish flew before the *Wallaroo's* bow.

In Avarua, the major town of the Cooks, cargo was unloaded and the local passengers went their way. Loaded down again with cargo and passengers—all islanders returning home—the schooner sailed east to the southern group of islands.

8

"Those who believe that the beach-comber or copra trader of the South Seas is necessarily a scoundrel, err grievously. There is proportionately to their numbers as much honesty, sobriety and energy amongst the traders as amongst any body of business men. They have their black sheep, no doubt; let the community which has none throw at them the first stone." *Admiral Cyprian A. G. Bridge, Royal Navy, Pacific Station*

Pukapuka Atoll.
"Harry, look at the bloody fools. Don't they be knowin' we're here?" McCombs said.

"Well . . . yes . . . maybe," the schooner captain answered.

"Maybe? They've got eyes, ain't they?"

"Well, Davie, you know how it is. They've been a long time without a ship, and—"

"Then why don't they come out, now we're here? Squattin' on the beach like a bunch of dummies. We've been standin' off since first light."

"They'll come along directly. Anyway, Alberti will." Captain Houchins reached for his binoculars.

"Alberti? He be nothin' but a bloody *kanaka* now. Lost what little mind of a white man he had."

"Alberti? He's the trader, isn't he?" Reggie asked. "What's a *kanaka*?" He and Tooks stood behind the captain and the supercargo on the wheel deck. The young man remembered his father using that word, but never knew the meaning.

Tooks tapped Reggie on the shoulder and placed a finger to his lips and pointed to his ear.

"Quiet, laddie," the supercargo said over his shoulder. "Just watch and listen. Lots to be learned doin' that. Your questions will be answered in their own time."

"Alberti a *kanaka*? I wouldn't say that about all white men, Davie," Houchins said. "If you were alone here for months, years sometimes on end, the way Alberti is, never seeing a white face—"

"Me? Here? I wouldn't be such a damn fool. Didn't Auckland send a new resident agent out since we were here last? There's a white face for him."

"Resident agents. Ha! There isn't one of 'em but what is the two ends and a bight of . . . a scoundrel." The captain tossed his cigar butt over the fantail. "We should've had that cargo, but we were laid up in Whangarei." Houchins nodded towards the island. "There's Alberti now."

"Well, it's about bloody time," McCombs said.

Both men raised their binoculars. An outrigger came out from the center of the island and headed for the gap in the reef.

"Maybe you're spot on, Davie. Looks like Alberti's come unhinged."

The canoe approaching the reef had three native paddlers, but in the middle was a white man sitting upright in a chair fixed astraddle the gunwales. An umbrella, lashed to the back of the chair, shaded the white-suited, pith-helmeted occupant from the sun.

Doctor Dozier joined the others around the wheel. He looked a bit haggard. "These Cook Island girls are very demanding." The Frenchman smiled and added, "Medically speaking, *bien sûr.*" He placed his travel bag and a white box with Red Cross markings on the deck.

McCombs lowered his binoculars. "That's not Alberti. He's over there on the beach."

The others looked toward the shore where a white man stood near the waterline waving his hat. Of average height, but quite thin and bare-footed, he wore shorts and an open shirt.

"Righto, lads. That's our man." The schooner captain removed his cap and waved at the trader.

A shout from the bowsprit turned the attention of those around the wheel back toward the canoe working its way through the reef opening. The canoe that was now upside down and its occupants swimming in the surf.

"Ha! That's one for the books, Davie, me boy. When's the last time you knew of a Pukapuka canoe capsizing in the gap? Something funny here." He turned to the first mate.

"Mister Marsten, the dinghy over the side, if you please. There's a good lad."

"Come, Reggie," Tooks said. "We go save the *Papa'ā.*"

After Reggie and the first mate pulled the white man into the dinghy, they rowed back to the schooner. The man patted his pockets and looked around in the surf. He shook his head.

"God almighty, I hate this place! Now I've lost my best pipe, my only decent tobacco, *and* my hat."

Looking over the man's shoulder as he rowed, Reggie watched the three island paddlers right the outrigger and start towards shore. One wore the agent's pith helmet.

When Tooks and Reggie helped the agent up the schooner's side, the captain, the supercargo, and the doctor didn't go forward to meet him. Soaked to the skin, the short, slightly obese and balding bureaucrat followed Reggie to the wheel deck.

"Elrod Swint, Resident Agent for Pukapuka, and the king's representative in these waters, thank you very much. Did you bring the doctor and the drugs? And what is the nature of your cargo?"

"I'll leave the formalities to you, Doctor . . . and Mr. McCombs." The captain turned and walked to the fantail. He lit another cigar.

"*Bonjour,* Monsieur Swint, I am Doctor Claude Dozier with the *Polynesie Française* medical service." The Frenchman extended his hand. "I have the necessary serum for the vaccinations. How many cases are there?"

The agent squinted and looked the doctor up and down. He didn't take his hand. "A bloody Frog? Couldn't they send an English doctor?" He looked to the supercargo, who shrugged his shoulders.

"Welcome aboard, Mr. Swint. I'm McCombs, the supercargo. How can I be of service?"

Doctor Dozier stepped between the two men. "I must insist, Monsieur Swint, how many typhoid patients have been confirmed? Have they been isolated?" A head taller than Swint, thirty pounds heavier and quite fit, Dozier, both hands raised waist high, looked like he was about to toss the agent over the side.

Swint backed away—his expression of arrogance changed to one of fear. "Three. The island nurse is dealing with them . . . Monsieur Doctor. They're in a hut on the far end of the island. I want nothing to do with this."

The doctor turned to the captain, who'd been watching from the fantail. "Captain Houchins, I must go ashore immediately."

The captain strode forward and ordered, "Mr. Marsten, lower the long boat. Reggie, help the doctor with his kit." Houchins took the doctor by the arm and led him to the ship's waist. He ignored the agent as he passed. Reggie grabbed the doctor's gear and followed.

Miffed by this slight, Swint turned his attention to the supercargo. "Your cargo, sir?" He put his hand to his head, and then patted his pockets again. "I can't believe I've lost my hat. I've had it since Calcutta. And my pipe—my favorite pipe." He looked over the side of the schooner. "All down there, I suppose."

"Mr. Swint, sir. Not to worry. These are just minor inconveniences of life in the tropics. Do come below to my trade room, and we'll get everything sorted."

"But your cargo, sir. McCombs, is it? I'll need to see an inventory."

"Of course, Mr. Swint, in good time. But first we must get you out of these wet clothes. And some warmth in your body." The supercargo escorted the resident agent below.

Back on deck, Reggie approached the captain. "Sir, may I ask a question?"

Captain Houchins didn't answer. He watched the crew lower the long boat over the side and puffed on his cigar. A big smile creased his face when he turned to Reggie.

"I'd give a guinea to be a speck on the wall below in the trade room right now, lad." He laughed. "Davie will be plying His Majesty's Resident Agent with cheap Flipo rum after offering him a new pipe and a bucket of *tabac*. And a new *chapeau*." He reached out and placed a hand on the boy's shoulder. "What's your question, lad?"

"Why didn't the islanders come out when we arrived?"

Oroa, one of the Pukapuka girls came up from the trade room with Swint's wet clothes and laid them out on the main mast boom to dry.

"Ha! There's another one for the books, Reggie, me lad. Davie's got island lovelies undressing his nibs below decks."

Captain Houchins and the doctor climbed over the side and into the long boat, where four rowers waited. Reggie handed down the doctor's gear.

"Come aboard, lad. You should meet Alberti. I'll answer your question as we go to shore."

Reggie went over the side and sat in the bow of the long boat. Tooks stood above at the railing.

"You have the helm, Mr. Marsten," the captain said to the first mate. "Allow no one aboard or ashore until we sort out this typhoid business. I'll return directly or send word." He ordered the rowers, "Push off."

The captain and the doctor sat in the stern sheets of the long boat on either side of the Maori helmsman. Houchins asked the Frenchman. "Are we in time, Doctor?"

"Perhaps, Captain," Claude Dozier said. "No one has died. I estimate we are in the third week of the disease. These are very healthy people, and the infected ones were isolated early on. I am most pleased that there is a nurse who seems to know what she is about. Unfettered, this could have spread throughout the entire population. Then there would have been a major problem."

The captain looked forward and remembered Reggie's query. "Your question, lad, about the Pukapukans not coming out to meet us."

Reggie nodded and smiled. *He remembered.*

"They're a strange lot these Pukapukans. Trace their families from Samoa, not Tahiti. Never been able to sort them out, even though I can muddle through with their lingo." He paused for a moment. "What if a canoe capsizes in the reef passage, for example. The Pukapukans ashore would gaze at the people dashing about in the water and say, 'Look, their boat's capsized. They are in the water. It is something new. Well, it was their idea to go out there. Let's sit here and see how they get themselves out of the water.' It's not that they're uncharitable or self-centered or anything like that. Rather the reverse, in fact. It's just that the idea would never occur to them to do anything."

Captain Houchins threw his cigar butt away. "It's the same with our arrival. It's something new. 'Let's see if they're coming for a visit. Nothing to get excited about'." He lit another cigar. "Strange lot these. At any other island we'd have a hundred canoes around the *Wallaroo* before we dropped anchor."

Under the power of the *Wallaroo's* rowers, the long boat shot through the reef gap and was soon on the beach. A crowd surrounded the craft. Makea, the island's *ariki*, placed leis over the heads of the three white men. Doctor Dozier immediately recognized the nurse by her white cap, even though she wore a *pareu*. They hurried off toward the far end of the island. Two island men carried his bags.

The trader pushed his way through the crowd and greeted the captain with open arms.

"Well met, you ol' pirate," Albert Freshour said. "Good voyage? I was hoping you'd get the contract. You're here sooner than I expected." They shook hands and hugged. "Who's the kid?" He nodded at Reggie.

"My replacement. A stowaway out of Auckland, or was it Whangarei? Can't remember. He wants to be a copra schooner skipper, but we're doing what we must to push him out of it. Davie has him under his wing, so you know he'll be corrupted straight away.

"Reggie, lad, meet a good friend, even if he's a Yank. Came to the islands a decade or more ago to write the great novel of the South Pacific, but he's not a bad lot and a good trader."

The American looked over their shoulders. "Where's Davie?"

"Still aboard. Entertaining your man Swint."

"Well, I hope you brought him lots of bully beef. He won't eat anything native."

"Not getting on well with this one then, are you, Alberti?" Houchins said.

"He's an ass, this one is," the trader said.

Some of the islanders started to slide outrigger canoes into the water. The captain spoke to the *ariki*.

"Tell your lot no one goes aboard until the doctor gives the okay."

Makea walked away to talk to his people.

Reggie followed Houchins and Freshour up the white pebbled beach to a single-story building made of rough boards with an unpainted iron roof— the S. L. Livingston Company's store and warehouse, and the trader's home. It sat among the coconut palms and had a covered porch along its front.

"Won't even try to learn the language," Alberti continued. "Won't eat anything except what comes out of a tin. The village mamas offered him wonderful meals—fish, pig, all their best. He wouldn't have any of it." They walked up the steps to the porch and into the store. "So they brought it all to me. What a feast!"

When they entered the main room of the store, Reggie looked at the shelves behind the counter—canned goods, bolts of colorful cloth, kerosene lanterns, hatchets, saws, knives of various sizes, jars full of stick tobacco, a rack of umbrellas, and three Singer treadle sewing machines. There were spools of thread and sewing needles next to a line of brown beer bottles with wire-fastened porcelain stoppers. All like what he'd seen in the trade stores on other islands, except the beer.

"Welcome to the finest watering hole in this quadrant of the South Pacific," the trader said with wide spread arms. "What'll you have?" He pointed to the bottles on the shelf. "We have some properly-aged home brew, some not-so-old home brew, and a batch of new stuff."

Alberti walked behind the makeshift bar—a wooden plank lying across two stacks of packing boxes. Above his head hung a hand-lettered sign: *The Danger Island Cantina*. Makea joined them.

What's a cantina?

"That jerk even wanted to close down my bar."

Two islanders came into the store. The trader opened bottles for them. They laid some coins on the bar, which Alberti scooped up and examined. "Frog francs." He shook his head and dropped the money into a cigar box.

What's wrong with the coins?

Four small children, naked except for *pareus*, burst into the store and surrounded the schooner captain. Houchins thrust his hands into his pockets, and then held out closed fists to the urchins.

"Which hand?" he said with a grin. The children paused for a moment. The oldest, a girl of maybe ten, pointed to his left hand. The five glass marbles in his palm disappeared in an instant, and the children flew out of the store to start their game. Houchins handed Alberti five marbles from his right hand. "For later," he said. "Davie has more aboard. How do they manage to lose 'em between visits?"

Alberti shrugged and laughed. "*Tamanu* seeds make a good substitute. Fancy a pickle?" He placed a large glass demi-john of green floating things on the bar. "Left over from the Battle of Verdun, I expect." No one took a pickle. "Got them off a Frog tramp steamer that passed through some months ago. That's probably where the francs came from." Alberti opened four bottles of the aged beer. "Let's go sit outside." He handed a beer to each of the others. Seated in comfortable chairs made of local materials, the trader continued his tirade about the resident agent.

"Didn't come for a visit until he'd been here two weeks or more. Don't think he likes the idea of me marrying an island girl and having a brood of half-breeds, as he called them." He took a drink from his beer. "It almost came to a head when he said that." The American stood and walked to the porch railing. "I've still got my old Colt .45 service revolver, and I almost thought about finishing him off." He took another pull on the bottle. "Could've dumped his body off the outer reef. No one the wiser."

He can't be serious. Kill a man for a slight like that?

Makea nodded, as if in approval, smiled at Reggie and winked.

"Speaking of firearms, Alberti. What happened to the gun rack you had?" Houchins said to change the subject.

"Full of umbrellas now. Got a few old Mausers and a shotgun or two stashed away in the warehouse. The Bible thumpers and Wellington bureaucrats don't cotton much to the idea of islanders being armed. The days of booze and guns are past, I'm afraid, Harry. Now, it's all sewing machines and canned goods."

"Well, Albert, my old friend, we'll have to live with these things. Did bring you some makings for your home brew though." Houchins stood and joined his friend at the railing. He lit a cigar and handed one to the trader. "Times are a changing. RA's come and go, and you've survived worse, I know." He lit Alberti's cigar. "They come with big dreams about how they'll change their world and it usually doesn't happen. Some do great things. Some are just lotus eaters, and some just putting in the time until their pension. But, we have to live with' em and their foibles. Mustn't let 'em interfere with our trade. Heard bad things about the Japs up north in the old German islands. Stopped all outside shipping. Some say they're building big military bases everywhere. Not good." He looked out to the lagoon. "Now, what's all this?"

A lone crew member of the *Wallaroo* was rowing the schooner's dinghy through the reef gap toward the beach.

"Reggie, my lad, go see what that's about."

"Aye, aye, sir," Reggie said, and went down to the beach to wait for the dinghy. Under one of the palm trees he passed two island girls who gave him big smiles. *Wonder if we're staying the night.*

Reggie pulled the dinghy up onto the beach. Tupai, the crew member, handed him a folded piece of paper—a note from McCombs: *Harry, I've got this Swint sod sorted. He won't be any bother. Can we come ashore or is the plague still rampaging amongst the natives?*

"Will you wait here, *inē*, Tupai?" Reggie said. "Must take it to the captain." The crewman nodded. Reggie felt uncomfortable giving orders to the crew—he was one of them. Even though he was a white man, he was still just a crew member. The rowers from the long boat remained on the beach making new friends among the island girls. Tupai joined them.

As Reggie walked back up the beach, he saw the palm groves around the store had filled with islanders. They weren't going into the store, just sitting under the trees and waiting. He'd been told by Davie that there were three villages on the island; the other *motus* around the lagoon only used to raise crops or coconut palms. To Reggie, it looked like everyone on the atoll had assembled at the store. He wondered why. The government office was in the middle village, not here.

The doctor came through the coconut grove next to the store and joined Reggie.

Dozier bounded up the steps to the porch. He smiled. "*Mes amis,* I think we have, how do you say, nipped it in the butt."

There was a pause, and then the others laughed, but not the *ariki*, who didn't understand the joke.

"So, a lot of needle jabs in their posterior parts, right, Doctor?" Alberti said.

"*Non. Dans le bras.* In the arm." He looked confused by their laughter. "Did I say something humorous?"

"Not to worry, Doctor," Houchins said. "We understand. What needs doing?" He read the note from the supercargo.

The doctor noticed the bottles in their hands. "Beer? *C'est la bière?* Is that beer?"

"*Oui,* Monsieur *Docteur, c'est la bière. Une bonne bière,*" Makea said. "A good Pukapukan beer."

"*Parlez-vous français,* Monsieur?" Dozier asked the chief.

"*Un peu,* Monsieur *Docteur, mais l'anglais est* . . . easier for me."

Alberti went inside the store and took a well-aged brew off the shelf. Back on the porch, he opened the stopper and handed it to the Frenchman.

"*Merci beaucoup,* Monsieur." Dozier took a long pull on the bottle.

Houchins offered him a cigar. "How do we sort this out? The jabs, I mean. How can we be of assistance?" He lit the doctor's cigar.

"*Bien.* Monsieur Makea, I must have your people assemble at the government office in Roto village. There, Nurse Tupou and I will conduct an examination, administer the vaccinations and complete the necessary paperwork. It is absolutely essential that every inhabitant of this atoll complete this procedure."

"Yes, I know this to be true. I must talk to my people first, Doctor," Makea said. He left the store and went out into the crowd among the coconut palms.

"He's a good man, Doctor," Alberti said. "Best to give him some time with his folks. They'll come around when they're ready."

"How long will this take to be done with?" the captain asked. "I need to be clear of Toka reef before dark."

"We may finish today, *mon capitaine,* but I have my doubts. And there will be examinations for some time to determine if the disease has been stopped." He spread his hands and shrugged. "I must stay until the end, *n'est-ce pas?*"

"Well, the contract was just to deliver you here. How will you get on to Pape'ete then? We won't be returning for some months."

"A few days ago, there was a French Navy warship nearing Tongareva—Penrhyn, as you call it—on a courtesy visit. I heard that on the wireless while aboard the Clipper en route to Aitutaki. They heard some transmissions in French and asked me to translate. If Monsieur Swint can be persuaded to communicate with them via wireless, they may rescue me from this plague, if I word the message properly." He grinned.

"What about my boys? They've been on the beach for a bit and chatting up the local damsels, I'm sure. Do they need to be jabbed again?"

"*Non, mon capitaine.* Your men are *bon,* as are you, *mon ami.*" He handed his empty bottle to Alberti. "*Maintenant,* now, I must go to work." He held out his hand. "*Bon voyage, mon capitaine.*" The doctor shook hands with the captain and Reggie. He held Reggie's hand for a moment and said, "Young man, you can do worse than learning from these men. They are honorable men. That's important in this world." With a wave of his hand, he jumped down the porch steps and ran to catch up with the flow of islanders heading toward the other village.

"Well, that's a Frenchie I could learn to like and respect," the trader said.

"He's a *pied-noir*—French, but born and raised in Algeria," Houchins said. "Understand they're looked down upon by the Parisians—French, but not quite French. Much as are our half-breed islanders. He was posted to Indochina for some years before ending up in the islands. Only spent the days with him between Aitutaki and here, but he has a top spot in my log."

"You met him in Aitutaki? How'd that happen?" Alberti asked.

"The planets seemed to be in line for this one, mate, if you believe that rubbish." Houchins lit another cigar. "We'd just tied up at Rarotonga and were off loading copra from the southern group, when the commissioner came aboard in a rush and offered us a lovely sum to dash north to Aitutaki, pick up some typhoid drugs, and carry on to here. Ol' Rupp said he would weigh the cargo and pay us when we returned. We did take aboard some home brew makings for you, Alberti. Can't let an old friend down, right? And some cases of canned goods for Swint, now that I know his name."

"The drugs were at Aitutaki?" the trader asked. "How'd that come to be?"

"Remember what I said about the celestial bit? That Yank airline, Pan American, was doing a route survey, they called it, to open a new service for their flying boats from Sydney to Honolulu. Their clipper flew the typhoid drugs and Dozier from Auckland to Aitutaki and landed in the lagoon. They were waiting for us when we arrived. As quick as could be we hauled anchor and beat north to you." The captain finished his beer and set the bottle on the railing. "Did pick up a couple of Pukapuka lovelies who needed passage home. Don't remember why they were that far south, but it didn't matter. They've kept the doctor and Davie entertained." He laughed.

"I've got some copra for you. Time to take it on board?"

"No, Alberti. Sorry, ol' friend. Need to be south of here as soon as possible. And as quick as can be. No extra ballast. We'll up anchor and be gone before dark. May make a quick call at Suwarrow along the way, but need to get to a safe anchorage—Aitutaki or Raro—before the cyclone season kicks in."

"Suwarrow is it?" Albert asked. "Still looking to find Mair's gold, are you now?"

"Right you are, mate. Always the chance a blow has uncovered something. Be lovely to stay longer, but needs must. Next time we'll let some barnacles grow on the anchor chains. We did bring you the makings, and Swint's Spam," he said again. "I'll send' em along as soon as we are rid of your RA. Come, lad," he said to Reggie. "Time to go aboard."

"Can I ask question, sir?"

The captain paused and put his hands in his pockets. "Haul away, lad."

Reggie turned to the trader. "Mr. Alberti, what was wrong with those French coins? And would you really have shot the government man?"

Albert Freshour took a step back, shook his head and said, "You've got a deep one here, Harry." The trader went back to the bar and opened the cigar box. He took out some coins, returned to the porch and handed them to Reggie.

"Some souvenirs from Danger Island. Your good captain will explain their value later." Freshour paused for a moment, and then said, "Would I have killed the ignorant *pommy* for his slur about my family? No, but the idea did raise some possibilities. No. I saw enough killing in France in '18. Those are very good questions, young man. You'll go far. If, of course, you don't spend too many years with this old pirate and his partner in crime, Davie McCombs."

* * *

Davie and Resident Agent Swint, who wore a new Panama hat, waited in the schooner's waist when Reggie and the captain returned in the longboat. Two outrigger canoes lay alongside. The two Pukapuka girls stood close to the supercargo.

"Mr. Marsten, make to get underway," Houchins said to the mate. "Mr. Swint, your kit will go in the canoes, along with yourself. No time to have my boats go and return. Weather's getting nasty. Must be away." He turned to Reggie and winked. "Stay close, lad. Have a special cargo for you."

The agent climbed over the side to one of the canoes. The girls joined him. They headed to shore.

"Right, Davie. What've we got for Alberti?" the captain asked the supercargo.

"His makings, of course. A bag of marbles for the kids, cigars, and a couple cases of Gordon's. He does like his gin, even if he is a Yank. Some ammo for his Mausers and shotguns, and a box of books."

"A great reader, Alberti is," Houchins said. "Right. Over the side then, Reggie. The canoe will take his nibs to the center village, while you slip ashore close in and give Alberti his cargo. They'll secure it in the long boat as soon as Swint is off a bit."

They watched the islanders paddle through the reef and toward the center village. When the RA's canoe rounded the point, Reggie was away in the long boat. The supercargo stood at the rail and shouted, "No time for chitchat, laddie. Alberti will be waiting. Give him my regards, but drop your cargo and make speed back. We're getting underway."

The trader was at the waterline with two islanders when Reggie's rowers brought the longboat parallel to the beach. Alberti and the Pukapukas unloaded the cargo and pushed off the boat.

"Hope we meet again, Reggie," Alberti said. "Good luck treasure hunting."

On the schooner, the crew hoisted the sails as the longboat was brought on board. Reggie joined the captain and first mate at the wheel. The wind had increased in strength.

"I'll have a course heading of 270° until we clear Toka reef, Mister Marsten, if you please," Houchins said. "Reggie, me lad, a lesson for you. See that smudge of a sandbar off the port bow?"

Reggie could barely make out a white gleam in the choppy sea.

"That's the west end of Toka reef. It runs pretty near four miles out from *Motu Kotawa*. That's that bit of island with the palms further along the lagoon." He pointed to the south with his cigar. "Many a not-so-bright skipper has gone aground there. That's why Pukapuka is also known as Danger Island. We always give it a wide berth and never try to close on the lagoon's passage at night." He lit his cigar. "It's best to lie off to the west and make landfall at first light."

The *Wallaroo* heeled to port as it sailed close-hauled away from the atoll.

9

Suwarrow Atoll

A stiff northwest wind astern pushed the schooner over the increasingly rough sea. Rain squalls swept across the *Wallaroo*. They were two days out of Pukapuka. Captain Houchins stayed at the wheel and chewed his cigar, which he had to re-light often. He took the occasional sip from a near at hand bottle of rum and laughed heartily whenever a freak wave broke over the bow drenching a crew member. Free from his other duties, Reggie stood by the captain—watching, listening, learning.

"Reggie, go below and fetch me another of these brown turds from Mr. McCombs. There's a good lad." The captain tossed the stub over the fantail.

Reggie went down the steps to the trade room. The supercargo sat at his table making entries in a ledger. A square hurricane lantern swung above his head.

"The captain would like another brown turd, Mr. McCombs."

The supercargo smiled, turned to a cabinet behind him and pulled out a box. He opened it and took out two cigars. "Getting a bit rough up there, is it? Best only take one." He placed the second back in the box. "The other'll get too wet to light." He handed a cigar to Reggie. "Ask the captain when he thinks we'll raise Suwarrow." Reggie returned to the stern.

"Here, Reggie, my lad, you take the helm while I light this." Reggie was thrilled whenever they allowed him to take the wheel. He loved feeling the power of the ship in his hands.

"Mr. McCombs wants to know when we'll raise the island. Suwarrow, he called it?"

"Soon, lad. Should see it soon. Tell him not to fret. He's a bit of a granny sometimes. Always worrying during the cyclone season. We'll be in the lee of Anchorage Island before nightfall." The captain took the wheel from Reggie, and the boy went below again.

"The captain says we'll be in the lee of Anchorage Island before dark, Mr. McCombs. What's on Suwarrow? Is there a trading station there?"

"Trading station? No. Not there. Come here, laddie." He took the pipe from his mouth. "Let me show you what Suvarov atoll, or Suwarrow as most people call it now, looks like." McCombs tore a page out of the back of his ledger and drew a big circle.

"We don't even have a decent chart of the god-forsaken place. This ain't exactly accurate, but near enough for our purposes. It's just a wide reef with a bunch of little islands, *motus* they call 'em—not really islands—scattered around it." He drew some small circles around the reef. "Most only a yard or two above the high water mark with a few coco palms. The biggest is Anchorage Island here." He drew a larger circle on the top part of the atoll and used the stem of his pipe as a pointer.

"There's a narrow passage through the reef on the east side of it, wide enough at high water for the *Wallaroo* to run inside. The lagoon is five or six miles across. The word is there's lots of pearl shell in the lagoon. *And* lots of sharks. An outfit from the States tried to make a go of harvesting it some years ago. No one lives there, but could be divers from Manihiki about trying their luck. There's a house of sorts and water tanks in the center of it. Used to be a coral jetty on the leeward side." He drew a line on the sketch. "But cyclones wreck it when they come through. The smaller *motus* have coco palms, but Turtle Island and *Motu Tou*," he pointed to a circle north of Anchorage Island and another on the west side of the lagoon, "are the only other places with any amount of vegetation. On an ebb tide you can walk the entire circuit of the atoll on the reef except the passage, but who'd want to?

"Some fellas about seventy years ago . . . English, I think . . . found a stash of doubloons on Anchorage Island. Word is a chest full of Spanish gold coins was found later on one of the *motus* by a chap named Mair and reburied." He relit his pipe. "That's what the captain's so excited about, wants to find the buried treasure of Suwarrow. 'Mair's gold' he calls it. Crazy idea, if you ask me, but he's the captain. Waste of time, I say."

"Buried treasure?" Reggie felt a twinge of excitement. "What's a doubloon?"

McCombs stood and stepped over to the shelf on the port bulkhead. He ran a gentle hand across the bottle containing the model of the *Fisherman-Maréchal Foch*.

"Mr. Zane Grey heard about the lost treasure from some Europeans on the beach in Pape'ete, but he was a rich man and only interested in hauling aboard prize fish. I remember one of his party talking about taking a look, but he, Mr. Grey, would have none of it. Wise man. He knew a fool's errand when he heard it." McCombs took a pouch of tobacco from the shelf and returned to the table.

"A doubloon? Very old Spanish gold coin." He tapped his pipe against the table leg, dumped the dregs in an ashtray, and used a pen knife to scrap out the bowl.

"Found sometimes on wrecks of the Manila Galleons. They used to haul cargo between the Philippines and Peru. Old stuff. Very rare." McCombs leaned back in his chair, filled, and relit his pipe.

"Yes, laddie. Every time we pass near enough, we stop in for a look. We'll drop anchor in the lagoon, and his nibs'll spend a day or two going from *motu* to *motu* hoping a blow's uncovered something. No trade and too many sharks in the lagoon to be looking for shell. Waste of time, I say. The wind's shifted to the northwest, the barometer's dropping. We're into the cyclone season. Time to be heading to Raro or back to North Island."

"Do you think a cyclone's coming, Mister McCombs?"

"Spin a coin, laddie."

"What's the difference between a cyclone and a hurricane?"

The supercargo laughed. "No difference. Everything north of the equator is a typhoon or a hurricane—depending on which side of the date line you are. Everything south of the equator is a cyclone." He lit his pipe.

"You'll hear them used all mixed together. Sort of depends on where you're standing and who's talking."

A shout from above brought Reggie and McCombs up on deck. The supercargo joined the captain at the wheel. Reggie ran forward to where Tooks stood balanced on the end of the bowsprit. He pointed toward the south.

"Look there, Reggie. Suwarrow." Reggie didn't see anything, but then a few low blurs appeared on the horizon—blurs that became a low green line and a line of white surf.

The following sea and ever-increasing northwest winds thrust the *Wallaroo* through the passage. The captain barked commands and the crew scurried to drop sail. The ship's engine came to life, and the schooner motored into the lee of Anchorage Island. Tooks and Reggie stayed perched on the bowsprit watching for coral heads—coral heads that could rip the bottom out of the schooner. Tooks pointed toward the palm covered island off the starboard side as they passed.

"Pearl divers stay there," he said. "Maybe some there now."

Reggie looked at the empty lagoon, "Where's their ship?"

"No ship," Tooks said. "It put them here and come back later. Sometimes many months." He nodded toward the blackening sky. "Bad weather come. Soon."

Those of the crew on deck looked at the narrow strip of coral beach on Anchorage Island. Reggie went aft and stood by the wheel.

"No one about this time," Captain Houchins said to McCombs. He handed his binoculars to the supercargo. "Their cutters would be in view on the beach if they were."

McCombs turned and scanned the center of the lagoon. "Unless they're out there pearlin.'" With a smile and a wink, he handed the binoculars to Reggie. "They're probably wise enough to be out of it during cyclone season. Not like some I could mention."

"Ha! You're an old woman at times, Davie, my friend. Look at that sky," Captain Houchins nodded toward the northwest. "We're better off here in the lee than outside." He turned to the boy. "Reggie lad, tell Tooks to assemble the crew aft. I need to have a word."

The crew gathered around the wheel in the stern of the ship. Y Ling, wiping his hands with a dirty cloth, mumbled in a mixture of English, Spanish, and Chinese about being taken away from his cooking. Cachero, the engineer, looked up at the darkening sky, then toward the island and shook his head.

"Well, lads, looks like we're in for a bit of a blow," Houchins said. He took a drink from the rum bottle. "Secure the ship double tight. I want two more wraps on the booms. We'll drop another anchor forward and two astern."

After the first anchor caught, the wind swung the schooner around, its bow pointed toward the Anchorage Island. "Best to stay below if it gets rough. Won't be able to launch a boat to pick you up if you go swimming in the lagoon." He laughed and took another drink. "Get 'er done, lads!"

Reggie turned to the captain. "Sir, may I go ashore and pass the storm in the pearlers' house?" A hard wind and rain would come with the storm and he wouldn't be able to sleep on deck. Reggie didn't like the idea of a day or two of copra bugs and cockroaches.

"House?" McCombs laughed. "Not much of a house, laddie. More of a shack."

"Suit yourself, lad." Houchins said. "Take the small dinghy. And find a big tree."

Tooks helped Reggie lower the dinghy over the side.

* * *

When the light craft grated on the crushed coral beach, Reggie stepped out into the kind, warm water. Small, almost transparent, fish nibbled at his legs as he dragged the boat up on shore close to the nearest coconut palm. He tied the dinghy's painter around the base of the tree. Reggie looked back toward the schooner. Tooks still stood at the rail. Reggie waved.

"*Find a big tree.*" He wondered what the captain meant. He turned and looked at the barrier of dense vegetation blocking his entry to the interior of the island. There must be a way through somewhere, he thought. He found a break in the wall of young coconuts and *pandanus*, and followed an overgrown path to a clearing in the center of the island. The dense jungle softened the roar of the breakers on the outer reef, as did the ruckus from the hundreds of sea birds nesting in the trees and flying overhead. The air was damp—heavy with jungle smells of rotting vegetation and wet soil. A brick water tank with a galvanized–iron roof was the first thing Reggie saw as he entered the clearing. Where's the hut, he wondered. The clearing was mostly a tangle of vines and bushes, but someone had made an attempt at a garden, and a few banana and mummy apple trees were about. The only clear ground was under five gigantic *tamanu* trees on the far side. Beneath the *tamanus*—as tall and majestic as English oaks—stood the remains of the pearlers' hut: two wooden walls and a tin roof.

Reggie stood looking at his accommodations for the night. Maybe this wasn't such a good idea, he thought. Well, I don't want them all laughing at me if I run back to the ship. I'll just stick it out. He found the old door to the hut under some palm fronds and dragged it inside to sleep on. It started to rain and the wind increased, bringing with it the sound of the sea smashing against the barrier reef. Reggie huddled in a dry corner of the hut. He took the blue Player's Navy Cut cigarette tin from his shirt pocket. Debris blown from the surrounding trees fell on the hut's roof. He lit the cigarette. I hope no large limbs break off and crash through, he thought.

In the fading daylight, Reggie watched the tall coconut palms on the other side of the clearing bend almost horizontal in the ever increasing wind. Then it was dark, like someone had pulled a blanket over the sky. Rain came sideways into the hut. Lightning illuminated the clearing, and Reggie saw he was not alone. Four, maybe five, coconut crabs scurried toward his corner of the hut. Weighing over two pounds with pincers that could take off a man's finger, they didn't seem afraid of the human presence. The sky lit up again and Reggie saw the rat. As he grabbed a piece of old wood to defend against these invaders, a coconut palm crashed down on the hut.

Reggie crawled out from under the debris. Sea water flowed in through the jungle on the ocean side of the clearing. "Bugger this!" he said to himself. "I'm goin' back to the ship."

Out in the clearing, now a dark whirlpool of wind and rain, another flash of lightning showed him the way to the lagoon. He held his arms over his head as protection from the fronds and coconuts that streamed by like missiles. Twice he stumbled over coconut palms that had fallen across the path.

He burst through the last of the bushes and fell on the beach. "Where's the bloody dinghy?" he yelled. He searched for the tree that he'd tied it to. The lightning was almost constant now, striking off to the west beyond the reef. He crawled along the beach and found the hole in the crushed coral where the tree had been. Reggie looked out into the lagoon—no dinghy. The *Wallaroo*, with a single reefed storm jib, was being battered by combers that poured in through the reef's gap. Can't swim out in this, he thought. Reggie saw that the sea had broached the reef at the north end of the island. The skipper's last remark came back to him, "*Find a big tree.*"

Reggie turned to go back to the clearing, but a coconut, thrown like a stone from a catapult, struck his head. He fell to his knees. Dazed, he crawled toward the path. Grasping the stump of a decapitated palm tree, he pulled himself to his feet and looked back at the lagoon.

"*Where's the ship? It's not there!*" He waited for the lightning but still couldn't see the schooner. He stumbled back to the clearing. Knee-deep sea water flowed around the remains of the hut and the water tank. Reggie stood at the base of the tallest *tamanu* tree and looked up. Shouldn't be too hard, he thought. Lots of low branches. He climbed the wet trunk until he was about twenty-feet above the clearing. There he wedged his body in a crook between two thick limbs. With his face against the tree limb and arms wrapped around it, he hung on and waited.

The tree swayed back and forth. Coconut palms ripped from the island's weak soil slammed against the *tamanu* near his head. Pummeled across his back and shoulders by coconuts, he almost lost his grip several times. Gonna have some tales to tell when this is over, he thought. He saw the sea rising around the base of his tree. May have to climb higher. Peering up in the darkness, he saw another perch he could reach. The tree swayed more violently now. If this goes, I'll just hang on. At least it'll float.

Reggie didn't know how long the storm lasted. His arms and legs ached. One side of his face was rubbed raw by the tree bark. He may have fallen asleep, but he didn't think he had. The wind lessened, the lightning stopped, but the rain continued. He thought the sky was getting lighter. At the base of the *tamanu* he saw sand, covered with the fronds, brush, and coconuts, but no water. Above, birds returned to the high branches. Maybe this is the eye of the storm that Mr. Coombs talked about, he thought. That means more to come. Best wait a bit longer. He looked about the clearing.

The hut was gone, as was the roof over the water tank. Fronds and floating coconuts covered its surface. Most of the palms and jungle on the seaward side of the island had been washed away. He could see the reef. The sea still seethed and smashed against the coral barrier, but the combers no longer rolled across the island. The sky cleared, except toward the west. *If this is just the eye, I should see storm clouds all around,* he thought. *Think I'll take a chance and go to the lagoon for a look. I can always dash back if it gets ugly. The lagoon. Bloody hell, the ship!*

Reggie didn't need a path to find his way to the lagoon this time. He stood on the beach where he'd come ashore the evening before. No sign of the schooner. The almost still waters of the lagoon were filled with debris. Floating among the fronds and trees were hundreds of dead seabirds. More dead birds and coconuts littered the beach. *Where's the Wallaroo? It couldn't have left. They wouldn't leave without me. Maybe it's across on another part of the lagoon.* He shaded his eyes with his hand. *Can't see to the other side. Need to get up higher.*

Reggie ran back to the *tamanu* tree and climbed as high as he could, higher than before. He looked to the west and south. No sign of the schooner. Some of the smaller *motus* around the barrier reef were gone, washed away. Across the lagoon, maybe five miles, a larger *motu* still had some trees. To the north he saw a few trees still stood on the closest *motus*. For the first time Reggie realized he might be *alone*. He climbed down, dropped the last couple of feet to the ground, and collapsed on the sand. He tried to stand, but his legs wouldn't respond. He felt dizzy. He sat at the base of the tree and leaned back against its trunk.

The western sky was brilliant with red and orange when he opened his eyes. *I must have fallen asleep,* he thought. *God, I'm thirsty.* Reggie took inventory. *Still got my shoes. And my knife.* "Fire and steel. That's the two things a man should always have," Captain Houchins said often. Reggie fingered the canvas sheath on his right hip. *Glad I listened to Tooks and had the strap sewn over the hilt. I've got my knife, but what about fire?* He patted his shirt pocket. *The cigarette tin was there. Lost my hat. Most likely out on the lagoon somewhere.* He put a hand in his pocket and brought out the French francs. *Don't believe they survived.*

Reggie held onto the trunk of the tree, stood, and looked around for a drinking coconut. The little green gems were everywhere. He opened a half dozen with his knife and emptied their contents, both liquid and meat. *At least I won't starve to death,* he thought. *Wonder how long a man can survive on coconuts?*

He returned to the lagoon side of Anchorage Island. Seated on a fallen palm log, he stared out across the water. *What do I do now?* he asked himself. *Am I the only one who survived? Could someone be alive on the other side of the lagoon? How long can I live on coconuts and raw fish? I'm sure I can catch or spear a fish. There're masses of birds here abouts. Should be able to snare a few. And there's the eggs. But I need fire. My matches won't last long. I wish I'd paid more attention when Tooks showed me how to make fire during our visit to Mangaia. But no, Mister Know-It-*

All said, "Why rub two sticks together when one has matches or even a lighter?" He did show me how to find sea urchins and sea slugs on the reef. And snails. That I remember.

The rain returned. Reggie collected an arm load of palm fronds and built a lean-to shelter over the log. He crawled inside. The rain still dripped in, but he was out of the wind. I've never been this alone before, he thought. Will anyone ever know what happened to me? While he slept even the nocturnal wandering of multitudes of hermit crabs around and over his body didn't disturb him.

* * *

Reggie woke with a start. Had something run across his face? Not the rat, he hoped. He crawled out from under the lean-to. When he stood, his body felt like someone had backed over him with a lorry—twice. The left side of his face burned and was tender to the touch. I must look a fright, he thought. Who cares? Not important. He took off his shirt and inspected it. It wasn't quite in shreds, but getting near. Should keep most of the sun off. His canvas trousers would now pass for short pants. He was thrilled that his shoes had survived.

The morning sun glared off the water. A firm breeze rattled the fronds on the remaining palms. Gulls and other seabirds feasted on the dead fish and feathered carcasses littering the beach and lagoon. *Am I really alone?* He stared across the lagoon. *Must take another look.*

Reggie walked back to the clearing. Coconut crabs scurried into their underground burrows as he passed. Surprised they weren't all drowned during the flooding, he thought about trying to catch one. They're good grub, but not raw. He reached down and picked up a drinking nut. The liquid tasted wonderful, as did the meat.

Climbing the *tamanu* tree again—each movement now painful—Reggie wondered what he should do next. Should I stay here on Anchorage Island or try to walk around to the other side of the lagoon, hoping someone else had survived? If another ship comes to Suwarrow, it'll stop here. But it would be maybe many days or weeks—or even months—before one comes. Maybe the pearl divers from Manihiki will return. From his perch in the tree, he saw the wide reef that enclosed the lagoon. It didn't look like the storm had ripped any gaps through it. The supercargo said one could walk the entire circuit except at the opening where the *Wallaroo* had entered. During an ebb tide I should be able to make *Motu Tou* easily in a few hours, he thought. I'll start tomorrow morning at first light.

Reggie spent the remainder of the day scouring the island for anything useful. He gathered a pile of fronds near his lean-to. Half-buried in jungle debris and jammed between the trunks of a smaller group of *tamanus*, he found the hut's door and dragged it to the beach. The tin roof he discovered under a pile of fronds and palm logs near the water tank. This joined his growing inventory of building materials on the beach. He cleared all the flotsam out of the tank and tasted the water. Too salty, he thought. Maybe when I return, I'll clean it out and collect rain water. He'd already thought about the proper shelter he would build.

When the sun was high in the sky, he improved his lean-to, laid some dry palm leaves in the bottom, and added the door and tin roof to the frond covering. It didn't look like it was going rain that day. Later in the afternoon, as the setting sun once again painted the sky with brilliant colors, he returned to the site with an arm load of drinking nuts. Before the last light faded he worked again on his shelter. I should stay dry tonight if it rains, he thought. He wondered if he would have any unwanted visitors. The coconut crabs and rats, if they're alive, should have lots to eat without bothering him.

10

Awake before dawn, Reggie walked to the other side of the island. Far out on the northeastern horizon he thought he saw a ship's light. He kept watching it, but when it didn't move, he realized it was probably a star or planet. Wishful thinking never got me anywhere, he thought. As he crossed back to the lagoon side of the island, he decided he'd need a stout walking stick for his trek around the reef. The sky had lightened when he returned to the small grove of *tamanu* trees where he'd found the door. He cut off a straight, six-foot limb.

Back at the lean-to, he inspected the contents of his Player's tin. Ten left, but only seven matches. Should I smoke a cigarette? No. Don't want to waste any matches until I'm ready to have a fire. He closed the tin. He hoped it wouldn't rain today. After a filling breakfast from four drinking nuts, Reggie took his stick in his right hand, a drinking nut in the other, and started walking north along the lagoon edge of the reef. I'll save this nut until I find another, he thought. Should find some on the other *motus* and along the inside of the reef. *Give anything for a bacon'n egg sandwich about now.*

The width of the exposed reef surprised and pleased Reggie. He figured it was as wide as five or six rugby pitches. And much easier going than he thought it would be. The ocean swells slammed against the outer edge and shot up sheets of foam and spray. Reggie kept to the lagoon side. This isn't a stroll in the park, he said to himself. The coral is fairly level but jagged and sharp-edged. Glad I didn't lose my shoes in the storm. I still must watch my step. Don't want to find any of those tasty sea urchins by stepping on them.

When Reggie reached the bend in the reef where it turned toward the south and west, he'd drunk three nuts and eaten two sea urchins. How long have I walked? he wondered. A couple of hours, maybe. The sun's still climbing, about halfway to noon. Think I can see the trees on *Motu Tou*. Probably not. Too far away. Maybe just a mirage off the lagoon. It's hot, even with the breeze. Wish I hadn't lost my hat. Almost wish it would rain.

The sun was directly overhead when Reggie stopped on a long raised strip of crushed coral and sand, which had been a tree-covered *motu*. Three small palms and some brush had weathered the cyclone. He sat in their shade. Not much farther, he thought. "Those trees down there must be *Motu Tou*," he said out loud while pointing to the south. Who the bloody hell am I talking to? Am I comin' unhinged? Must be the sun. I'll just sit here a piece and cool off. He leaned back against the base of the palm. He'd dozed a bit before a gull landed in the palm above and loosened a coconut.

What the hell? Reggie said to himself. He looked down at the coconut in the sand next to his thigh. Now I know why Tooks said to never sleep under a coconut tree. Poor Tooks. I wonder what happened to him? He was my best friend. Wonder what happened to all of them? And the ship. Reggie stood and stepped away from under the nuts above his head. He shaded his eyes with his hand and looked south across the lagoon. Could it be over there? Can't see the reef on that side. Too far. Maybe I should go around to the south rim if I don't find anyone on *Motu Tou*. He looked down at the shadow creeping out from the palm trees. Need to push on. He gathered up two drinking nuts and his stick.

During his circuit of the reef, Reggie's attention was on the lagoon searching for any signs of survivors from the schooner, or where he placed his feet. He did look out to sea from time to time watching the ocean and the weather, in hope-against-hope that he might see a ship. How would I signal it if I see did one? How could I tell anyone that I'm alive? Reggie started to realize he might be on Suwarrow, alone, for a long time.

What's that? Reggie saw a white pole protruding out of a tidal pool near the seaward edge of the reef. He was almost to *Motu Tou*. It looked like the shaft of an oar. As he approached the tidal pool, Reggie saw that the oar was jammed upright in a crevice in the coral. The oar had three red-blue-red rings halfway along its white shaft. Not from the *Wallaroo*, he knew. Reggie placed his stick and drinking nut on the reef and grasped the oar. He wiggled it back-and-forth until it came loose from the coral. While holding the oar in his hands, he saw that part of the blade was broken off. He inspected it closely to see if there were any identifiable marks—what ship it was from or where it was made? Nothing. About six feet in length and badly scraped, he knew it had been at sea for a while. Wonder where it came from? he asked himself. Off which ship? Still pretty solid. I'll take it along. Don't know what use it will be. Maybe part of my new shelter.

Reggie emptied his drinking nut, picked up his stick and the oar, and walked toward *Motu Tou*. He was more careful where he placed his feet on this last stretch of the reef. Palm logs and fronds thrown up on the coral from the lagoon hid many of the holes on that pockmarked surface.

Less than a mile away, *Motu Tou* seemed to have survived the cyclone with little damage. It hadn't been swept clean like the smaller islets on this side of the reef. Piles of logs and other debris were jammed up against its lagoon side. The western most *motu* of the atoll, and oriented west-to-east, the cyclone's force had flowed around *Motu Tou*. Reggie began to think that the storm had just struck Suwarrow a glancing blow. He looked to the south where the reef curved around back toward the east. No *Wallaroo*. Could it have been swept over the reef by the storm? No. He turned to face the center of the lagoon. It must be out there. Mister McCombs said that parts of the lagoon were very deep, and divers used breathing rigs to harvest the pearl shell.

Reggie didn't believe that a ship of that size could just disappear . . . just be gone. And all his friends. Reggie felt a sense of loss that he hadn't known before. He'd never had friends, mates, whom he'd worked, eaten, joked, laughed, drank, argued with, and learned from just disappear. This can't be right. Why him? Why did he survive? Tooks had said that Tangaroa could be a cruel god. But what about my god? Why did he let this happen? Maybe they don't care. Maybe they don't exist? That's what Mister McCombs believed. Maybe we're on our own in this world. Weren't Y Ling, a Buddhist, and Cachero, the Catholic, always arguing over religion? It sounded like they talked in circles.

Reggie skirted a jumble of logs and walked close to the lagoon edge of the reef. A shark's fin broke the water's surface a few yards away. He reached down into the palm tree debris and broke loose a coconut. "Up yours, mate," he shouted as he threw the nut at the shark. *No one could have survived out there—too many sharks. I must be alone.*

11

As he left the coral of the barrier reef, Reggie thought the brush on *Motu Tou* looked thicker than on Anchorage Island. A grove of tall *tou* trees rose from the center of the island in among the palms. On a stretch of sand above the crescent-shaped bay on the lagoon side, Reggie saw what looked like a brown log. A brown log with a red top.

"Oh, my god! It can't be!" He dropped the oar and ran along the beach. Tooks always wore a red shirt. "Tooks! Tooks! Are you alive? Tooks, it's me, Reggie!"

Reggie fell to his knees next to his friend's body. The Maori's face, half-buried in the sand, was turned toward him. Reggie grabbed Tooks's shoulder and hip, and rolled him over onto his back. The man cried out as if in pain.

"Tooks, it *is* you! You're alive! Tooks, are you injured?"

His friend's eyes opened. "*Vai. Vai.*" He spit sand from his mouth.

"*Vai?* What's *vai?* Speak English, Tooks. What's wrong?"

"Water. Want water."

"Righto, mate. Just a minute." Reggie ran to the lagoon and found a drinking nut. Kneeling again by his friend, he cut open the nut. He raised the man's head and held the nut to his lips. "Drink this."

Tooks opened his mouth. Reggie poured the cool liquid between his lips. Tooks gagged and lost most of the fluid. He took the nut from Reggie and held it over his mouth.

"Steady on, mate. There's more of that about." Reggie ran along the beach collecting drinking nuts. He dumped a pile of the little green gems next to Tooks and started cutting them open. He looked down at his friend. *Tooks's alive. I'm not alone.* He handed another nut to his shipmate. Tooks drank it down without gagging and reached for another. Reggie carved out chunks of the meat from the nuts and handed them to his friend, who devoured them between drinks. Tooks's breathing was labored. He rested his head back on the sand and closed his eyes. His face twisted with pain. Another groan escaped his lips.

"What's wrong, Tooks? Where does it hurt?" Reggie looked at the man's body, but didn't see any injury. No blood or anything on his shirt or canvas shorts.

"*Tōku vaevae.* My leg. Broke."

"Oh, shit! Which one?"

"*Maui.*" Tooks patted his left thigh. Reggie saw a bulge on the calf below the knee. A light touch on it caused a cry from his friend.

"Damn! Sorry, mate. Don't move. Must think for a minute. Must remember."

Reggie stood and stared down at his friend. *How'd we do that?* His memory raced back to the day when Ioapa, a farmhand, fell off their wagon and broke his leg. Reggie's father had been a medical orderly during the war. Reggie helped him set Ioapa's leg before they took him to the hospital in Whangarei. *Can I do this? There were two of us then. I held Ioapa under his armpits when Father pulled on his leg. But, I'm alone here. How can I do it? And what will I use for a splint? We used pieces of board and leather straps. There's nothing like that here. Think. Must think. What do I have?* He looked around at the storm debris on the beach. *Maybe the rigid stems of the palm fronds might do. I don't need much length. The thick bits should work. But what will I secure them with? Maybe can I find a length of line from the Wallaroo? No. I need something now. Don't have time to scourge around the reef. Wish I knew how to make rope from the trees like the Maoris. No time for that.*

Reggie stripped the branches off several fronds. *These should work. But how to secure them? My belt'll work. Nobody's goin' to mind if I run around starkers. And, my shoe laces! Reggie, you're bloody brilliant.*

He knelt next to his friend again and looked at the bulge on his calf. He didn't want to touch it until he had to. The skin wasn't broken, but it seemed like the bones had separated a bit. There was a reddish tinge to Tooks's dark skin. I have to straighten 'em before I splint 'em, he thought. *God, I wish my father was here.* He leaned back on his heels and closed his eyes. *I don't know if I can do this. What if I make it worse?* He remembered his father telling about how he would take the time to make soldiers more comfortable even though he knew they were dying. "As needs must," he'd said. "You can't just stand about and watch them die."

Reggie laid the palm frond stems alongside the leg to see where he should chop them off to fit between Tooks's knee and ankle. As he bent over the Player's tin fell out of his shirt pocket.

"Cigarettes? You have cigarettes, Reggie?"

Reggie, so wrapped up in his doubts about setting Tooks's leg, hadn't looked at his face. There was a hint of a smile and a sparkle of anticipation in his eyes. Tooks had placed a hand behind his head and watched Reggie closely. He held up two fingers, in the shape of a V, with his other hand and tapped them on his lips.

Reggie picked up the tin. "Righto, mate, but I didn't want to use the matches. We'll need fire and—"

"No worries, mate. We will have fire." He grinned and pointed a finger at Reggie. "And *you* will make it. A cigarette, Reggie, *'inē*. Please."

Reggie lit a cigarette and handed it to Tooks. The Maori pulled hard on the cigarette, held the smoke a long time before releasing it with a rush.

"You must have one, Reggie."

"No, mate. A bit off yours, but I'm saving the smokes. I know you can teach me how to make fire, but you can't make cigarettes."

Tooks laughed and grimaced with pain. He passed the cigarette to Reggie, who took a short drag and handed it back.

Reggie felt dizzy for a moment. He closed his eyes and thought about what he had to do. "Tooks, we must set this leg and splint it, or it won't heal right. You'll be a cripple for life."

Tooks's head was back on the sand as he enjoyed the cigarette. He looked up and offered it to Reggie. Reggie shook his head, "You finish it."

How am I going to do this? What do I tell him? This is going to hurt like hell.

"Seen before," Tooks said. "Watched crew's leg fixed on *Tiare Taporo*, Captain Andy's schooner. Two men hold him and supercargo pulled leg straight. He yelled a lot." Tooks softly stubbed out the cigarette in the sand. He handed Reggie the butt. "Save. Make more smokes later."

Reggie placed the butt in the tin. "What'll we use for cigarette paper?"

"*Pandanus* leaves make good cigarettes."

How can I keep Tooks from moving when I pull on his leg? Reggie asked himself. Maybe I could drag him up the beach to a tree where he could get a grip on something. No, I don't want to move him. *I'll bring a tree to him!* Reggie went to the jumble of palm logs driven there by the storm. Must find the biggest one I can move, he thought. He found one he could barely lift, dragged it up to Tooks, and positioned it lengthwise behind his head. Tooks watched all of this with a calm expression.

"I'm going to kneel behind you and try to roll this log under your shoulders. Can you raise yourself up a bit on your elbows?" The islander nodded and pushed his shoulders up from the sand. He let out a cry of pain.

"Sorry, Tooks." Reggie tried to roll the log, but it was too heavy. I need a lever, he thought. No. No time to look for anything. He grasped one end of the log and dragged it forward. He did the same with the other end. Tooks lay back on the log. Both men breathed hard.

"That was the easy bit," Reggie said. He dug out a hole in the sand under the log behind Tooks's shoulders. "Wrap your arms around the log, mate."

Reggie moved around and knelt on the sand facing his friend. *God, I pray I do this proper.*

Tooks's arms were wrapped around the log. He smiled and said, "Do it now, Reggie."

He took the man's foot in one hand, grabbed the ankle with the other, and pulled.

Tooks yelled.

Reggie thought he felt the bones move. He released his grip.

Tooks was breathing hard.

"I have to check the leg. This'll hurt."

Tooks nodded, his eyes closed. Sweat poured off his face.

Reggie placed his hand on the bulge and pressed down.

Tooks yelled again.

"I'm so sorry, mate." Reggie thought the bones felt like they were straight. *What do I know? Can't do more. Don't think I've made it worse.*

Reggie sat back and removed his canvas belt and the shoe strings. He positioned the two splints alongside the leg and secured them over the bulge with the belt. Tooks let out a groan of pain.

"Steady on, mate. Almost sorted." He wrapped and tied off his shoe strings above and below the break. The young man's heart raced as he sat back on his heels and looked at his friend. He wiped the sweat from his forehead.

Tooks smiled. "Well done, *teina*. All of Cooks call you *Doctor* Reggie."

"What's *teina*, Tooks? And how will anyone know what happened?"

Tooks started to laugh, but grimaced in pain. "*Teina*—brother. Now you my brother, Reggie. Before *taeake*, friend. Now you family." Tooks groaned again. "More *uto*, please, *teina*."

"*Uto?* Oh, right, a drinking nut." Reggie opened several nuts and handed them to his friend. "What happened to the ship, Tooks?"

"*Huripari*, cyclone, come. Ship drag anchors. Longboat ripped off deck. Main mast break and fall on deckhouse. All crew hanging on and praying to Tangaroa and Christian god. Supercargo go overboard. Ship pushed across lagoon, bottom ripped out on reefs. Foremast break, fall on Tooks's leg. Ship roll over, all crew in water. Ship sink. I grab plank from deckhouse and pray. Storm bring me here."

"What happened to the captain?"

"Not know. Never see him. Maybe he drunk in cabin. Sink with ship."

Reggie stood and looked out across the lagoon. Dark clouds were coming from the northeast. Rain, he thought. It's getting on toward sunset. Need some shelter.

He spent the remaining daylight dragging palm logs up to where Tooks lay. He collected armloads of fronds and built a hasty lean-to. The rain arrived as he slid under the cover and lay next to his friend. He opened more nuts and shared them with Tooks.

"You all right? How's the leg feel?" His roof wasn't doing a very good job of keeping off the rain.

"Leg hurt. You do good, Reggie. Tooks always remember, *teina*."

"What about the others? Think any made it.?"

"No, *teina*. All *toremi*, drowned, or *mako*, sharks, get them. This an evil place."

"Evil? Why evil, Tooks?"

Tooks held his hand over his face to keep off the rain. "Tomorrow, Reggie, I show you how to make good roof." He tried to shift his body, but groaned in pain. "Many men come here, many *Papa'ā*. All after pearl shell. Suwarrow have best pearl shell in Cooks. Most *mako* too. Lagoon deep. No one dive deep because of sharks. Many tried. One man make fort on Anchorage Island, bring cannons. Other *Papa'ā* bury gold here. Many die. Evil place."

"But, I thought Mister McCombs said men from Manihiki come and dive here."

"Yes, Reggie. That people have no sense. Many die. They take shell from not deep water too. Young shell. Not good."

"I don't understand, Tooks. What's wrong with taking young shell?"

"Take young shell, not have more shell later."

"So, it's like sheep farming, isn't it? If we killed all the lambs, we'd have no sheep later."

"You smart boy, Reggie. Learn fast. Tomorrow we make fire, have good *kaikai*, and make good shelter." Tooks looked closely at Reggie. "What happened to face?"

Reggie touched the crusty scab above his left jaw. "Made love to a tree during the storm." He rubbed the knot on his right temple. "And lost a fight with a flying coconut." Both men laughed.

"How you find me, Reggie? How you come here?"

"Walked the reef around from Anchorage Island. Needed to see if anyone was alive. If I was really alone."

"See nothing?"

"No. Just an old oar, not from the *Wallaroo*. Nothing else. Maybe I'll look farther around tomorrow. Think others could be alive?"

"No. Maybe, but, yes, you must go look."

* * *

Before dawn Reggie crawled out from under the lean-to. The rain squalls had passed over the atoll, and the sky was clear of clouds. Wet and chilled, he stood holding up his shorts with one hand. He walked around to the ocean side of the *motu*, and his eyes searched the western horizon for lights that might be a ship. We must find a way to signal any vessel that comes close to the atoll, he thought. But with what? Tooks said he would make a fire. Maybe we can make a smoke signal or something. *Make a fire. Yes!* Then we can cook something to eat. I know I can spear a fish like Tooks taught me when we went night fishing on the reef on Mangaia. And the coconut crabs. I saw some run into the brush before dark. There's plenty of sea urchins and snails. And sea slugs. Lots of fat ones in the reef pools. Mister McCombs called them *trepang*—said Chinese traders would pay a good price for dried ones. Mister McCombs. I can't believe they're all gone. All drowned. I should look farther around the reef. Maybe someone else survived.

Reggie looked at the sky. The wide swath of the Milky Way stretched like a belt of crowded bright dots from horizon to horizon. At least I'm not alone, he thought. Where's the Southern Cross? Always have a hard time finding it. The eastern sky slipped from black to indigo when he walked back to the lean-to. Tooks slept. Reggie picked up his knife and went into the brush. He needed a belt and knew he could find a vine or something that would work. He cut a length that was pliable enough and inserted it through the loops in his shorts and the knife's sheath. This'll do, he thought. When it dries out and breaks, I'll cut another. Pleased with himself he pushed his way through the brush to the center of the island. Fat coconut crabs scurried into their lairs. "Your days are numbered, lads," he said. There was little brush on the flat ground under the stand of *tou* trees and coconut palms. I'll build a proper shelter here. But how do I move Tooks? He'll need crutches. Reggie scoured the vegetation until he found two lengths of stout wood with a flat or forked end. He returned to the lean-to and stuck the crutches upright in the sand. What about the oar? He walked back toward the north end of the *motu* and found it. Before returning to the lean-to, he went onto the reef again and speared a couple of urchins with his knife. Breakfast. Tooks was awake when he returned. He held a drinking nut over his mouth.

"G'day, mate. How's the leg."

"Still broke." They laughed. "Where you go, Reggie?"

"Over to the other side." He nodded to the west. "Looking for ships." Reggie broke open the sea urchin shells and handed the morsels to Tooks. "Think we should move to the center of the island. Good spot there under some big trees. I made you some crutches." He pointed to his creations.

"You good *teina*, Reggie. Think of others first."

"I have to take care of you, mate, or I won't survive."

"No, *teina*. I know you survive alone if happen."

"I want to go on around the reef to see if anyone else is alive."

Tooks nodded. "Put some *utos* here and go. You must look for others. We make fire when you come back."

Reggie opened a half-dozen drinking nuts and placed them next to his friend. He picked up his stick and walked south off the *motu* along the reef. The lagoon edge of the reef was cluttered with debris from the storm. Within a mile from *Motu Tou* he found pieces of wood and a tin bucket that must have been from the *Wallaroo*, and lengths of line. He piled these up on the reef to collect when he returned. One short bit of frayed cord he cut and replaced the vine around his waist. He wondered where these pieces of rope had been on the schooner. Had he pulled on it, handled it, or secured it off somewhere before? Who else had touched it? He still couldn't believe they were all gone.

The sun neared its zenith when he saw the glint from glass in a reef pool. What's that? he wondered. There's a bottle floating there. Using his stick, Reggie brought the bottle to where he could grasp it. My god, it's the *Marshall Foch*—Mister McCombs's ship in a bottle! He turned it over and over in his hands. It's all in one piece. Nothing broke. How wonderful!

Reggie looked out to the center of the lagoon. "Mister McCombs, you may be gone, but you live on with this. I'll never forget what you taught me." His eyes filled with tears. He placed the bottle under his arm. "This I'll always keep safe."

Farther on, Reggie found a large portion of sailcloth among the debris. This'll make do for part of the shelter's roof, he thought. He placed it on the coral and continued his search. At the southernmost bend of the barrier reef, he gazed across the lagoon toward Anchorage Island and to the east. Maybe after he got Tooks settled in a proper shelter he'd make the rest of the circuit—a two-day journey at least. He didn't believe anyone else had survived. Reggie turned toward the open ocean. The storm swept everything to this side of the lagoon. Or over the reef.

On his return to *Motu Tou* Reggie collected as many green coconuts from the storm debris as he could carry in the sailcloth. Urchins he speared and dropped in the bucket along with a mess of snails.

Tooks had pushed some of the fronds aside and was sitting up leaning against the logs. He greeted the young man with a big smile. Reggie dropped the weighty bag and an armload of planks and line next to the lean-to.

"How's the leg? Let's take a look." Reggie pushed a frond aside. *I have no idea what I'm doing.* The swelling may have increased—he couldn't tell for sure. "Well, mate, it doesn't seem any worse." He nodded toward the pile of bits from the reef. "Lots of good kit. But this is the best." He showed Tooks the bottle.

"Where you find this, Reggie?" Tooks's eyes opened wider.

"In a reef pool. Saw the sun shining off it." He offered it to Tooks.

"No." He held up both hands." This only yours, *teina*. Special gift from Tangaroa. Must protect . . . save. Don't know meaning. Must ask Aunt Ngere when we return to Raro."

"I don't understand, Tooks. This some kind of superstition thing, like Tangaroa?"

Tooks frowned and shook his head. "No laugh at Tangaroa, *teina*. Me good Christian, but old gods still here. Maybe not on top no more, but still here. Think Tangaroa like us or we be in *mako* belly. Christian god too busy with big business, so other gods take care of us on Suwarrow."

"Who's this Aunt Ngere? Why is she important?" Reggie handed Tooks a handful of snails he'd collected on the reef and opened an urchin.

"Very famous reader of signs. Went to Hawai'i long time. Learned all *Papa'ā* ways of reading signs. Brought special cards that show future."

"Tarot cards? Seen those at the fair in Whangarei. My father said they were a bit of a flim-flam."

"What is flim-flam, *teina?*" Tooks's brows furrowed.

"A trick. A way to skin . . . to cheat . . . the punters, as Mister McCombs would say." Reggie nodded toward the lagoon. "He didn't believe in gods either."

"Mister McCombs no say nothing now, Reggie. Supercargo only pray to one god . . . Yankee dollar."

"But I learned a lot from him." Confused, Reggie thought everyone on the *Wallaroo* liked the supercargo. Especially the captain. They always behaved as old friends. He never heard a cross word exchanged. Reggie pointed across the lagoon. Storm clouds covered the eastern horizon. "We need a better shelter."

"Just put more fronds and sailcloth over us, *teina*." Tooks tried to shift his body, but stopped and moaned in pain. "Not move tonight. Maybe tomorrow under big *tou* trees. Build good hut. Make fire."

"But there's a squall coming." Reggie pointed to the darkening sky.

"Just rain. Not *huripari*, cyclone." Tooks extended a hand. "*Inē*, please, *teina*, a cigarette."

Reggie opened the Player's tin—nine smokes and six matches left. He lit a cigarette, inhaled a lung full, and then handed it to Tooks. The islander leaned back on the sand and enjoyed his smoke. Tooks offered Reggie a final drag, but he shook his head. Reggie placed the butt in the tin.

Reggie showed Tooks the line he'd found. "I'm going to take off my shoe strings and put this on. Should have a better purchase." He cut two foot-long lengths.

Tooks nodded. "Take belt too."

"Think we'll wait a bit on that one." Reggie hitched up his shorts. "This line'll do for now."

With the crutches and the oar as an A-frame, Reggie raised the roof of the lean-to. Not much, but high enough so they could sit up. Fronds in layers along the sides and the sailcloth over the top and down the front opening protected the two castaways from the squalls that passed during the night. The shelter wasn't waterproof—the wind shifted fronds about— but they were mostly dry when they awoke the next day. Both men shivered from the early morning chill.

"Today we make fire, Reggie. No like cold."

Reggie pushed aside the sailcloth door. No wind, and the waters of the lagoon like glass. High, scruffy clouds skidded across the sky above the northern horizon. On the crushed coral and sand beach Reggie saw, like a disorganized spider web, the faint tracks of the hermit crabs' nightly treks spread out in all directions. He stood at the water's edge with the tin bucket. Massive schools of blue parrot and silver needle fish scattered when he waded in to pick up a large black sea slug lounging in the shallows. He knew he needed to make a spear. If we have a fire today, this should be our last cold breakfast, he thought. He walked along the shoreline until he came to the edge of the reef, where he collected more urchins and snails. Above the island, flocks of seabirds swirled in and about the trees. Reggie thought they must be rebuilding their nests. Maybe some survived the storm and he could find some eggs and nestlings. They'd be tasty roasted. He added two nuts to his stash before heading back to the shelter.

Tooks was sitting up and doing something with the palm leaves.

"What you makin', mate?"

"Hats. One for you and one for me." He looked skyward. "Too much sun not good."

"I've got our breakfast." Reggie emptied the bucket next to the lean-to. Tooks saw the sea slug.

"*Rori. Trepang.* Good. Must save skin. Sell to Chinese trader."

"Why do Chinese traders buy sea slug skins?"

Tooks laughed until the pain in his leg stopped him. "Chinaman, he think if man put chopped up bits of *rori* skin in woman's food, make her want to have love with him. If he old man, *rori* bits in his food make him good lover again."

"Does it make do? Does it work?"

Tooks laughed again and grabbed his leg. "No make joke, Reggie. Hurt too much to laugh."

"Sorry, Tooks. Are we going to make a fire today and move in under the trees?"

"We eat now. Then see if Tooks can move." He reached out and picked up the sea slug. "Your knife, *teina.*"

Tooks cut a small hole in the end of the *trepang*, and squeezed out a mess of white stingy innards. He threw them aside. "No good for *kai*, to eat." He slit open the sea slug length-wise and scraped out a brown mass. "This good *kai*." Tooks cut the gooey mass in two and handed half to Reggie.

Reggie hesitated but thought this can't be any worse than the urchins and snails. He took the offering. Rubbery and salty, he got it down his throat as quickly as possible. They finished the rest of the meal with two drinking nuts.

"Now, *teina*. Help me stand. We go find big trees for shelter."

Reggie handed Tooks one of the crutches and moved the fronds and sailcloth aside. Kneeling behind the Maori, he grasped him under the armpits and stood. Balancing on his good leg, Tooks wrapped his left arm around Reggie's shoulders.

"You strong man, *teina*." Tooks hadn't cried out in pain.

"Been wrestlin' sheep since I could walk."

The two men made their way to the center of the *motu*. As they passed through the brush, coconut crabs scurried away to their holes in the ground or at the base of trees.

"See where *kaveu* go, *teina*. You catch later. Good *kai*, but need fire first."

Under the stand of *tou* trees in the islet's center there was little vegetation, almost parklike. Reggie lowered his friend to the ground at the base of a tree, and they discussed where to build their shelter. A gap of about eight feet separated two of the tallest trees. Low-lying branches and crooks just below shoulder level would support a cross-beam. Tooks said the back of the shelter should face the lagoon—the prevailing winds and rain would come from that direction. Reggie cut and stripped a pole for the crossbeam and three more for the slant supports on the backside of the lean-to. Tooks pointed out the best vines in the surrounding vegetation to use for tie offs.

"We need many fronds, Reggie. Many. Your knife and some *utos, inē*, please, *teina*."

After bringing Tooks the drinking nuts, Reggie carried several armloads of fronds to the site. Tooks told him how to position them on the supports so the rain would run off.

"Reggie, bring me the oar and your stick next time, *inē*."

On subsequent trips back-and-forth from the lagoon beach to the *tou* tree shelter, Reggie carried the oar, his stick, the sailcloth, and other salvage from the *Wallaroo*. The ship-in-the-bottle he laid on the ground next to Tooks. "Keep a sharp eye on this, mate," he jested. "Don't fancy any crabs skyin' off with it." Reggie looked up at the flocks of sea birds infesting the island's trees.

"*Tapukus*, young birds, up there, Reggie. Good *kai*. And eggs. Show you how to get them."

"How long have we been here, Tooks? I've lost count of the days."

"What day you find me, *teina*?"

Reggie had to think for a moment. "Third day after the storm, I think. Not for sure, mate."

"Six, maybe seven days. Mark stick with knife. One day or two not make important."

"Why'd you want the oar and my stick?" Reggie said.

"Bring old nut husk, Reggie," Tooks said ignoring Reggie's question.

He smiled. "Put oar and stick here." He patted the ground by his side. "Now, go get many more fronds and drinking nuts. Pull fronds in lagoon up on beach. They dry soon."

Reggie scoured the *motu* for fronds. The storm had stripped many of the palms bare. On the lagoon side, he pulled dozens up onto the beach and found more debris from the schooner, mostly bits of wood and lengths of line. How long will we be here, he wondered, as he looked out across the lagoon. I'm not alone now and won't starve. That's good. Why did Tooks want my stick and the oar?

When he went along the shore, Reggie filled the tin bucket with urchins, snails, and sea slugs. He threw up young coconuts floating at the water's edge onto the beach to collect later. As he walked back through the brush to the shelter, Reggie smelled the smoke. He dropped the bucket and the fronds he was dragging and ran to the island's center. Tooks sat against the tree where Reggie had left him, but now smoke rose from a hole in the sand between the Maori's legs. Reggie tripped on a fallen palm log and landed face-down on a frond.

Tooks laughed. "Come, *teina*. Eat good *kaikai* now." Tooks fed chunks of coconut husk into the fire.

Reggie got up and joined his friend. "You said I would make the fire, Tooks."

"Yes, *teina*. You will. Rain come. Fire stop. Make new fire."

"But how'd you do it?"

Tooks picked up the oar and showed Reggie a long, narrow trough he'd carved in the blade. "Not hard wood." He picked up Reggie's stick. "Hard wood. You push hard wood in not hard wood." He did it. "Make very fast. Have coconut pieces here." He pointed to the end of the trough. "Make very fast. Make fire." Tooks smiled. "Next time, *teina* make fire."

"The rain, Tooks. What about the rain? How do we keep the fire goin'?"

Tooks pointed to the lean-to. "Dig fire pit at open end of shelter. Put up sailcloth and fronds. Keep rain off. I show you. Get water for drink too."

Reggie spent most of the day dragging fronds to the shelter and layering them on the top and sides of the lean-to. When Tooks was satisfied with this, he had Reggie use some stout poles and the sailcloth to rig a covered porch over the lean-to's opening. With a piece of board from the schooner, Reggie dug a fire pit beneath the porch. Tooks sent him out to the reef to find and bring back large pieces of coral. At the shore, Reggie saw dark clouds building up in the northwest. Rain's comin', he thought.

Tooks told Reggie to place dry palm leaves in the bottom of the fire pit, and then some coconut husks. The chunks of coral were laid on this bed. Tooks wove a palm frond leaf torch and had Reggie light it from the small fire between his legs. The wind started to increase, and both men looked up at the darkening sky.

"Hurry, *teina*. Rain come." He pointed to the fire pit.

Reggie transferred the fire to the pit. In moments, the flames were baking the coral pieces. The rain arrived. Reggie helped Tooks into their new shelter. The Maori looked at Reggie's handy work and nodded.

"Good, *teina*. We stay dry now." Rain water poured off the sides of the sailcloth, but not on the fire. "When rain stop, split two fronds. Lay here and here. No sleep on sand."

Reggie went out into the rain and got the bucket. He dumped out the remaining slugs, snails and urchins under the porch, and placed it under the runoff. When the bucket was full, he grabbed a handful of sand and scrubbed its insides. He dumped the bucket, filled it again, dumped it again, and then filled it a third time. "Now we have water, *vai*, Tooks."

Tooks showed him how to make drinking cups from coconut shells. Reggie made a dozen of these and placed them around the sides and back of the shelter to catch rain water running off the fronds.

The rain squall passed over the *motu*. Reggie continued to drag fronds, small logs, and coconut husks to their new home. He placed everything within Tooks' reach, so he could feed the fire.

"Reggie, we have special *kaikai* today. Then we have cigarette." He smiled and pointed across the clearing. "See hole at bottom of tree? Big *kaveu* live there. I see him go in. You kill." Tooks tossed a coconut husk onto the fire.

"How do I kill it, Tooks?"

"Take stick, sharpen end. Go to hole. *Kaveu* close, you use knife. *Kaveu* not close, use stick. Stab here." He pointed between his eyes. "No use hands. *Kaveu* very strong *unga*. Chop off finger."

Reggie sharpened one end of his stick and walked over to the tree. He saw the coconut crab just inside its lair. Its claws looked too dangerous to put his knife and hand in that close. He brought the crab back to the shelter on the end of his stick.

"What now, mate?"

"In fire, *teina*. On the rocks." Tooks laid a frond over the crab.

Reggie brought Tooks cups of water while the crab cooked.

"Tomorrow you get fish, *teina*."

"Get fish with what, mate? I don't have a pole or line or bait or nothing."

Tooks laughed until his leg hurt. "*Teina*, you catch fish same way you catch *kaveu*. Remember when we go night fishing on reef at Mangaia? Make long stick to get fish. More long than this, he pointed to Reggie's walking stick."

"Righto, mate. I remember. We speared some big ones that night. Not me, sorry to say, but you and your mates brought in quite a haul."

"In morning we make *korare*, fish spear. Time for *kai* now."

They devoured the baked meat from the crab and wiped up grease drippings with soft core bits from the drinking coconuts. Urchins and snails added to the feast. When they finished their meal, the sun had set. The breeze shifted a bit, and the shelter filled with smoke—an annoyance, not uncomfortable. The swelling in Tooks' leg had gone down some, and Reggie's face had healed. They shared a cigarette and talked about their families.

Tooks could recite his family lineage back many generations, as far in the distant past as the great migration, when the fleet of canoes—*vakas*, he called them—sailed out of Muri Lagoon on Rarotonga for New Zealand.

Reggie didn't know much of anything about his family's history, only a little of his father's service in the Great War. His mother came from North Island. Wellington, he thought. He'd never met any other relatives, except his uncle Clyde. It wasn't a subject discussed in the Pobjoy household. He wondered why.

* * *

The next morning Reggie stood on the edge of the reef with his new fish spear. He'd cut a slender ten-foot pole. Tooks had fashioned a barbed end from the rib of a palm frond and fastened it to the pole with a vine.

"Look for blue parrot fish," Tooks said. "They stupid fish. When scared, hide head in coral. Keep backside sticking out. Easy to spear." After several unsuccessful attempts, he speared a parrot fish. And a second. Reggie dropped his spear on the beach and ran back to the shelter.

"Tooks. I did it, mate!" He held up the eighteen-inch beauties. "They must be 'bout two pounds each."

"Good, *teina*. Make you a Maori soon." Tooks pointed to a *pandanus* tree at the edge of the clearing. "Bring some green leaves, Reggie. Wrap *ika*, fish, before we cook."

Tooks cut off the tails, roughly filleted the two fish, and wrapped them in the leaves. "Put on rocks. Cover with green palm." He ran a thumb along the blade of Reggie's knife. "Not sharp now. Much cutting."

"Can we eat those spiky pineapple-lookin' things on the *pandanus* tree?"

Tooks frowned. "Can if not have nothing else. Taste bad, very bitter. Make belly hurt."

When Tooks said the fish were done, Reggie used a piece of board to remove them from the fire. They unwrapped the fish and tore the treat-of-a-meal apart with their fingers.

Afterwards, Reggie sat cross-legged under the porch feeding bits of wood into the fire. Tooks lay under the roof on the palm frond bed.

"How many smokes left, *teina?*"

Reggie opened the Player's tin. "Seven. And the scraps."

"This special day, *teina*. You spear fish."

They shared a cigarette.

"Tooks, our new home here under the trees is most comfortable, but how will we know if a ship comes?"

The Maori was silent for a few minutes before he spoke. "*Papa'ā* not same as Maori with time. Maori think about today, *Papa'ā* think about tomorrow. *Papa'ā* have clocks, calendars . . . Maori have today. Tired, sleep. Hungry, eat. Need food, go fish. *Papa'ā* think about next day, next week, next year. You want leave Suwarrow soon. I know this. Tooks not in hurry. We have *kaikai*. Have water. Have roof. We wait for divers from Manihiki come back. Maybe, when leg better, build *vaka* and sail back Raro."

Reggie thought about what he'd been taught in school about the islanders.

"Were the Maoris cannibals, Tooks?"

Tooks frowned again and shook his head. "Not a good thing to speak of, *teina*. Missionary John Williams stop all that in Cooks. But he get eaten by bad people in New Hebrides. Not Maori. *Papa'ā* bring good things to islands: Christian god, schools, doctors, radio, books. Stop fighting on islands."

The palm fronds above their heads rattled in the breeze. Tooks looked up and sniffed the air. "Rain, *teina*."

A squall came ashore. Reggie placed the bucket and coconut cups around the shelter.

As the rain beat down on the palm frond and sailcloth roof, Tooks looked at Reggie. He thought there was sadness in the young man's eyes.

"What you do when we go back to Raro, Reggie?"

Reggie hadn't thought about the future—busy each day with food and fire. Maybe, I'm becoming a Maori, he thought.

"Don't know. Want to see more islands. Want to see many places. My uncle Clyde has been everywhere. He told me about Tahiti and Singapore and Calcutta. They all sound grand. Maybe I'll find a berth on a tramp or another schooner." He turned to his friend. "Have you been to Singapore or other places?"

"Pape'ete many times, *teina*. Calcutta, Singapore, no. Suva and Apia, yes." Tooks looked at Reggie and nodded. "Need build big fire. Tell ship we here. Tomorrow we go to reef, north side of *motu* and find good place. Tooks need walk. Sit too much."

"Sure you're ready to have a go, mate?"

"Yes, *teina*. Use two crutches tomorrow. Put more husks on fire, *inē*."

* * *

Reggie awoke before first light, stoked the fire, and added a husk and a few dry palm leaves. He went out to the reef—the waters of the lagoon still like glass, the sky in all directions clear of clouds—with a basket Tooks had made from palm leaves. He collected drinking nuts, snails, and urchins for breakfast. How long will we be here, he wondered. He remembered his plan to walk the reef to the other *motus* on the eastern side of the lagoon. Maybe no sense doing that. No one there. What about going back to Anchorage Island? Tooks might be able to do that in a bit. There's a water tank, and any ships would stop there first. And lots of coconuts and crabs. *Motu Tou* was small, and Reggie worried about that. How long could they stay here before they needed to find food elsewhere? But there's always fish in the lagoon and bits on the reef. We have water, and I can go to another *motu* for nuts if we need them. Best stay here. For now.

He carried breakfast back to the shelter. Tooks stood by the porch using both crutches. He smiled when Reggie showed him what he had collected off the reef.

"*Teina*, you become Maori now. Have *kaikai*, then go find place for big fire."

Reggie spent all morning gathering fronds and logs. With a short plank from the *Wallaroo*, he dug a deep pit and built a teepee-shaped pyre over it. He piled coconut husks in the pit along with palm leaves, and he covered the outer log layer with fronds. If they saw a ship, Reggie would carry fire from the shelter and light the signal. Tooks sat on a palm log, watched, and gave advice. When he and Reggie were satisfied with their signal fire, Tooks said they should make a small shelter by the pyre so one of them could watch for ships during the day.

12

Reggie carved a mark on his stick—another week gone. Tooks spent more time walking. He only needed the use of one crutch now. Reggie made the trek around the reef to the *motus* on the east side of the atoll but found no evidence of other survivors. Every time he looked out across the water toward Anchorage Island, he thought about his friends who now lay at the bottom of the lagoon. And the *Wallaroo*. I'll return someday, he said to himself, and put a marker or something to honor them. Tooks will come, too, and maybe we'll have a sort of Maori ceremony.

Reggie became a proficient reef hunter. Daily he speared fish and the odd small octopus. Along with the usual urchins, snails and sea slugs, bird's eggs and young nestlings from the trees overhead were added to their diet.

After a meal of fish, octopus, *trepang*, and *tapukus*, the two castaways spent the night at the beach shelter on the north side of the *motu*. High wispy clouds raced across the northern sky. They shared a cigarette. There were three left in the tin.

"When we return to Raro, *teina*, you meet Tara, my sister. She twelve now, I think. Make good wife for you."

"Twelve? Tooks, she's just a kid. You can't marry someone who's only twelve."

Tooks laughed. "Not marry, *teina*. Just meet. You come back in five . . . six years from Singapore, Calcutta, other places, and she wait for you."

"That's not how we do it, Tooks. Wait. Didn't I see her on Raro before sailing to Pukapuka? I met many of your family on the pier."

"Yes. She there. She fancy you. She say you come back some day, and she be your *va'ine*, wife."

"No, mate. This is crazy. I only saw her for a second."

"Not matter, Raro women know these things."

* * *

A sound woke Reggie—a different sound. Beneath the booming of the surf on the outer reef he heard something in the scrub brush. It sounded like someone throwing sand into the bushes. The moon was full and at its zenith. He rose, looked over at Tooks, who slept like a child, and walked toward the sound.

He hadn't gone more than ten yards when he saw a dark shape, low to the ground, moving toward the lagoon. *What the hell is that?* He ran. *It's a sea turtle. What a find! Fresh meat!* Reggie ran and stopped in front of it. The turtle ignored him and continued its march to the sea. Reggie went to its left side, reached down and tried to lift it. *If I can turn it over, we'll have food for a week!* He couldn't shift it. *This thing must weigh over 300 pounds!* The turtle stayed its course. *A lever. I need a lever!* He ran to get his stick.

By the time he got back the turtle was entering the water. Reggie splashed in alongside of it, but the water was too deep to use the stick. He grabbed the turtle's shell near its neck, but the sea creature was now in its own element and turned to attack its enemy. Reggie pulled his hand back just quick enough from the turtle's beak.

"Piss off, chum! I'll keep these fingers, thank you very much." He stood waist-deep in the lagoon and watched the turtle disappear into the still waters.

"*Honu*, turtle." Tooks stood behind him on the beach leaning on his crutch. "*Hēki*, eggs. Put down eggs. Good *kai*." Tooks explained that the turtles came ashore to lay and bury their eggs in the sand above high water. "Easy to find. *Honu* make path."

They followed the groove in the sand up to the brush.

"Dig here," Tooks said.

Reggie cleared away some sand and exposed the eggs—dozens of them. Reaching into the sand, his hand touched something solid and square. *What's this?* He pushed more sand away.

"Tooks, there's something else here. It feels like a corner of a box or chest or something."

"Good, Reggie. You find Captain Harry's treasure. Now we be rich, have many schooners and *va'ines*." He laughed and started back toward the shelter. "Tomorrow."

"Why not now, mate?" Reggie thought his friend would want to see what was in the box.

"Too dark. Wait for sun. Box not goin' away."

At first light, and after a breakfast of turtle eggs, they went back to the site. Tooks leaned on his crutch, and then lay on the sand, as he watched Reggie uncover the chest. Reggie tried to lift it out of the hole twice, but it was too heavy. There was a large padlock on the chest. Reggie bashed it with a coral rock, which shattered with no success.

"Damn!" He drew his knife from its sheath. The outer layer of the chest was leather, hard and cracked. He worked to cut a piece off, but there was an inner metal layer he couldn't penetrate.

"There's iron or something under the leather, mate. Don't fancy breaking my knife." Reggie sat back on his heels and shook his head. "We don't have the right gear, Tooks."

"We come back. Someday."

"Righto, mate. It'll be here, won't it? But we have to mark this spot so we can find it again."

Reggie looked across the lagoon towards Anchorage Island. He thought that if he could plot the direction from there and another island to here, where the two meet would be close enough. He raised his left hand palm outward, spread his fingers, and measured the distance between Turtle Island and the north end of Anchorage Island. *If only I had a compass*, he thought. He considered marking the closest palm or *tamanu* tree with his knife, but thought better of it. *Don't want to give any clues to other visitors. And the trees may be carried away or blown down by another cyclone.* Reggie then paced off the distance from the chest to the north end of the *motu* and walked back to the hole. *The treasure will have to wait. At least we have the eggs—that's a real treasure.*

It took several trips to the shelter to collect all the eggs in the basket.

* * *

Reggie slept well that night, his stomach full of baked turtle eggs. In the morning, he walked back to where they'd found the chest. Better double check my fingers, he thought. His hand trembled when he lowered it. Black smoke rose from Anchorage Island. No. Not from the island, but beyond— out to sea. *There's a ship out there!* He scampered back to the shelter, whooping and hollering all the way. "Smoke! Tooks, there's smoke! A ship!"

Tooks hobbled toward the signal fire. Reggie joined him and used the last two matches from his cigarette tin to light the pyre. Smoke from their signal fire rose slowly in the still air.

"Are they putting a boat ashore?" Tooks asked.

Reggie shaded his eyes with a hand. "Can't tell, mate. Too far away."

"Go hide chest," Tooks said.

"What? Why, mate?" Reggie was confused.

"Bad men. Maybe bad men come. Take treasure. Leave us here. Maybe kill us. We get ship. Come back someday. Go." He waved Reggie away.

Reggie ran along the beach to the chest. On his knees he scooped sand, coconut husks, and coral bits into the hole. He grabbed a palm frond, swept it back and forth across the spot, and laid the frond, two palm logs, and more fronds on top. He climbed the nearest tree as high as he could. *They must see our smoke. Is that a boat inside the lagoon? No. Too far away.* He waited. *Yes! Yes! There's a boat!* As he slid down the truck of the tree, he lost his grip and landed on his ass in the sand. Jumping to his feet, he hurried back to the fire.

"There's a boat in the lagoon, Tooks."

They stood on the beach and waited. A column of thick dark smoke climbed skyward from their pyre.

"Look." Tooks pointed. "Boat come."

Reggie couldn't see anything. He raised his hand again to shade his eyes from the glare off the water, and then the white speck across the lagoon grew larger. A whaleboat steered straight for them.

"Yes! Yes! I see it, Tooks. We're rescued." Reggie took off his shirt and waved it over his head.

"Not talk about treasure." Tooks tapped the side of his nose with a finger.

The whaleboat's exhaust let out a belch of grayish-black smoke as it slowed before scraping ashore. A white man wearing a seaman's cap stood in the bow. He gave the two castaways a suspicious look. Besides the helmsman, there were two other men in the boat; one had a rifle.

"Speak English, do you?" The man's right hand rested on the butt of a revolver stuck in his belt.

"Yes sir," Tooks answered. His right hand squeezed Reggie's shoulder.

Could these be bad men? Reggie thought. They have guns. What can we do? He unfastened the strap on his knife.

The white man looked past Tooks and Reggie toward the trees. "Any more of you about?"

"Why you ask, sir?" Tooks said.

"Can't be too careful these days." He took his hand off the pistol. "How you come to be here?" He placed a hand on the boat's gunwale and hopped over the side. "The name's Slough, second mate on the *Cadosia,*" he said, extending his hand to Reggie.

Reggie stepped back, nodded toward his friend and said, "This is *Mister* Tooks Marsten, first mate of the *Wallaroo.* I'm just the cabin boy."

Slough didn't offer his hand to Tooks. "The *Wallaroo,* eh?" He looked out at the lagoon. "And where your ship be now?"

"Out there with the *makos,*" Tooks said.

"Cyclone do her in, did it?" He looked down at Tooks' splinted leg. "My boys'll give you a hand aboard when you're ready."

"No." Reggie stepped forward. "I'll take care of it, Mister Slough."

Slough smirked. "You're a feisty one for a little man, *cabin boy.*"

Tooks laid his right arm across Reggie's chest, holding him back. "Reggie no cabin boy now. He my *teina,* my brother. You come to help us, Slough? If no, then be away. We stay until next ship come with good men."

"Hang on a bit, mate." Slough looked back at the other men in the boat. They—islanders also—didn't seem pleased with the exchange to this point. The man with the rifle had set it aside. The helmsman shook his head and said something to the others in a language Reggie didn't understand. Slough faced the castaways. "Right. Tooks . . . *Mister* Marsten, can we go back to the ship and let the captain sort this out?"

He stood aside and motioned for them to board the whaleboat. The other crew members nodded and smiled. They helped Reggie lift Tooks into the boat.

Reggie started to climb in when he yelled, "No, wait!" He ran into the trees and returned with the bottle in his hand. "Don't want to piss off Tangaroa."

Captain Edvard Nordfors, master of the British-flagged freighter *Cadosia,* sat across the table from the castaways and grinned as he watched them make short work of their meal. In the crew's mess, Reggie and Tooks washed down a platter of roast mutton, fried potatoes, and a half loaf of bread with two chilled bottles each of *San Miguel.*

Nordfors inspected the *Maréchal Foch* in the bottle from every angle. "Fine piece of work this," he said. "Made by the supercargo . . . a McCombs, you say?"

Reggie nodded as he worked on a second slice of mince pie.

"Didn't know the man, I'm sorry to say. I had met your Captain Houchins one time in Pago Pago, me thinks. Liked his rum . . . and smoked fat cigars, if I remember right. Bit of a character, as most schooner skippers are." He placed the bottle on the table. "She was a fine ship, the *Maréchal Foch.* Crossed wakes with her once when she was on a rum run to the States during that prohibition business. Heard she broke up on a reef in the Australs some years back." Nordfors took a pipe from his coat pocket, filled and lit it. "I've radioed Avarua about you. They sounded chuffed. Me thinks you can expect a rousing welcome."

13

The *Cadosia* was less than a mile outside the barrier reef on its approach to Avarua's Avatiu Harbor when a flotilla of outrigger canoes, lighters, and various other craft—some under power, some under sail—came out from the island and surrounded the freighter.

Weeks earlier, Resident Agent Swint had informed Avarua when the *Wallaroo* departed for Rarotonga. Long overdue, and with the passing of the cyclone that missed the southern group of islands, the authorities and Tooks' family had been concerned about its fate. Captain Nordfors' wireless message was cause for celebration.

Rarotonga's Avatiu Harbor didn't have facilities for larger ships. The *Cadosia* anchored offshore and had her cargo ferried in by lighters. The captain insisted that Tooks be strapped onto a stretcher before being lowered over the ship's side in a basket to a waiting lighter. Tooks had been offered a proper crutch by the ship's purser. He declined and continued to use the one that Reggie had made for him on Suwarrow. Reggie followed him in a bos'un's chair. Tooks' mother, sisters, and cousins waited in the lighter. Tooks was smothered with flowers and kisses.

Reggie sat in the bow of the lighter. Tooks, lying in the cargo bay, shushed everyone and pointed to his fellow castaway.

"That is Reggie, my *teina*. I am here because of him. He is now family, my *teina* . . . my brother."

As the lighter entered the harbor, Tooks told the story about the cyclone and their time on Suwarrow. At the quay, Tooks, still on the stretcher, was lifted up out of the lighter and slid into the back of an old Ford pickup truck. Tooks waved away other family members, except his mother and Reggie, and the truck raced around the island's rim road to the village of Titikaveka.

Flowers were abundant, with red and white blossoms prevailing. Children, decorated with wreaths and crowns of flowers, and waving great bunches of the glorious bloom, ran from every quarter to meet the castaways.

On the south coast of Rarotonga, the celebration preparations began well before the *Cadosia* dropped anchor outside the reef: a pit dug, a pig butchered, the fire started, stones laid, old mats ready. The space around his mother's small cottage near the lagoon's edge was swept clean of fronds and husks. Tooks' father's grave, in front of the house, was festooned with flowers. Family and friends arrived with food and more flowers.

Before Tooks arrived and off loaded from the truck, vehicles of all descriptions had assembled at his mother's home. People came on foot, bicycle, and motorbike—a new addition to Cook Islands transport.

Dignitaries of a sort arrived. Doctor Landers, the government medico from the island hospital—an ex-pat who had fled a boring practice in the American Midwest—examined Tooks' leg. "Reggie did an excellent job of setting it," he said. "No need to re-break or cast it."

A representative of the Resident Commissioner and Vernon Rupp, the S. L. Livingston Shipping Company agent on Rarotonga, wanted to know details about the loss of the ship and disposition of its cargo, but Tooks' relatives shooed them away. A local stringer from an Auckland newspaper was allowed to join the celebration. She, a distant cousin, wore a skimpy *pareau* and a big smile.

The feast, the music, and the dancing lasted until the early hours of the following day. Tooks told the story many times about Reggie saving his life and their days on Suwarrow after the cyclone. Tooks' sister, Tara, kept Reggie well supplied with food and drink. Reggie was polite and appreciative but showed her scant notice; his eyes roamed over the older girls performing the suggestive hulas, and the Auckland stringer.

Some time after midnight, Reggie was in desperate need and slipped away to the bushes near the beach. He just had the buttons on his shorts fastened when he heard someone behind him.

"Sorry, Reggie. I didn't mean to startle you." It was the newspaper woman. "I'm Matarena, but everyone calls me Marty. Will you give me a few minutes for a short interview? My readers on North Island will love this story."

"Okay. I needed to get away for a bit. How will you write here in the dark? "

"A good reporter is always prepared." She took a notebook and flashlight from her bag. "If we sit close, you can hold the torch while I scribble." They sat on the beach.

She wanted some background about where he was from and when he went to sea. Reggie talked about the farm and his desire to see other places. He didn't mention Rosie Harbittle. When describing the time on Suwarrow, he explained why he'd decided to spend the night on Anchorage Island, a decision that saved his life. She was especially interested in how he knew how to set Tooks' broken leg. Reggie had never been this close physically to an attractive woman. He enjoyed the fragrance of her hair and the view of her substantial cleavage. She asked what his plans were for the future. He wasn't sure but wanted to see more of the world.

She closed her notebook and gave Reggie a kiss on the cheek. "I can't pay you for the interview, Reggie, but maybe this . . . ." She stood, untied her *pareau*, and let it drop to the sand.

* * *

"Tara favors you," Tooks said the next day at breakfast in his mother's house.

"Nah, mate. She's just a kid. We talked about this on Suwarrow. Who was that girl who danced last?"

"Marama, a cousin. But she's married to Hono, a constable. Sorry, *teina*." He smiled. "There are others. How was your interview with Cousin Marty?"

"Quite enjoyable, *teina*."

They went to Rupp's office in Avarua and gave an account of the storm and the loss of the *Wallaroo*. Captain Nordfors, also present, listened to their story. He was most impressed by Tooks' portion, relating how unselfish and resourceful Reggie was. The young man, embarrassed, said he couldn't have done without the Maori's help and knowledge.

"Well, son," Nordfors said, "What are your plans?"

"Don't rightly be knowin'. Would like to be seein' other places . . . other islands."

"I'd like to sign you on as apprentice seaman on the *Cadosia*. We're sailing to Fiji and Samoa, and then to wherever we can get a cargo."

"What about Tooks? Is there a job for him?"

Before Nordfors could answer, Tooks said, "No, Reggie. Don't want to leave the Cooks. Take the captain's offer . . . it's what you told me on Suwarrow you wanted. You will return someday."

Nordfors turned to the shipping agent. "What about this copra you mentioned, Rudd? I can surely get a decent price for it farther west."

"Sorry, Captain. The company has a contract with an outfit in Auckland for all copra from the Cooks." He said to Reggie and Tooks, "I'll send it on to North Island on the next available ship. The company will try to find the kin of Captain Houchins and the rest of the crew from the schooner. I'll make sure they hold back a portion of the profits for you two. It'll take some months before that is sorted."

Rudd gave Reggie a packet containing his passport and seaman's papers. "Came on a ship from Auckland shortly after you went north," he said. "Been holding them for you . . . almost sent them back." Reggie had filled out the paperwork in Auckland. McCombs recommended the items be sent on to Avarua, not knowing when they would return to North Island.

"I'll be takin' your offer, Captain. When are you sailin'? I have to collect some things from Tooks' home."

"Later this evening, Reggie. I'll have a boat waiting for you at the pier."

From Rupp's office, Reggie and Tooks went to the Resident Commissioner's office. They dictated and signed a detailed typed report about the loss of the *Wallaroo*.

At Tooks' house, Reggie put the ship in a bottle and the French coins in a bag, and then paused. "Tooks, *teina*, I be wantin' you to keep these safe for me." He handed the bag to his friend. "I don't be wantin' to lose them."

"You sure of this, *teina*? These be very special."

"Yes, Tooks. Maybe Tangaroa will be makin' sure I return to secure them. And I be wantin' you to keep my part of the copra money. Probably won't amount to much."

14

That evening, as a gorgeous sunset painted the western horizon with a mass of color, the *Cadosia* raised anchor and left Rarotonga.

They sailed west to Suva, Apia, Pago Pago, Batavia, and Rangoon. Reggie sent postcards to his folks and Tooks from every port of call. Some weeks later, they took on a cargo of tea in Ceylon. Ashore in Colombo, Mister Slough, the second mate and now a good friend, introduced Reggie to a well-known house of pleasure run by a Madam Sati.

Making port in Cape Town, they loaded a cargo of lumber and wheat for England. North of the Cape Verde Islands, they heard a news report on the ship's wireless—war had started in Europe.

Two days from the Isles of Scilly, Reggie was doing bridge duty as helmsman. Captain Nordfors stood behind him listening to the war news with Artur Vika, the radio operator. The radio room's door opened directly onto the bridge. Additional lookouts had been posted on the bridge and in a crow's nest above the ship's superstructure.

"Ahoy the bridge! Periscope off the starboard quarter," shouted the seaman in the crow's nest.

"Vika, A distress signal. Now! Send our location." Nordfors turned to the navigator. "A plot quickly. Give it to Vika." The second mate came into the bridge.

"Slough, the Swedish colors. Quickly, man." Slough yanked the flag out of a locker and dashed to the stern. Mister Woglum, the first mate, joined them on the bridge.

The U-boat surfaced some thousand or more yards off the starboard side. Officers and lookouts appeared on the conning tower, and crew members manned the submarine's deck gun.

"What ship?" the Germans signaled by lamp.

"Bring me the Aldis, Mister Woglom," Nordfors ordered. Using the hand-held signal lamp, the captain signaled back to the U-boat, "*Gunvor.* Out of Stockholm."

The U-boat ordered the *Cadosia* to stop and standby to be boarded. Nordfors ignored the order and signaled that they are a neutral vessel.

A shot across his bow from the U-boat's deck gun forced Nordfors to stop the engines. The U-boat launched a rubber boat with a boarding party. Captain Nordfors ordered the crew to load extra food and water into the lifeboats. As the boarding party neared the *Cadosia,* the signal lamp on the U-boat flashed. The rubber boat stopped, turned around, and headed back toward the submarine. Crew members on the freighter heard the German officer in the rubber boat yell, "*Schnell! Schnell!*" Captain Nordfors ordered the engine room to get underway at best speed. The rubber boat crew paddled like men possessed. The submarine moved closer to pick up the boarding party.

"What's happening, sir? What's happening?" Reggie asked the captain.

Woglom pointed toward an aircraft in the distance. "It's a Sunderland!"

The aircraft banked and headed for the ships. The German rubber boat crew scrambled aboard the submarine, and it started to submerge.

The Sunderland, a four-engine Royal Navy seaplane, dropped down low to the waves. The U-boat was disappearing fast.

"Radio from the Sunderland, Captain," Vika yelled. "Change course hard to port, max speed. The U-boat may try to hide under you . . . us."

"Hard aport, Reggie. Engine room," Nordfors shouted down the voice tube, "give me all you can. Now!" The U-boat was gone.

Four barrel-like objects fell from under the wings of the seaplane as it passed over the U-boat's last position.

"Depth charges," Nordfors said. Four eruptions appeared on the surface.

"Not seein' any oil or debris," Woglom said. He handed the binoculars to the captain.

"Right. Hard to starboard, Reggie. We'll make this Nazi play our game."

The Sunderland banked and came back toward the ship. Reggie heard voices from the radio.

"They're returning to refuel, Captain. They said to keep changing course—zigzagging. Another plane may be out later since they made a positive sighting."

"We were lucky this time, Captain," Woglom said. "Think they'll try again?"

"Hope not, Mr. Woglom. Tell the lookouts to keep alert." Slough came back into the bridge.

"Should we hoist the Union Jack, Captain?"

"Not yet. We'll stay under false colors until we enter the Channel."

"I'll be leaving the ship in Plymouth," Slough said. "Don't relish being sunk like in the last war."

"What happened, Mr. Slough?" Reggie asked.

"Torpedoed off Ireland in '17. Spent two days on a life raft . . . no food, no water. Not wanting to go through a second time."

"Don't be scaring the lad, Slough," the captain said.

"I think I'd like to fly," Reggie said.

"Never flown before, son?"

"No, sir. Never been in an airplane."

"Well, if you get called up, ask for the RAF."

Reggie hadn't given much thought about being called up. It would happen, he knew. He didn't want to go into the infantry. Many times his father had talked about how miserable he'd been in the Anzac Brigade in the first war. Would I have a better chance of joining the RAF if I volunteered, he wondered.

Shortly after the *Cadosia* tied up in Plymouth, Reggie drew his wages, left the ship, and headed to an RAF recruiting office.

15

"How old are you, son?" asked the sergeant. Reggie had finished the initial in-processing, including a physical exam, and was being interviewed.

"Nineteen, sir."

"Not English are you?"

"No sir. New Zealand."

"Why do you want to join the RAF?"

"I be wantin' to learn to fly."

"I see. Well, son, there's a Royal New Zealand squadron posted up north near York. Would you like to join your fellow countrymen for this little set-to with the Nazis? Most likely over with by Christmas."

"Yes, sir. I be likin' that."

"Right then. I'll give you travel orders and a rail voucher. You'll have military priority on anything going in that direction."

The train ride to the north of England was in the dark. It took all night after many stops before pulling into the York railway station. Even if the journey had been during the day, Reggie wouldn't have seen anything of the English countryside or cities. Blackout curtains covered every window. In a driving rain, a bus took Reggie and the other recruits to RAF Elvington on the south edge of the city.

"Sorry, Pobjoy. No need for pilots at present," said the flying officer who interviewed him. "Thought we'd be ferrying these 'Wimpies' back home, but somebody started a war." He leaned back in his chair and lit his pipe. "What we need are air gunners and radio operators. That's what you'll do. You should fit nicely in the tail of one of these buses. That's all. Report to the sergeant outside."

Disappointed, Reggie left the headquarters building. He heard a voice call his name.

"Reggie? My god, how'd you happen to turn up here?" Dee-Dee Dearlove walked over to him and extended his hand.

"Well, stone the crows! Mister Dearlove. So good to see you." Reggie took his hand.

Flight-Lieutenant Dearlove looked around and said, "Reggie, other ranks are required to salute officers."

Reggie stepped back and saluted. "Sorry, sir."

"Okay, that's enough of the military protocol crap. How in the world did you did you end up here? And, Reggie, me lad, you're a bit of a celebrity here about with the Kiwis."

"Sir, I don't be understandin'."

"Suwarrow. There was a lengthy piece in a newspaper we received from Auckland. You did some amazing things on that atoll."

Marty must have enjoyed our romp on the beach. "I haven't seen it. Is there a copy about?"

"Should be one in the Mess. You haven't told me how you came to be here in Yorkshire." Reggie gave him a short history of his journey. He didn't include the night spent at Madam Sati's in Colombo. They walked to the Nissen hut that housed the Officers' Mess. Inside the building, airmen were loading the mess gear into boxes.

"What's going on, Jones?" Dearlove asked.

"A bit of a flap, sir. The squadron is being posted to somewhere in the south."

"Well, Reggie, I must go to Ops to find out what's happening," Dearlove said. "Chat with you later." Reggie didn't see his friend again for over two years.

* * *

Reggie completed nine months training without catching sight of an airplane, except the ones flying over the base. Nor did he put his hands on a gun. There were plenty of lectures, aircraft recognition tests, and cross-country running to keep in shape. Then came a barrage of inoculations for tetanus, yellow fever, smallpox, and flu. Finally, with a grand celebration, he received the three stripes of a sergeant aircrewman.

From Yorkshire, Reggie traveled to the squadron's new base in Bassingbourne, and his operational training began. Upon arrival, he was sent to see the squadron gunnery sergeant. His name was Daniel Croxall—forty-five and hard as nails. He was a big man with a head of fiery red hair. An aerial observer and later a pilot in the last war, he now was the squadron's senior air gunner. Originally from South Island, he had stayed in England after the war, married a local girl, and worked at a brewery in York. When the war started, he walked into the squadron headquarters and offered his services.

He took Reggie straight to a Wellington to see what he knew, or rather, what he didn't know. He spent the morning and afternoon showing Reggie everything. The Wellington, affectionately known as a "Wimpy," was a two-engine medium bomber that carried a crew of six.

Intense training continued on the ground and in the air. He learned the complexities of the weapons, twin .303 caliber Browning machine guns mounted in the electrically controlled turret. As the "tailend Charlie," Reggie would have the loneliest position in the aircraft.

One morning at breakfast, a flying officer sat next to Reggie. "You Pobjoy?" he asked.

"Yes, sir."

"I've got you in my crew," he said, and then bombarded Reggie with questions: How much morse did he know? Could he find everything in his turret in the dark? Did he know how to launch the flares? What did he know about dinghy drill? Did he know how to bail out? Could he map read? Could he operate the emergency hand pump for the under carriage? Did he know where the petrol cocks were? And much more . . .

Reggie was exhausted when they finished.

"Well done, lad. You'll do," the officer said. He extended his hand. "Welcome to the crew. I'm Yarborough, but everyone calls me 'Yarb'." He leaned back in his chair and lit a cigar. "Finish your breakfast, and I'll introduce you to the rest of the crew. We're on tonight."

Reggie gulped down his food. *My first mission! Hope I'm ready.*

They walked to the squadron briefing hut where the rest of the crew waited. Hinckley, the wireless operator, was from Russell in the Bay of Islands; the navigator, Estes, was from South Island; 'Mac' McCartney, the nose gunner, was a Scotsman who had immigrated to New Zealand in the '30s; and last was Spenser, the waist gunner, from Auckland. They all welcomed Reggie warmly to the crew.

Yarb went to the front of the hut and pointed to a map of northern Europe. "Sorry to disappoint, lads, but tonight's mission is a NICKEL run over Holland, Belgium and northern France."

A NICKEL operation or "nickeling," as the crews called it, was a leaflet-dropping flight over occupied countries. The leaflets were in bundles of 1500, each about the size of a large brick. Each bundle consisted of packages of twelve leaflets held together by a rubber band. Over the target areas, a crew member would feed the bundles down the flare chute.

"Bloody waste," Hinckley said. "More free ass wipe for Jerry." Everyone laughed.

"We're due to take off at 18:50. Be in the crew room at 17:00. Get some sleep, write letters, or read a book. No booze. Any questions? No? Dismissed."

Reggie went to the crew quarters and wrote letters to his parents and Tooks. He tried to sleep but was too excited. Mid afternoon the crew received a weather briefing and went to the mess for tea. Reggie wasn't hungry but ate all he could, partly to keep warm, and partly because he didn't know where or when the next meal would be. After tea he returned to the barracks to put on warm clothes.

The nose and tail turrets were the coldest positions in a Wellington, and gunners wore more clothes than the other crew members. In addition to usual vest, pants, and shirt, he donned three pullovers, a roll-top sweater, and four pairs of socks. These were covered with his tunic, flying suit, and scarf.

Before he left the barracks, he made a final check to see that he hadn't forgotten anything. All personal papers were left behind, in case he was taken prisoner. Into his kit bag or pockets went a revolver, torch, cigarettes, thermos flasks of hot coffee, money, a clasp knife, matches, and an extra scarf and gloves.

Transport waited outside the crew room, and they piled in with their belongings. Reggie started to sweat under all his layers of clothing. The ground crews waited by the airplane to help the flight crew stow their kit.

It was still light, so Reggie gave a final polish to the perspex round his turret before climbing in. His parachute was stored in the fuselage just outside the turret. He could reach it by opening the turret door and stretching behind him. Reggie put on his helmet and plugged in his intercom.

The engines were being run up and tested; the whole tail shook and vibrated. Yarb called through the intercom asking if he was okay and ready to move. Reggie heard him call up each member in turn. The engines roared as Yarb opened the throttles. The Wellington moved slowly at first and then rapidly. As they climbed, the ground appeared darker to Reggie. The bomber circled the aerodrome and gained altitude. They turned east toward the Channel.

"What's our ETA to the Dutch Coast, navigator," Yarb asked.

"Seventeen minutes," he answered.

"Thanks. Is everyone feeling all right? How are you in the tail, Reggie? Feeling cold?"

"Not too bad, sir. Can't see much though."

They were flying through cloud cover. Reggie thought it was like going through a tunnel in a train. The clouds disappeared behind them, and Reggie could see the English coastline like a gray streak in the darkness below. At ten thousand feet he turned on his oxygen and felt warmer and more comfortable.

"Reggie and Mac, it's time for you to zap a few seagulls before we reach the Dutch coast," Yarb ordered. The airplane shuddered as both gunners let go several short bursts to test their guns.

"Guns checked, Yarb," Reggie reported.

"Guns checked, skipper," Mac said. "No sign of a welcoming party. Maybe the *Luftwaffe* boys are all in bed."

"Don't count on it, Mac," Yarb said.

As they crossed the Dutch coast, enemy searchlights filled the sky looking for the airplane. The pilot took evasive action, banking left, and then right to avoid the beams.

"Time to turn south, Yarb," the navigator said. The Wellington banked hard to the right.

Yarb said, "Get ready for the first drop, Spenser."

"Ready, Yarb," he answered.

Reggie knew the waist gunner had untied the bundles and was waiting to feed them into the flare chute.

"Okay, Spenser, let'm go."

Reggie saw the sky behind and beneath the airplane fill with white confetti as the rubber bands that held the bundles together were torn off by the slipstream.

As they crossed into Belgium, more searchlights hunted for them. Spenser continued to feed the leaflets into the chute.

"Almost to France, Yarb."

"Right. Almost done, lads."

Then Reggie was blinded when a searchlight found the Wellington. Enemy anti-aircraft batteries locked on them and laid a carpet of flak in their path. The shells exploded like puff balls, deadly balls of fire spitting out shrapnel that peppered anything within a couple of hundred yards.

The "Wimpy" suddenly flipped to starboard, as if slapped by a giant hand, and started to lose altitude.

"Fire, port engine!" yelled Mac. Reggie knew the pilot would be pressing the fire extinguisher button. The airplane was hit again.

"Starboard engine gone," someone shouted.

Losing altitude fast, Yarb's voice came over the intercom, "Bail out! We're going down. Bail . . ." the intercom went dead.

Reggie opened the turret door, grabbed his parachute, and snapped it into position on his chest. He tore off his helmet and turned the turret sideways. The strength of the wind forced the door free, and he fell backwards through the opening.

He pulled the ripcord and watched his parachute inflate above him. *Bless you, Tangaroa.*

Floating down he looked back at the plane. Its port engine was ablaze. Reggie didn't see any other parachutes.

My God! My mates. Didn't anyone else get out?

Still caught in the beams of the searchlights, anti-aircraft fire surrounded the Wellington. Reggie's heart almost stopped when the bomber exploded. He watched the wreckage fall earthward. Looking down, he saw the ground coming up fast and prepared to land. At least, he thought, I don't see any water.

Reggie landed in a field at the edge of a forest. He dragged his parachute into the trees, removed his flying suit, and covered both with leaves and branches. He stood behind a large tree and listened. In the distance he heard the clanging of a fire brigade vehicle or ambulance.

Hope the plane's wreckage didn't land in a village. Don't believe I've lost my mates. I'm alone again, just like on Suwarrow.

Reggie heard movement and a branch snap. He drew his revolver. The movement stopped; he heard voices speaking French. Someone came closer.

"English? English?" a girl's voice asked. A torch lit up the ground near his feet. "English?" the voice said again.

He stepped from behind the tree and saw a man and a young girl. They saw his pistol.

"Friends. Come," she said. The man turned off his torch.

She took his hand. He holstered his revolver. "My parachute?" he asked.

"He will bury it. Come, English, we must go quickly."

Reggie followed the girl through the forest to a road where a van waited, its engine idling. He climbed into the back and the van sped away.

The back of the van was filled with baskets full of baguettes, freshly baked and warm to the touch. What a wonderful smell, he thought. Reggie, hungry, couldn't resist breaking off the end of a loaf. He left a half crown in the basket.

The van stopped in a village. Reggie transferred to a sedan. He had no idea where he was. Somewhere in France, he thought. After two hours, he arrived at his next location.

* * *

Reggie was hungry when he woke. He hadn't eaten, except for the piece of baguette, since the afternoon before. The woman said she'd bring him something. *What next? Wonder where I am. Somewhere near Paris?* The room was up in an attic, barely large enough for the single bed covered with a faded blue blanket—no pillow—and the ceiling sloped down to the top of a small window. It was dark when he'd arrived in the boot of an old car. The driver hurried him past a sty with two sleeping pigs and through the rear door of the building. A thin, dark-haired woman led him up three flights of stairs and into a small room. He lay down on the bed without removing his boots and slept. And slept.

Light forced its way through a gap in the flower print curtain covering the window near his head. On top of the dresser sat a carafe of red wine next to a plate of bread and cheese. Reggie ate a piece of bread and followed it with a chunk of the strong-smelling cheese. He washed both down with a long drink of wine. *Not too much at once. Have to keep my wits about me.* He finished the bread and cheese and took another small drink of wine. Bending down beneath the rafters, he walked to the window and pulled the curtain halves apart just enough to see out. He jumped back, hitting his head, and spun around when he heard a key in the lock. *Damn, I'm buggered!* His hand went to the revolver on his belt. The door opened. The woman came in, her finger to her lips.

"Quiet, Monsieur. You must be quiet."

Reggie rubbed the top of his head. "There's a German officer down there. He came in."

"*Oui*, Monsieur. Many come here, but you are safe. But you must be silent. Stay away from the window." She looked at the empty plate on the dresser. "Enough to eat? *Bien.* I'll bring more later." She took the plate and carafe, closed the door behind her and locked it.

Reggie went back to the window and peeked around a corner of the curtain. A wide river flowed past just beyond the street in front of the building. The arched spans of a railroad bridge filled his view to the right. A gray German Army staff car was parked below his window. He watched an officer get in and drive away.

Reggie sat on the bed and wondered how long he would be here. *Where to next?* He lay down again but couldn't sleep. *What happened to my mates? Did any survive? I didn't see any other parachutes when I floated down from the Wellington. Maybe they didn't make it.*

He must have drifted off, because when he woke it was dark again. He heard the key in the lock. His hand went to the revolver's handle. The woman came in with another plate—some cold ham, another baguette, and more cheese. She placed a pitcher of water and a glass on the dresser. "No more wine," she said. "You will be leaving soon."

"Where am I?"

"It is better you not know, Monsieur."

"Right. I understand. But what be that big river out there?"

"*La Seine.*"

"Where am I be goin'?"

"*La Cité* . . . Paris."

"Paris? Isn't it full of Germans?"

"*Oui*, Monsieur. It is easier to hide you there than in a small village."

"I guess that be makin' sense. When do I go? And what about the German officer?"

"Soon. I will come when it is time. The . . . German is gone."

"Please. What be your name?"

The woman hesitated. "I'm sorry, Monsieur. *Mais,* it is best you not know any names."

An hour later Reggie heard heavy footsteps on the stairs. *That's not her.* He sat up on the bed, took his pistol from his holster and cocked it. He heard the key turn in the lock. It wasn't the woman who entered this time but a man—older, dressed in a well-cut suit, and wearing a fedora.

"Cheerio, mate," he said extending his hand. Seeing the pistol in Reggie's hand, he added, "No need for that, mate. I'm on your side. One of the good guys."

Reggie kept his Webley pointed at the man's chest. *Do I trust him or shoot him?*

"These folks been taking good care of you? I'm Harry Cole. I'm here to take you into Paris."

"You're English. What're you doing here?"

"Just a minor cog in the system, mate. Helping get chaps like you back into the war. From Paris, you'll be passed along to friends in Vichy France, and then across the border to Spain."

"What if I shoot you? And why Spain?"

"If you shoot me, it'll piss off a lot of folks in the War Office. I've been sent here to help you chaps get back home. From Spain, you'll go to Portugal, and then home. Ready to go?"

Behind the inn a black Citroën sedan waited, its engine running, its boot open. Cole pointed. "In you go, mate. A bit cramped I'm sorry to say, but it'll only be for an hour or two. Stay quiet."

Reggie climbed into the sedan, lay on his right side, and tucked his knees up against his chest.

"Might be best to let me have your Webley." The Englishman held out his hand. "If you're found out by the *gendarmerie,* they'll be most put off by it."

Reggie handed his pistol to Cole, who closed the lid. The sedan began to move.

It rained hard for part of the journey, and the trunk lid leaked. Reggie's left side was soaking wet when the sedan stopped and the trunk opened. He knew he must be in the city, because it had sounded like they were driving on cobblestones. A man said, "*Vite!* Monsieur, quickly." He led Reggie through the door of a *pension* and into a small office. They went into another room, obviously a bedroom, where the man pulled a large armoire away from the wall exposing a door. "In here, Monsieur."

Reggie found himself in a tiny room with no light. He turned on his torch. The room was filled with luggage and boxes. A short cot rested against one wall.

"Wait here, Monsieur," the man said and closed the door. Reggie heard him push the armoire back into place.

Reggie scanned the room with his torch but didn't see a wall switch or a light fixture anywhere. There was little free space to move around. He sat on the cot and lit a cigarette. It felt like there was something under the cot. He reached down and pulled out a small green leather valise. He opened it and removed some papers—typed sheets and carbon copies—and they were in English. *Wonder what these are doing here.* One of the copies had a title, *Up in Michigan, EH.* They looked to him like stories somebody had written. Too tired to read more, he stuffed the papers back in the valise and laid down. *Must try to sleep. What happens now?*

Reggie didn't know how long he'd slept when he heard the armoire being moved. The door burst open, and a light blinded him.

"Stand up, English. Hands up," a voice shouted. A German soldier grabbed him. Another man wearing a long black leather coat slapped handcuffs on his wrists. They searched his pockets and, not too gently, patted him down. He was pushed toward the door. Reggie saw the man in the leather coat reach down and examine the valise. He took it with them. Outside, Reggie was forced into at the back seat of a black car. A soldier with a submachine gun sat next to him. The man with the leather jacket sat in the front seat next to the driver.

"The war is over for you, English," he said.

16

Sylvia Beach stood behind the display shelf in the window of her bookstore. She thought it might rain and considered closing for an hour or two to have lunch with her friend, Adrienne. A long, gray Mercedes-Benz stopped outside. The driver, a German soldier, jumped out, hurried around to the curb side and opened the rear door. A tall officer got out of the back seat. He straightened his coat, stomped his feet, and walked up to the window. He stood for a moment, and then came into the shop.

"Good afternoon, Madame," he said in perfect English with no hint of accent. "I want to buy that copy of *Finnegan's Wake.*" He pointed to the book in the window.

"It's not for sale."

"Why not?" He removed his leather gloves and slapped them in an open palm.

"I'm keeping it."

"For whom?" He slapped his gloves again.

"For myself. It's my last copy."

"But surely you can get another. I've read all of Joyce—*The Dubliners, Portrait of an Artist, Ulysses.* All except this one."

"I'm sorry, Monsieur, but it's not for sale."

The officer raised his right hand and looked like he was about to say something, but he spun on his heel and marched out of the store. His driver, who was leaning against the rear of the staff car, barely had time to throw his cigarette into the gutter and open the door.

Sylvia removed the book from the display shelf and placed it under the counter. So, it begins, she thought. After the Germans occupied Paris the previous summer, most of her international clientele fled to other borders. Even Gertrude Stein and Alice B. Toklas now rusticated somewhere in the unoccupied countryside. But they were Jews. Would that make a difference? Other Americans in the city refused to leave, but it was only a matter of time before the United States entered the war, and they would be compelled to leave or be interned. She still had her French customers who wanted English language literature, so she would survive for the moment. But how long would the Nazis allow foreign works to be sold?

German visitors had been few and infrequent. Many had been educated in the United States or England. Her shop was on a back street away from the usual tourist venues, so most of the *Wehrmacht* customers were just curious or had an interest in English literature.

"Sylvia! Sylvia!" Adrienne rushed into the bookstore. "Turn on your radio. Hitler has declared war on America!"

Sylvia, up a short ladder, dropped the two books she was shelving. "When?"

"Just now." Adrienne knelt to pick up the books. "What will happen to you? Will you be arrested? What about the shop . . . the books?" She held up the dropped volumes.

"I don't know, *chérie*." Sylvia stepped off the ladder and reached out a hand for the books. She turned and placed them on a stack of waiting-to-be-shelved fiction. "We'll have to be patient and see what happens." Sylvia knew she had influential friends in the French literary establishment, and so far she hadn't been bothered much by the occupation. But now she was an enemy alien. How would that change her life? She had no desire to flee to Switzerland, Vichy, or Spain, even if it was possible. Paris was her home. She would wait and see.

As a foreign national of a belligerent nation, she was ordered to appear weekly at the local police precinct.

"*Bonjour*, Phillipe, *ca va?*" Sylvia greeted the same bored, elderly *gendarme* seated behind the glass partition.

"*Bonjour*, Mademoiselle Beach. *Bien. Et vous?*" He slid the required form across the counter toward her and offered a pencil.

"*Merci*, Phillipe, but I'll use my pen." Warned by friends that forms filled out in pencil were sometimes altered, Sylvia always used her fountain pen. She took it from her purse, and then noticed that her name and address were already in place, and at the bottom of the form someone had written *She doesn't own a horse.*

"Phillipe, what is this nonsense about a horse?"

"*Je ne sais pas*, Mademoiselle. The *Gestapo* added it since your last visit. Do you *have* a horse, Mademoiselle Beach?"

* * *

The German officer returned.

"Where is the *Finnegan's Wake?*"

"It's gone," Sylvia said.

"You sold it?"

"No. It wasn't for sale."

"So that's the way it is going to be, is it? All right, Madame. We're coming to confiscate all your goods today." He turned and stomped out.

What is it with these Germans and their boots? Sylvia ran across the street to Adrienne's bookshop.

"Adrienne! Where are you?"

"*Ici, chérie.*" Adrienne shouted from the toilet niche behind the second row of shelves.

"They're coming to steal my books!" she shouted in return.

Adrienne appeared, adjusting her skirt. "I saw the big Nazi car. What did he want? *Le même, n'est-ce pas?*"

"*Oui*. My Joyce. But I won't give it up. What am I to do?"

"Let's go talk with Madame Hinfrey. I believe there is an empty apartment above."

They found Madame Hinfrey, the concierge. She offered Sylvia, rent free, the use of the vacant fourth floor apartment above the bookstore.

With a collection of boxes and clothes baskets, Sylvia, Adrienne, another friend Solange, and the concierge, started shifting Shakespeare and Company up the five flights of stairs. A carpenter, who lived around the corner, came and removed the bookshelves, display counters, and light fixtures. Adrienne called a house painter friend. He arrived with his son and started painting the outside of the building a different color.

Sylvia dropped an empty clothes basket on the floor and reached for a desk chair to carry upstairs. How many trips was that, she thought. She heard a footfall behind her. She turned. A German officer stood silhouetted in the open doorway, his face in shadow. *Damn! We've been caught!*

"*Bonjour*, Mademoiselle Beach." The officer stepped forward into the light. "Sylvia? It's me. Klaus."

"Who?"

He removed his hat, smiled, and ran a hand over his chin.

"Klaus . . . Klaus from Eisenstadt. Without the beard and mustache. What's happening? Are you moving?"

"Klaus. Oh yes. Klaus. Nice to see you." She paused. "You're in the German Army? But you're Austrian."

"After 1938 it's all the same."

"Yes, of course." She reached down to pick up the chair. *Does he know what's happening? Has he been sent here to spy on us?*

"Let me help you with that," he said. "Are you moving the bookstore?" He picked up the chair.

Sylvia hesitated, and then said, "Who's asking? Klaus the German officer . . . or Klaus the Austrian artist?"

"What's going on here, Sylvia?"

What do I say? Where are his loyalties? He was a friend and known as "the Good German" by the other artists and writers. She told him.

"What was his name?" Klaus said. "His rank? What does he look like?"

Sylvia didn't know his name and didn't know the military ranks, but she described him and the car.

"Faistenhammer. Major Faistenhammer. The swine. I'm sure of it," Klaus said. "He's very proud of his English, went to school in New York or Boston, I think. Speaks it to me all the time, and corrects my errors in pronunciation. Faistenhammer's a pompous Prussian ass. We're both on General Potzdorfer's staff. And that was probably the general's staff car he was using."

Klaus put the chair down and picked up his hat. "You keep working, Sylvia. I'll see if I can delay his return. I'll be back later. Or tomorrow. *Au revoir.*"

17

Sicily, August 14, 1943.
Assigned to the staff of General Huber's XIV Panzer Corps, Klaus witnessed the heroic but futile defense of Sicily against the Allied invasion. The Americans under General Patton were advancing down the north coast toward Messina, and the British under Montgomery were plodding up the east coast. In Rome, Mussolini abdicated, and the Italian forces on Sicily collapsed. General Huber ordered an evacuation of his corps across of the Straits of Messina to the Italian mainland.

Klaus stood on the bridge of the ship and shared a glass of wine with an Italian naval officer named Francaviglia.

"Your Italian is excellent, *Herr Hauptmann,* with a touch of northern accent."

"*Grazie, Tenente,* as is your German. My mother was from the Alpine region near Villack."

They watched the coast of Sicily disappear in the distance. It was dark and the sky overcast. The evacuation took place at night to stay hidden from Allied aircraft. British bombers made attempts to find the ships, but most of their bombs fell harmlessly in the sea. They looked up when they heard aircraft overhead. Of the stick of bombs that straddled the ship, only one found its target. All Klaus remembered was a blinding flash of light and the noise.

* * *

When he woke all he felt was the pain—his right leg, his left arm, his chest, his head—everywhere the pain was horrific. His right hand searched his body for missing pieces. The rocking motion from side-to-side didn't help. *Where am I? Why can't I stop moving?*

"*Guten Morgen, Herr Hauptmann,*" a sweet voice said. Klaus attempted to turn in the direction of the voice.

"Don't move, *Herr Hauptmann.* Lie still. I'll bring more morphine," the sweet voice said.

"Wait, *bitte, Fräulein,* where am I?"

"You're going home. You're on a hospital train. We should cross into Austria tomorrow morning."

* * *

German Army hospital, Vienna.
"*Guten Morgen, Herr Hauptmann.* How are you doing today?" asked the nurse. "Lean forward a little so I can adjust your pillows. You have a visitor."

An *SS* officer with the rank of *Hauptsturmführer* stood at the foot of Klaus's bed holding his chart.

"*Guten Morgen, Hauptmann von Reichenhall.* The officer moved around to the side of the bed and offered his hand. "I'm a friend of your father." They shook hands.

"I'm Dr. Aribert Heim. I know your father from party meetings in Eisenstadt and Vienna. He told me you were here and asked me to check on your care." He looked at the chart. "You seem to be on the mend. Most likely you'll be home for Christmas."

"*Danke, Herr Doktor.* How is my father?"

"Very well. He is doing great things for the *Reich.*"

"What *is* he doing? He's not much of a letter writer. He hasn't joined the army again, has he?"

"Oh no, Klaus." He laughed. "May I call you Klaus?"

"As you wish, *Herr Doktor.*"

"Your father was a hero in the last war. Now he has been very instrumental in helping us identify enemies of the Fatherland—Communists, radical intelligentsia, Jews, and other undesirables."

"And what happens to these 'undesirables'?"

"Sent to *Arbeitslager* to work in the war production factories. I'm returning to my position at Mauthausen. That is why I wanted to meet you. Your father raved about your language skills, and we could definitely make use of them in the *lager*. We have many workers from other countries—French, British prisoners of war, some Russians, and many others. You have done your duty to the Fatherland in France and Italy. It's an opportunity to stay close to home. And it would be much better than the Eastern Front, *nicht wahr?*"

"*Ja, Herr Doktor. Vielen dank.*"

"The Mauthausen commandant, *SS-Standerten Führer* Franz Ziereis, is a personal friend of mine, and I am certain I can arrange for the necessary orders." He wrote something on a card and placed it in a book. "Here is a small present for a heroic comrade. I'm sure you have already read it, but this volume was personally signed by the *Führer*. My address is on the card. Enjoy your Christmas. Write to me. *Auf Weidersehen.*"

The officer left the ward. Klaus held up the book. *Mein Kampf.* He shook his head. *Why would I want to read this rubbish again? Signed personally by the Führer. Who cares? Wonder when I can safely toss it in the nearest dustbin? Undesirables? Jews? Maybe the stories I've heard are true. I must ask father about this.*

* * *

Klaus's parents and Mattie with their son, Siegfried, were on the platform when the train arrived from Vienna.

"Welcome home, son. We're so proud of you. A hero of the Fatherland," his father said. "But the cane?"

After he had kissed and embraced his mother and Mattie, he said, "Nothing serious. Just my leg . . . still a bit stiff. No pain, though." He handed his cane to his father and lifted his son. "What a fine looking young man you have become, Siegfried. You've grown so big."

That evening, after the best meal Klaus had had in months, his mother and Mattie went into kitchen. He and his father sat in the parlor and enjoyed a glass of schnapps.

"I'm surprised at that wonderful *repas,* Father. I heard talk in the hospital about food shortages."

"Not for senior party officers, son. Did Dr. Heim visit you?"

"Yes, Father, he did."

"Did he tell you about the secret weapons the *Führer* is building at Mauthausen?"

"No, he didn't mention that."

"Well, son, we will soon have weapons that will destroy our enemies and win this war."

"Father, I have seen the might of the Allied armies and their air forces. The skies over Sicily were filled with their planes."

"Son, you must *not* speak of these things to others. It is a minor setback. We're building an airplane that will sweep the skies of their bombers."

"What about the Russians? Other patients in the hospital said they are unstoppable."

"Defeatist propaganda, son. I assure you that we will be victorious. The *Führer* has promised that." Klaus's mother and Mattie joined them. She held a letter.

"This came for you in the morning post, son. It looks very official."

"*Danke.*" Klaus opened the envelope and read. He handed it to his father.

"What is it? Good news?" Mattie asked.

"Oh yes. I've been assigned to General Kitzinger's staff . . . in Paris."

"And promoted to major," his father said, beaming.

"Thank God it's not the Russian Front," his mother said. Mattie agreed.

That night, after he had planted the seed for their second child, they lay holding each other close.

"I've missed you so much, Klaus. Things have been horrible. There are food shortages for most, and many of our friends like the Weismanns have been taken away. Your father said they were enemies of the *Reich*. Even *Pfarrer* Benedict has been arrested. How can an old priest be an enemy? What harm can a priest cause?"

"Try not to think about that, *liebchen*. We must think about you and Siegfried. Have you heard from your parents in Innsbruck?"

"Yes. Mother writes often. They are enjoying their new home in the Alps near the Swiss frontier."

"Good. I want you to plan a visit to them soon."

At breakfast the next morning, Klaus confronted his father.

"What's this I hear about our friends like the Weismanns and *Pfarrer* Benedict being arrested?" His father was reading a newspaper. He didn't look up.

"Who told you this?"

"Mattie."

"Son, women shouldn't talk about things they don't understand."

Klaus reached across the table and pulled down the newspaper. "Is it true, Father?"

"Son, these are dangerous times. There are many enemies of the *Reich* among us. Some have openly criticized the *Führer's* policies. It's not good for the morale of the people. Hurts the war effort."

"But *Pfarrer* Benedict? Has he criticized the *Führer?* How can an old priest be an enemy of the state?"

"Ah, yes, Klaus. *Pfarrer* Benedict, I believe, was sent to Mauthausen to provide spiritual comfort to the workers. Many are Catholics." He picked up his newspaper.

I know he's lying. Must get Mattie and Siegfried away from here. But I may need his help.

"Father, Mattie has expressed a desire to visit her parents in their new home near Innsbruck. I'm sure you can assist in arranging that."

"But, of course, son. There will be no problems getting travel permits for both of them."

Part Two: 1944-1950

18

South bank of the Seine across from Argenteuil, Winter, 1944.

"I think it's going to snow."

Jacques looked up at the darkening sky. He flicked his *Galuoise* into the river.

"Doesn't matter. We have to stay until someone else shows up. It's supposed to be Pierre, but that fat pig is always late. And it's getting cold."

"You don't like him much, do you?" Louis said. This was his first time on the *vedette*.

"Have you ever tried one of his baguettes? I know there are flour shortages, but his are a disgrace to all other French bakers. They're like cardboard. And have a funny sour taste to them. Inedible."

"*Oui, mais—*"

"Look! What's that? It's a Horch. Damn Nazi staff car. And it's stopping at the inn." Jacques lifted a pair of opera glasses from his fishing creel and took a quick look across the river.

"One officer with a basket . . . like he's making a delivery."

"There'd be more soldiers if it was a raid, *n'est-ce- pas?*"

"*Oui*, but we still must report it."

"*C'est vrai*, but I've never liked spying on my friends."

"*Oui, mon ami*, but the inn had many foreign visitors—including Germans—before the war and some during the occupation. Jules just wants to make sure which side they're on."

"But what about all the Allied airmen they've helped?"

"*C'est vrai, mon ami*, but some of those airmen were later caught by the *Gestapo* in Paris. Jules is trying to find out who the traitor is. That's why we watch the inn. *Voila!*" He pulled a large carp from the river. "And get in some good fishing, *n'est ce-pas?*"

* * *

Klaus was apprehensive about how he might be received at the hotel. He'd arrived in Paris after the first of the year but had delayed this visit until now. His duties hadn't allowed him to visit the hotel during his previous assignment in 1941.

Snow crunched under his feet when he got out of the staff car. His basket contained some gifts. He thought the American cigarettes and chocolate might smooth any ill feelings. The bell over the door jingled as before when he opened it—just as he remembered. Madame Gaultier came from the kitchen.

"*Bonjour*, Madame Gaultier."

"Monsieur?" She didn't look pleased.

"You don't remember me, Madame? Klaus…Klaus von Reichenhall… from Eisenstadt. I stayed here many times before the war. I brought my wife . . . "

Before he could finish she turned her back to him and shouted, "Constance. Come here."

When her daughter came into the room, Madame Gaultier returned to the kitchen.

"*Oui*, Monsieur. May I help you?" Constance asked.

"*Bonjour*, Constance. Do you remember me? Klaus from Eisenstadt."

She looked him up and down. Any semblance to a smile was replaced by a frown. "Yes, I remember you. Mother said you had visited with your wife just before the war."

"She didn't seem pleased to see me."

"It's the uniform, Klaus. You're a German soldier."

"After 1938, one had no choice."

"One always has choices, Klaus."

"Not under the Nazis."

"Yes, we know. We've been under their heel for almost four years. Are you a Nazi, Klaus?"

"No, and never will be."

"But you're soldier . . . an officer . . . a major."

"Yes, but only a staff officer. I work in an office and translate captured documents. I've never fired a gun. Never hurt anyone. I have to carry a pistol, but it's not loaded."

"I think you're losing the war."

"Soon, I hope. I just want to go home."

Can I trust him? How much do I dare tell him. Must be careful.

"Come, let's sit," she said. "Would you like a glass of wine?"

"Yes, Constance. That would be good."

Constance brought a bottle of wine and glasses.

"It hasn't been easy for us, Klaus. My father has been arrested by the *Gestapo*."

"When? For what?"

"They said he was a member of the *Maquis* . . . you know, the *résistance*."

"Was that true . . . the *résistance?*"

"Perhaps. I mustn't talk about it."

"Your husband . . . How is he?"

"Gone. Sent to some labor camp. I haven't heard from him in over a year."

"What is his full name? Maybe I can learn something. And I'll see if I can get your father released."

"Pierre Louis Renaud. He was taken away in November, 1942." She started to cry. "I'm sure he's dead. No one has returned from those camps."

"I must ask this, Constance. Is he a Jew?"

"No. Just a butcher. He had no politics."

"I'm ashamed about what is being done to the Jews. All our Jewish friends and neighbors in Eisenstadt were sent to the camps. I have found out what happened."

"It's true then? They're death camps?"

"Yes. It makes me sick, Constance. I just want this horrible business to be over."

"What about your family?"

"That worries me, especially if the Russians come to Austria before the Allies. I've written to Mattie and told her to stay with her mother's family near Innsbruck. It's close to the Swiss border. They should be safe there. I hope she gets my letters." He reached across the table and took her hand. "May I come back again, Constance? Sometimes I need to get away from the war."

"Of course, Klaus. You'll always be welcome."

* * *

"Who is this Nazi who comes to visit so often?" asked Jules, the leader of the *Maquis* in Argenteuil. "I'm not comfortable having him here."

Three other men seated around the hotel's kitchen table nodded in agreement, but not Gaultier, Constance's father.

"He's Austrian, not German, and definitely not a Nazi. He used to stay here and paint when he was a student before the war."

"Doesn't matter if he *was* an Austrian, he's a German officer now and an enemy of France." Jules said.

"Maybe he's *Gestapo*," said Benard, a plumber, "spying on us."

"That's ridiculous," Gaultier said. "He's just a soldier. I believe he may have been responsible for my release. I could've been shot."

"Perhaps he could have an accident," Jules said.

Constance, outside in the pig sty, listened at the open window. She looked down at the hog she'd just killed. Enough of this silliness, she said to herself. She slammed open the door to the kitchen and strode to the table. The clatter of her wooden shoes echoed off the walls. Blood covered her apron, her bare arms and hands—even a splash or two on her face. She pointed her knife at the *Maquis* leader and around the table to each of the others.

"Anyone who harms Klaus will have to answer to me. He's not a Nazi. He's a friend. *C'est tout!*"

19

Stalag VIIB, Lamsdorf, Germany, Summer, 1944.
When Reggie was captured in 1941, he was sent to *Stalag Luft1* near Barth in northern Germany. From there he had attempted to escape twice, hoping to find a boat to Sweden. After his second attempt and recapture, he had been transferred to *Stalag Luft III* in eastern Silesia near the Polish border. For reasons he never understood, he was further transferred to *Stalag VIIB* at Lamsdorf.

"*Wunderbar. Ist wunderbar,* Sergeant Reggie." Johan, the German *Luftwaffe* guard, held the ship in a bottle of a two-masted schooner in his hands, turned it around, and looked at it from every angle. "Very fine." Johan put the bottle on the table, removed his cap, and pulled a faded blue handkerchief from a pocket to wipe his brow.

"A problem. Just a small one, I'm afraid. I hope." He pointed at the small hand printed nameplate on the front edge of the wooden stand. "She is no longer my . . . how do you say . . . favorite."

"Who's not? The ship or the girl?" Reggie sensed some profit in this. "I can always be flogging the ship to someone else. It's a corker, right? Won't be findin' better in the *stalag.*"

"*Nein. Nein.* It's not the *Schiff. Nein,* it's perfect. It's the name. Greta *is* no longer my favorite. It is possible to change the name to Hilda, *ja?*"

"What happened to Greta, Johan? Figured you two for the long stay. There be another chap?"

"*Nein,* Reggie. It's the war. Greta's husband has returned from the Ukraine. He was with an engineer unit. He's being sent west to France. She will follow him. She's from Alsace, so is part French anyway. The food and wine are better in France, I suppose. I will miss her—such great—how do you say?—breasts." He held his open palms in front his chest.

Engineer units being redeployed from the Ukraine to France. Nice tidbit of news to pass on to London.

"Johan, you old dog. You never be tellin' me Greta had a husband. How many other Russian Front widows are you comforting?"

"Hilda is not a widow, as you say. She's the daughter of the baker in Lamsdorf. Her father supplies some of the bread to the camp. I met her during the conduct of my duties."

"Duties? What duties are those, mate? To have your way with all the young girls in the province? Ha! How much of our Red Cross packet chocolate does it takes to get a local girl to drop her knickers?" Reggie was having fun.

"The *Schiff,* Sergeant Reggie. Will you change the name, *bitte?*"

"For sure, *mein Freund,* but there's another problem. It's unlucky to change the name of a ship. It can be done, but certain gods, very greedy gods, must be appeased."

"*Was?* What do you say? What kind of nonsense is this? This is only a model, a toy. There is only one god? Who are these other gods? This is stupid."

"The Maori god for the sea, Tangaroa, for one. It's bad luck to change the name of a ship. If you have to do it, you must write the old name on a piece of paper, fold the paper, and place it in a small cardboard or wooden box. Burn the box. Scoop up the ashes and throw them into the sea on an outgoing tide. If you live on a lake, do it at night and only during a new moon. River dwellers should send the ashes downstream."

"That is absurd. You foreigners have some strange customs. I have told the other guards about your skill. Could you make more for them?"

"For you, mate, anything, but I'll need some more bottles and better supplies."

"What supplies?"

"Ink, carving tools, papers, instruments, and other bits and bobs. If I could go to Lamsdorf, with an escort, of course, I could find these things."

The forgers in Section K would love this.

Before Johan could answer, he was ordered by an officer to go to the front gate. Reggie followed him. A truck with new arrivals entered the camp. The other prisoners gathered to see who had joined them.

The first officer off the truck was Dee-Dee Dearlove. Reggie pushed his way through the crowd and ran to his friend.

"Dee-Dee!" Reggie skidded to a stop, came to attention and saluted. "Sorry, *Squadron Leader* Dearlove."

Dearlove returned the salute then hugged his friend. "None of that, Reggie."

"Must be keepin' appearances up for the Krauts, sir. Where'd you be catchin' it?"

"Flak over Berlin," he said. "Had to crash land in a field somewhere in Poland. How are you, Reggie? We heard you'd survived and were behind the wire."

"As best as can be, considering. Lost a bit of weight. The rations have been crap this past year."

"Are the Red Cross packets getting through?"

"Not as often as before. *Frtiz* steals most of them. They're just as hungry as we are."

Reggie was going to tell Dee-Dee about the camp, but the guards separated him and three other officers from the rest of the new arrivals and herded them toward the officers' compound.

"Chat with you later, Reggie."

"Yes sir, be lookin' forward to it." Reggie saluted again.

What a small world. Four years ago we were sailing the South Pacific together without a care.

20

German Army Headquarters, Paris, August 17, 1944.
Klaus searched his desk for any personal items he wanted to take. He removed the photograph of Mattie and their son from its frame. That and her letters to him he stuffed in a briefcase.

"The Vichy Frogs are pulling out, *Herr Major*," said Corporal Wagenknect, Klaus's driver. He placed a cup of *ersatz-coffee* on the officer's desk. "And so is our embassy."

"Yes, Hans, as are we. General Kitzinger has ordered all of us to join his headquarters in Nancy. Get my car ready."

"*Ja wohl, Herr Major.* But what about the files?"

"Leave them. We haven't the time to burn them."

"Will we be coming back?"

"I doubt it, Hans. The Americans are too close."

"What about this?" Hans held a small green valise.

"What is it?" *I don't have time for this.*

"Don't know. It's been stuck in the back of a wardrobe for months. It's full of papers in English, I think."

"Let me see it." Klaus put it on his desk. "Go get my car, Hans. *Schnell!*" He opened the valise and dumped its contents. Klaus rapidly read through the papers, and then leaned back in his chair. He took a deep breath. *Gott in Himmel! This is Hemingway. The lost manuscripts. I must save them.*

With the manuscripts back in the valise, he grabbed it and his briefcase, and left the office.

* * *

North of Paris
Second Lieutenant Ken Meier, age twenty, from Dolph Junction, Oregon, loved his "Jug," the nickname of the P-47D Thunderbolt fighter plane he flew. The "Jug" was fast and armed with eight .50 caliber machine guns; a short burst was usually enough to send any *Luftwaffe* aircraft spiraling earthward in flames. Ten five-inch rockets mounted under the wings rained havoc on *Wehrmacht* tanks and the unlucky railway engine.

Meier and his wingman, Second Lieutenant Antonio "Tony" Crowe, known as "Birdman," from Burlington, Iowa, headed west, back toward their base near Thurleston, South Devon. Flying low and fast across France, they looked for targets of opportunity. Both pilots had joined their squadron two weeks before and were anxious to see some action.

Ahead and off to his right, Meier saw a gray sedan drive off a road and disappear in some trees behind a stone building.

"See that, Ken? Looked like a Nazi staff car." Crowe was behind and above Meier.

"Want me to bust the barn?"

"Nope. Let's do a buttonhook. Try to catch 'em in the open."

"Gotta be careful, Ken. Some of our boys've pushed forward out of Paris."

"If it were our boys they wouldn't be hiding, right?"

Corporal Wagenknect looked up through the trees as the American planes passed overhead. He lit a cigarette. "I don't think they saw us, *Herr Major*."

"I think you're right, Hans. Let's get going." Hans guided the car back onto the road. Klaus looked at his map; he hoped the bridge at Neuville was still standing. He thought they should be there in a half hour.

Klaus felt quite comfortable leaving the Hemingway manuscripts with Constance. She was an honorable woman, no hint of avarice in her soul, and educated enough to know the potential value of the hold—not just the literary value. Even if I don't survive the war, she'll make sure of their survival. Probably bury them in her pig sty for safekeeping, he thought with a smile.

They drove less than a kilometer before the rockets exploded in the road on either side of the Horch. A chunk of shrapnel pierced Hans's brain. The car careened to the right, dropped its front wheels into the ditch alongside the road and flipped over. Upside down and shaken Klaus was uninjured until a burst of .50 caliber rounds from Crowe's "Jug" tore through the car's floor boards and smashed his right thigh. He crawled away from the Horch and passed out.

* * *

"Sarge, there's a Kraut officer over in the ditch with a busted up leg. Looks like he's lost a lot of blood. It's pretty bad. The other one's dead. Whatcha want to do with him?"

"Put a tourniquet on the leg and drag'im up here to the road. If the medics get here in time they'll take care of him. If not, another hero dies for the fatherland."

Sergeant Boyce, the squad leader of the American Army reconnaissance unit, watched two of his men strip off Klaus's leather belt and fasten it around his leg above the knee. They dragged him up out of the ditch and laid him in the grass verge at the side of the road. One of the men jumped into the back of the squad leader's jeep.

"Look, Sarge, got me a nice souvenir." The soldier showed his NCO a brown leather holster with a Walther pistol inside. The other soldier climbed back into the cab of the squad's armored half-track.

"Keep it out of sight, Murray, or some officer'll confiscate it," Boyce said. "All right, let's go. Stay alert."

As the Americans drove off, they didn't see four men come out from behind a farm house near the road. Two of the men carried rifles; a third held a German Luger pistol in his left hand—his right coat sleeve was empty and pinned back on itself above the elbow. The fourth, a mere boy of twelve, ran over to the wrecked Horch, yanked open the rear door on the driver's side, and leaned in. With a big smile he straightened up and held a MP-40 submachine gun above his head. He shouted to his friends,

"A Schmeisser! Now I too can fight." He reached back into the car and pulled out a canvas ammunition case with several loaded magazines. The other three partisans walked across the ditch and stood over Klaus.

"This one's still alive." One of the men bent down and slapped Klaus's face. "Should we finish him off or just remove the tourniquet and let him bleed to death?"

The sound of approaching vehicles made them pause. The boy hid behind the Horch.

"*Amis, pas des Boches*," the older partisan said. A column of Sherman tanks clanked past. Armored half-tracked vehicles and trucks full of infantry followed the tanks. A jeep left the column and stopped by the partisans. An American officer with a small silver cross on his helmet got out of the vehicle. He saluted the civilians.

"*Bonjour, mes amis. Vive la France.*" He looked down at Klaus. "*Est-il mort?* Is he dead?"

One of the Frenchmen kicked Klaus in his injured leg; he cried out in pain.

"*No, padre, pas encore.*" The other partisans laughed. The chaplain turned to his driver.

"Flag down the medics, Bill."

The driver watched the vehicles pass and directed an ambulance in behind their jeep. The soldier in the passenger's seat had a red cross on a white background on the front and side of his helmet.

"What ya got, Chaplain?"

"Wounded German officer. Someone's put a tourniquet on his leg."

"Well, let's take a look." The medics got out of the ambulance and examined Klaus.

"Lost a lot of blood. Jim, get a stretcher." The driver went to the rear of the ambulance, opened the door and pulled out a stretcher. He laid it down next to Klaus.

"Put some sulfa on the wound. I'll give him a shot of morphine." As a notice to other medical personnel, the soldier stuck the needle of the empty syringe through Klaus's collar and bent it back.

"Okay, let's roll 'im onto the stretcher," he said. Klaus cried out in pain again. "Chaplain, you and your driver take the back end. Right, on three, lift." They slid Klaus into the back of the ambulance.

Another jeep left the column and stopped.

"What's going on, Doc? One of my boys? Howdy, Chaplain."

"Afternoon, Colonel. Not one of ours . . . wounded German major. Think these Frenchies had other plans for him." The chaplain nodded toward the partisans. A burly man in an Army uniform with a war correspondent's patch on the shoulder of his field jacket climbed out of the back of the jeep.

"Let me talk to 'em," he said.

The American civilian walked over to the three partisans. He handed out some cigarettes and spoke to them in French. The colonel looked at his wrist watch and the column of vehicles passing by.

"How bad off is the Kraut major, Doc?"

"Pretty bad, sir. Probably won't make it. I gave 'im some morphine. His leg's a mess."

"Well, take him along. Run him back to Division when you get some more wounded." The war correspondent walked back to the jeep.

"What'd you find out, Hem?"

"They don't know shit. The Kraut's staff car got jumped by our flyboys. This bunch has just been layin' low and pickin' off stragglers."

"All right. We've been here long enough. Good work, men," the colonel said to the medics. "Let's go, padre."

The regimental commander's jeep sped off down the road followed by the chaplain's.

* * *

"Do you know who that was?" One medic said.

"Of course I know. The colonel."

"No. Not him. The civilian. The newspaper guy."

"No. Should I?"

"That was Ernest Hemingway, the writer."

"What does he write?"

"Books, you moron. Novels. He's world famous. They make movies outta his books."

"What movies?"

"Didn't you see *For Whom the Bell Tolls?* I saw it in the States before shippin' out."

"What bell? Don't get much chance to go to movies sheep ranchin' in Montana, or read books for that matter. What's it about?"

"The war in Spain. It was about an American who . . . oh, never mind. Let's go."

21

"Man must always make an effort, so that he may deserve to be called man, but he is much less master of his own person and destiny than he imagines." *José S. Saramago*

Paris, Fall 1944.
Émile Patrice Plude wasn't sure how he would be received by his father's distant cousin, Pascal Culon. Rain sheeted down around Émile as he stood under the canopy outside the frosted glass and wood framed double doors of Bistro Béroud.

His Aunt Marie had written to Pascal about a job for Émile before she sold the family farm in the Dordogne. They'd received no answer—not unusual with the post disrupted by the war. The capital had been liberated, but the functions of government were still in disarray. Émile had dreamed about going to Paris. He could have found work on other farms in the Dordogne but wanted to do something different with his life—see more of the world.

The two-day train journey from Bordeaux had been exciting but uncomfortable. Exciting, because this was the first time he'd ridden a train farther than to Bergerac and back to La Linde, his village. Uncomfortable, because the train was over-crowded with people returning north to Paris and other liberated parts of the country. The passengers were mostly families who had fled to Vichy France, Spain, or Portugal after the French defeat in 1940. In deference to the elderly and mothers with children, Émile stood in the aisle or on the platforms between the cars for the greater part of the journey.

A young woman, quite fashionably dressed, joined him on the platform and extracted a silver cigarette case from her purse. "Have you a match, Monsieur?" She looked at his ill-fitting Sunday suit, scruffy shoes, and floppy peasant's black beret. "No, probably not." Before Émile could answer, she turned to another man, who lit her cigarette. With her back to Émile, she carried on a conversation with the man, interrupted by giggles and laughter.

Must think I'm only a kid. Don't know how to talk to girls . . . women. I'm ready to be a man. Been ready for some years. Maybe I'll learn how in Paris.

Above average height and well-built for a sixteen-year old, Émile had the large, strong hands of a man from the country and dirty-blond hair trimmed short by a bowl-cut from his aunt before he left the farm.

At the station's information kiosk in Paris, he asked directions to the rue Jean-Louis. He rode the Métro to the Rennes station and walked up into a wet night. A policeman pointed him in the direction of the bistro. The rain stopped for a moment, but Émile's trouser legs were soaked when a taxi sped past close to the curb. Clutching his cardboard suitcase under his left arm—the old rope handle broke during the shuffle on the train—he reached for the bistro's door handle when it swung open. Light, music, and

a fog of tobacco smoke assaulted him as he moved aside to allow a couple
to exit. The man, well-dressed in a black raincoat and fedora, looked him
over and shook his head. The woman, who wore a long red coat and
yellow hat, was over-perfumed and wore an abundance of makeup. She
laughed and said something that sounded like "peasant just off his wagon"
to Émile—her accent strange to his ear.

Émile stepped into the bistro. Plaster faux-Roman statuary was
scattered around the room among glass-topped tables and wooden chairs
with woven cane backs. Posters and paintings showing scenes of Paris life
hung on the walls. Several couples and pairs of men occupied, maybe, half
the tables. The bar, white marble with a zinc top, ran across most of the far
wall, less a space for access to the kitchen and toilet. Behind the bar, a bald
brawny man wearing a stained apron and white shirt with sleeve garters
poured a drink for a man sitting on a stool. A cigarette dangled from the
bartender's lower lip. He looked up and saw Émile.

"Hey! Close the door. This isn't a *pension*. Try down the street."

"*Bonsoir*, Monsieur. Are you Pascal Culon? I'm Émile Plude from La
Linde. Your nephew . . . Amelia's son." He closed the door.

The man on the bar stool turned and looked at the new arrival.
Swarthy of complexion and well-dressed, he had a thin moustache and
streaks of gray in his hair. Émile noticed his shined shoes. He said
something to Pascal that caused both men to laugh. The man finished his
drink, shook hands with the bartender and turned to leave. He stopped
when he got near Émile, sniffed and said, "Most definitely from the
country. I'll leave you to deal with your rustic relative, Pascal." Waving a
hand over his head, he said, "Consider my offer, *s'il vous plaît. A bientôt.*" He
stubbed out his cigar in an ashtray on one of the tables. "Welcome to
Paris," he said to Émile and left the bistro.

Pascal Culon came out from behind the bar and greeted Émile.
"Welcome to Paris, nephew." He wiped his hands on the apron before he
took Émile's hand. "We received Marie's letter, and I thought Francine
had answered, but the post the way it is . . . ." He shrugged his shoulders.
"But, you're here, and most welcome. How are things in the south?" He
took Émile's suitcase, grasping the length of twine that kept the box from
falling apart. "Come sit at the bar. A *pastis*, perhaps?"

Pascal poured a portion of the licorice-flavored liqueur into a glass. He
placed a pitcher of water next to the glass. "Your pleasure, nephew."

Émile had had *pastis* before, but just on the sly with other farm workers
at a local bar. Only wine was allowed on the farm.

Pascal turned to the small window in the wall behind the bar and
shouted, "Francine, come out. Amelia's son, Émile, is here." He turned
back to the bar and poured two more glasses of *pastis*. "We must celebrate."

A short, buxom woman with graying hair came into the room wiping
her hands with a dish towel. She stopped for a moment and looked at
Émile.

"What a handsome young man you are, Émile." She lunged forward
and gave him a hug and three kisses on his cheeks. "We always do three

when it's *spécial.* And this is *spécial.* How is our cousin Marie? We hope she got a good price for the farm." She turned to the bar and added a bit of water to her *pastis.* "So, *Salut,* and welcome to Paris. Are there many shortages in the south?" Francine asked.

It was past closing time and the other customers had left. Two men—very fancily dressed, Émile thought—remained at a corner table filling out some kind of forms.

"No, not really. When you live on a farm, you have all you need—eggs, milk, vegetables, fruit—everything. We had problems sometimes getting petrol for the tractor, but a few chickens in the right hands usually solved that."

"So you know how to pluck a chicken or butcher a pig, do you?"

"*Bien sûr,* Auntie. Why do you ask?"

"We have a source of fresh meat, but sometimes it is very fresh—alive—and we'd love having someone who can take care of that." She looked at Pascal who shrugged and shook his head. "We city folks have lost the skill of . . . how you say . . . country doings." She finished her *pastis.* "Before, when the markets were open and filled with what we needed this wasn't necessary, but now we need a man from the farm to do it." She nodded to her husband for a refill. "Out back in the alley is a place where you could prepare the birds and pigs."

One of the men at the table in the corner interrupted their conversation about butchering. "Hey, Pascal. Got another pencil? This one's finished." He threw the stub at the bar. Pascal took a pencil from a glass behind the bar and hurried to the table.

"Care for another drink, Messieurs?"

"Any Calvados?" one asked. Pascal nodded.

"Here, Pascal." The other man showed the racing form to the owner. "What nag should I pick for the second race?" He handed Pascal a pencil. "You pick."

"But, Monsieur, you know I know nothing about the horses. It would be foolish—"

"Pick one, Pascal. Just pick one."

Pascal made a mark on the form. He handed the pencil back to the man. "*Bonne chance,* Monsieur."

"Half is yours if we get lucky, Pascal. And I'll have a Calvados also."

Pascal returned to the bar to get the drinks.

Who are these men who can stay past closing time and order Pascal about like a servant? They must be betting on horse races. How do they do that? They're wearing nice clothes and have shined shoes.

Émile's thoughts paused when two young women came in. Dressed like the woman he'd seen leaving the bistro earlier, they went straight to the table with the two men. They both slapped wads of money on the table. One of the women lit a cigarette. The other turned toward the bar, saw Émile and said, "*Chérie,* look at the new pretty boy."

Francine moved in front of Émile, almost like a bodyguard. "Stay away from my nephew, Claudine. He's not for you."

The girl shrugged her shoulders and turned back to the table. The men laughed and one said, "*Bien,* now back on the streets."

The girls left the bistro—one threw Émile a kiss.

Francine took him by the arm. "Come, nephew. I'll show you where to put your things."

There was an alcove behind the bar in a storage room. Francine showed Émile the single, thin-mattress bed and the small armoire for his clothes. He would use the bistro's toilet and could bathe upstairs in their apartment. His wages would be minimal, plus a portion of the bar tips. And, of course, his meals were included. What would he do? Everything.

When they returned to the bar, the men were gone. Pascal went around the room clearing the tables and turning off lights. Francine poured Émile another *pastis.*

"Those girls—women. Are they prostitutes?" he asked. Émile had heard about the ladies of the night in Paris.

"*Oui,* nephew, and you should stay away from them," Francine said. "There are many nice girls in Paris. I'm sure you'll find one."

"And those men. Do they work for them? They gave them money."

"*Bien sûr.* It is part of doing business in this *arrondissement,* unfortunately. But business is business and times are difficult." She took a sip from her glass. "Pimps. They're pimps. A low class of creature that prey on unfortunate girls. Scum, mostly. They all work for Carlo Pioletti, a Corsican gangster. But, he has kept us supplied with wine and spirits, and fresh meat throughout the occupation. In return, we allow his business to be conducted here. His thugs do keep other riffraff away. We may sell out to him someday. He owns the rest of the building." She looked up over her head. "Pascal will want to retire to the coast in a few years. But, that's no concern of yours. Just stay away from his girls and be polite to his pimps."

* * *

Émile did everything—swept the sidewalk outside the bistro before it opened for the day, washed dishes, scrubbed pots and pans in the small kitchen, cleaned the tables and mopped the floor after closing, or if a patron got too drunk and threw up. When needed and at the end of the evening, he mucked out the toilets. But in between his daily chores, Francine taught him how to cook, how to bake, prepare a menu, and organize special meals. Once a week he washed the windows inside and out, and dusted the statuary and around the pictures.

"Are all these pictures about Paris?" he asked Pascal.

"Most. They're prints of scenes from the last century done by Louis Béroud. The previous owners knew him, loved his work, and renamed the bistro in his honor when he died in '30. They told me he used to come here often before the last war." He pointed toward two on the wall left of the bar. "Except those over there."

Émile walked over to the pictures for a closer look. He'd dusted them many times, but hadn't paid any attention to their content. "They're almost the same, aren't they?"

Pascal came out from behind the bar and stood next to him.

"Good eye, nephew." He pointed. "The one on the right is a Monet... a copy, of course, of the railroad bridge at Argenteuil. The other was done by a young German artist, Klaus . . . something. Many art students try to capture the same scenes as the masters."

He laid a hand on Émile's shoulder. "It's been some years since I've thought of him. He was in love with one of our waitresses. Don't remember how that ended up, but she gave the painting to us before she left for America with her parents, the previous owners . . . Jews, you know." Pascal walked back and began arranging wine carafes on the bar.

"Jews? I don't think I've ever met a Jew." Émile straightened the chairs around a table. "What are they like?"

Pascal laughed. "What are they like? You *are* from the country, nephew. They are no different from you or me . . . most good, some not so good. Just people."

Émile stopped and looked at Pascal. "Didn't we send many of them to camps during the Occupation?"

"Many? No, nephew, we sent thousands to concentration camps and to the death camps. It is a national disgrace we, the French, will never erase."

"What's a disgrace, *mon chéri?*" Francine came into the room with a demijohn of pickles for the bar. She smiled at Émile.

"I was telling our nephew about the Nazis and Petain's criminals rounding up and deporting French citizens just because they were Jewish."

She looked at Émile with curiosity in her eyes. "Were you not aware of this in the Dordogne?"

"No, Auntie. We knew the news on the wireless was mostly propaganda, so we didn't listen to it often."

Francine turned on her husband. "What made you talk about this? The war is almost over. The Americans are across the Rhine, and the Russians are close to Berlin."

"Nephew asked about the paintings—the Argenteuil bridge." He pointed. "The one by that German—."

"Klaus wasn't a German. He was Austrian and a fine young man." Francine said.

"Austrian, German, they're all Nazis . . . all the same."

"You must be getting senile, *mon chéri.* Don't you remember he came here at Christmas last year and brought us English cigarettes and chocolates? You didn't have any qualms about selling the fags to Carlo's hirelings for an exorbitant price." She turned and stepped closer to the painting, shook her head and said, "I do hope he is all right." Facing her husband again, she said, "What's this about the Jews?"

Pascal took a deep breath. "I was explaining to our nephew about the Schleins and how they had to . . . decided to . . . go to America. And I *do* remember that Nazi officer coming here with his gifts, as you call them. He was probably trying to impress Carlo's whores or one of our waitresses." He poured himself a *pastis.*

"You're *fou, mon coeur,* but I love you anyway. Klaus was no Nazi. Just a young man caught up in a horrible war. He had no interest in our girls.

Remember, he brought his new bride here for a visit before the war." She took the dust cloth from Émile and said, "Come, nephew. I must finish the *cassoulet*. The beans are soaking, but the three fat ducks in a cage out back need to be plucked and cleaned."

Cousin Pascal may be the owner, but Francine is the boss.

* * *

After the city's liberation, it didn't take the soldiers from the Allied armies any time to find the Bistro Béroud. They seemed to come in droves—Americans, British, and Free French. Carlo made sure that Pascal had an ample supply of cheap wine and watered-down whiskey. But it wasn't the lure of cheap booze and good food that brought the soldiers to the bistro. There were other pleasures on offer. The American Provost Marshall tried to declare it off limits, but a few dollars—not francs—passed from Carlo's hands to influential members of the new government, and the Bistro Béroud—a monument to the honor of a great French impressionist they insisted—and all its amenities, remained available to the liberators.

Pascal hired two more waitresses to handle the crowds. One, Angelique, a young girl from a village near Caen, quickly made friends with Émile, another import from the country. When he brought drinks and meals to the tables, Émile overheard Angelique speaking English to the American soldiers, but never to the British.

In the kitchen after she brought dishes to be washed, he asked her, "Angelique, I didn't know you spoke English? But why only to the *Amis*?"

She turned to him, and he saw hatred in her eyes. "The British bombed my village during the invasion, killing my parents and younger brother. I too was injured." She pulled up the sleeve of her blouse and showed him a fresh scar on her arm. "A friend took me west to the Americans, and they healed my wound." She pulled her sleeve down. "I've no love for the British."

"How did you learn to speak English?"

"I don't speak English, Émile." She smiled. "I speak American." She went back into the bar.

After closing, Angelique and Émile sat at a table. Pascal and Francine had gone up to their apartment for the night. Émile still had things to finish, but Angelique asked him to sit for a moment. She was waiting for an American soldier to return and take her to a party.

"You asked where I learned to speak English . . . American?"

Émile rested his mop against another table. "*Oui*, how did that happen? Was there an American school in your village? I've heard the *Amis* have schools here in Paris."

She lit a cigarette and offered him one. He shook his head.

"*Mon père* spent many years in America. He worked in the vineyards in California before the first war. During the war, because of his knowledge of American English, he liaised between the French Army and the *Amis*. He insisted that we . . . Patrice, my brother, and I . . . learn to speak like Americans." She looked at the clock on the wall behind the bar, and then at the door. "He wanted to take all of us to America someday, but this war ended all that. And now they're all dead."

"I'm so sorry about your family. I too have no love for the British. My father was killed at Oran."

"Oh no. That was a betrayal and a tragedy." She looked at the clock again. "I don't think my Yank is coming back for me tonight." She lit another cigarette. "Émile, would you have a glass of wine with me? I'm not ready to go back to my place quite yet."

Émile jumped to his feet and draped a cloth over his arm. "*Bien sûr,* Mademoiselle Angelique, *à votre service.*"

She laughed and looked at the door again. Behind the bar, Émile opened a locked cabinet and withdrew an opened bottle of *Côtes du Rhône* from Pascal's *spécial* stash. He brought two glasses to the table. She took a sip.

"Émile, *mon chéri,* this is not the usual plonk with toe nails left in it." She took another sip, reached across the table to touch his hand. "You are a good boy, *mon chéri.*"

A boy? I'm not a boy. I've never been with a woman, but I'm not a boy.

He stood. "I must complete my chores and turn off the lights." He grabbed his mop and started to walk away but turned and asked, "Are you staying longer?"

Angelique finished her wine, looked again at the door, and then said, "If you'll sneak another," she held up her glass and smiled, "I'll give you your first English lesson. Perhaps, a tutorial on body parts and their functions?"

Émile's small bed barely survived their exertions in applied biology. He was asleep when she left.

When Émile awoke, still naked under the duvet, he looked at the alarm clock by his bed. It was almost eight o'clock. He had to get up and sweep the street outside the bistro, but he lay back down—just for a moment.

I am now a man. I made love to a woman. Oh, she smelled so wonderful! Her kisses, her touches, and her beautiful breasts and long legs. Not her first time, bien sûr, but wonderful just the same. How did I do? Hope she enjoyed it. Wonder when we can do it again?

He'd finished his outside chores when Francine came out of the kitchen. Émile hummed a favorite tune as he went around the room straightening chairs and picking up overlooked cigarette butts from the night before.

"You're very cheerful this morning, nephew. Sweet dreams, was it?"

"*Ah, oui,* Auntie. *Très* sweet."

Soon after the bistro opened for the day, an American soldier came in. He was tall, blond, and stood with his hands on his hips. Émile, working behind the bar washing out some wine glasses he'd missed the night before, nodded and smiled.

"*Bonjour,* Monsieur."

The American looked around and walked to the bar.

"Hey, kid, is Angelique around?"

"*Pardon,* Monsieur, *mais, je ne comprends pas. Je ne parle pas anglais.*" Émile shook his head and shrugged.

"No English, huh? Okay. Tell her Mark was here. No, wait. I'll write a note." He grabbed a paper napkin from the bar, took a pencil from his breast pocket and wrote a few lines. "My outfit is pulling out today. Don't know if I'll be back." He offered the napkin to Émile. "Make sure she gets this."

Émile shook his head again. *Wish I could speak American.*

"Angelique…you know her, don't you, kid?"

"*Ah, oui,* Monsieur. . . Angelique." Émile nodded.

"Good. Here's something for your trouble." He flipped a coin in the air.

Émile caught the coin and took the napkin.

"Great catch, kid. Make sure she gets this."

"*Oui,* Monsieur. Angelique." He looked at the coin—five francs. "*Merci,* Monsieur."

The soldier left. Émile folded the napkin and slipped it in the pocket of his apron. He felt a pang of jealousy.

She won't be in until later. Should I give her the message? Wonder what it says. Could just throw it away. She'd never know. But, when he comes back and asks her about it, what would I say? If he had shown up last night, I . . . we wouldn't have . . . He laughed. *I owe him that, bien sûr!*

"What's so funny, nephew?" Pascal came into the bar with a case of wine. He placed it under the bar.

"*Rien,* Uncle. Nothing of importance. An American soldier just left. He gave me a note for Angelique." Émile took the napkin from his apron and handed it to Pascal. "I don't know what it says, but he was very concerned that she gets it."

Pascal looked at the note, shrugged and said, "Probably another proposal of marriage. The Yanks use that as a way of getting in our girls' knickers." He shrugged again. "*C'est la guerre.*" He opened a bottle of wine and started to fill the carafes on the bar. "The Germans were the same." He opened another bottle. "But, the Yanks have more to offer."

Three French soldiers came into the bistro. They wore American-style uniforms, but with Free French insignia on their shoulders. That was not the only difference—the *képi blanc* of *la Légion étrangère,* the Foreign Legion. Pascal brought glasses and a carafe of red wine—the good stuff, not the plonk—to the table. After perusing the *menu fixe,* one asked, "What about Madame Culon's famous *cassoulet?*"

"I'm so sorry, Messieurs, *mais,* this is not on the *menu fixe.* If you would be so kind as to return after, say, seven, the *cassoulet* will be available." He reached forward and filled their glasses. "Another carafe, Messieurs? *Offert par la maison, bien sûr.*"

Émile, behind the bar slicing lemons, watched and listened.

La Légion étrangère. I've heard of them. They are everywhere in exotic places throughout the French colonies: Africa, Indochina, and other places I've never heard of. I know I'll have to do my national service. Maybe I can do it in la Légion étrangère.

"Émile, bring these heroes of France another carafe."

"*Oui*, Uncle." Émile brought another to the table.

"*Merci beaucoup*, son," said an older légionnaire with a bushy, speckled grey moustache that curled up at the ends. His face, especially around the eyes, was heavily creased, like someone who'd spent many years in the sun. He looked closely at Émile. "Done your time yet?"

"No, Monsieur, I'm only seventeen."

"You look older, doesn't he, Miguel?"

A légionnaire with a quite dark complexion, raised his head and looked at Émile. "No, *Père* Pierre, he's just a kid." He smiled and said, "Pay him no mind, boy. This old desert rat's always trying to shanghai fresh blood into *la Légion*." He lifted his glass so Émile could fill it. "When your national service time comes, learn a trade—truck driver, carpenter, mechanic—anything but infantry. No future there."

The third légionnaire asked, "Are the oysters fresh, Monsieur?" He was smaller in stature than the other two, and his accent different to Émile's ear.

His skin is almost yellow and there is a slant to his eyes. Must be from an Asian colony.

"*Oh oui*, Monsieur. Arrived from the coast this morning," Pascal lied. He didn't know when Carlo's people bought them. The basketful arrived earlier that morning with fish and live fowl. He assumed it all came from *Les Halles* market but didn't ask any questions.

"*Bien*," the older soldier said. "We'll have a dozen each."

"Good choice, Monsieur." Pascal turned to Émile. "Open three dozen, nephew, *s'il vous plaît*."

"*Oui*, Uncle. *Tout de suite*." Émile set the carafe on the table and went into the kitchen. He hated opening oysters—nearly jabbed the oyster knife through the palm of his left hand the first time he did it. But Francine, listening at the window, already had several finished. He helped with the rest, stabbing his hand only once.

"You're getting better at this, Émile. It just takes practice." She arranged the oysters on three platters and placed a sliced, freshly-baked baguette in a basket. "Off you go."

Émile carried two platters into the bar. Francine followed with a third and the bread. The légionnaires stood when she approached their table.

Madame Culon blushed and wiped her hands on her apron. "*Merci beaucoup*, Monsieur, but . . . how do you know of my cooking?"

"From an old sergeant major when we were in Dakar. He said when we get to Paris . . . no doubt in his mind we would get here . . . we must have Madame Culon's *cassoulet* at the Bistro Béroud on rue Jean-Louis. If you were still here, *bien sûr*. And you are, and here we are."

Madame Culon clapped her hands to her cheeks, shook her head and blushed again. "What was his name—the sergeant major? Is he here with you? Can he come tonight? I'll prepare something *spécial*." She looked from face to face.

"I'm so sorry to disappoint you, Madame, but our comrade, Étienne Agellier fell outside of Toulon in August." He pulled a fourth chair to the table. "Please join us."

"Étienne. Yes, I remember him." She sat. "Émile, another glass, *s'il vous plaît*." She brushed the hair out of her eyes, wiped away a tear and smiled at the soldiers. "At least he died on French soil."

Émile brought another glass and carafe.

"He was a regular here while on recruiting duty for the *la Légion* before the war." She drank from her glass. "A wonderful man. Enjoyed my cooking. Used to bring prospects here for an evening of drinks and girls. Think he had a family in Paris or close by. Don't remember all of it." She filled her glass and raised it. "A salute to Étienne. And to all the heroes of France."

They stood. Pascal began singing *La Marseillaise,* and other customers who had entered the bar joined in.

* * *

Angelique read the note from Mark. Émile watched her tear it into small pieces and let them fall to the floor.

Not good news. Something more to clean up. What did the note say? Must have been bad news. I'll ask her later.

For the remainder of the day, Angelique avoided Émile. When she came into the kitchen while he was performing his *plongeur* duties, she didn't chat with him as before. He greeted her as usual and smiled, but she acted aloof as if she was superior to a mere dishwasher.

Women are such strange creatures. Perhaps what we did was not important for her, as it was for me. I have much to learn.

The légionnaires returned for the *cassoulet.* And three of Carlo's girls. After a welcoming carafe of the best vintage, Pascal switched to the house wine. No one noticed—except Émile.

Angelique became the favorite of an American logistics officer and quit work two weeks before Émile's eighteenth birthday. There was a celebration of sorts at the bistro where she flashed around a gaudy engagement ring and raved about her new life in Paducah, Kentucky.

22

Stalag VIIB, January, 1945.
Reggie glanced sideways out the window of Hut 23. He smoked a cigarette. Sixteen fellow *"Kreigies,"* as the Germans called the Allied prisoners of war, sat at desks working on forged travel documents and maps. An officer, who had been a junior don at Cambridge, rambled on with his lecture on American literature of the twentieth century. If any German guards, known as "goons," approached the hut, Reggie warned the airmen. They would hide their work in a secret drawer under their desks and open the books they were studying. The officer talked about Hemingway. Outside, Kevin Vaughn, a Welshman from Cardiff, tended a garden near the hut. If he saw a goon approach, he would start doing stretching exercises with his hoe.

Listening to one of several clandestine radios constructed by the *Kreigies,* Reggie knew the war was going bad for the Germans. Italy had surrendered, the Americans and British Armies had crossed the Rhine, and the Russians were in Warsaw.

"The chap is the most famous Yank writer of the twentieth century," the don continued. Reggie only half listened. "And has earned his spurs, as they say, about life. Wounded in Italy in the last war, he's been through three wives, hunted big game in Africa, caught record-setting fish in the Caribbean, was a war correspondent in the Spanish Civil War and in China, and is now with the Americans in France. But, he has had some bad episodes. In 1922, a suitcase filled with the beginnings of a novel and many short stories was stolen from a railway carriage in Paris—never recovered or found."

A goon walked toward the hut. Reggie stomped his feet and the paperwork disappeared inside the desks. The German guard entered the hut.

"*Guten tag, Feldwebel* Grabenhorst," the don said, intentionally promoting the corporal to sergeant. "Would you care to join our little discussion?"

The guard looked around. "*Nein,*" he said and left.

"Now that that's sorted, we'll continue." The airmen brought their handiwork back onto the desk tops.

"Enough about Hemingway's private life. Let's look at one of his best, in my opinion, short stories, 'Up in Michigan'."

What'd he say? I be knowin' that one. When did I see it? Right. The valise with the English papers in Paris. Well, stone the crows!

* * *

During the third week of January work parties started returning from the east. They said the Russians were only days away and headed in their direction. The camp loudspeakers announced they were to be evacuated.

Reggie thought this might offer chances to escape again. The guards, with pistols at the ready, gave the prisoners two hours to gather their belongings. At six o'clock, in the dark, the march started to an unknown destination. In the chaos, Reggie searched for and found Dee-Dee.

"We must be stickin' together, mate."

"Right you are, Reggie. I'm not my whole self today."

"What is it, Dee-Dee?"

"Stomach cramps. Some diarrhea."

"That not be soundin' good."

As the column of one thousand men began filing out, every man was issued a Red Cross parcel and German rations. The rumble of artillery could be heard in the distance. All night and the next day they trudged down the never-ending road. Finally after dark on the second day, they stopped for a ration of hot vegetable soup. The column had covered fifty kilometers from Lamsdorf. Another eighty-three kilometers brought them to *Stalag VIIIA* at Görlitz where they waited a few days for small groups of stragglers to join them.

"Reggie, I can't go on. It's dysentery. It's returned."

"They'll be loading sick chaps on a train. I'll stay with you. Can't abandon a fellow Kiwi."

Packed like sardines in freight cars with stretcher cases, the combined body warmth reduced the suffering from the freezing weather. The train passed through Dresden, which had been badly damaged by Allied bombing. At Halberstadt, the train sat on a siding, but no rations were issued.

When an air raid alarm sounded, Reggie carried Dee-Dee out of the car and down to a ditch beside the track. A pair of roving Mustangs flying low and looking for rail targets dove across their train to attack a locomotive on the next track. Reggie lay on top of Dee-Dee. The American fighters returned and blew up their train's engine.

Reggie helped his mate to his feet, and they joined a column of men who could still walk. Another prisoner—Reggie never learned his name—helped him carry Dee-Dee.

The second week in March, the survivors arrived at a *stalag* in Ziegenhain. They were housed in large tents, and Dee-Dee was taken to a hospital.

On Good Friday, March 30, US Army tanks liberated the camp. Days later, Reggie, Dee-Dee and other airmen were taken by truck to an airfield. US Army Air Corps C-47s waited for them.

"We're goin' home, mate."

"Thank you for taking care of me, Reggie."

"No worries there, *teina*."

"*Teina*? What's that, Reggie?"

"Cook Island Maori for brother. We be brothers now, mate."

23

Paris, 1946.
Émile registered for national service at the local police precinct. A few weeks later, he was called up. When interviewed by an ancient sergeant, he said he wanted to join *la Légion étrangère.* The NCO stared at him for a moment, and then laughed.

"No, son. You don't want to get mixed up with that bunch of criminals." He stamped Émile's papers and said, "You'll go to the 159th—Berlin."

After an issue of uniforms and equipment, and a few days' instruction in how to march, salute officers, and look like soldiers, Émile and sixty-three other recruits were herded onto a train to Berlin.

The war had ended the year before. France, now an occupying power in Germany, established military bases throughout the country, most on the southern border along the Rhine River. The moribund German government was obligated by treaty to pay for the occupation forces. The French Army took advantage of that, so the recruit training of the soldiers sent to their brigade in Berlin was conducted in Berlin. The four major Allied victors—the United Kingdom, France, the United States, and the Soviet Union—maintained garrisons in the former enemy's capital city.

The train ride to Berlin exposed Émile to the devastation of the war. Passing through Frankfurt and other German cities, he saw mile after mile of rubble and the shells of bombed-out buildings. The train stopped for long periods on sidings where repair work was still being completed. Except for Bordeaux on the coast, the countryside of the Dordogne had been untouched by the war. Émile had heard on the wireless about the devastation in other parts of France, but this was his first glimpse of what it must look like.

When the train rolled slowly into Berlin, Émile and the other inductees crowded at the windows of their carriage gawking at the ruins. At a still partially damaged railway station—only the girders and frames of the domed ceiling remained—they transferred to trucks. Their route through the city took them past block after block of destruction. The once-wide boulevards—now used to collect the rubble from adjacent buildings—allowed only a single lane of traffic.

The convoy passed through an archway that announced their arrival at *Le Quartier Napoléon.* Formerly the barracks and hospital of a *Luftwaffe* unit, the *caserne* had been badly damaged by Soviet forces during the battle for the city. It now served as the headquarters of the French garrison in Berlin.

* * *

Émile's day began at five a.m. with an hour of physical exercise. After a quick breakfast—coffee and a croissant—the recruits prepared for the daily barracks inspection. The remainder of the morning consisted of drill and weapons training. After a mid-day meal of soup, bread, and a sausage or two, he worked on fatigue details clearing the rubble from damaged buildings in the *Quartier*. Germans in dark blue clothing, under supervision of armed soldiers, assisted in the clearance of the rubble. Émile learned they were German prisoners of war.

Every night he walked guard duty for an hour or two around the boundaries of the *Quartier* with an experienced soldier or NCO. They often met and chatted with Berliners, females mostly, who were willing to exchange favors for food, chocolate, or cigarettes.

Three weeks into his training, Émile was ordered to the regimental headquarters.

What have I done wrong? I've been a good soldier. Followed all the orders. Passed inspection . . . most days.

Émile stood at attention in front of the sergeant major's desk. The NCO paged through some papers, and then looked up.

"Be at ease, son. You're not in trouble." He pointed at the document on the desk. "Your dossier states that you were a *sous-chef* in the Bistro Béroud in Paris."

"Yes, sir. For two years. It's on the rue Jean-Louis, and—."

The NCO raised his hand. "I'm not concerned about its location, son. Any *sous-chef* from a Paris bistro or Lyon will fill our needs." He took a cigarette from a pack on the desk, lit it, and leaned back in his chair. "*Le Club des Sous-Officiers* is in need of a cook."

"Yes, sir. I'd be willing to try it."

"Try it? You have no voice in this, son. That's what you'll do. This *is* the army." He snubbed out his cigarette. "No more guard duty or fatigue details for you. You'll be billeted in a room above the club." He closed the folder on his desk. "Report to Sergeant Masneri. He's in charge of the club's staff. Major Favre may want to interview you. He's the *président* of the club, but I don't see any difficulties. He's a Parisian, so he should be pleased with my choice."

Émile saluted and left the regimental headquarters. *No guard duty. No inspections. No fatigue details. Thank you, Pascal and Francine for taking me in. I must write to them about my new position.*

* * *

"Your immediate supervisor is Corporal Dubonnett, the chef," said Sergeant Masneri. "He'll tell you your duties and work hours." He stood. "Come, Plude. I'll give you a tour of your new home."

Le Club des Sous-Officiers occupied a three-story building that had formerly been the officers' mess for the *Luftwaffe*. Remarkably undamaged by the fighting, it didn't take the new occupants long to bring it up to their standards. As in any army, the noncommissioned officers were quite adept, expert even, at scrounging and acquiring comfort items unavailable to others.

The breakfast and luncheon room, the enclosed patio, and the main bar were furnished with contemporary tables and chairs. The lounge was filled with comfortable chairs and sofas from the *Bauhaus* school. The ballroom had an abundance of antique tables and chairs. When officers visited *Le Club,* they always commented on the elegance of the furnishings. One overly self-important officer commented that some of the items, especially the antiques, should be moved to the officer's mess. After a word to the commanding general by Major Favre, that officer never appeared again in *Le Club.*

The garrison's *sous-officiers* lived on the second floor of the building. Émile shared a garret room on the third floor with three other soldiers—two were *sous-chefs* and the other a supply clerk.

"No German nationals are allowed above the ground floor," Masneri said. "The cleaners and other staff are Polish refugees for the most part. Two have a room in the attic. They have pretty much free run of the place, so keep any valuables locked away. There's a safe in my office if you need to use it."

24

"Given any more thought to my offer, Reggie?" Squadron Leader Dee-Dee Dearlove joined Warrant Officer Reggie Pobjoy at the rail of the *S.S. Orion.* Two hours out of Auckland, they watched the western sky slide from black to gray. The sun would be up shortly. Reggie threw his cigarette into the sea.

Porpoises—sometimes olive-grey, sometimes steel-blue—played about the ship's forefoot, leaping and plunging in the bow wave, scraping themselves against the bow plates, turning cartwheels in twos and threes.

"I appreciate your offer, Dee-Dee, but I'm not believin' the life as a bank clerk is the one for me. Me thinks I'll be goin' back to the Cooks for a bit." Reggie turned to face his fellow *stalag* survivor. "There be some old business there to sort out . . . and a buried treasure to recover, if someone hasn't beat me to it."

"Buried treasure? You never mentioned that before." Dearlove reached into his breast pocket and pulled out a cigarette case. He opened it and offered it to Reggie. "So that's the draw to the Cooks for you . . . buried treasure? I had visions of you just lounging about among the palm trees with a bunch of native girls and writing your memoirs."

"Native girls? Now that's something I haven't thought about. Not such a bad idea after the years inside the wire, is it?" He took a cigarette from the case.

"We made a good run at catching up in Paris, and especially in Colombo, did we not?"

"That we did, mate. Madam Sati provided us the best of the house—surprised she remembered me after all those years. We were lucky not to miss the sailing."

"So, Reggie, what plans?"

"Home for a visit, and then be catchin' a boat to Rarotonga. Got some old friends to look up. And maybe stay around for a bit. Those folks treated me very well when I was there before."

"No sheep ranching then?"

"Not on your life, mate. That's why I left Whangarei the first time."

"About this buried treasure . . . I assume you're serious . . . our bank could be quite helpful in any transactions that might arise from its discovery."

"Dee-Dee, you swine, you're already starting to talk like a banker, and we haven't been demobbed yet." They both laughed. "But you're at the head of the queue if it comes to that, mate."

As the *Orion* entered Waitematā Harbor, a navy band, crowds, and Maori dancers greeted the ship. Naval vessels in the harbor sounded their horns; fireboats shot water about. Dearlove's family met them on the pier. Reggie spent the night with his friend's family in their posh home overlooking the harbor. Dee-Dee and his brothers worked on Reggie to join them at the bank, an island rep, perhaps. Reggie said he would keep the offer in mind and asked them to find out about ships going to the Cooks. The next day the two RNZAF officers were de-mobilized at an air force base outside of Auckland.

Reggie called the Parua Bay Hotel and asked if someone could send a message up the hill to his folks at the farm. Reggie rode the train to Whangarei and was met by his father, mother, younger brother, Malcolm, Jr, and sister Margo. His father had bought a Ford sedan during the war. No wagon and team this time.

During his time behind the wire, Reggie had received only four letters from home. He'd written many more, but they had received only two. From one, Reggie learned that Rosie Harbittle had married a sheep farmer and had three children.

After dinner, Reggie and his father walked up to the bluff above the house. Reggie looked across Parua Bay. A flat-bottomed scow plodded up the river. His father hadn't said anything about his running away to sea until now.

"This is where it all started, isn't it, son?"

"Right you are. It seems like a long time ago."

"Have you gotten the roaming spirit out of your system?"

Reggie turned to face him. "Father, I know you be wantin' me to settle down here and help with the farm, but I've still one more voyage to take. Goin' back to the Cooks. For how long I can't say."

"Look around, son. This will be all yours someday. It's a good life . . . an honest life."

"Yes, Father, I know, but I still don't want to be a sheep farmer. The sea's in my blood now. When I was in the *stalag*, my thoughts weren't about sheep but the islands." Reggie offered his father a cigarette. He refused. "Give it . . . the farm . . . to Junior. He loves it here."

"I'll not be arguing with you, son. You've been through enough. We're just chuffed you came out of this war unharmed. Your mom cried for days after they told us you'd been shot down. Happy we were when we learned you were a prisoner of war. But some of the tales we heard were horrific."

"The *Luftwaffe* treated us well, considering."

"Well, son, it's getting late. Let's go down. I . . . we . . . want to hear your stories, especially about the cyclone business on that atoll."

Reggie called Dee-Dee from the hotel. He said ships to the Cooks were rare, but the RNZAF made occasional flights to Rarotonga—a runway had been built in 1943. Reggie returned to Auckland.

* * *

In August 1947, a C-47 Dakota, flown by 41 Squadron, RNZAF, landed on Rarotonga with Reggie on board. After handshakes with the crew and promises to meet in the future for a pint and war stories, Reggie left the plane. He shouldered his knapsack and followed the coast road through Avarua. A two-masted schooner lay at anchor in Avatiu Harbor. Before Reggie could raise his thumb, an islander stopped and asked where he was bound. Yes, he knew where Tooks Marsten lived in Titikaveka and dropped him off on the road by the house.

Reggie looked at the single-story, cinder block building with a tin roof and a wide porch. Its back side faced the lagoon. The doors were open and he could see through the house to the reef. Voices and chopping sounds came from the back. He walked around the house through a stand of banana and breadfruit trees, and startled a long-legged orange tabby snoozing in the shade.

Tooks and two boys were cutting open coconuts. Halved husks lay on wooden racks drying in the sun. Reggie took the knapsack off his shoulder.

"*Kia orāna*, Tooks. "

Tooks jumped up and turned. He stared at Reggie.

"My God! It's you, *teina*." Running to his adopted brother, he grabbed Reggie and lifted him off the ground. Tears filled his eyes as he held him at arm's length.

"Reggie, you've aged. Where have you been? Have you been in the war? How did you get here?"

"One thing at a time, mate. You be lookin' good. How's the leg?"

"Good, *teina*. Good as new. You did a wonderful job, *Doctor* Reggie."

"I be truly sorry for all the pain I caused you."

Tooks dismissed it with a wave of his hand. "Have you been in the war, Reggie?"

"That be right. I was a prisoner of war for some years, but no permanent damage."

"For that I'm pleased. You must tell us the story."

"I'm most pleased the war didn't come to the Cooks."

"Yes, Reggie, we were lucky. Many islands up north were destroyed."

"Who be these two lads then?" Reggie asked and nodded toward the boys standing behind Tooks and staring wide-eyed at this young *Papa'ā*.

"The tall good looking one on the right is my nephew, Billy. James, his younger brother, is the other. Good lads they are. Come and shake hands with my *teina*."

They hesitated, so Reggie stepped forward and extended his hand. Billy's grip was firm and Reggie returned the pressure. He was gentler with James.

"No more copra. Clean out the pit and start a fire. And kill a pig," Tooks ordered. He turned to Reggie, spread his arms, and said, "So many years, *teina*. What brought you back?"

"The islands, Tooks. The ship in a bottle . . . the *Maréchal Foch*. And to see my brother . . . my *teina*."

"Yes, the bottle. It's in the house . . . and other things."

When they turned to go inside, Reggie saw a girl standing in the doorway.

"Remember Tara, my sister, Reggie?"

"*Kia orāna*, Reggie. You've returned," she said, her face beaming. "I knew you would . . . someday."

"*Kia orāna*, Tara. Yes, I remember you. You were just a kid."

Tara, now a young woman, had dark eyes and long dark hair flowing down her back, but her features were more Caucasian than Polynesian. She wore a colorful *pareu*, which did little to hide her mature figure. Reggie was smitten.

Two small children came out of the house and stood next to Tara. Tooks said something to them in Maori and they ran off in different directions.

"Sent them to tell the family that my *teina* has returned."

Tooks and Reggie went through the house and sat on chairs on the front porch. Tooks spoke to his sister in Maori, and she went into the house and returned with two beers and a wooden box. She sat on the floor and handed Reggie the box. He opened it, and inside was the ship in the bottle and a small cloth bag. Reggie opened the bag and emptied coins into his hand.

"The Frog francs Alberti gave you on Pukapuka," Tooks said. "Remember?"

"My god, I'd forgotten about these." He fingered the coins. "Whatever happened to him . . . Alberti, I mean?"

"He's here on Rarotonga . . . in hospital."

"In hospital? What happened?"

"Some kind of lung . . . breathing thing."

"TB is it?"

"Might be. Don't know for sure."

"Must go see him."

"Yes, of course you must. Ask him about his time on Suwarrow.

"Suwarrow? What was he doing there?"

"Don't know the all of it, but he and his family survived another cyclone about five years back."

"Well, stone the crows! Another cyclone. That should be an interesting tale. I have to talk with him."

"Yes, *teina*. Tomorrow. Today we must celebrate your return to the islands."

Throughout the afternoon the Marsten clan gathered at Tooks' home. They feasted on fruit, fish, pig, and taro dishes. Tooks insisted he stay with them as long as he liked—he was family. As they sat around the fire pit in the back garden, everyone bombarded Reggie with questions about his adventures. They wanted to know all the details of his voyages after he'd left Rarotonga before the war. And about the war. News of the outside world came infrequently to the islands. With Reggie's approval, the ship in the bottle was passed around. They all agreed that it had been a good omen and proved that Tangaroa had favored the two castaways on Suwarrow. Tara sat next to Reggie all evening and made sure he had plenty of food and a beer when needed. He had a hard time keeping his eyes off her. Reggie was festooned with fragrant leis and a floral wreath crown. Tooks' mother thanked him again for saving her son's life. He even had to demonstrate how he set Tooks' broken leg on *Motu Toa*. No mention was made of the chest. The festivities lasted well into early morning hours.

Soon, family members started to drift away to their homes or made themselves comfortable on woven mats and went to sleep.

"I saw a two-master anchored in the harbor," Reggie said to Tooks. He could hardly keep his eyes open, but couldn't move—Tara slept, her head in his lap. The eastern sky was brightening, hinting at another colorful South Pacific sunrise.

"The *Moana Tama*. I'm first mate on her. We're waiting for a cargo."

"Is she available for hire?"

"Yes, *teina*. To where?"

"Back to Suwarrow."

The next day, Reggie had a stone cutter prepare a headstone.

At Avarua's small hospital, Reggie needed to don a paper surgical mask before he entered the tuberculosis ward. When he entered, he saw that the Yank was a mere shadow of his former self. Always thin, Albert Freshour was emaciated. He reminded Reggie of the Jewish refugees he'd seen from the concentration camps. Freshour coughed when Reggie sat next to him, and then turned to face his visitor. Reggie raised his mask. A spark of recognition filled Freshour's eyes and he smiled.

"My God, it's young Reggie." He coughed again.

"*Kia orāna*, Alberti." They shook hands.

"You're looking fit, Reggie. Not been in the wars?"

Reggie relayed his story to the American. *How many times have I told this?*

"Was very sad hearing about Harry Houchins and Davie McCombs. And the rest of the *Wallaroo's* crew. You and your Maori mate were lucky . . . lucky as we were there four years later."

He coughed violently. Reggie handed him a glass of water.

"Thanks. You didn't have any luck finding Mair's gold, did you?" He tapped the side of his nose with a finger.

Should I mention the chest? No. Not until we finish that business. Maybe not then either. The fewer who know about it the better.

"No. No joy there." *Hate lyin' to this man, but the chest may be full of rubbish.*

"I rooted around a little after the storm, checking the bases of palms that had been ripped out but didn't find anything. Too busy looking after the kids." He coughed again. "Most likely just another southern ocean myth."

"The kids. How are they? Who be lookin' after them?"

"Relatives. Lots of family here on Rarotonga. No worries about that."

"How long will you be here, Alberti?"

"Don't know. Some time probably."

"Tooks—my mate from the *Wallaroo*—and I are goin' back to Suwarrow."

"I won't ask why . . . sure you have your reasons. Kick the sand around a bit while you're there. Maybe you'll find something. I have no desire to return to that place." He started to cough again, and the nurse told Reggie it was time to leave.

"I'll be back, Alberti, when we return from Suwarrow."

* * *

Tooks introduced Reggie to the schooner captain. Tooks described him as a bit of a rogue, but totally honest, trustworthy, and could keep a confidence. Like Albert Freshour, Randy Johanson was a Yank who fell in love with the islands and had married a local girl. The *Moana Tama* was the only ship calling at the islands since the war's end.

"So it's Mair's gold you're seeking, is it?" Johanson asked.

They sat outside the large war surplus Nissen hut that housed the island's Returned and Serviceman's Association. When Tooks told the RSA's secretary about Reggie's war service, he couldn't pay for a drink.

"That be right, Captain," Reggie said. "I be wantin' to hire the *Moana Tama* to go have a look."

"Suwarrow was pretty messed up by a cyclone in '42. Made a run up there in '45 taking provisions to some coast watchers. Still in sad shape then. Takes awhile for the atolls to recover."

"I'd still like to give it a go." Reggie looked at Tooks, who nodded. "A cut of what we find is also on offer."

"Well then, I believe we have a deal."

"But wait, Captain Randy, and I don't be meanin' to be suspicious, but can you vouchsafe for the rest of the crew?"

The old seaman and Tooks both laughed.

"Hell, son, except for Ned, the engineer, they're all Tooks' relatives. No problems there."

25

The cyclone season had ended when the *Moana Tama* anchored in Suwarrow's lagoon. Reggie and Tooks stood at the helm next to the captain.

"Ten years, *teina*," Tooks said, "Almost ten years."

"Right you are, mate," Reggie said.

They looked at the dense foliage of Anchorage Island.

"The coast watchers' place may still be standing," Captain Randy said.

"Let's be takin' a look," Reggie said.

The three men rowed ashore in a dinghy and forced their way through the brush to the center of the island.

"Much better shape than when I was here last," Reggie said as he inspected the wooden cabin with the tin roof.

"You'll have to tell Freshour about it when we return to Rarotonga," Randy said.

"Will do. He'll be chuffed."

* * *

The *Moana Tama's* long boat, propelled by an outboard motor, crossed Suwarrow's lagoon. In the bottom of the long boat were shovels and other tools they might need to recover the chest.

After dinner the evening before, Reggie showed Captain Randy and Ned the headstone he'd had carved in Avarua. It commemorated the captain and crew of the *Wallaroo*. Reggie and Tooks planned to place it at the center of *Motu Tou*. When the long boat slid up onto the beach on the north edge of the *motu*, Reggie jumped ashore and stood looking out into the lagoon.

"We have returned, Captain Houchins . . . and Mister McCombs. You're not forgotten," Reggie said with tears in his eyes.

Tooks joined him on the beach and put his arm around his friend. "Come, *teina*, let's place the stone."

Reggie retrieved the stone from the long boat, and they all went through the brush to the base of the tall *Toa* trees where they had built their shelter. There was no evidence of their previous occupation. The clearing was cluttered with palm fronds and branches from the trees that towered above.

"Mostly likely blasted away by that other storm," Captain Randy said. "Sorry, lads."

"This be as good a place as any," Reggie said, and he and Tooks laid the headstone at the base of a *Toa* tree.

"One more thing, *teina*," Tooks said and motioned to the young man standing behind him. He handed Tooks a canvas bag. From it Tooks pulled out a stone carving of Tangaroa and a length of wire. Reggie understood. Tooks handed the carving and bag back to his nephew. "Up you go, Billy," Tooks said. "As high as you can."

Billy climbed as far as he could and secured the carving to the tree trunk with the wire. He slid back down to the ground.

"Let's go find the chest," Reggie said, and they walked back to the beach.

Reggie went to the north edge of the island where it met the reef. He paced back to a spot near his friends, looked north across the lagoon, raised a hand, and spread his fingers. He lowered his hand, turned, and pointed to the sand.

"Dig here."

Tooks' nephews brought the shovels from the long boat. They cleared away palm fronds and pieces of rotted logs, then started to dig.

"How deep you think?" Captain Randy asked. He sat on a log and lit his pipe.

"Not very," Reggie said. "The sea turtle not bein' great sappers." The others laughed.

A loud clunk made the diggers pause.

"Damn, that be quick!" Reggie said as he dropped to his knees, and pushed—almost threw—the crushed coral aside to expose the cracked black leather and rusted iron straps on the chest's top.

"I'll be damned!" the captain said. He stood and looked in the hole.

"Well, stone the crows! I can't believe it's still here." Reggie leaned back on his heels. "Four years in the *stalag* I'd thought of little else." He looked at his Maori brother. "Tooks, how can this be happening? No one found this after ten more years?"

"It's Tangaroa, *teina.* He save it for us."

The other crew members reflected their excitement as they quickly uncovered the chest and removed the soil around it. Reggie examined their find and pulled on the leather handles fastened to each side—they ripped off in his hand. The rusted padlock was still intact.

"Secure the six-foot pry bar from the long boat," the captain ordered. "We'll need a log so we can use it as a lever."

Two crew members carried a log to the hole. Billy brought the steel pry bar. They removed enough beach soil from the sides and one end so they could get grip on the chest when it was lifted. They pried it loose, and four of them lifted it out of the hole and placed it to the side. The bottom of the chest creaked when they lifted it. Reggie brought a hammer from the long boat. Captain Randy had watched all this with a smile on his face.

"Before you bust it open, Reggie . . . Tooks . . . you should know that this can't be Mair's gold."

"What?" Reggie lowered the hammer. "Why not?"

Captain Johanson knocked his pipe against the heel of his shoe. "Mair found his gold coins and jewels on Anchorage Island at the base of a coconut palm . . . not here." He filled and relit his pipe. "At least, that's what the stories say."

"Then what the hell be this?" Reggie pointed at the chest with the hammer.

The captain laughed. "Reggie's gold . . . or whatever is in it." He pointed toward the chest with his pipe.

Reggie swung the hammer and the lock flew off to the side. The others moved closer to the hole. Reggie attempted to open the lid.

"Rusted shut. Hand me the bar." Reggie pried open the lid to find the chest full of sailcloth bags. He lifted one. It came apart, and silver coins spilled out. "Rotted through," he said.

"Secure the burlap sacks from the long boat," Johanson said. A crew member ran to the boat and returned with an armful of sacks. "Let's take a look at those." The captain held out his hand, and Reggie gave him a fistful of coins. Johanson examined them. He shook his head. "Chilean dollars . . . pesos. Not worth anything. You might get a bit of silver from some of them, but these copper ones are counterfeit. Sorry, lad." He dropped the coins in a burlap sack. "Try another, Reggie."

Reggie lifted a bag with both hands from the chest, tore it open, and dumped out its contents. The sunlight reflected off gold.

"Now that's more like it," the captain said. He picked up a coin. "You've struck pay dirt here. American gold double-eagles . . . twenty dollars . . . 1875 . . . worth a pretty penny, these are." He looked up at the sky and shook his head. "Winds picking up. Weather might get nasty. Let's haul this lot back to the ship where we can sort it out proper like."

"Right you are, Captain," Reggie agreed. He carefully lifted and loaded the three dozen bags into the sacks. "My god! Look at this," Reggie said. The bottom of the chest was covered with gold and silver ingots.

"Well. I'll be damned," the captain said holding up one of the ingots. "This lot's probably worth more than the coins." He turned it over in his hand. "Chinese. These look like Chinese markings." He handed it to Tooks.

"Not Jap," Tooks said.

They'd loaded all the sacks and tools into the long boat when the captain said, "Fill in the hole, lads. We don't want any evidence of our find. I say we take the chest out and dump it in the lagoon. Unless you want it as a souvenir, Reggie. Bottom's all rotten."

Midway across the lagoon they dropped the chest over the side and it sank out of sight. When they returned to the ship, Johanson saw that the dinghy was drawn up on Anchorage Island's beach.

"Who's ashore?" he asked a crew member who had remained aboard.

"The engineer . . . Ned. Said he wanted to take a look at the hut."

Almost on cue, Ned pushed his way out through the island's brush, waved to the ship, and rowed back.

The long boat and dinghy were secured on the schooner's deck. Ned leaned against the rail looking at the island.

"What're you doing, Ned? We need to get underway," the captain said.

"Sorry, skipper. Just thinking about the future."

"Well, no time to be gee-gawkin'. Get the engine cranked up."

The *Moana Tama* motored through the gap in the reef and headed west. Once it cleared the atoll, the captain ordered the helmsman to set a course to the southeast. The sails were raised, and the engine stopped. Tooks and Reggie stood at the port rail as they passed Suwarrow. Ned joined them.

"Be thinkin' we'll ever return, Tooks?"

"Maybe, *teina*. Maybe."

"I will," Ned said. "Someday."

"Whatever for?" Reggie asked.

"Tired of civilization, I am. Especially since the war."

"How would you survive, Ned?"

"Funny you asking that, Reggie, after what you and Tooks did. I've lived in the islands long enough to know how the natives do it. Right Tooks?"

"Yes, engineer. It is possible."

"Just need a bit more kit, and I believe I could be most comfortable. The coast watchers during the war planted a vegetable garden, some apple trees, and raised chickens. And the water tank is fixable."

"How would you get here?" Reggie asked.

"Don't know that for sure. Haven't thought that far ahead."

A stiff wind pushed the schooner southeast toward Rarotonga. The atoll receded in the distance and was soon below the horizon. A rain squall sent the men below.

The crew had unloaded the burlap sacks from the long boat and carried them down into the main cabin. Reggie, Tooks, and the captain sat at the gimbaled table. Ned watched from a side berth. One by one they emptied the sacks on the table, tore open the canvas bags, and dumped out their contents. They separated the coins into stacks by type and value.

"This is a bloody mother lode," the captain said. Tooks and Reggie were speechless. "You lads are set for life. The ingots themselves are worth a fortune."

Each bag contained about one hundred coins: silver and copper Chilean pesos, gold five-pesos—also from Chile, American twenty-dollar gold double eagles, Hawaiian silver dollars, British gold sovereigns, and French gold twenty-franc pieces. There was one hundred each of the gold and silver ingots.

No one had spoken while they sorted the treasure. The captain stood and took a bottle of rum from a cupboard. He poured a glass for each man.

"A toast to a wonderful future, lads." They all raised their glass and threw down the rum.

"Think I'll be giving some serious thought to retiring," Johanson said.

"But what about the *Moana Tama?*" Reggie asked.

"Well, I don't know. She's had a good life," he said, "but not getting any younger. Does have a few more years left in her." He poured another glass of rum. "More than I've got, probably. Think I'd enjoy not being away from the family so often." He drank. "Wouldn't mind sitting on my porch and watching the whales pass."

"We'll buy her," Reggie said and looked at Tooks, who nodded.

"You serious, lad?"

"Right you are. You said on the way out here that the islands needed a ship to help the economy."

"That be true, Reggie. Inter-island shipping came to a halt during the war. The government used to provide a ship but hasn't found the money or desire to start it again. The islands are chocked full of copra for the international trade. And there's a market for fruit and vegetables if you can get them to Auckland or Fiji."

Ned stood over the table and said, "Anyone have any idea what all this is worth?"

"Not a clue," the captain said. Reggie and Tooks shook their heads.

"If you be willing to sell us the *Moana Tama*, Captain," Reggie said, "there's one last voyage we'd be likin' you to make as skipper." He pointed to the stacks on the table. "We be needin' to get this lot to Auckland. I've a banker mate who will help us sort it out proper like."

Reggie reached down to the pile of French coins and picked up a larger one that wasn't gold. "What be this, I wonder?" Engraved on one side of the piece was the image of a horse-drawn wagon crossing a bridge. It was dated 1838. On the obverse side, surrounded by a laurel wreath, was written *Compagnie des Ponts d'Asniers et d'Argenteuil.* He handed it to the captain.

"Strange shape," Johanson said fingering the eight-sided coin. "Not sure what it is. Not worth much. The French used to flim-flam the natives with fake coins, but they usually had some king on them. Most surely French—the writing says that. Might be a bit of silver in it. Don't know. Maybe your banker mate can find out."

Reggie took back the coin and put it in his pocket. "I'll be keepin' it as a souvenir. Reminds me of a bridge I saw in France."

26

An overnight stop at Rarotonga to take on fuel and provisions interrupted the voyage to Auckland. Ned agreed to stay on board until they returned from New Zealand.

"We be plannin' to open a store in Avarua, and we'd like to hire you to help run that operation," Reggie said.

"Yes, guv. I'll do that . . . until I get my kit together for Suwarrow."

"As long as it takes, Ned. And we'll be pleased to haul that cargo for you." They shook hands.

Tooks emphasized to the crew—his kin—the importance of not talking about the treasure when they returned to Rarotonga. He would ensure they received their share of the find, but not all at once. People would get suspicious with too much money being thrown around.

From Avarua, Reggie sent a telegram to Dee-Dee Dearlove about their pending arrival. He also asked him to tell his parents that he'd be up for a visit.

En route to North Island, Reggie spent many hours chatting with Captain Randy about the island trade. He also spent time getting to know the schooner. Almost identical to the *Wallaroo*, the *Moana Tama* had its idiosyncrasies—same as any sailing vessel. The captain gave Reggie and Tooks a list of repairs and replacements that should be taken care of.

"It'd be best to replace the bilge pump," he said. "This one's a bit cranky. She hasn't been out of the water for some years, so a look at her hull is in order. The sails are in good shape, but you'll need a new storm jib. We blew out the old one in a storm on a run home from Pukapuka some months back. Also, you might think about hiring a full-time cook. The galley's a bit of a mess, as you know, but the boys manage to keep us fed between stops."

"What about a radio?" Reggie asked.

"Well, son, I've never seen a need for one," Johanson said. "The only regulations to operate commercially in the Cooks is the old Inter-Island Boat Travelling Ordinance. Before sailing you have to sign a declaration that there is enough food and water on board . . . and a compass." He lit a cigar. "But, having said that, the new Resident Commissioner has been making noises about making a radio an additional requirement."

* * *

When the *Moana Tama* entered Auckland's harbor, Deerlove waited for them when they tied up at the government pier. The treasure, now in two small wooden crates, went to the bank. The schooner, moored in a dry dock, had its hull cleaned and inspected, a new bilge pump installed, and a storm jib purchased along with a radio. Reggie and Tooks passed an afternoon with Stephen Carlile of the bank's legal team drafting the paperwork establishing the Southern Cross Trading Company, Ltd. They would be equal and co-owners with Captain Johanson as a silent partner.

They drew up a bill-of-sale transferring ownership of the *Moana Tama* to the trading company. The bank would handle all future financial transactions and provide legal services when needed.

Dee-Dee told Reggie that his parents now had telephone service. He called his dad and said he and Tooks would be up for a visit in a day or two. Reggie had two more things to take care of. He placed an advertisement in the local papers for a cook and an engineer.

While the schooner sat in dry dock, Reggie and Tooks drove north to Whangarei in a new Ford pickup truck. It was a gift for his dad and brother. Before going up the hill to the farm, they stopped at the Parua Bay Hotel for a drink. At the end of the hotel's pier, they looked out at the bay's mud flats, now exposed at low tide. To the east, fog started to roll over the Whangarei Head.

"This be where it all began, Tooks."

"Yes, *teina*. Tangaroa must have made the engine quit so we'd end up here and meet you."

Reggie laughed. "He must have been on holiday when my 'Wimpy' got hit by ack-ack in '41."

They drove up to the farm and received a warm welcome from his family. His brother, Malcolm junior, was chuffed when his older brother handed him the keys and title to the truck.

* * *

Dee-Dee had some good news for them when they returned to Auckland by train.

"Found you a cook, Reggie. Bit of a rascal, but his credentials are good. Ex-para. Jumped into Arnhem in '44. Spent some time behind the wire as we did. He'll be by at 10:00 tomorrow for you and Tooks to interview." He handed Reggie a paper. "Here's the value of the gold and silver bars. You two are wealthy men."

"Well, stone the crows!" He handed the paper to Tooks. The Maori was silent, but his eye brows raised. He just nodded.

"It'll take a while to sort out the value of the coins. We'll be working with a trusted antique coin agent in Singapore. I'll keep you informed of our progress." He shook his head. "Unfortunately, no joy finding an engineer that wants to sign on to a copra schooner."

* * *

The next morning Reggie and Tooks sat in plush high-backed chairs behind a highly polished table in the bank's small conference room. They each had a paper listing the prospective employee's qualifications. Tooks looked at the paper.

"Why all the fuss, *teina?* We're just talking with this chap, right?"

"Too right, mate. But we're a business now and there are certain ways we have to handle things."

"It all seems a bit fancy to me, *teina*."

"I be agreeing with you on that, brother, but here we'll do it their way. Back on Raro, we'd be inviting the chap to have a brew and a chat." There was a knock on the door.

A man of average height, quite tanned, marched to the front of the desk and saluted. "Malfrey Pinchot-Wiggins, known to me friends as 'Wiggie', at your service, Captain . . . Captains.'"

Tooks chuckled, and Reggie returned the salute. "No formalities here, mate. Please be havin' a seat."

"Thank you very much, sir." He sat in the chair offered.

Reggie looked at the paper. "It be sayin' here that you were in the war."

"Aye, sir. Formerly sapper corporal in the 1st paras. Went into the bag at Arnhem."

"Wounded were you?"

"Aye to that. Just a bit of shrapnel in me leg and back. Don't slow me down none."

"What be bringin' you to this part of the world?"

"That's an easy one, sir. I've always had a hankering to see those islands in the South Pacific. Your banker-*wallah* mate said that's what you're all about. I've been a *sous-chef* and acting purser on many ships. Worked me way east from Liverpool to Auckland. Nothing posh mind you, but I can burn the beef and fry eggs with the best of them."

"You were an oiler on the *Inverness Castle* from Liverpool to Cape Town." Reggie pointed to the paper.

"Aye. Nasty job that was. My first berth."

"Be knowin' something about engines, do you?"

"Not really my bailiwick, Captain. Did do a short stint in the regimental motor transport platoon before we made the jump."

Tooks stood and walked over to the window. Reggie knew he was getting bored.

"Captain Tooks?" Reggie said. Tooks turned and nodded.

"Wiggie, we'd be signin' you on as cook and assistant engineer. The present engineer is aboard until we return to Rarotonga. When you're not burnin' the beef, become familiar with ship's mechanical parts. Are we agreed?"

"Aye aye, Captain. I'll not let you down. Where be the ship now?"

Reggie gave him directions to the dry dock. "We be wantin' you to give the galley a close look . . . needs fixin'. Give us a list of what bits you'll be needin'."

* * *

The return voyage to Raratonga was uneventful. Captain Randy enjoyed being a passenger, and Reggie insisted he use his former cabin for his final trip on the *Moana Tama*. Wiggie dazzled everyone with a full English breakfast their first morning afloat. Tooks and the other islanders were surprised at the quantity of food offered.

Several calm periods afforded Ned the opportunity to teach Wiggie about the ship's engine as the schooner motored northward toward the Cooks. Billy also showed a keen interest. James served as cabin boy and helped Wiggie in the galley. When they passed by the Kermadec Islands, Reggie told Captain Randy about his first meeting with Dee-Dee Dearlove.

Some days out of North Island, Reggie tested the new radio and successfully raised both Avarua and Auckland on the emergency frequencies.

Heeling over—her starboard rail almost in the water—the *Moana Tama* seemed to fly across the waves, like she relished the clean, freshly painted and re-caulked hull. The bilge pump worked to perfection.

Reggie spent most hours at the helm getting used the feel of the ship. Tooks stood at his side and made suggestions about the trim of the sails.

"This be the answer to all my dreams, brother."

"Yes, *teina*, it is a good life. Cook Islanders love the sea."

"But I'm not a Cook Islander, Tooks."

"Yes, Reggie. You are now. Tangaroa made it happen."

Over meals in the main cabin, Captain Randy told tales of his years in the islands and his life at sea before settling in the Cooks. Wiggie and Reggie talked about their war experiences. Ned had many questions about life on Suwarrow.

On the morning when the green jagged mountains of Rarotonga appeared on the horizon, Reggie radioed Avarua of their arrival. Wiggie started the engine as the sails were dropped just outside the breakwater. The pier in Avatiu's harbor was crowded with Tooks' family and other islanders. Reggie saw Tara and told himself this was going to be his home.

"Think there'll be a big celebration tonight, *Captain* Reggie," Randy Johanson said joining him at the wheel. "These Rarotongans love to party."

"Your plans?"

"I'm going to look for a nice property on the west side of the island. Will build something more posh than what I have now. Looking forward to enjoying the sunsets while sitting on my porch."

"And your family?"

"I think I see them there in that mob. The wife will be pleased to have a proper kitchen. And maybe some schooling in Auckland for the oldest."

One piece of sad news awaited them—Albert Freshour had died. Reggie arranged for a headstone to be placed in the small military cemetery next to the RSA building. One evening at sunset, the *Moana Tama*, without fanfare, slipped out of the harbor. Once past the island's barrier reef, the American's body was sent to Davy Jones's locker—his last wish. Captain Johanson and Ned were on board for the burial. They had known Freshour for many years and thought of him as a friend and fellow islander.

* * *

The next few years passed quickly. The Southern Cross Trading Company was a welcome asset to island commerce in the Cooks. The company established its headquarters and a store in Avarua and opened trading stations on most of the islands. The demand for copra on the international market increased. Many of the islands outside of the Cooks had suffered devastating damage to their coconut plantations during the war in the Pacific. The *Moana Tama* was able to handle the copra, passenger, and general cargo trade, but a ship with refrigeration was needed for the fruit and vegetable crops. Reggie and Tooks flew to Auckland to find such a ship.

27

Paris, 1948.

By the time the French Army duty train arrived in Strasbourg, Émile had sobered up enough to reflect on his time in Berlin and his future. The celebration by the train load of soldiers ending their two-year national service had gone on for most of the journey from Berlin through West Germany, and now to the French border. Here, they would transfer to trains for Paris or to wherever their demobilization stations were.

What to do next? Pascal and Francine are selling the bistro to Carlo Pioletti. Will I have a job waiting for me? Francine said in her last letter that Carlo wanted to meet with me about my prospects. Maybe he'll hire me. I am now better qualified than before I came to Paris. Learned so much in the sous-officiers' mess. Corporal Dubonnett was a master chef. Always wondered why he was in the army. There were rumors about some tryst with a diplomat's wife while he was posted in Algiers. Sergeant Masneri proved to be a comrade when he caught me in bed with one of the Polish cleaners. "Good choice," he said. "Had her myself."

When Émile came up from the Rennes Métro station, rain soaked his uniform cape as he walked to the bistro. He stood under the awning for a moment. The fogged-up windows and whispers of music brought back memories.

Just like the first time. But I'm not the country kid from La Linde this time.

He opened the door and strode up to the bar. An attractive young woman with short blond hair, too much eye make-up, and lipstick greeted him, "*Bonsoir*, Monsieur . . . Monsieur soldier, what would you like?"

"*Bonsoir*, Mademoiselle, is Pascal or Francine about?"

"*Oui*, Monsieur, they—"

The sliding window to the kitchen slammed open. "Émile! Émile! Pascal, Émile's here!" The window slammed shut.

Moving faster than Émile had ever seen her move before, Francine flew out of the kitchen, tossed away a dish towel, and grasped him on both arms. Three kisses and a hug. Pascal followed and repeated the greeting. Customers looked up from their meals and drinks.

"Nephew, so wonderful to see you. Welcome home. How you've been missed!" Francine took a *serviette* from the bar to wipe her tears. Pascal made no move to wipe away his tears. He removed Émile's wet cape and hung it on a coat rack in the hall. Émile handed him his army cap. Instead of placing it on the rack, Pascal set it on his own head and saluted. "Reminds me of when I was a *poilu* in the first war." He pointed to a table and said, "Musette, two bottles of our best champagne, *s'il vous plaît.*"

When the bottles were opened and brought to a table with three glasses, Pascal addressed the others in the room, "A word to all, *s'il vous plaît.*" He raised his glass. "Our beloved nephew, son of a veteran of Oran, has returned after his national service. His time was spent in Berlin amongst our historical foes, but now our friends against a common enemy.

Please, welcome his return by joining us in a glass, *sûr la maison, bien sûr.*"

Musette opened more champagne—not the good stuff. Émile noticed.

She's a smart one. Knows the business. Not just a pretty face.

Émile watched her as she went from table to table with the glasses and the wine.

Is she just a waitress or one of Pioletti's girls?

She joked and laughed with the male patrons. One pinched her. She squealed and playfully threatened to hit him with the bottle.

One of Pioletti's girls, bien sûr.

"What's happening in Berlin, Émile?" Pascal's question jerked his attention from Musette.

"About what, uncle? I haven't heard any news."

"The newspapers are full of it, and it's been on the wireless. The Russians have stopped all travel in and out of Berlin. You escaped just in time, nephew."

"There were some incidents and harassment by the Russians and their East German flunkies, but never a complete blockade," Émile said. He watched Musette return to the bar.

Who cares about the stupid krauts and commies? I've done my bit. Time to get on with my life. Damn! Hope this doesn't interfere with my demob tomorrow.

Francine touched his arm. "We're so glad you're back and away from there."

She looked up when the door opened and a young man, wearing a trench coat and tweed flat cap, entered the bistro and went straight to the bar. Francine nudged Pascal with an elbow and nodded in the direction of the bar. Émile saw the man pass Musette a piece of paper. She took off her apron, got a raincoat from the rack by the toilet, gave a forced smile to Pascal, and went out into the night.

The young man moved as if to go behind the bar, but Pascal stood, stepped in front of him and said, "What would you like, Andre? Let me get it for you."

"A *pastis.*"

The pimp threw back the drink and left the bistro. It had stopped raining.

Pascal rejoined Francine and Émile at the table.

"Watch out for that one, nephew. He's a bad sort, meaner than the others." Pascal finished his glass of champagne and refilled it. "He's Carlo's nephew, Andre, and one you'll have to deal with if you work here."

"I don't remember him from before."

"No. He's new," Francine said. "Came up from Ajaccio two, maybe three months ago." She pulled him close. "Likes to beat up his girls. Heard Carlo isn't pleased with him damaging the merchandise. Bad for business. Carlo can be quite ruthless if you cross him, relative or not. Many years ago . . . maybe before you were born . . . a waitress worked here named Constance." She paused, looked up to smile and say *merci* to some departing customers. "She wouldn't do tricks but took money from Carlo and disappeared. A best friend of hers . . . another waitress, Marla, who did do tricks, who Constance stayed with after her boyfriend died, or maybe killed by Carlo's thugs . . . was found floating in the Seine below Pont Neuf with her throat cut."

"And what about that British traitor two years ago?" Pascal said. "He used to come in here for the girls during the Occupation." He finished his wine and shook his head. "There are so many stories . . . many are just that…stories. You don't know what to believe."

"What happened to the traitor?" Émile asked. "Did the Allies get him?"

"No, nephew." Pascal lowered his voice. "The story is that he was a deserter from the British Army who worked for Carlo fingering Allied airmen who were passing through Paris. The *Gestapo* paid well for that information. After liberation, he became a potential embarrassment and problem for Carlo."

"So, what happened?"

"Shot by the police just before you went on national service. You must have read about it. Everyone figured that Carlo told them where to find him."

"I'm sorry, Uncle, but I don't understand how this Carlo could have had British deserters working for him and fingering Allied pilots to the *Gestapo*. Why hasn't he been arrested, charged, brought to justice? He's a war criminal, *n'est-ce pas?* At least a collaborator, *non?*"

The last customers left the bistro. Pascal no longer whispered. "People like Carlo never are brought to justice. They are too powerful, have too many politicians in their pocket. He supplied female accompaniment to De Gaulle's minions and the Germans before them. He is not above the law, he is beyond it—he makes his own laws."

Maybe I don't want to work for this gangster Pioletti. I'll still meet with him after I'm demobbed to hear his offer.

"Enough of this, husband," Francine said. "It is what it is. And it will soon be all behind us. Our arrangements with Carlo have been distasteful at times, but always profitable." She clapped her hands to her cheeks. "Oh Émile. Nephew. I've been so negligent. Have you had any supper? No, *bien*, there's a bit of *cassoulet* remaining." She stood and turned toward the kitchen. "I'll warm it for you."

Émile spent the night on his old cot in the storeroom. The next morning, after coffee and croissants with Pascal and Francine in their apartment above the bistro, he rode the Métro to the army headquarters at Château de Vincennes. A cursory physical exam and the signing of many forms ended his active service. He turned down offers for reenlistment. Future obligations as a member of the reserves would take place at the château—he gave the bistro's address as his residence.

The sun had broken through the morning mist off the Seine as he left the bistro, but now, when he came up from the Métro, rain.

Why is it every time I arrive here it's raining? An omen, perhaps?

Under the awning, he shook out his army cape before going in. He hung the cape and his hat beside two trench coats on a rack inside the door. Pascal, opposite two men sitting at the bar, pointed.

"Here's our soldier. Back from the wars against the Russian bear."

Carlo Pioletti and his nephew, Andre, turned on their stools.

Pioletti must color his hair. Looks like the same slick-backed greasy black as before. Andre's hair's the same. It's like they're wearing a uniform—the same two-piece suits, patterned neckties, and crisp white shirts. And highly shined shoes. A gangster pimp's uniform.

"The closed sign, *s'il vous plaît*, Pascal." Carlo lit a thin cigar.

Pascal scurried from behind the bar, crossed the room, and flipped the sign on the window. Carlo left the stool and extended a hand to Émile. Andre didn't move.

"Welcome home, Émile," Carlo said. "Let's sit at a table."

Émile shook his hand and pulled out a chair at the nearest table.

"What would you like to celebrate your return to civilian life? A *pastis*, perhaps, or maybe champagne, *non?*" Carlo put out his cigar in an ashtray.

"I had a bit too much champagne last night. A small *pastis* would be fine."

"One can never have too much champagne, but . . . ." He turned. Pascal, behind the bar, was already pouring the *pastis*.

Carlo's offer was simple and specific: Émile would have total control of the menu, kitchen and bar staff, and daily running of the bistro. Sartène, a fellow Corsican—who Émile remembered from before—would continue to be the principal supplier. Carlo would provide the waitresses, who might work flexible hours, but Émile could hire others, as needed, on a temporary basis. Andre would close out the bistro each night and collect the receipts. Carlo's accountant would go over the books at least once a month. There would be no problems with the police or riffraff, or the silly tradition of strikes. Carlo gave him the phone number of the *commissaire* at the local precinct. Émile could move into the apartment over the bistro after Pascal and Francine retired—rent free. Carlo would make a room available for him at the *Pension Benoit* if he didn't want to continue sleeping in the storeroom.

Carlo wrote down a figure on a napkin and slid it across to Émile. "*C'est bien?*"

Émile looked at the figure. *Very generous. More than I expected. Do I want to work for this gangster? What else would I do? I have a chance to expand my skills as a chef. Do I care about what else goes on? Many Parisian bistros probably have the same arrangement. I'm not breaking any laws. Can't go back to being a pig farmer in the Dordogne. I have a place here. I'm good at this. Maybe I'll move on somewhere in the future, but this is my life for now.*

"*Très bien*, Monsieur Pioletti." They shook hands.

* * *

Francine couldn't stand for long periods. She sat by the cash register at the end of the bar and handled all the money while Émile did most of the cooking. He also tended bar in the evenings and acted as the night manager. Émile and Musette fell in love. She still did tricks from time-to-time. Émile didn't like it but loved her, so he tolerated it. They took long walks along the Seine and talked about leaving Paris. She had a sister, Annick, who lived in Marseille, and suggested they flee to the south to start a new life. Émile was not sure about this idea—Carlo may have influence in Marseille. Determined to change her life, she planned to tell her pimp, Andre, that she was finished doing tricks.

* * *

Émile rolled onto his left side, gently fondled Musette's right breast, then placed a soft kiss on its nipple. *How many other men have done this? If someone had told me six years ago, when I was preparing to leave La Linde, that I would be in love with a prostitute and managing a bistro in Paris, I would say they were fou.*

Musette pushed his hand away and rolled over onto her stomach. "Not now, *mon chéri*, I must have more sleep. It's getting light. Go start the soup or something." She smiled. "Come back before lunch."

* * *

It had been four months since Francine and Pascal retired and moved to a cottage on the coast of Brittany.

Down in the bistro the lights were on. Émile made himself a cup of coffee. Krakow, the Polish *sous-chef* was outside sweeping the sidewalk under the awning. Krakow was new but not young.

He waited outside the door one morning a month ago when Émile opened for the day. A rumpled felt hat and shabby army overcoat made Émile think about Carlo's promise to keep the riffraff away.

"*Bonjour*, Monsieur. Are you Monsieur Émile Plude?" He removed his hat.

"*Oui*, and *bonjour* to you, Monsieur. How can I be of service?" Émile recognized the Polish accent he'd become quite familiar with in Berlin.

"I have a letter." He reached inside his coat and brought out a crinkled envelope.

As he attempted to smooth out the creases, Émile was surprised to see the franking from *Le Quartier Napoléon* in a corner of the envelope. He reached out a hand.

"*Pardon*, Monsieur." Taking the envelope from the man, he opened the door and bid him enter. "You have come from Berlin, *n'est-ce pas?*"

"*Oui*, Monsieur." He stood inside the bistro and looked from side-to-side.

"Please, Monsieur, remove your coat and have a seat. I'll bring some coffee, or would you prefer something stronger?"

"Coffee's fine, Monsieur."

Émile brought two *bols de café* to the table. He read the address on the envelope: *Monsieur Émile Plude, Bistro Béroud, rue Jean-Louis, Paris*. He slit open the envelope with a dinner knife and unfolded the single hand-written sheet. It was from Major Favre, the *président* of *Le Club des Sous-Officiers*.

Shortly after being offered his new position, Émile had written to Sergeant Masneri and Corporal Dubonnett at *Le Club* in Berlin. He thanked the *chef* for all his help and training, and asked that his sentiments be passed on to Major Favre. And he'd invited anyone from the brigade, who might be passing through Paris, to have a drink with him at the bistro. During the past two years, several comrades from Berlin had done just that. From their visits, he received first-hand information about the Berlin

Airlift and what was happening in *Le Quartier.*

Major Favre's letter introduced Ignacio Krakow, a Polish displaced person and former freedom fighter against the Germans. He'd worked at the French garrison for five years in a number of jobs: common laborer, driver, *plongeur,* interpreter, and bartender at *Le Club.* Desiring to leave Germany and emigrate to France, he'd been provided with the necessary papers, but he would need full employment. Without that, he might be sent back to Poland. Any assistance Émile could offer would be greatly appreciated. Major Favre closed the letter with a congratulatory note about Émile's position.

Krakow had finished his coffee and leaned back in the chair, his piercing black eyes focused on Émile. The young man laid the letter on the table. He smiled and asked, "Can you cook?"

Krakow's head shook like he was surprised by the question. "*Oui,* Monsieur. I have been a cook."

"*Bien.*" Émile stood and extended his hand. "Welcome to Paris, Monsieur Krakow. And welcome to the Bistro Béroud."

Krakow grasped Émile's hand with both of his. "*Merci beaucoup,* Monsieur. I am forever in your debt. You will never regret this, I promise you." Tears formed in the corners of his eyes.

"It is my pleasure to assist a fellow Berliner," Émile said. "Have you somewhere to live?"

"No, Monsieur Plude. I have just arrived."

"There is a place in the back storeroom where I spent my first two years before my national service. But I think a man of your age would prefer something more comfortable. The owner, Monsieur Pioletti, has a *pension* nearby. I'm sure I can arrange a reasonably priced situation for you."

A week later Émile helped Krakow in the kitchen. Out front in the bar, Musette waited for any late night customers. A miserable wet evening—no business in over an hour. Émile hoped they could close early. Andre, Carlo's nephew, should arrive soon to check the receipts, collect the cash, and pay their weekly wages.

Émile started to wash up the dishes and platters stacked at one end of the counter by the sink. Tuan, the Vietnamese dishwasher, hadn't shown up for work. Émile thought about sacking him.

"You don't mind doing the work of a *plongeur?*" Krakow said.

"No." Émile smiled. "This is how I started, as a *plongeur.* I came to Paris in '44 from La Linde . . . that's in the south near Bourdeaux . . . after my aunt sold the farm."

"Remember to scrape the meat and vegetable bits into the big one," Krakow said pointing to the large metal pot resting on the stovetop. "Good for tomorrow's soup."

Émile laughed. "*Bien sûr,* Krakow. Just like in the army. Even in *Le Club* we added one day's leavings to the next day's luncheon soup." He and Émile hadn't talked much before this evening. "Makes no difference. If it tastes good, the patrons don't know if it comes out of a pot or a tureen."

"You're a good boy, Émile. I've watched you. Someday you'll be a great chef—*cordon bleu.*"

"You're a strange one, Krakow. What's Polish cooking like?" Émile didn't know how old the Pole was. His papers said fifty. There was a lot of grey in his beard and his hair. His eyes looked older, and he was usually very quiet. But, he'd only been there a week.

"Polish cooking? I have no idea. I worked in the kitchen in the camps. There we threw in whatever we had—old shoe leather, rotten turnips, sometimes a skinned rabbit or dog—into the pot and boiled it."

Émile stopped scraping the dishes. "You were in a camp? You mean a concentration camp? Where? When? How did you end up in Berlin?"

Krakow ignored Émile's questions. He poured a pitcher of water into the soup pot and stirred the mixture with a wooden ladle. He then reached up to take a drink from the glass of wine he'd placed on the self above the stove.

"Why were you in the camps? Are you a Jew?" Émile asked.

Krakow lifted the ladle out of the pot and pointed it at Émile like a conductor's baton—or a weapon. Drippings splattered his shoes. He opened his mouth to speak, but stopped and turned toward the wall separating the kitchen from the bar. "What's that?" he said.

They heard Musette scream from the outer room. Émile dropped the plate he held—it shattered on the floor. He grabbed a carving knife out of the rack on the counter and rushed out of the kitchen. He turned the corner into the bar and saw Andre punch her in the stomach and push her back against one of the fake plaster statues that decorated the room. The pimp laughed and raised his hand to strike her again.

"No!" Émile yelled. "No! Never again!"

Andre turned his head to look back over his right shoulder. Émile rushed across the room and thrust the knife into the pimp's back—he felt the blade hit bone.

Andre cried out, spun around and backhanded Émile with his raised fist. Émile fell across a table. The pimp tried to reach the knife with his left hand as he drew a revolver from his belt with his right hand. He raised the gun and pointed it at Émile. Musette, back on her feet, lunged forward and grabbed Andre's right arm, forcing it down. The shot went into the floor.

Andre turned. Musette clawed at his face with her finger nails and kneed him in the groin. The gun fired again. Musette fell away from Andre onto the floor. Blood spread across the front of her pink blouse. Andre stood staring at her. Émile grabbed an empty wine bottle off the table and broke it on the table edge. That sound woke the pimp from the shock of shooting his girl. He turned, and Émile shoved the broken bottle into his face. Staggering back, the pimp raised the gun and fired.

The bullet missed Émile but shattered a bottle of cognac and the mirror behind the bar. Andre tripped over Musette's body and fell backwards. The impact drove the knife point out through his chest. He dropped the revolver and looked down at the bloody end of the blade sticking out of his white shirt. Émile stood over him holding the broken wine bottle.

What have I done? Have I killed a man? Musette is bleeding. I must...

Krakow pushed Émile aside, picked up the revolver, and shot Andre through the left eye. The pimp's body jerked once, and then lay still. The cook stepped over him and knelt down next to Musette. He checked her wrist and neck for a pulse. Krakow looked up at Émile and shook his head.

What's happening? He shot Andre in the face. Musette can't be dead.

"She's gone, *mon ami* . . . Which is what you must do. Be gone." Krakow stood, wiped the gun clean with the end of his apron, knelt again and placed the revolver in Musette's right hand. He closed her fingers around the butt and, holding the hammer down with his apron-covered left hand, pressed her index finger against the trigger.

What's he doing? Why can't I move? I must do something for Musette.

"Now, Émile, you must go quickly. Someone will have heard the shots. This is what you must do." Krakow hurried behind the bar and emptied the cash register. He came back and seized Émile by the shoulders and shook him—the young man stood like he was frozen in time.

"Wake up! She's dead. You can't change that. You must save yourself. I've done enough to confuse the *flics* for a while, but Carlos will be after your head for killing his nephew. There isn't time to create a lie, and you're not a good liar anyway. I overheard that Carlo wasn't happy with your relationship with that girl, so your life isn't worth a *sou*."

Émile seemed to regain his senses. "Confuse the police? What do you mean?"

"Look at the pimp—knifed in the back, face mangled by a broken bottle, and shot by a dead girl." Grabbing Émile by the wrist, he forced the cash into his hand and closed the fingers. He took the wine bottle from Émile's other hand and wiped it clean with a corner of his apron. "I never told you this, but I was once a *flic* in Warsaw many years ago. I know how to foul up a crime scene. Now, there's one more thing. Very important."

"*Quoi?* What?" Émile looked at the bills in his hand and down at Musette, and then at Krakow.

"You must hit me—not too hard. Just enough to make it look real, *n'est-ce pas?*" Krakow turned his back to Émile. "Use a chair, but not too hard, *s'il vous plaît.*"

Émile stuffed the money into a trouser pocket, picked up a wicker chair and swung it at Krakow's back. The Polish cook fell across a table and onto the floor.

"I'm alive, Émile, *merci.* Go now! I'll take a little nap until someone comes."

Émile wanted to go up to the flat and get some things, but he heard a police siren. He threw off his apron and grabbed his coat from the hall rack. He paused to look back at Musette's body one last time before he ran out the back door into the alley.

Where to go? Have to get out of Paris. Home—La Linde? No. They know where I'm from. What about Annick, Musette's sister in Marseille? Does Carlo's web reach that far?

Émile ran to the Rennes Métro station and stumbled down the stairs to the platform. On the train he caught his breath. *Why was I running? No one knows what happened yet. The police will still be looking around and talking to Krakow. What will he tell them? A good story, bien sûr. Krakow, a former policeman. Never would have thought that. What will happen with Musette? Would they know about Annick? I must tell her what really happened.* At the *Gare de Lyon* Émile bought a third class ticket on the night train to Marseille.

Émile walked through three carriages before he found a compartment with three sailors and a légionnaire. He wanted to hide in a crowd. In the station he'd bought two bottles of cheap red wine, a baguette, and a half dozen packets of *Gauloises.*

The sailors slept. The légionnaire nodded in greeting when Émile entered the compartment. He sat next to the soldier. Émile wanted to offer him some wine but realized he had no way to open the bottle. The légionnaire laughed, seeing Émile's predicament, and pulled a corkscrew out of his coat pocket.

"One should be prepared for any emergency," he said and handed the tool to Émile.

Émile removed the cork and offered the bottle to the légionnaire.

"*Merci beaucoup, mon ami,*" He took a long pull on the bottle and gave it back to Émile. "Going far?"

"To Marseille." *Merde! Should I tell strangers where I'm going? What if they're questioned by the police.*

"I also," said the soldier. "On holiday, are you?"

What lie should I tell? "No, I'm going to visit an old friend. He has a fishing boat in Marseille, and I'm hoping to find work with him. And you?" *Must change the subject.*

"I'll only be there until I ship out for Sidi Bel Abbès."

"Where is that?" Émile asked.

"Algeria, *mon ami.* A bit more wine, *s'il vous plaît.*" Émile passed the bottle.

"What's it like there?"

The légionnaire took another long pull on the bottle. "Hot, dry, and sand you could not imagine. The flies are the worst—get into everything, as does the sand. Miserable place."

"Why are you going there?"

"*La Légion, mon ami.* That's where my regiment is. But I've heard rumors that we may go east to Indochina."

"Would that be better?"

The légionnaire laughed. "Better to leave the quiet desert for a war in the jungle? I think not."

"What war? Who are we fighting?"

"Communists . . . Vietminh. Don't want to be a colony of France any longer." The légionnaire leaned back and closed his eyes.

When the train left the station in Lyons, Émile had a tinge of fear when two men in overcoats and fedoras looked into the compartment more than once—police or Carlo's thugs?

* * *

A light rain fell when Émile arrived in Marseille. *Why's it always raining when I get to a place,* he wondered. At the tourist information kiosk he asked for directions to the bar where Annick worked. The rain stopped as he walked to the waterfront. The bar was closed. *Too early,* he thought.

Making a circuit of the harbor to pass the time, he watched the fishing boats depart in search of their daily catch. He passed a recruiting office for *la Légion*—also closed. Its windows displayed posters of smiling légionnaires in heroic poses against backgrounds of exotic-looking tropical locations.

Émile completed his tour of the waterfront and arrived back at the bar as it opened. The woman who had unlocked the door was dressed in a tight pair of slacks and a low-cut sweater that revealed an impressive cleavage.

"*Bonjour,* Monsieur," she said and went behind the bar.

"*Bonjour,* Mademoiselle, does Annick Vauvert still work here?"

She gave him a puzzled look. "I am she, Monsieur . . . Annick Vauvert. Why do you ask?"

"I am Émile . . . Émile from Paris. Musette's—"

"That Émile?" She came out from behind the bar, grabbed his arms and planted a kiss on each cheek. "So wonderful to finally meet you. Why are you in Marseille? Is Musette with you?" She looked over his shoulder toward the street. "She writes about you often."

Émile looked around the room—no one. But a bead curtain on a doorway suggested another room or back door. "Are we alone, Annick?" He lowered his head and withheld a sob as tears filled his eyes.

"*Oui, mon cher.* What is it, Émile?"

"Let's sit. I have some sad news."

They sat at a table. Controlling his sobs, but not his tears, he took her hands in his. "Musette is dead."

Annick pulled away from him. "Oh, What . . . how?" She started to cry.

"The pimp, Andre." Émile told her what had taken place last evening.

She pounded her fist on the table. "He was a monster . . . had to run away to his uncle in Paris because the *flics* here were after him." She leaned forward again and took his hands in hers. "She wrote me about your plans to run off together. She sounded so happy in her letters." Annick then held her head in her hands and sobbed. "My poor little sister . . . she sounded so happy. She wanted to quit this rotten life and run away with you, Émile."

He touched her cheek. "How did you know Andre?"

"*Mon cher,* this bar and others in Marseille belong to Pioletti or some other Corsican bastard. They control the harbor." She looked toward the door and nodded like she'd reached a decision. "I must go burn her letters about you. My life won't be worth a *sou* if they think I've talked to you." Annick got up from table. "Émile, you must leave here. They know Musette was my sister, and they'll come asking questions."

"Where will I go?"

"I'm sorry, *mon cher.* That is not my concern. I'm glad you gave my sister some happy moments, but I fear, Émile . . . fear what they will do to me if I help you. Now, please just go."

Émile hurried away from the bar more afraid and confused than ever. He almost ran. *Where will I go? What will become of me?* He stopped to light a cigarette in front of the recruiting office. The lights were on inside. Without hesitation, he threw away his cigarette and went in.

Part Three: 1954-1964

Chapter 28

Hanoi, French Indochina, March, 1954.

"Anyone seen that Nazi pig, Vater?" Violating the unwritten rule about never mentioning another légionnaire's past brought silence to the bar in Hanoi's *Club des Sous-Officiers.*

"*Pardon moi,* comrades. I forgot myself," said the *adjutant-chef* from the air force. "A *pastis, s'il vous plaît.* It's Andre, *n'est-ce pas?*" the NCO said to the bartender. Andre LaLande was Émile's name in the Légion.

The NCO turned to face the other members in the club bar. "*Alors, mes amis,* the German swine in question owes me several thousand francs, and I fly home tomorrow. I've been searching for him these past three days. His battalion said he's had some kind of medical emergency and couldn't receive visitors. I hoped he'd jumped into Dien Bien Phu and got his balls shot off. That's where all my money went, *bien sûr.* Horny bastard."

That brought a guffaw from an NCO at the end of the bar. "Medical emergency? You might call it that. He stuck his dipstick in the wrong crankcase, he did." The assembly laughed. "He's been sent to hospital in Saigon."

"Flying home tomorrow, are you? Not volunteering to jump into the frying pan?" another NCO asked.

The *adjutant-chef* turned to face his questioner. "How long have you been here . . . not the bar . . . but in Indochina? One month? Six months? I came out in '45 just in time to see the Jap surrender. And I'm going home to plant a truffle orchard in the Dordogne. Any problems with that, comrade?"

Émile listened to all this as he did every day. *A truffle orchard in the Dordogne? That's interesting. Never heard of such a thing. Maybe I can learn something.* He served drinks to other NCOs before he came back to earth. *I'll never be able to return to the Dordogne. Pioletti knows I'm from there. His goons will be watching, checking, waiting forever. Unless he dies.*

* * *

Upon his arrival in Hanoi from his training and skirmishes against rebel tribes in Algeria, Émile had been assigned as bartender in *Le Club des Sous-Officiers.* He also supervised the Vietnamese cooks in preparation of special French dishes. Did he feel guilty that he wasn't out in the jungle fighting the Communists? No. Émile enjoyed working in the club, life was good, and he had no desire to be a hero. He joined the Légion to escape and hide, not fight.

Sean O'Conner—if that was his real name, Émile wondered—sat at the bar. He was a special friend to Émile and his best mate Claude Rondeau. Sean, an Irishman who claimed to be an IRA big shot, said he had to join the Légion to hide from the British security services. He instructed both Frenchmen in English during their training at Sidi bel Abbes and the voyage to Indochina. Émile was a quick study and tried hard to learn a language that might be most helpful after he left the Légion.

Claude worked as a supply clerk in the regimental storeroom and helped out in the club opening beers, washing glasses, and getting free drinks. He said they should be doing more, not just counting stock and pouring booze. They argued about this frequently, when Claude wasn't complaining about the A-bomb tests in the South Pacific. Before joining the Légion, Claude worked for a Catholic mission on Puluwat, an atoll in Micronesia.

Émile knew the war was going badly. The *sous-officiers* in the bar complained about the incompetence and stupidity of French generals— one couldn't defeat the Vietminh with the same tactics used against the Germans, even with American air support. The strategy of the war was beyond Émile's comprehension. He was just hiding from his past. He hadn't given much thought to what he would do when his five years were up. Not back to France, *bien sûr*. But what? Somewhere he wouldn't have to look over his shoulder.

"*Attention, s'il vous plait!*" The room went quiet. Several légionnaires stood. A staff officer had entered. He walked to the bar and accepted a glass of red from Claude. The *sous-officiers* remained silent when he turned to address the room. It was a rare occasion when a staff officer, or any officer for that matter, entered the Légion's *sous-officers'* club, unless invited. Émile knew the *commandant* had lost the lower half of his left leg during the landing near Toulon in 1944. As a captain, he'd been the commander of Émile's company during his combat training in Algeria. Émile knew the officer would rather be in Dien Bien Phu if he was able, or allowed.

"General Leon is asking for volunteers to escort a medical team into Dien Bien Phu tonight. A surgical team has been assembled and elements of the 6th Colonial Regiment will accompany them, but there is space for seven volunteers. No need to be parachute trained. You will receive all necessary instructions at the aeroport."

Claude elbowed Émile in the ribs. "Come, comrade. Let's go die for France. This is probably a suicide mission. But what glory!"

The officer asked for a show of hands. Claude grabbed Émile's wrist and forced his arm up and raised his own.

"Are you *fou?*" Émile pulled his arm down. He owed his life to Claude, who saved him from capture, torture, and death by the Tuaregs on a patrol in the *Sahel.*

* * *

Hanoi's Bach Mai airfield was ablaze when Émile, Claude, and the other volunteers arrived in the back of an open truck. A C-47 "Dakota," damaged from enemy ground fire, had made an erratic landing and struck a fuel tanker. From the wings forward the fuselage was a ball of fire. Firefighting crews attempted to retard the flames, and others pulled wounded out of the back of the airplane.

"We should go help," Claude said. He started to climb over the tailgate of the truck but was stopped by a sergeant.

"Stay where you are! You'll get your chance to be a hero in a few hours." The truck continued along the runway to a hanger. Inside the hangar, paratroopers of the Colonial Regiment helped the medical team don their parachutes. After a quick briefing on how to land and the pre-jump commands, the seven volunteers donned their parachutes.

"Aren't we getting a second chute if there's a problem with first?" Claude asked.

An NCO from the 6th said, "The jump altitude will be too low for a reserve chute to deploy. Pray that your main opens."

In addition to their MAT 49 submachine guns, the volunteers had a kit bag of medical supplies attached to their parachute harnesses.

The sixty-seven soldiers crammed into the Fairchild C-119 "Packet" transport aircraft included a ten-man hospital surgical team, fifty paratroopers from the 6th Colonial Parachute Battalion, and seven volunteers who had never jumped before.

When the C-119 rose from the runway for the hour and a half flight to Dien Bien Phu, Émile thought it took a long time for the plane to get off the ground. And it shook and rattled so much he thought they might issue screwdrivers and spanners to the passengers. He looked across the interior of the plane to Claude. His friend smiled and gave a thumps-up. *What the hell am I doing here?* When they argued about volunteering in the club, Claude played his trump card—"I saved your ass in Algeria. Now you can repay the debt."

One of the pilots came back into the cargo area and talked to the senior medical officer. Then he turned and spoke to a captain from the 6th Regiment, who was sitting next to Émile. He had to yell to be heard.

"It's goin' to be a hot one. Ground fire's heavy tonight. We'll be makin' a lot of evasive maneuvers. It'll get a little jerky. Make sure your guys keep their seatbelts on," he said in English.

The captain nodded and turned to Émile. "American. C.I.A."

We have American spies flying our airplanes? What's going on here? This war is crazy.

The plane made a violent dip down to the left, almost throwing the pilot off his feet. He grabbed a stanchion and gave thumbs up to the jumpers before returning to the cockpit. Gaining altitude and banking right, the plane leveled off. A soldier from the medical team leaned forward and vomited on his boots. Émile started to feel nauseous, but took several deep breathes and closed his eyes. *If I survive this I will do everything I possibly can to disappear. The world has gone mad.*

The plane made more uncomfortable dips and banks. Other soldiers threw up. Reducing speed, the "Packet" leveled off and the jumpmaster stood in the center of the plane. He held up his palm and shouted, "Five minutes."

A crew member opened the doors on each side of the aircraft. The jumpmaster leaned out and looked forward. He stepped back, turned and faced the jumpers. "Two minutes." A light over the doors glowed red. He looked out the door again, then turned and yelled, "Stand up!" The jumpers unlatched their seat belts and stood facing the jumpmaster, holding onto the cables above their heads. "Hook up!" They fastened their static line snap hooks onto the cables. "Check equipment!" Everyone checked the snap hooks and parachutes of the jumper in front of them and their own equipment. They all gave a thumbs up to the jumpmaster. One soldier in the rear of the plane started to sing *"La Marseillaise."*

The jumpmaster took a quick look out the door, turned and shouted, "Stand in the door!" He pointed to the jump doors. The two lines of jumpers shuffled forward. The first man on each side took his place in the door. The light over the doors changed to green.

"Allez!"

Émile was third in his row of jumpers and followed the captain out the door. The force of the prop blast almost flipped him upside down, but he looked up and saw his chute had opened. The sky was crisscrossed with green tracers from the Vietminh gunners in the jungle around Dien Bien Phu.

Mon Dieu, they're trying to kill me!

Émile saw an explosion in the sky and thought the plane had been hit. He looked down. It was difficult to make out any features in the dark. As tracers passed close to him he instinctively ducked. That's dumb, he thought. Below, fires burned around the airstrip and enemy artillery joined his reception. An explosion engulfed him in heat and smoke. He hit the ground unprepared for the landing.

Pain, noise, movement, more pain, more noise. Voices yelling. Émile opened his eyes long enough to see an angel. And then nothing.

* * *

When Émile opened his eyes again he saw a white ceiling. *Am I dead? Is this heaven?* The pain in his head was a constant throbbing. He raised his hands to his face and wiggled his toes. Relieved he was in one piece, he tried to turn his head, but the excutiating pain stopped him. People were talking near him, and he heard a scream a way off.

"*Bonjour*, Légionnaire LaLande." Another angel's face appeared above him. "Welcome back. We were worried you wouldn't rejoin us." The nurse adjusted his pillow and brought a bottle with a siphon to his lips. "Try to drink this. You're very dehydrated."

"What? Where am I?"

"You're in Grall Hospital . . . Saigon." She put the bottle down and lifted a bowl. Spooning a portion of the soup, she placed it between his lips. The savory meat and vegetable mixture tasted like ambrosia to him. The pain in his head seemed to subside.

"What happened? How did I get here?"

"You sustained a major head injury on the drop into Dien Bien Phu. Fortunately, they were able to evacuate you on the last flight out of that hell hole. All serious head patients are brought straight here to Saigon." She fed him more soup.

Émile raised his knees. "Can I walk?"

"Not yet. The doctor must examine you first."

The nurse fed him the rest of the soup. "Dien Bien Phu has fallen. You are one of the lucky ones." Tears formed in her eyes. "Ten thousand brave Frenchmen are now in the hands of the enemy." She walked away.

Claude? What happened to Claude? Is he alive? A prisoner of the Vietminh? How can I find out? Blackness returned.

The nurse's face was over his when opened his eyes again. She smiled and said, "Welcome back. You have a visitor, Légionnaire." Claude's face replaced hers.

"*Bonsoir,* Andre. *Ça va,* comrade?"

"*Bien. Très bien,* you worthless offspring of a Tuareg whore." They laughed. "Look what your heroic shit got me into."

"*Mais,* but the glory, *mon ami.* We are heroes of Dien Bien Phu. A *Légion d'honneur,* I'm sure, must be forthcoming." Claude sat on the bed. Émile— shocked—saw the sleeve of Claude's hospital gown's left arm was empty and pinned back on his shoulder.

"*Mon Dieu, mon ami!* Your arm. What happened ?"

"Improper exit position, some fat-assed twat, who had never jumped, told me. I hope his nose has recovered from my right cross." They laughed again. "I got tangled up in the static line or something. Mangled it right up, it did. Those medicos on the ground were my saviors, but they couldn't save all of it. I thought I was for Charon's barge."

A week later, Émile was allowed to walk for a few minutes with assistance. The ward, filled with seriously wounded, was a depressing site to him. Many wouldn't recover. He and Claude took slow walks in the hospital's garden and shared cigarettes. They could now take their meals in the hospital's dining room.

On his bed, a large box awaited him when he returned from breakfast one morning.

"Here are your things from Hanoi," the nurse said. "Would you like me to open it for you?"

"*Non, merci beaucoup.* I can manage." Émile opened the box and pulled out his dress uniform coat. From an inside pocket he removed his wallet and checked the contents. *The francs are all here!* He was sure some Vietnamese "slicky-boy" from the club would have stolen them after he left for Dien Bien Phu.

"We'll get your uniform cleaned and pressed before you return to France," the nurse said.

"France? Not back to Hanoi?"

"No, Légionnaire LaLande. You're scheduled to be sent back home until you're fully recovered."

"What about Sidi bel Abbes? Can I go there?"

"I'm afraid not. All head injuries are sent to the hospital in Marseille. You'll have a lovely sea voyage home. Wish I was going with you."

Marseille. I can't go back to France. Carlo's people may find me. Must get away again.

That afternoon in the garden, Émile and Claude sat on a bench observing and commenting on the physical attributes of the nurses who attended to other patients in wheelchairs or in need of a helping hand.

"Hey! Look there. Isn't that Vater—that Nazi swine who was sent down here for the 'cure'?"

Émile had only seen Vater a few times in the club in Hanoi but remembered his abusive personality, especially with Vietnamese waitresses.

"*Oui, mon ami,* that's him for sure. Look at the way he keeps sliding his hand down to the nurse's ass." Émile lit a cigarette. "She must not know why he's here."

"Maybe they had to cut it off." Claude laughed. "That'd make a lot of women happy."

"Claude . . . comrade. I don't want to go back to France. What can I do?"

Claude was quiet for a moment. He lowered his voice. "People talk to me. Tell me lots of things. Apparently a one-armed man is not considered a threat." He lit a cigarette. "There's a Chinaman in the *Chợ Lớn* district who is an artist of creation—forged papers, passports, etc. For a few francs—quite a few, actually—one can become a new person. I'm told he relishes getting French Army identity papers." He stubbed out his cigarette. "I'll get his address for you."

During their time in Algeria, on long desert patrols and boring ambush positions, they had told each other why they'd joined the Légion. Claude knew all about Pioletti and admitted to the impregnation of a missionary's wife on Puluwat, which caused him to flee. When he arrived in Pago Pago, American Samoa, he went to the French consulate and enlisted.

"Where should I go?"

"Go to the islands, *mon ami.* The antipodes. Life there is good, and people don't care about your past, or look closely at your papers." He stood. "Or try Australia. It's a whole continent. Lot of places to disappear to. I need a drink." They walked inside to the hospital's small bar.

"What about you, Claude? What will you do?" Émile ordered two glasses of red from the Tonkinese bartender. They sat at a table overlooking the garden. Other ambulatory patients occupied tables around the outside terrace.

"I will return to France and to the welcoming arms of the *Madeleines.* He raised his glass in toast. "To all the beauties who will repay this poor disfigured veteran for his service against the Asian hordes." He took a drink. "And against the many bad guys we had the pleasure to send to join their seventy virgins."

"That reminds me of something," Émile said. "Sometime after I crashed on Dien Bien Phu, I remember seeing an angel. No, not a vestal virgin, but a woman's face looking down at me. Was I dreaming? I don't know."

"Galard—Flight Nurse Genevieve de Galard. You must remember her. She came to the club with the other nurses and pilots." He requested another glass—the limit allowed patients. "I heard she didn't get out, so she's certainly behind the wire with the others."

* * *

"Great news, comrade," Claude said one morning. "The Angel of Dien Bien Phu, Genevieve de Galard, has been freed. And she's coming here to see us." Claude was in his dress uniform.

"I must get up and change," Émile said. He started to get out of bed.

"No, *mon ami*." He placed his hand on Émile's chest. "It's more impressive if you're supine when she arrives."

An hour later Flight Nurse de Galard made her way through the ward, accompanied by an entourage of doctors, nurses, French Army brass, and a batch of reporters and photographers. Not a striking beauty, but looking smart in her flight nurse dress uniform, she stopped and chatted with each patient. Some she recognized and called by name. Others she pretended to remember and gave words of comfort. Claude stood at attention next to Émile and saluted when she stopped at the end of his bed.

"I should salute *you*, Légionnaire," she said. "And who is this?" She took the clip board with Émile's chart from the end of his bed. "Going home soon, I see. How is your head? Worse than a bad hangover, I expect?" Everyone laughed.

Claude took a step forward. "Mademoiseille de Galard. Will you marry me?" Others—not the French officers—laughed again.

Émile shook his head. "Pay no attention to him, Mademoiselle. He's still a bit *fou* from his injury."

Galard gave Claude a kiss on his cheek and said, "I am honored by your proposal, Légionnaire. *Mais,* I've had several today, so you'll have to get in the queue." She placed the clipboard back on the bed frame. "I hope you have a swift recovery, Légionnaire LaLande." She kissed Émile on the cheek. "Watch out for that one." She nodded toward Claude and winked. The VIPs continued on their tour and left the ward.

"Now you can dress, comrade." He held up two pieces of paper. "Day passes, Andre. Come, let's go take advantage of the delights of *Tu Do* street. And we can visit the Chinaman."

The streets of Saigon, awash with people, mopeds, and taxis, reminded Émile of Hanoi. It was hard for him to believe that a war was going on. They rode a three-wheeled bicycle taxi to a bar recommended to Claude. It was filled with French soldiers dancing and chatting up the Vietnamese bar girls.

After a glass of disgusting wine, Claude said, "The Chinaman's shop is close by. Let's go see what he has to offer." Fending off the advances of two girls, they left the bar and walked down a series of alleys and side streets until Claude, looking at the address, said, "This is it. Don't forget to haggle."

The shop reeked of incense and cooking oil. The obsequious forger, so tiny in stature a strong wind might blow him away, quoted a price for a passport. Claude shook his head. "Too much, you ol' pirate. Try again." Émile raised his hand telling his friend to stay quiet. He made a counter offer. The Chinaman reduced his original price. "*C'est bien,*" said Claude, interjecting himself into the negotiations again. "But how about the bonus of a French Army identity card? And, perhaps, other documents with official signatures and raised seals?"

"Agreed," he said and turned to Émile. "Monsieur, I must take a photograph for the passport. You'll want to remove your uniform coat and use one of those shirts from there." He pointed to a rack of shirts and trousers.

Émile found a nondescript beige shirt that fit. While buttoning it, the Chinaman examined his head and said, "We must do something with that bandage. Perhaps you can remove it for a moment, *non?*"

"I'll do it," Claude said. He unwound the dressing. "You're looking *bon, mon ami.*" He examined the wound. "Healing nicely, it is." The Chinaman took two photos.

"Why two photos?" Émile asked.

"Always best to take two, if one isn't good enough." He laid the camera on a table. "A name, Monsieur. I need to know what name you want on the passport." He handed Émile a scrap of paper and a pencil. "Please write it down for me, *s'il vous plait.*"

Émile searched his memory for a name. "DeGroote . . . Jean-Philippe DeGroote."

"And from which country do you want the passport?"

Merde! He hadn't considered that. Not France, *bien sûr*. He knew his English wasn't good enough to pass himself off as a Brit. "Switzerland. Can you do a Swiss passport?" Émile was quite sure he could pose as someone from one of the French-speaking cantons.

"*Ah oui.* That is not difficult. I must have some information about you."

Émile wrote his date of birth, the color of his eyes and hair. He baulked at his religion and where he was born. "What religion should I use, Claude? And where am I from . . . my hometown?"

"Roman Catholic. I can teach you the rituals. Used to be a Catholic myself." Claude thought for minute. "Martigny. It's close to the border with France near where I was born, Les Perrons. I know it quite well. Used to have a girlfriend in Martigny, but that's another story. I'll tell you everything I remember about Martigny before you leave."

"And now, Monsieurs, the payment." He held out his hand.

Émile gave him all his francs, and Claude made up the shortage.

"One week, Monsieurs. Return in seven days."

As they left the shop, Claude said, "I kept back enough for a taxi."

"How can I ever repay you, comrade?"

"No problem there. I know a corporal in the finance office who can finagle an advance on our pay. Leave it to me."

In the taxi, Claude asked him, "Who's this DeGroote guy? Did you make it up?"

"No. Jean-Philippe DeGroote was a classmate and close friend back in La Linde." Émile went silent, and then continued, "He drowned in the Dordogne during our last year in school. Brilliant musician he was. Could play any wind instrument—oboe, clarinet, saxophone—all of them."

When they arrived back at the hospital, Émile's travel orders were waiting for him. *Ten days. I leave in ten days. I pray the passport is finished before then.* When the nurse came to change his dressing, she asked if he had removed it. "Just for a moment or two," he lied. "The damn thing itches."

* * *

Every day during the next week, Claude drilled his friend on Martigny and Catholic rituals. They found an atlas in the hospital library. Émile studied the towns and villages in the area.

They were sitting on a bench in the garden one afternoon. Claude had finished his tutorial for the day. He asked, "What are your plans for getting out of Vietnam? Are you planning to jump ship in Suez or somewhere else?"

"I didn't have a plan until just now. Look at this." Émile showed him the Saigon edition of *Match*. He pointed to an article about a Chinese firm that was recruiting workers to go to the Carolines. Salvaging sunken Japanese ships from the harbor in Truk was the purpose. "The Carolines. Wasn't that where you were?"

"*Oui, mon ami.* Nasty place it is . . . Truk I mean. But it's the islands, Andre. Perfect place for you to disappear. The Chinaman most certainly knows someone who knows someone. I'll get a pass tomorrow and go see him."

"Should I go with you?"

"No. It's better if I go alone. One never knows . . . the security police could be watching him."

Claude joined Émile in the hospital canteen early that evening. "You're all sorted, as our Brit comrades say. The Chinaman has a nephew who is first mate on the ship taking the workers to Truk. I do believe all these Chinese are related." He gave Émile a folded piece of paper. "This is a letter of introduction." Émile opened the letter. It was written in Chinese characters.

Emile shook his head. "How do we know what this says. It could be a trap."

"Not to worry, *mon ami.* I emphasized to the gentleman that if anything happened to you, some very angry légionnaires would pay him a visit."

* * *

"Today's the big day, Andre. I have a present for you . . . the Chinaman, actually." He handed Émile a manila envelope. Inside were various blank official documents and identity cards.

"How did you manage this?"

Claude shrugged. "I make friends easily." He was already in his dress uniform. "Come. Get dressed. It'll be your last time."

"What will you do when you get back to France?" Émile asked while he dressed.

"We'll have to wait and see. Maybe I'll become an activist, as they called themselves, and protest against the A-bomb tests. *La Légion* has decided to retire me medically with a small pension. I'll probably stay with my cousins in Paris for a while."

"I didn't know you had cousins in Paris."

"I haven't told everything about my former life, have I?" He reached out his hand. "Let me have your identity tags."

"Why? What are you going to do?" He handed Claude the tags.

"Don't ask. I'll tell you later." He took the tags and removed Émile's chart from the end of the bed. "I'll be right back. Get ready." Claude left through the door to the next ward. He returned a few minutes later and replaced the chart. "Here are your tags, Légionnaire Volantes."

"What have you done?"

"I'll tell you in the taxi." Claude took him by the arm, and they left the hospital.

"Well, what about the tags and why were you messing with my chart? And who is this Volantes?"

"Volantes, bless his soul, is in another ward full of guys not expected to make it. I switched charts and removed his tags. Yours are now hanging by his chart. This should confuse the staff long enough for you to be well away on your sea voyage to the South Pacific."

"But about his family back home. This isn't right, Claude."

"*Mon ami*, you are the family I'm looking out for. Don't worry. The staff will sort things out eventually. I'm sure his fingerprints are on file somewhere. If need be, I'll drop a few hints to certain people."

In the forger's shop Émile took off his uniform and hung it on the rack. "You can keep this. And these." He handed the Chinaman the identity tags and the envelope.

"*Merci beaucoup*, Monsieur." He removed the documents, examined them, and nodded. "Very fine. Yes, these will do nicely." He opened a desk drawer and held up the passport. "I sincerely hope you appreciate the work put into this. It is one of my finest creations."

Émile inspected the passport and handed it to Claude. "*Très bien, Grand-père.*"

After he finished dressing in civilian clothes, Émile inserted the passport and a few francs into the sealskin pouch he had bought.

Claude gave him the address of his cousins in Paris, which Émile slipped into the pouch. "Just in case you ever return to Paris. It's an old family address. They've lived there for decades."

"I seriously doubt that will ever happen. But you never know. Maybe I'll send you a postcard from paradise." They laughed. "Now, *Grand-père*, how do I find this ship?"

Outside in the alley Claude said, "I'll take my leave now, *mon ami. Bon voyage.*" They shook hands and hugged. "When I get to Paris, I may try to find out what I can about this *mafioso* Pioletti. *Adieu*, Jean-Philippe DeGroote. *Bonne chance!*" Claude saluted, turned and walked away. Émile watched his friend blend in with the crowds at the street corner, and then he turned and headed for the Saigon River, the city's port.

Back in the shop, the forger placed the documents and identity tags in a drawer on top of the second photo of Émile.

* * *

Hotel Gaultier, Argenteuil, 1954.

Constance was in the kitchen finishing the last of the breakfast dishes when she heard the bell over the door ring. Her overnight guests had departed.

"*Bonjour,* Constance," said the postman. "Here're your newspapers and some other things. You have a letter from Switzerland."

"*Bonjour,* Paul. *Merci Beaucoup.* Would you like a coffee?"

"*Merci,* Constance. Not today. I'm a bit behind in my deliveries. *A bientôt.*"

She picked up the letter and looked at the postmark. *Geneva. Visitors booking a room perhaps?* She turned the letter over and read the return address, Klaus von Reichenhall, 13B Hauptstrase, Eisenstadt, Austria. *That's strange. Why the Swiss postmark? Oh ! It can't be. Ten years! It's been almost ten years.* She tore open the envelope. The writing was in French.

Mon cher Constance,

I do hope this reaches you. Are you well? I would have written sooner, but life here has been somewhat difficult these past years. We have been under Soviet occupation since the end of the war. All post to other countries has been subject to inspection by their secret police. A colleague of mine, who is traveling to Switzerland to attend a symposium, will post this from Geneva. Fortunately, things are changing and the Russians will be leaving soon.

Mattie and I have two sons and a third child is expected in a few months.

I was captured by the Americans shortly after leaving Argenteuil in 1944 and didn't return home until 1946.

I teach languages at a collegium. Life is getting better.

All these years I have wondered about the souvenirs I left with you. I truly hope you still have them.

How is your family? I'm sorry I wasn't able to determine what happened to your husband. I hope he was able to return after the war.

My best to your parents. They were always most kind to this poor artist.

When you have a moment, we would thoroughly enjoy receiving a letter from you.

ton ami,

Klaus

Mon Dieu! Klaus is alive! He survived the war. How wonderful! But the name—von Reichenhall. She was confused, and then she remembered. Her mother had told her his real name, Klaus von Reichenhall . . . *from* Eisenstadt, after his visit with Mattie in 1937. She went to the hotel's desk and took some stationery back to a table. *What should I tell him?* She didn't want to be the bearer of bad news. Not after all these years. Her father had been killed fighting with the *résistance* against a Nazi *SS* unit that was planning to destroy the bridge at Argenteuil; her husband had died in the slave labor camp at Mauthausen in Austria. No, she wouldn't write that. Yes, his souvenirs, as he called them, were still hidden in a chest in the attic under her wedding dress. She *would* mention that her mother emigrated to America.

Sitting at the table, she pushed aside the latest edition of *Paris Match* Paul had brought, and started to write. Later, after returning from the post office, she perused the newspaper and saw an article about the awarding of the Nobel Prize in Literature to an American author, Ernest Hemingway.

29

Pape'ete, Tahiti, French Polynesia, 1957.
The cavernous interior was already crowded when Heinrich Vater pushed through the doors of Quinn's Bar. He side-stepped to the left and stood for a few moments while his eyes adjusted to the change in light. He looked across the room searching the long zinc-topped bar for the man he sought.

When he first saw the man a week ago boarding a copra schooner at the wharf, he was sure he recognized him from somewhere in his past. The man went below decks. Vater hadn't boarded the vessel. He wasn't sure why he hadn't done that—he had the authority. But something made him pause. Vater had a remarkable memory for faces—couldn't always place a name with it, but eventually the thread would join. A skill that was most useful for a colonial *gendarme.*

The thread became complete later that evening. As he left the bar at the Hotel Maret, a French Army officer coming from the lobby called his name, "Vater? Sergeant Vater? It *is* you, isn't it?"

The officer turned to his wife. "A moment, *ma chérie.* An old comrade." He left his wife and walked over to Vater.

Heinrich saluted. The officer returned the salute and extended his hand.

"Not remembering me, are you, Sergeant Vater? Jules Rappe, a green, snot-nosed lieutenant in the 13th Demi-Brigade when I knew you in Tonkin."

Vater's memory for faces failed him this time.

"*Bien sûr,* Monsieur Captain, it's been a few years." They shook hands.

"Yes, and I see you have done well for yourself—a *sous-officier* in the *gendamerie.* Come, you must have a drink with us."

"Another time, *bien sûr,* Monsieur Captain, I'm already late for an appointment with the magistrate." *I must get away from this officer. Any conversation would certainly be about Indochina, and he had been at Dien Bien Phu. I seem to remember a brief encounter with him in some bar in Hanoi before I flew to Saigon. The past is sneaking up on me.*

"Good to see you again, Monsieur Captain. This is a small island. I'm sure we'll meet again soon. Madame." Vater saluted and hurried away.

"Who was that, Jules?"

"An old comrade from Indochina. With us at Dien Bien Phu, I'm sure." Rappe searched his memory. "Well, no matter. The details get fuzzy sometimes."

"You did have a great head injury, Jules. I'm surprised you remember anything."

"I always remembered you, *mon coeur.*" He took her arm and they walked into the hotel restaurant.

Vater hadn't walked more than a hundred meters along the street before he remembered. *The man on the copra schooner. It's LaLande. LaLande, who was at Dien Bien Phu. LaLande, who I saw in Saigon. LaLande, who knows I wasn't at Dien Bien Phu. What if he meets the captain?*

* * *

Émile wanted to get out of French Polynesia—too many Indochina veterans, too many people, too many officials. The *pension* where he worked was filled with men working on the new international airport being built on the island. Afraid he'd be recognized and turned into the authorities, he wanted to find another place to hide.

So far, no one had questioned his forged passport. Passage to Tahiti had cost all the little money he'd earned salvaging sunken Japanese ships in Truk harbor. He realized it was stupid on his part to come to a French island instead of New Zealand or Australia. His job as breakfast cook at Madame Flynn's on the edge of town didn't pay much but came with room and board. Earlier that day he'd talked to a copra schooner captain about his destination, but he was going north to the Marquesas, not west to the closest non-French islands.

During his time away from the *pension's* kitchen, Émile visited many of the remote villages on the island, always searching for a place to disappear. He heard stories about a crazy American—Ernest Darling, "Nature Man" the natives called him—who had lived up in the mountains with an island wife forty years before. Offered a vast fortune by a rich relative to return to the States, Darling chose to remain in Tahiti until his death. Perhaps, I can find a refuge here, he thought. Émile made friends with a few of the local fishermen. He went out with them in their cutters at night to fish for squid and learned how to sail.

Returning from the waterfront that evening, he stopped at Quinn's and looked in through the open doors. The orchestra—three guitars, drums, a string bass, saxophone—was rendering "Rose of San Antone," with Polynesian whoops and hoots.

In the last half of the 20th Century, Bangkok's Mosquito Bar's disreputable reputation was only rivaled by Quinn's Bar in Pape'ete. Patrons were often entertained by the dancing and brawling "Suzie No-Pants."

The dance floor pulsed to the action of the dancers; two thirds of whom were several dozen Europeans and Tahitians wearing garlands of flowers. They were totally indifferent to the fact that ladies and gentlemen from a cruise ship, sitting at an isolated section of tables reserved for them, had traveled halfway around the world to inspect them. French soldiers and sailors stood at the bar or danced with the girls—the notorious unkempt and completely unrestrained "Quinn's Girls."

Elsewhere, crowded in booths and knee to knee around tables, were tourists from the hotels, French men and women in garish clothes from the holiday camp on Moorea, and sunburned young men from the yachts. A table full of Swedish tourists, in particular, seemed to be dazed. A half-caste beauty, whose skimpy *pareu* barely covered her large breasts, squirmed among the press of bodies, taking photos with a flash camera.

Pushing through the crowd to the bar, Émile found a vacant stool and ordered a beer. In the mirror behind the bar he saw Vater. *Merde!* His right hand moved instinctively to the handle of his sheath knife—a nervous reaction whenever he sensed danger. A sweet voice said, "*Bonsoir,* Monsieur," and as he turned a light blinded him. He blinked, saw the exposed flesh, and then the camera.

"Five francs, if you want a copy, Monsieur." She raised the camera again. "Perhaps a smile in this one, Monsieur?" He covered his face with his hands. "No. No, please. No pictures. But I'll buy you a drink, *n'est-ce pas?*"

"*Merci,* Monsieur, but not while I'm working. Perhaps later when you buy the photos?" She winked and slid back into crowd. Émile looked back to the mirror.

Vater sat at an upper level table near the wall drinking a bottle of *Hinano* beer with a young Tahitian woman in a very tight red *pareu*. On her head, somewhat askew, perched a crown of ginger blossoms. The girl performed her usual exertions: pouting, hunching her shoulders, wrinkling her pug nose, tilting the ginger lei even more precariously over her forehead. Émile thought she looked cheap and well-used. He recognized her as the girl who had moved into a bedsit down the hall from his room at Madame Flynn's.

The music came to a thudding halt, like a stampede stopping short at the edge of a cliff. The musicians stood back to catch their breath; the dancers moved off the floor. Voices, laughter, the clink of glassware were suddenly audible. Only temporarily. The musicians shifted position; the guitarists stepped forward; the saxophone player took up a ukulele; the drummer tucked a leather-topped drum between his knees. A pause, then four quiet chords on the ukulele; four quick chords from the guitars: the *tamure!*

Quinn's had filled to capacity. Faces flickered and glimmered among the lights and colored shadows; the music was secondary to laughter, whoops, and shouted conversations. A fight started. With dexterity approaching elegance, a pair of bouncers flung the combatants into the street.

Émile pulled his floppy hat down to cover more of his face. *Is Vater a threat? Would he even recognize me? It's been—what?—over two years, and my hair is much longer.* He left his unfinished beer on the bar and slipped out through the crowd into the night.

While he walked along the harbor quays, Émile thought about how he could get away from Tahiti. He looked out at the harbor—the tide was ebbing and the wind blew from the north. How far to the British islands, he wondered. Cutters of various sizes were tied up to the the quays. He inspected several, looking for water casks. On a ten-footer he found a full water cask and baskets of fruit. *Moorea* was written on the stern. Must be going back across the channel after an evening in town, he thought. *My passport! Merde! I have to return to the pension to get it.*

Before going up to his room, Émile went into the kitchen and filled a sack with baguettes. Upstairs he pulled the pouch containing his passport from under the mattress and placed the strap over his head. He packed his meager belongings into a small valise. As he looked around to see if he had forgotten anything, he heard the screams from down the hall. *What the hell is that?* His memory flashed back to Paris when Musette was killed.

He ran down the hall and kicked open the door where the bar girl stayed. She lay on the bed naked, her wrists tied to the headboard frame. Vater straddled her, naked except for his under shorts. He glared at Émile. "LaLande?" He looked surprised and confused. "I know you. Get out!" The girl screamed again. Vater hit her with his fist.

"You get out, Vater. Leave her be, you pig!"

Vater moved faster than Émile expected, jumped off the bed and charged him. Émile sidestepped and tripped him. Vater fell by the chair holding his uniform and pistol belt. He reached for his gun. Émile drew his knife as he lunged forward and stabbed Vater in the throat, puncturing his jugular vein. Vater staggered to his feet grasping his neck. Blood spurted between his fingers. He took two steps toward Émile and collapsed. A pool of blood spread around his head.

I've killed him. Good riddance. I killed Andre in Paris and others in Algeria, but always in self-defense. This was no different, but easier. Why?

Émile cut the girl loose. She was unconscious. He carried her to his room and laid her on the bed. Back in her room, he rolled Vater's body over. He placed a pillow over the policeman's face to muffle the sound, and shot him in the face with his gun. Using Vater's vest, he wiped the pistol clean and placed in the dead man's hand. That should confuse the other *flics*, he thought. "Bless you, Krakow," he said.

Émile grabbed his bags and went down the outside back staircase. He ran toward the waterfront. At the quay he took the bloody sheath knife off his belt and threw it into the bay. *Shit! That was stupid. Maybe there's one on the cutter.*

On board he untied the lines, raised the sail, and slipped slowly away from the quay.

30

The South Pacific west of French Polynesia, 1957.

"Cap'n! Cap'n! There's somebody out there!" Mateo, a Filipino deckhand, pointed to the north. Captain Marlow Drayton, the master of the inter-island freighter *Dorado*, rose from his chair on the bridge and stepped to the starboard rail. Through his binoculars he saw what looked like an overturned lifeboat. A man rose on one knee by the keel of the boat and waved a white cloth.

"All stop!" Drayton ordered. "Lower a boat, Henri. Go pick 'im up . . . and his craft."

One of *Dorado's* motorized lifeboats returned with the man—a white man—and his righted and bailed out boat, a small de-masted cutter, in tow. Henri, the first mate, helped the man climb up the gangway ladder that had been lowered down the side of the freighter. The man collapsed on the hot steel deck.

"Get some water down there!" the captain ordered from above. "Pull 'im out of the sun." Two crew members and the first mate lifted the man and carried him into the shade next to a bulkhead. The ship's cook ran over with a bucket of water.

"Cool 'im off. Save a little for 'im to drink," said the mate.

The splash of water made the man shake and roll over.

"Give 'im a drink, Kwan."

The cook lifted the man's head and poured some water into his mouth. The man grabbed the bucket and lifted it.

"Not too much, man," the mate said. "You had a bit in the whaleboat. There's plenty more where that came from. Steady on."

The man wore only a ragged open white shirt and canvas shorts. An oilskin pouch hung by a strap around his neck. Barefoot, hatless, and burned by the sun, his lips were cracked and swollen. He sat up, leaned against the bulkhead below the bridge, and reached out for the bucket. Kwan gave him another drink.

"Where's he from? Speak English, does he?" the captain asked.

Kwan looked up to the bridge, "He say 'We, miss-sir, he speakie English a little'."

"A Frog, eh? How'd he get out here? Not to mind. Bring him up to the bridge."

"What about his boat?" the mate asked.

"Bring it aboard. Secure it on the forward cargo hatch."

The freighter's passengers watched all this from the railing outside the ship's salon.

"Well done, Captain!" shouted one of the British travelers and gave a thumbs up.

Captain Drayton nodded. Two crew members helped Émile up to the ship's bridge. Kwan followed with a pitcher of water.

* * *

Seated in his chair on the bridge with the castaway opposite in a folding chair, Captain Drayton watched Émile drink from the pitcher. The *Dorado* was underway again.

"Now, Frenchie. Let's hear your story," he said and pointed to the pouch around Émile's neck. "And I'll have a look at your papers."

"Not French . . . Swiss . . . Bora Bora." Émile had the presence of mind not to say Tahiti. The other island was the first name that came to him. He took his passport from the pouch and handed it to the officer.

"Speak English, do you now? Well, you're a long way off course, lad. Fancy a cold beer?"

Émile, half-dead from his three days clinging to the bottom of the cutter, knew he had to keep his mind clear.

"No beer, *s'il vous plaît*. Just water, *merci beaucoup*." Émile drank deeply again and tried to stay awake. "Some sleep, *s'il vous plaît*, Captain. I would like to sleep."

"Yes, of course. Where are my manners? Take 'im below, Kwan. Put 'im in the purser's spare bunk. We'll have a chat later. And get him some tiffin."

Émile fell onto a bunk in the small cabin. His mind raced: *What do I tell them? Who am I now? How did I get here? Do they know about Vater on Pape'ete? I have to get my story together. So tired. Must sleep.*

* * *

When Émile awoke, a plate of cut sandwiches, a bowl of fruit—a mango and two bananas—and a chunk of white cheese sat on the small cabinet next to his bunk. Alongside a pitcher of water was a bottle of *San Miguel* beer.

He sniffed the cheese—no idea what it was. Didn't care. He was hungry. The sandwiches, a banana, the cheese, and half the *San Miguel* were gone when the cabin door opened. A balding, red-nosed, middle-aged man in an almost nautical uniform came in. His yachting-style cap, and his pressed and creased white, short sleeve shirt with blue shoulder boards, accented by crossed gold keys, contrasted with his well-worn canvas shorts.

"Sorry, old boy. Would've knocked, but must get some bits from my kit. It is my cabin anyway, right? Feeling more shipshape are you? I've got some cream here for your burns." He placed a jar on the cabinet. "Stinks a bit, but does the job."

"*Merci*, Monsieur, for all this." Émile waved his hand toward the plate and beer.

"Not my doing, mate. Thank the captain. You're dining with him this evening. And with the paying passengers. They're all agog to hear your tale, so make it a good one."

"A good one? *Je ne comprends pas.* I do not understand. What do you mean?" He stood from the bunk. "*Pardon*, Monsieur, but I do not know your name? Who are you?" He extended his hand. "*Je suis . . . pardon . . . I* am Jean-Philippe DeGroote from Switzerland."

"Sorry, mate. Malfrey Pichot-Wiggins. That's me. My friends call me 'Wiggie'. I'm acting purser on this leaky barge. For a bit, anyway . . . until we close on Rarotonga. Used to be *sous-chef*, but got kicked topside after that Paluan *kanaka* jumped ship in the Marquesas."

Wiggie eyed Émile up and down, turned to a wall cabinet, and drew out a white shirt and a pair of duck trousers. He threw them on the bed and pulled a pair of canvas shoes from under his bunk.

"We're about the same size, mate, so these should do for this evening's soirée. There's a razor in the basin, and the shower's aft along the passageway on the port side." Wiggie looked closely at Émile's blistered face. "You may want to wait a bit until your skin's sorted before scraping it."

"*Merci beaucoup* for the use of your clothes. Wiggie? What did you mean about making it a good one?

Wiggie closed the cabinet and turned to face Émile. "I've been around the islands for quite a time since I got out of the paras. Seen lots of folks, lots of places. To me, it isn't natural for a white man to be floating around on an overturned cutter this far from land. Either you're a sailing dunce or you're running from something. Don't matter none to me, mate. But the folks topside will expect, at least, a plausible story."

* * *

"Right you are. Here's our castaway," Captain Drayton said as Émile entered the ship's salon.

The salon, a cramped little room, was barely large enough for a table with a seating of eight. One corner had a short bar with four stools for four thin people. A bow-tied islander in a starched white shirt attempted to fulfill the passengers' requests from the ship's limited inventory—beer, gin and rum always in good supply. Two small cocktail tables were pushed out of the way next to the bench seats during meals. Between meals the long table rested against the opposite bulkhead and functioned as a writing desk.

"Take the end berth." Drayton directed Émile to an empty chair at the opposite end of the table. "We're all together in this, I'm afraid," he said to the six passengers seated around the table. "Haven't had the opportunity to interview our new arrival since he came aboard, so his tale will be as fresh to you as to me. Let's hope it's a good one."

The captain lifted a gray-green passport. "Our guest is . . . Jean-Philippe DeGroote from Switzerland. I'll leave the rest to him." He laid the passport on the table. "But first, some introductions." He nodded toward a large woman seated on his right. "Miss Abigail Lithwick, a Yank from Iowa and noted literary scholar. She joined us in Pape'ete. On her way to Auckland to educate the Maori in Kiwi land."

The obese American woman—a multi-colored muumuu attempted to hide her bulk—laughed. "Not just the Maori, Captain. Anyone who'll listen." She smiled at Émile, "*Bonsoir*, Monsieur DeGroote."

Émile nodded and returned the greeting, "*Bonsoir*, Madame Leftwitch?"

What a grotesque woman. Her face is as big as an overripe melon with two small, beady dark eyes and her nose . . . large with flared nostrils . . . must be some African blood in her veins somewhere.

The woman laughed with her whole body. Her ponderous breasts rearranged the table setting when she leaned forward. "Not Left-witch, Monsieur. Lith-wick. And it's Mademoiselle not Madame."

That's not a surprise.

"Next is the God Squad," the captain continued. "Reverend and Mrs. Boniface Archambault. They've come to the islands to preach to the converted. Will be with us until Nouméa. Must not be any sinners remaining in Quebec."

Archambault, attired in a black suit coat, black shirt, and a spotless dog-collar—in spite of the temperature and humidity—frowned and lifted himself halfway out of his chair. His wife, a nondescript, shapeless middle-aged woman in a flower-print dress, giggled and took another drink of wine. The captain turned toward the other guests.

"To larboard, we have Major Percival Martingale, formerly of the Queen's Gurkha Rifles, and his lovely wife Penelope. They're on a round-the-world cruise." The major rose from his seat, bowed imperceptibly and sat. Dressed in military-cut khaki mufti, the only items missing were his rank insignia and medals. His wife, over-adorned in jewelry, obviously had spent a great deal of time with her hair and makeup. She wore a simple low-cut, black, sleeveless dress that displayed sun-damaged arms and an unremarkable cleavage. She didn't make eye contact with Émile, just stared at the nearest porthole.

"And last but not least, our resident scribbler, John Spreadborough." A quite thin man, in his late thirties, with very black hair and large brown eyes, looked fixedly at Émile, as if trying to commit his visual details to memory. "Mr. Spreadborough's a fellow Yorkshireman from my home port of Whitby. He's done several cruises with us . . . usually popping off on some atoll for a month or two until we return . . . either writing his next best seller or just sampling the native wares." Drayton smiled and reached for his wine glass.

Spreadborough stood, shot a glare at the captain before turning to face Émile. "I would very much like to hear a detailed description of your adventures, Monsieur DeGroote. At your convenience, of course. Always most interested to learn about a person's experiences in the islands."

"Right you are. That's done. I believe turtle soup is the first course this evening. Right, Kwan?" Drayton said to the cook, who waited in the hatchway with a large tureen. Wiggie took the place of the islander behind the bar. "So, Jean, let's hear your story."

Émile stood, but the captain motioned for him to sit. The cook maneuvered around the table serving the soup.

"*Bonjour, tout le monde,* everyone. You must excuse me if I act confused, but I am not used to so much attention. *Normalement,* I am below decks with the crew, not at the table of the captain. My name is Jean-Philippe . . . Jean-Philippe DeGroote. I *am* Swiss from Matigny, a small town near the frontier with France and Italia—"

"We've been there," Major Martingale said. "Haven't we, Penny?" He looked at his wife, who shrugged. "That's where ol' Boney crossed the Alps into Italy, isn't it?" He glanced around the table for confirmation. The others shrugged or ignored the outburst. "Sorry, ol' man. Do carry on."

"I am not an important person. Just a *sous-chef,* a cook. Nothing more." *How did I get to the South Pacific? That was the easy bit, but how did I get here? I don't want to mention anything about Vietnam or the Légion. Or do I?*

"*Alors,* I was trying to sail to Bora Bora from Pape'ete. I was offered a position at a new establishment there . . . a man from Marseille needed a chef for his tourist hotel. I was tired of Pape'ete and wanted to move on to Raiatea, which is where I thought I would make the first day. A friend offered me the use of his boat, but . . . a storm . . . a storm *incroyable.* I was forced to the west for two, maybe three days, *et mais,* how you say, a rogue wave took the mast and flipped the boat. I was *sans rien,* everything: water, food, compass, clothing, *sans rien. Mais,* I saved my papers." He pointed to the passport on the table in front of the captain.

Drayton had raised an eyebrow when Émile talked about making Raiatea in one day.

"That's a good story, Jean," the captain said. "But what brought you here to this side of the world? You're a long way from the Alps."

"I am not at all political, but I did not like what was going on in France after the war. I decided to go abroad to seek my fortune."

"Wait a minute, Jean-Philippe," Spearbourough said. "You talk about France as if you're French. Aren't you Swiss?"

Merde! I've slipped into my French persona. How do I get out of this? Must change the subject.

"*Pardon,* Monsieur, but Martigny is on the, how do you say, frontier with France, and after the war, full of refugees. When I finished my military service, it was difficult to find a position. I was a cook in the army." *At least that's not a lie.* "In our *bataillon,* there was a *prêtre* . . . a priest . . . who was to be sent out to the Carolines." He turned toward Captain Drayton, "You are familiar with them, *non?*"

Drayton nodded. "Right nasty place the Carolines. Truk *was* the jewel of the old German colonies in Micronesia until the first war."

What do I tell them next? Maybe the captain will keep talking, so I can think. What was the name of the island Claude was on? Pulu-something. Yes! Puluwat.

"The Japs turned it into a huge navy base, and the Yanks bombed the hell out of it. Still a bit of a mess. Needs a lot of sorting." Drayton drank some wine and continued, "Haven't been in there for a year or two. Harbor's full of sunken Jap ships." He looked at Émile. "So, you were on Truk then, Jean?"

"*Oui, mais non,* Captain. We stopped there for a short time. Our mission was on an atoll named Puluwat."

"Not familiar with that one. Never heard of it," Drayton said. He turned to the writer. "What about you, Spreadborough? You seem to know all the back alleys out here."

Merde! I have no idea where that atoll is. Must change the subject.

"Sorry, Captain. Never heard of it either. So many in the western Pacific. Difficult to know them all. Difficult enough just knowing the ones in French Polynesia." Spreadborough opened the notebook he'd placed on the table. "But, how'd you get there, Jean-Philippe? And what were your duties? What was your employment?"

"A ship from Marseille to Nouméa . . . *beaucoup* stops." *Okay, think quickly, what was I doing with a Catholic priest on his way to the South Pacific?* "My duties? Factotum. I believe that is the English word, *n'est-ce pas?* I was to be his chef until I could teach the natives our ways, and then secretary, driver, anything he needed."

"Driver?" the pastor asked. "Now, that's rich. It's odd to find an atoll with drivable roads, let alone automobiles."

Think. Think. "Oui, Monsieur. . . C'est vrai . . . mais . . . the priest . . . how do you say, Padre Claude . . . had only the one arm." *That's almost true. Claude did lose his arm after the parachute drop into Dien Bien Phu.* "There were no automobiles on Puluwat."

"Factotum? That's a posh word for someone's dogsbody, is it not?" Major Martingale glanced around the table. Miss Lithwick nodded in agreement. The others ignored his comment.

"Dogsbody, Monsieur? *Je ne* . . . I do not understand the word."

"A lackey, a servant."

"*Ah oui,* Monsieur. That was my position, and *très bon* until Padre Claude was taken by the shark." Everyone leaned forward and looked at Émile. *Now, I may have gone too far. Think. Think.*

"Bloody hell!" the major said.

"How disgusting," said Mrs. Major.

"God's will be done," said the pastor. His wife nodded in agreement and emptied her wine glass.

Miss Lithwick, mouth open, stared at Émile as if in disbelief.

Captain Drayton almost spit out his wine. Behind the bar Wiggie shook his head. Spreadborough spoke first.

"Jean-Philippe. Please. Some details. What happened?" His pen had already written 'shark attack' on a blank page.

"Steady on, ol' chap." The major said. "There're ladies present. Mustn't spoil their appetites. You and Jean can have a good chinwag later. Might like to hear the story myself over a snifter. What do say, Captain? It's your table."

After dinner, the ladies went to their cabins or out on deck. The men remained in the salon. Over a snifter of cheap Chinese brandy and cheaper Filipino cigars, Émile told the tale of Padre Claude's demise by shark. He also explained the reason for his departure from Puluwat atoll. The Vatican replaced all the diocese's positions with American clergy, who brought their own staff. Émile was given a small separation stipend and paid passage to Tahiti. He would have preferred Samoa or Fiji, but "the first available ship out of Truk" was the agreement.

Captain Drayton told him that they would talk in the morning about his prospects and that he might be more comfortable messing with the crew for the remainder of the voyage.

* * *

Wiggie opened the porthole in his cabin's bulkhead to let the smoke out. He threw the stub of his cigar into the sea.

"These Flipo turds are bloody dreadful, but . . . Don't care much for Pape'ete these days myself," he said to Émile. "Getting to be a bit too civilized, if you know what I mean. Not really civilized, but more like metropolitan . . . like any other big city, too many cars, too many foreigners, too much crime. Heard one of the Frog *gendarmes* got himself knifed last week. I was in Quinn's . . . You've been to Quinn's? Of course you have. No one spends any time at all on the beach in Pape'ete without a visit to Quinn's . . . when a whore came running in saying that one of their lot and a copper had topped each other."

What? How can that be? She was alive when I left.

"A right mess it was, according to the wharf scuttlebutt. He'd been opened up like a butchered pig, but got one shot off . . . in her mouth . . . before he packed it in."

This is all wrong. I put her on my bed. Vater was dead, I'm sure of it. I shot him. The knife. I threw it in the harbor. There was nothing to connect her to the crime. Wiggie seemed to be watching him closely, looking for a reaction to this bit of news. *Must be calm. Maybe it's just wharf scuttlebutt, as he says.*

"*C'est vrai*, Monsieur Wiggie. That is why I wanted to find another position away from Pape'ete."

"Fancy a real drink, Jean? Got a bottle of Scotch under my bunk." He wiped out two glasses from the wash basin. "And we can dispense with the 'monsieur', if you please.

"I listened to the bumbf you off-loaded on the punters this evening. Don't know if the captain was taken in by all of it, but the others surely had it for pudding." Wiggie lifted a bottle from a drawer under his berth. He poured two fingers of the amber liquid into the glasses and handed one to Émile.

This man sees right through me. Must be careful. Can I trust him? How much should I tell him? The truth or another story?

Émile accepted the glass, took a sip, and decided to take a chance. "Wiggie, what do you mean by 'bumpf' and 'punters'? I do not know these words. And what did I say that had anything to do with a dessert . . . a pudding?"

Wiggie stared at Émile for a moment, and then started to laugh, laughed so hard he put his glass aside and sat on the lower bunk. Maybe it was the wine at dinner and the brandy afterwards, but Émile also laughed. Wiggie starting spitting up his whiskey. Émile slapped him hard on the back. The purser caught his breath and leaned back in the berth.

"Bumpf. You've never heard of bumpf?" He grinned at Émile. "I don't know the Frog word for it, but the Yanks call it bullshit. Yes, bullshit. That's what you were feeding them up topside." He reached for his glass and took a sip. "And punters . . . they're the clueless paying public." He took another sip. "And they all took it down like a mess of sticky pudding." Wiggie tried to stand, but fell back on the bunk. "I'm about legless, I am." He laughed. "Need to get some kip." He handed his glass to Émile, stretched out on his bed and closed his eyes.

Émile poured the remainder of both whiskies back in the bottle. He slipped out of his shoes, climbed into the upper berth and lay there wondering what lies he would have to tell the captain tomorrow.

* * *

The porthole in Wiggie's cabin was at the same level of Émile's face on the top bunk. The morning sun woke him. He lay there for a moment, eyes closed, trying to remember where he was. The throbbing of the *Dorado's* engines played a duet with the throbbing in his head. He opened his eyes and looked around the cabin. A tray on the small cabinet held a steaming mug and a plate with a roll or pastry of some kind. Wiggie's gone about his duties, Émile thought.

Émile swung down from the bunk and paused to steady himself. He looked in the mirror above the washbasin. *What a mess. The cream seems to help. I don't think I should shave just yet. Why shave at all? No, it's time to grow a beard. A little bit of change might be a good idea.* He looked at his almost shoulder-length hair. *Wonder if there's a barber onboard?* He reached down, lifted the mug and took a sip. *Tea. Oh well, it is an English ship. And it does taste quite good.* He took a bite of the roll. *Tasteless. Oh, what I'd give for one of Francine's croissants.* He smiled. *I can bake better than this. Something to offer the captain when we have our talk.*

Wiggie came into the cabin. "*Bonjour*, Jean. How's your head, mate? I was a bit fuzzy myself this morning." He looked at Jean's face. "Not going to give the ol' razor a go, are you? Probably a good idea. Things are still a bit peely."

"Is there someone who cuts hair on board, a barber?"

"*Oui, Monsieur. Bien sûr, mon ami.* And that's all my French, Jean. Kwan can butcher your locks as well as the best of us."

Wiggie looked at the clothes Émile had slept in. He shook his head. "The captain wants to see you in his cabin topside. What you're wearing will have to do. He's seen you in worse, I must say. A bit of advice. Tell him the truth, as much as you can. He's a good and honorable man, and will do the best by you."

As Émile made his way forward and topside he thought about what he would tell the man who'd saved his life. *I'll wait to hear where the captain's questions lead.*

The door to the captain's cabin was open. Émile knocked on the bulkhead.

"What's that? Who? That be you, Jean? Come in."

The captain's cabin wasn't much larger than the purser's—only one bunk, a bit wider and longer, an additional cabinet, and small table with two chairs. A small refrigerator sat tucked in next to the washbasin. His desk, more like a small writing table, was just inside the door.

"Take a berth," the captain said as he rose from his desk and pointed to one of the chairs at the table. "A bit better are you now? Had some kip and some tiffin? Wiggie lookin' after you all right is he?" He pulled out a chair and sat facing Émile. "Ol' Malfrey's a proper bloke when he's not on the drink. Must've had a rough time in the paras. But he's a good one to fill in when a berth's open. Never stays aboard long though."

The captain poured himself a mug of coffee from the carafe in the middle of the table. He didn't offer any to Émile.

"Right, Jean. I need to hear your story. Not the rubbish you chucked about last evening, but what's really going on."

What do I tell him? I have the feeling he doesn't like the French, so I'll stay with the Swiss façade.

"*Merci pour tout,* Captain. Monsieur Wiggie has done a good job."

Captain Drayton laughed. "Mon-sir Wiggie? Ol' Malfrey will definitely start acting the swell if he hears that." The captain leaned forward toward Émile. "Right, son. Let's have it. I don't do Frog, so we'll have to struggle along with the Queen's English, which you seem to have a proper handle on. The mate, who's from the Seychelles, takes care of all our dealings with the Frogs. And I've got Kwan for the Chinese, and Mateo for the Flipos. We're a right little United Nations on this ship . . . Sorry, got side-tracked, Jean. Let's hear it."

"To be completely honest, Captain Drayton, I got in a bit of trouble in Pape'ete, and had to . . . how you say . . . flee the island—"

"You're not the bloke who knifed the Frog copper, are you? Wait! Don't answer that." He held up both hands. "I don't want to know." He took a drink of coffee, and then reached behind, took another cup from a small shelf and pushed it across the table to Émile. "Serve yourself." Émile poured a cup of coffee.

"Don't care for the Frogs much," Drayton said. "Think they waved the white flag a bit too early in '40. Lost me older brother and a few good friends at Dunkirk. Heard this Frenchie *flic* was ex-Nazi. Caused quite a ruckus in port. Customs wanted to board us after we got underway, but we had our clearance papers, so I told them to piss off."

Émile tried to keep up with this stream and find a place to jump in with his offer. A shout from the voice pipe above the desk stopped the flow. "*Captain. Bridge. Land. Penryhn Island.*"

Drayton looked up at the voice pipe, and then back to Émile. "You'll not be wanting to go ashore here, permanently that is. Nothing there for you, unless you want to become one of those lotus eaters who live off of the generosity of the natives." Drayton rose from the table. "About your passage. You said you were a *sous-chef.* Go make friends with Kwan. His cooking could use some help. But be careful. He likes to swing his meat cleaver about when he gets the wind up. Took a swipe at Wiggie a while back, but ended up on his arse with the blade at his own throat. Don't want to mess about with ol' paras." The captain put on his cap. "Your time on the *Dorado* is not in the ship's log, Jean. Or whatever your real name is. The ship's owners need not be involved in our private life here in the islands. The best port for you to go ashore is on Raro . . . Rarotonga. We're standing off at a couple of other atolls in the Cooks en route, but Raro is your best choice. And the harbormaster there is a friend and drinking mate of Wiggie. Shouldn't look too closely at your papers."

"*Pardon*, Captain, excuse me. Is there something wrong with my passport?"

Captain Drayton stopped before leaving the cabin. "No, Jean. It's quite good. But I wouldn't try to pass it off at Customs in Zurich or Paris."

* * *

Émile left the captain's cabin. *I should go below to the ship's galley, but I want to see the island.* A hatchway onto the starboard boat deck was a few steps away. He went through it. Spreadborough leaned on the railing near a lifeboat smoking a cigarette and looking toward the distant line of green— the first appearance of Penryhn Island. He turned to face Émile and nodded.

"*Bonjour*, Monsieur Jean-Philippe. Good tale you told last evening. Always like to hear local stories. Fancy a fag?"

Émile took the offered cigarette. The Englishman struck a wooden match on the bottom of the lifeboat and lit it for him. Émile hadn't had a cigarette since before his cutter capsized. The initial intake of nicotine made him a bit light-headed. He grasped the railing.

"*C'est bon*, Monsieur. *Merci beaucoup*. English?"

"What? Me? Oh, you mean the fags? No. American. Winston's. Not their best, but most available here in the islands. Probably a Filipino knock-off."

"You are a writer, *n'est-ce pas*, Monsieur?"

"*C'est vrai*, Monsieur Jean-Philippe, a chronicler of life on these islands of paradise . . . before they're ruined forever." He flicked his cigarette butt into the sea. "I hope you don't mind me addressing you as 'Monsieur'. I know you've been relegated to the lower decks and won't see the salon again except as a minion, but it's from the lower decks and among the minions that the real . . . the true stories . . . arise. All one hears in the salon is petty bourgeois claptrap and pseudo-posh rubbish." He lit another Winston. "Take our present congregation for an example. Major Martingale is a relic from a dying empire. His wife probably wishes he was still off bashing the Pathans on the Northwest Frontier, so she could enjoy the attentions of their Sikh majordomo."

He pointed toward the island. "We'll go around to the western approach and come in through that passage. Not many of these islands have an anchorage inside the atoll. But you probably know that, don't you?"

Émile nodded. *Must keep up the façade.*

"Penryhn, called Tongareva by the locals," Spreadborough continued, "is actually one of the largest atolls in the South Pacific. Spent a few months there in the past." The writer offered Émile another cigarette. He wedged it behind his right ear for later.

"Now that Bible thumper, Archambault . . . never understood why his sort is out here. More than enough sinners to go around back in Canada. Do they really think these people are so simple? Most were converted . . . I *do* hate that word . . . during the last century. Haven't seen any regression to paganism or cannibalism in my travels. Most are devout, if nothing else, especially in the Cooks."

"You have been a long time in the islands, Monsieur Sprea . . .?"

"Spreadborough, Jean-Philippe. Spreadborough. Old English family name, though there are a few Jacobins up in Scotland. But, none of that means anything to you, does it?"

Émile shook his head.

"Nor should it. Who your family was or did isn't important. What *we* do is." He flicked a second butt into the ocean. "What was your question? Right, how long have I been in the islands. Have to think. What's the date? Not the day . . . the year?"

"1957," Émile said. *How could a man forget what year it is?*

"Almost a decade. Came out in '49. Was working for an Anglo-Egyptian rag in Cairo as book reviewer—among other things—when an advance copy of . . . Sorry, Jean-Philippe . . . Are you understanding all of this?"

Émile nodded and smiled. "I will stop you when I get lost, *n'est-ce pas?*"

"Perhaps, I should slow it down a bit."

"No. Proceed, *s'il vous plaît.* I learned my English from a *très bon* tutor, but an Irishman. He spoke very fast and used *beaucoup de patois* . . . how you say? . . . slang." Émile laughed. "*Aussi*, his accent was quite strange . . . from other English I have met."

Spreadborough looked at Émile with a puzzled expression. "How'd it come about that you learned English from an Irishman? If you don't mind my asking."

Merde! Said too much again. Must be more careful. "*Bien sûr*, of course. *Prêtre* Claude and I had a course in English from an Irish monk before leaving for Puluwat. We spent *beaucoup* time talking to the English passengers on the voyage out, and that's when we found the difference in the language." Émile took the Winston from behind his ear and the writer lit it. "It is very much the same in Helvetia—Switzerland—where we have French, German, and Italian cantons, which all speak a different *patois* from those countries." *Thank God Claude told me all about his years in Switzerland before joining . . . Maybe he'll change the subject. What was he talking about? Ah, the ruin of the islands.* "You said that the islands are being ruined. How is that?"

"The A-bomb tests. Entire atolls wiped off the face of the Earth. You must know about the tests in the Marshalls. It's not *that* far from the Carolines, both in Micronesia. The Americans have conducted over fifty since the end of the war."

I remember things Claude had said about the islands. How he'd been opposed to the A-bomb testing in the Marshalls after the war. Claude wondered why the Americans had to come to paradise to play with their war toys, when they had vast deserts at home to contaminate. He also thought that if de Gaulle comes to power, we'll certainly do the same in Polynesia.

"I had a friend who was against the A-bomb testing. He thought the French may do the same in the future."

"Your friend was most psychic," Spreadborough said. "I've heard that Paris plans to spend millions building an international airport on Tahiti. The tourist trade doesn't justify that level of investment, but a support base for a South Pacific nuclear test site just might."

"Will not other countries be against such a thing?" Émile asked.

The writer laughed. "Jean-Philippe, de Gaulle and France don't care what other countries think, even the Americans. They lost Indo-china and will probably lose Algeria. After the Suez Crisis, they realize they're on their own."

"But what about the islands and their peoples?"

"After the last war, no one cares about a few sea urchins, palm trees, and the islanders. They used to ship the natives off to Peru to work in the mines. Now, they ship them off to refugee camps on Guam and Samoa while they blow up their atolls. The islands are not important when Paris and western civilization are threatened by the Russian bear."

"What does Russia have to do with—?"

"Who's got a cigarette?" Abigail Lithwick's bulk forced an increase in the space between the two men. Draped in a different colorful muumuu, she looked first at Émile and shook her head. "Not you, castaway." She turned to Spreadborough. "Your turn, mate." She held up two fingers. He placed a Winston between them.

"Love English manners, don't you, Jean-Philippe? Now, he'll offer to light it for me. Doesn't think we mere females are capable of lighting our own fags."

"*Pardon*, Mademoiselle, I always thought of it as a courtesy. I have lighted the cigarettes of my male friends many times."

"Well spoken, Jean-Philippe," Spreadborough said.

"What are you boys talking about? Thought I heard something about naked Ruskies." She smiled.

Both men laughed. Émile had a tinge of pride that he understood the joke.

"We were discussing the destruction of the South Pacific by your American A-bomb tests," Spreadborough said.

"Oh, not again? I've heard enough of that sad song since I left the States. We save your Limey asses from both the Germans and the Japs, and now you complain about us trying to protect you from the Reds. Sometimes I think I should've applied for a fellowship in Chile or Liberia. But, doesn't matter. I won't be around for World War Three, if it comes. Unless it comes sooner than later. I didn't vote for Truman or Eisenhower, so you can't blame me for what's happening."

Émile was puzzled. "Who did you vote for, Mademoiselle?"

It was the teacher's turn to look confused. "Well, this is a big surprise. A Swiss dishwasher who's interested in American politics." She looked at Spreadborough, but his face was vacant of emotion. Émile stepped away from her.

Why is this woman insulting me? Perhaps she doesn't enjoy associating with the crew, as I now am. Time to go to the galley.

"Not a *plonguer*, Mademoiselle. A *sous-chef*. I can cook." Émile turned to leave.

"There's no need, Abigail," Spreadborough said, "to be rude to our castaway, as you called him."

The American teacher looked to the writer, and then turned to Émile. "Oh, I'm so sorry. I didn't mean to offend anyone. It's just my warped sense of humor and too many days listening to the major brag about how they could have won the bloody war without our help. Pompous ass." She took a step forward, reached out and put a hand on Émile's shoulder. "I'm so sorry, *mon ami*, for what I said about you being *just* a dishwasher. I was a dishwasher once—my first year at university. Got to eat all the good stuff nobody wanted. Unfortunately it all ended up here." She pointed at her massive breasts and hips. They laughed.

The mate came out of the hatchway behind the three.

"What's this all about then?" His gaze focused on Émile.

Henri Fauré, the *Dorado's* first mate was born on Mahé in the Seychelles and had spent his life after the age of ten at sea. A tower of a man, close to seven feet tall and near three hundred pounds in weight, his powerful fists maintained discipline on Captain Drayton's ships. Abigail was first to turn and face him. She smiled and took a deep breath. His entire persona seemed to collapse.

"So sorry, Miss Lithwick. Didn't mean to disturb, but the captain desires your company and that of Mister Spreadborough in the salon, if you please." He almost bowed.

"All right, Monsieur Fauré. Thank you very much. Come along, Johnny. Let's go see what Bligh has in store for us." She grabbed the writer by the arm and they went forward to the gangway that led up to the salon.

The mate looked to Émile. "Right, *sous-chef* Jean-Philippe or whoever you are, get yourself below to the galley. The boat deck's for paying passengers only." He pointed toward the next hatchway.

"Yessir, Monsieur Mate. I did not know my way and those two asked to speak with me." Émile walked along the boat deck to the next hatchway. *If I had my knife, I could take this bully. He's big, but slow. They're always easy. Maybe I can find a knife in the galley?*

* * *

Rarotonga was still below the horizon when Captain Drayton summoned Émile to his cabin.

"Take a berth, lad." The captain nodded toward the small table. He poured two cups of coffee from the carafe on the sidebar. Adding milk and sugar without asking, he sat in the chair opposite Émile and slid a cup toward him.

"Jean, I've been most impressed by your skills in the galley. Kwan says you're a welcome addition, even if he is a bit green-eyed about it. Takes some of the pressure off him, any road. You're thinking about going ashore at Avarua, are you not? Just wanted you to know there's a permanent berth on the *Dorado,* if you be wanting it."

Émile took a sip of coffee. Too sweet. "*Merci beaucoup, mon capitaine,* for everything. *Mais,* I think it best if I go ashore on Rarotonga. Your next port is New Caledonia, *n'est-ce pas?*"

Drayton nodded and stirred his coffee. He stood, turned to his small desk and took Émile's passport from a drawer.

"I prefer to remain in the British islands," Émile said. *My papers may not pass a close scrutiny by the French authorities.*

"Will you be wanting the cutter then?" Drayton sat and handed Émile his passport.

Émile had almost forgotten about the boat he'd stolen. He shook his head.

"I thought not." Drayton reached inside his coat and removed something from a wallet. "No worries there. Weren't any registration numbers to be found." Drayton sat back in his chair and was silent for a moment. He leaned forward and slid two New Zealand ten-pound notes across the table. "Can't put a man ashore without a bean in his pocket. Don't want it known that Marlow Drayton is a mean cheapskate."

"*Merci beaucoup, mon capitaine.* I am eternally in your debt." Émile slipped the passport and the banknotes into his oilskin pouch. He didn't mention that Wiggie and Spreadborough had already loaned him a few pounds.

"There's a former servicemen's association on Rarotonga. You be a veteran, even if it was the *Swiss* Army." The captain had a smirk on his face. "But, no matter. Decent bar. Go chat with them. Wiggie'll know them all. Maybe they'll have something for you. Hate to lose you. You're a good hand. Something else going on, right?" He raised his hands. "Don't want to know about it. Folks should mind their own business. We'll slip you off after dark. Avarua's a sleepy little place. No one'll be the wiser. There'll be nothing to say you were ever on board. The rest of the crew knows the routine." He offered his hand to Émile. "*Bonne chance,* lad."

* * *

When the *Dorado* dropped anchor outside of Avatiu Harbor, no lighters put out from shore to meet them.

"What the bloody hell? This isn't Sunday." Captain Drayton scanned the harbor with his binoculars. "There's no one about at all." He put down his binos and reached for the microphone of his wireless.

"It's Anzac Day," Wiggie said. "The whole lot of 'em will be over at the RSA having a proper knees up." The purser had come to the bridge to bid farewell to the captain.

"Right you are, Wiggie, my friend. Forget these southern ocean holidays at times. So be it." He leaned back in his chair and folded his arms. "Not much cargo to off load. We'll use the ship's boats." He looked toward the harbor. "Might be a bit of fun to join the celebration, but needs must." Drayton turned to face Wiggie. "Sure you won't stay signed on? Could be a few extra pounds in it for you."

Wiggie extended his hand to the captain. "Much appreciated, Marlow, old friend, but I need to put my feet on dry land for a bit. Look me up when you return. I may be sick of civilization by then." They shook hands.

"Surprised the harbormaster didn't come out," Drayton said. "I tried to reach him by wireless an hour ago. Seems no one will be vetting our cargo."

"Berrynabor? He's an old Gallipoli hand. Probably led the march pass and is organizing the song fest at the RSA." Wiggie lowered his voice and motioned the captain to the port rail. "Brilliant time for our castaway to slip ashore." He pointed down to the cargo deck where Émile stood looking at the island and talking to Henri. "I'll see to him. You're going to miss his cooking and baking skills, are you not?"

"Aye, that's a true thing, Wiggie. The punters . . . the female ones, any road . . . were a constant presence in the galley. Bit of a bother. They wanted his recipes. Kwan was not amused." Drayton saw Spreadborough join Émile on the deck. "Those two have been thick as thieves, have they not?"

"Well spotted, Marlow. Think the writer's not as sold about Jean's tale as the other passengers. We're agreed on that—too many holes in the man's bucket."

"Did Spreadborough mention where he's bound for next?"

"Said something about hiring a schooner to Rakahanga."

"Rakahanga? There's nothing there. Got cleared off once by blackbirders and never quite recovered. Less than two hundred souls, last I knew. Was a trading station, but I heard they'd shut it. Well, no matter. Writers are a strange lot."

"That's the *Moana Tama* inside, is it not?" The purser pointed to the two-masted, white-hulled schooner anchored near a jetty.

"Right you are. One of the last of the copra schooners. Still part of the Southern Cross's fleet, I hear tell."

Wiggie smiled and nodded. "Yes, mate. Reggie Pobjoy has kept her in service. Nothing to compare with his new ships, but there's a bit of sentiment to all this. Somewhat of a love affair with the old island schooners, especially about the *Moana Tama*. She was my first berth in the Cooks. Reggie said she's the spittin' image of the *Wallaroo*." Wiggie lit a cigarette and offered one to the captain. "Did you be knowin' that one, Marlow?"

"No, Wiggie. Before my time."

"And what about a Harry Houchins or a Davie McCombs?"

"No, my friend. All pre-war, isn't it? Only been out here since '47."

"Well, my captain, those two were almost legends in the Cooks before the war. Put the stops to a typhoid outbreak in '38, they did."

"How's Pobjoy connected to all this, any road?"

"He was cabin boy . . . his first berth by the way . . . on the *Wallaroo* when she made the dash to Pukapuka with the medicos and drugs to stop the typhoid. He and Tooks Marsten, the first mate, were the only survivors when a cyclone sunk the schooner in Suwarrow lagoon on its return to Raro."

"Suwarrow? That's a bad luck place, if I ever heard of one. Met that

Yank writer, Freshour, first time I dropped anchor off here. Told me his story about the cyclone of '42. He and his brood were lucky not to come a cropper."

"Right you are." Wiggie stepped back and saluted. "Now, Captain Marlow, sir, if you'll have Henri lower a boat, I'll be on my way. I'll keep an eye on Jean until he gets sorted."

Marlow laughed and shouted down to the first mate, "Henri, the small lifeboat for our departing guests, if you please."

* * *

"Well, Jean, what do you think of the thriving metropolis of Avarua?" Spreadborough said.

"Much smaller than Pape'ete, *n'est-ce pas?* No one about. Seems deserted."

Wiggie joined them at the rail. "Anzac Day, *mes amis,* a big celebration of the Kiwis' and Aussies' service in the wars," he said, "The march pass and wreath laying at the cenotaph should be finished shortly. Everyone'll be watching the rugby match near the airfield or boozing it up at the RSA. Or both."

They watched the crew lower a lifeboat and gangway ladder over the side.

The waterfront was lined with open sheds and boat houses, which had slips that ran down into the harbor. Most of the other buildings—all single story—were painted white and had red roofs. A road, probably of crushed coral, Émile thought, ran behind the sheds. Other buildings and thatched huts sat scattered amongst the coconut palms on the coastal plain. Two jetties extended out from the shore. A flotilla of more than a dozen lighters was moored between them.

Émile looked at the verdant green mountains that rose out of the morning mist in the center of Rarotonga.

This is similar to Moorea across the channel from Pape'ete. How will I get on with these English? Wiggie's led me to believe that they don't look too closely at one's papers. He claims to know some important, or at least influential, people here. Maybe I'll find my bolt-hole somewhere in these islands.

The first mate stood in the stern of the life boat, one hand on the tiller. Another crew member held the boat close to the base of the ladder. Henri motioned for the three men to come aboard. Spreadborough, Wiggie, and Émile filed down the ladder and remained standing when the crew member pushed off. The lifeboat headed toward shore. Émile looked back at the ship, and saw the passengers standing along the railing outside the ship's salon. He raised a hand in farewell. Only Abigail Lithwick waved back.

31

The first mate eased the lifeboat up onto the shore between the two jetties. The three men hopped over the side onto the crushed coral beach.

"*Au revoir. A bientôt,*" Henri said.

"See you next time, mate," Wiggie shouted over his shoulder.

Spreadborough hurried across the beach between a boat repair shop and a small warehouse, heading for the Banana Court Hotel. He was nearly run down by a grandmother on a motor scooter. A young girl rode sideways behind her. The girl laughed and waved at the men. The writer dashed over the road and up the stairs of the hotel's verandah. Émile and Wiggie waited at the road's edge as an ancient Ford pickup truck, its cab and back filled with islanders, sped by. The driver honked, and everyone waved and shouted "*Kia orāna.*" Wiggie and Émile returned the greeting.

"What does *kia orāna*—did I say it properly—mean?" Émile asked.

"Well done, mate. Hello. Or G'day. Usual Cook Island greeting."

Several more islanders passed on bicycles or motor scooters. They were all going in the same direction—west.

Wiggie pointed after the last group. "That's where we're bound for, Jean. The RSA is down the road a piece by the airfield. Just a short stroll and a chance to get back our shore legs, and work up a proper thirst."

"Wiggie, *mon ami,* I look forward to joining this celebration, but I must get some things of my own to wear." Émile spread his arms and looked down. He still wore the kit Wiggie had loaned him—duck trousers, white shirt, and canvas shoes. "I want to purchase a hat to protect my face from the sun." His week-old beard helped some with the healing.

"Right you are, mate, but all'll be shut today. Most sure Reggie will have closed his store, but we'll take a peek as we pass by." The two men started walking west along the road. More celebrants passed.

"This is a major festival, *non?*" Émile said.

"That it is, Jean. There'll be a rugby scrum on the pitch near the airfield. And a right proper boozer at the RSA after. Lots of wonderful island grub. Most likely go on until first light tomorrow."

"This RSA, is it the serviceman's club the captain mentioned? He said you know everyone there."

"Ha! That's Marlow talking out of turn again. No worries. Yes, I do know some of the major players in these islands, but not all. Just follow my lead, mate, and we'll get you sorted. Here's Reggie's shop."

The sign above the overhanging roof that covered the verandah read Southern Cross Trading Company. Wiggie tried the door—locked. He looked through a window next to the door. "We're in luck. Good ol' Ned's inside." He rapped on the glass.

A quite thin, gaunt even, man unlocked the door and stepped out onto verandah. "We're shut, it's Anzac . . . Oh, it's you Wiggie." His face expanded in a giant smile. "Well done, mate. When'd you come ashore?" He extended his hand.

"Just jumped ship off Marlow Drayton's barge." He took the man's hand. "All right are you now? Thought you might be back on Suwarrow again. Given that up, have you?"

"No. Not at all. Had some offers for a book. Been putting aside a few bob and hope to go back next year. Who's your friend?"

Wiggie turned to Émile. "Jean, formally of the Swiss Army's Chef's battalion . . . and in need of some kit. Nothing too fancy or dear, if you please."

"*Kia orāna,* Jean. Welcome to Rarotonga. Been here before?"

"No, Monsieur. My first time." They shook hands. The three men walked into the store.

"What are you in need of, guv?" Ned asked Émile.

"A shirt or two, *bien sûr.* And short pants, maybe one pair of trousers like these . . . and some shoes . . . and a hat."

"Would you like island shirts or *pommy* shirts?"

"What is the difference? Sorry, I don't understand."

"Well, guv, the island shirts are more colorful, and the *pommy* shirts are basic white or a pale blue—more formal. Maybe, one of each would be good for a start." Ned pulled two shirts off a shelf and laid them on the counter. "What's next? Shorts?" He looked at Émile and said, "You're about average size. These should do." He added two pair of khaki shorts to the shirts. "For the trousers, you'll have to come back when Elaine is in to give you a proper fitting."

"Slow down, Ned. We haven't had an accounting of all this yet," Wiggie said.

"No worries there, Wiggie. There's an under-the-counter list of who Reggie says have no-end credit. If this chap's your mate, he's in the queue. What else you need, guv?"

"I'm on this list?" Wiggie asked. "No-end credit? Well, Bob's your uncle!" Wiggie reached for his wallet. "Been away for a bit. What's my ticket?"

Ned told him.

"As much as that is it? Right. Here it is." He handed Ned a handful of British pounds. "All done and dusted. And I may also come back for a proper fitting by our lovely Elaine." He winked at Émile.

"Thank you, Wiggie," Ned said, "Reggie'll be chuffed, and most likely buy a round at Skipper Jake's to celebrate."

"What's this Skipper Jake's all about then?"

"You've been away too long, mate. Remember Jake Cartwright, who came here a year or more ago from North Island?"

Wiggie nodded, but frowned like he was trying to recall the name. "Big man, blond hair?"

"Too right, mate. Jake served in Malaya with the SAS during the Emergency." Ned continued, "He's putting together a restaurant and bar along at the next cove. Skipper Jake's he calls it. He'll be up the road at the

RSA, if you're heading that way." He turned to Émile. "What else you be wanting, guv?"

"Some shoes. And a hat." Émile said. "And have you any knives?"

"Knives is it then? Lots of them here. What's your pleasure?" Ned pointed to a display case with dozens arrayed.

"My Swiss friend here is a gourmet chef, mate, and needs an example of your best cutlery," Wiggie said.

"Well, I don't know about the gourmet business, but there are a few blades more than better for filleting fish. Is that what you're about?"

Émile looked at the knives and selected a thin-bladed one. "That would be excellent for filleting fish, n'est-ce pas?" Then he pointed to a sturdy sheath knife with a six-inch blade. "And that one also, s'il vous plaît."

Wiggie, surprised by the second choice, remembered about the ex-Nazi copper getting butchered on Pape'ete. Maybe more to our "Swiss" friend than meets the eye, he wondered.

"So what's going on your feet then? Not much on offer, but can match those you're wearing." Ned pointed to Émile's feet.

"Oui, Monsieur, a pair like these and some, how you say, beach sandals."

"Jandles? Is that what you be wantin'?" Wiggie laughed. "You're getting to be a true Cook Islander quick as can be."

Émile was about to point to a floppy hat like the one he wore on Tahiti when Spreadborough entered the store.

"So this is where you all disappeared to? I take a moment to arrange for accommodations, and my friends abandon me. Quite uncivil for island folk, if you ask me." He looked at the pile of clothes, shoes, and knives on the counter. "New wardrobe, Jean? And new tools of the trade, n'est-ce pas? One for the kitchen and one for the belt."

What does this man know? But I don't believe him to be an enemy. More like a friend. Maybe not a friend, but a fellow traveler. Maybe a comrade. Not one who had shared experiences, but one who understands and accepts. Émile took a straw hat with a wide brim off a rack and laid it on the pile. "How much is all this together, Monsieur?"

Ned did a quick accounting with his fingers. "Well, guv, you won't get much change from a tenner."

Émile pulled a ten-pound note from his pouch and handed it to the clerk.

Wiggie laughed and slapped him on the back. "You're out to ruin my reputation, mon ami, paying up all at once like that. I bought an entire suit here on tick some years ago."

"Hard to fathom you ever owning a suit, Wiggie," Spreadborough said. "Best add a bar of soap and a teethbrush to that lot, Ned. The island's Ritz doesn't provide such amenities."

"Nice to see you again, Mister Spreadborough," Ned said as he placed the toiletries on the counter. "Your book selling well, is it? I've had an offer to write something about my time on Suwarrow and would fancy some advice about the publishing scheme." He reached behind, took a canvas belt off a rack and added it to the pile. "You'll be wanting this . . . no charge . . . to hold up your shorts, guv, and for your knife."

"You secured us a berth at the Banana Court, have you now?" Wiggie asked the writer.

"Right you are, Wiggie. Only one room with two singles, but they'll set up a cot. We can spin a coin for it."

"*Merci beaucoup,* Monsieur Spreadborough. I insist on paying my share of the tariff."

"We'll sort out those boring details later, Jean-Philippe."

"Monsieur Ned, is there a room where I may change my clothes?"

Émile appeared from a backroom in his new outfit—shorts, the flowery shirt, jandles, and his straw hat. He handed the borrowed clothes to Wiggie.

"You'll need a carry-all for the rest, guv," Ned said. He took a cloth bag out from under the counter and offered it to Émile. "I'll mark it down on Wiggie's account." They all laughed.

"Join us for a pint, Ned?" Wiggie said, as he stuffed the returned clothes into his kit bag.

"Another time, perhaps. Not much for crowds these days. Inventory to get sorted and all."

"Any chance of us stowing these bags here, mate? Still sleeping in the storeroom, are you?"

"No, Wiggie," Ned said and chuckled. "You *have* been away for a bit. I've a family now and a small place on the road near the police station. But, I'll gladly secure them in your room at the Banana Court on my way home."

"Right you are. Well, lads, time's a-wastin'. All this chatting is thirsty business. Let's be off." Wiggie headed out the door. "*Meitaki ma´ata,* Ned."

"Come by the Banana Court bar tomorrow when you finish here, Ned," Spreadborough said, "and we'll chat about the book trade."

Out on the road, a motor scooter ridden by two young women passed by. The passenger waved, and the flowered wreath flew off her head. She turned, laughed, and pointed to her head. Wiggie picked up the wreath and handed it to Émile.

"Jean, this'll go nicely on your new hat. Put you right in the proper festive spirit."

Émile laid the wreath over the hat's crown. *What beautiful women. Just like in Tahiti. Been a while. Maybe I'll find someone here.*

"Perhaps you'll have a bit of luck, *mon ami,*" Spreadborough said, "and she'll come looking to retrieve it."

"Right you are there, mate. She *was* a bit of all right," Wiggie said.

Avarua's Returned and Services' Association occupied a large Nissen hut, which sat across the road from the airfield. Awash with red, white, and blue bunting, the building had Australian and New Zealand flags displayed in abundance at every entrance. Window shutters along the sides were propped open. In the grassy space between the building and the lagoon's edge, tables and chairs were scattered about beneath palm frond shelters. Crowd noises flowed from the rugby match across the road on the other side of the airfield. The three heard singing as they approached the building.

"Roll me over, in the clover. Roll me over, lay me down, and do it again."

"Sure enough, that's Berrynabor leading that," Wiggie said.

"Gettin' on a bit to be such a randy ol' goat, isn't he?" Spreadborough said.

"It's the islands, mate. The women here make sure you're never too old."

The writer smiled and nodded in agreement.

"Wiggie, who is this Berrynabor? Someone I should meet?" Émile said.

"Not straight off, Jean. Truth be told, we should steer around him for a bit until we get you sorted. He's the harbormaster and will want to know who came ashore. Just keep it shut, smile, and follow my lead. If I say you're the bloody king of Araby, just nod and act stupid." Wiggie pointed toward a door halfway along the side of the building. "Right, lads. Into the breach."

Cigarette smoke, music from a ukulele band, and noise—noise from people talking, laughing, shouting, greeting friends—struck Émile when he entered the RSA. The building, ten yards wide and three times that or more in length, was packed with partiers. Flags from all the Western Allies, and some Émile didn't recognize, hung from the ceiling. Rows of banquet tables ran the length of the hall. A drinks bar, with patrons three-deep, occupied the back wall. A few round tables near the front by the raised stage—probably reserved for dignitaries, he thought—were empty.

Wiggie led his mates along one side toward the bar. He paused for a quick word and hand shake with several people who stood as they passed. Maybe, Émile thought, Wiggie was indeed known on the island. Others also greeted Spreadborough. As they neared the bar, two men with pints in hand turned and paused. Military medals were affixed above the left breast pocket of their jackets.

"Wiggie! What palm tree did you fall out of?" asked a wiry-built, sun-browned man.

"Should we associate with a ne'er-do-well *pommy* ex-para on this auspicious day?" asked the other, a big man with blond hair. Both men grinned

Wiggie laughed and turned to Spreadborough and Émile. "Gentlemen, I would very much like to introduce two of my very close mates, Reggie Pobjoy and Jake Cartwright. One is a pirate and gunrunner, and the other is a bootlegger and probably a white slaver. But they're mates, so there it is."

Wiggie got a handshake from each of the men.

Émile enjoyed the exchange. *This is the same banter he'd had with comrades in the Légion. Obviously, there're old friends, or fists and knives would have been in play.*

"How long you ashore for this time, you ol' barnacle?" Reggie asked.

"Who knows? I was *sous-chef* on the *Dorado*, but moved up in status to purser after a Paluan *kanaka* jumped ship in the Frog islands. Kowtowing to a passel of foreign punters about did me in." Wiggie nodded toward Spreadborough. "You be knowing this chap, of course."

"The scribbler? Of course. Well met. Do any publicity work, John?" Jake said.

"Why do you ask?" Spreadborough started to pull his notebook out of a pocket but stopped.

"About to open a new establishment down the road. Would like the word spread about a bit. Can't pay much, but an open bar bill might be on offer."

"And who's your mate with the fancy hat?" Reggie asked.

"Ah," Wiggie said, "Let me introduce you to Jean-Philippe, late of the Swiss Army culinary corps, and chef at many fine restaurants in Pape'ete. Presently *sous-chef* on the *Dorado*."

"Don't remember that many fine restaurants in Pape'ete, Wiggie," Jake said, "Pull the other one, mate."

"You goin' back onboard then? A bit of shore leave, is it?" Reggie asked Émile.

Émile didn't know how to answer. He looked to Wiggie, who shrugged and said, "Maybe not. It's a bit of a sticky wicket, Reggie."

Reggie looked hard at Émile, and then turned his attention to the writer. "John, I know you to be an honorable man. Not like some I could mention. And it's a pleasure to see you again." He held out his hand. "What's the story here? You're all being a bit too vague for my taste."

"Good to see you again also, Captain Pobjoy. May we sit somewhere private for a few minutes?"

"Right. This'll do." Reggie pulled out a chair at the end of an empty table. He motioned for the others to join him. "Get us a round, Wiggie. It's on the house, so no whinging."

Reggie and Jake listened while Spreadborough relayed his, and Wiggie's, knowledge of Émile's story. The two Cook Islands men glanced at Émile as the story unfolded. Émile remained silent throughout, but once his right hand caressed the handle of the sheath knife. Wiggie returned with a tray of pints.

The crowd erupted in cheers and applause when the ukulele band was augmented on stage by a collection of island drummers and a troupe of dancers—teen-agers and young children, girls and boys. The girls wore grass skirts and coconut shell tops to cover their prepubescent breasts. The boys also wore grass skirts. All had floral head wreaths.

The attention of the men at the table shifted toward the stage, and they didn't notice the large, balding elderly man, with a jowly face, who'd come in a door on the lagoon side of the building. "Happy Anzac Day, chaps," he shouted. Benjamin W. Berrynabor, the harbormaster, looked at each man at the table as if trying to place names with faces. "Wiggie. Off the *Dorado*, are you then? I see she's just outside . . . off loading cargo, is she not?" He swayed side-to-side, reached down and took a drink from Jake's pint. "Any passengers ashore?"

Wiggie nodded toward the writer. "Just one, your excellency."

"Don't be a prat, Wiggie. Just goin' about my business . . . I know Spreadborough . . . all the time goin' and comin.'" He looked at Émile. "Who's this new face then?"

How do I answer him? Will he demand to see my passport? Wiggie said to remain quiet and let him talk. I don't want to return to the ship.

"Not to bother, Ben. He's the ship's assistant cook. Was lookin' to secure a few fresh fruits and veggies. Forgot it was Anzac Day. Be going back aboard after a pint or two. Henri, the mate, should be along presently with a manifest."

"Right . . . Well done. Carry on. Just need to get meself a pint." The harbormaster nodded and turned toward the bar.

Wiggie watched Berrynabor until he was well immersed in the crowd at the bar, and then turned to his friends. "That should keep him sorted for a while."

"Well played, mate," Reggie said. The others nodded, except Émile.

"Wiggie, do I have to go back to the ship?"

"No, *mon ami*, you'll get so legless tonight you'll miss the *Dorado's* sailing." Wiggie looked at Reggie, winked, and raised his glass. "These things happen, do they not, *Captain* Pobjoy?"

"Well remembered, Wiggie. But that's another story." Reggie grinned.

"I most surely would like to hear *that* story, Captain Pobjoy," Spreadborough said.

Reggie laughed and said, "Having a writer underfoot is near as bad as a bloody journalist. And, John, we can drop the *Captain* Pobjoy, if you please. It's Reggie. Right, mate?"

"Oh, thank you very much, sir . . . I mean Reggie." He looked after the harbormaster. "I wonder if he knows of any vessels bound for Rakahanga?"

Another outburst of applause turned their attention to the front of the building. Three young women replaced the children on the stage. Dressed only in colorful short *pareus* and halter tops—coconut shells not providing adequate coverage—each wore a hibiscus behind the right ear. They started a dance that caused a raucous outburst from the crowd. The dancers twitched and waggled their hips in an unmistakeably suggestive manner.

"Want to secure a closer look, mates?" Wiggie said to Émile and Spreadborough. Without waiting for an answer, he said, "I'm for it." He took a pint in each hand and maneuvered through the crowd toward the front of the hall. Émile followed.

"Aren't those tables up front reserved for toffs?" Spreadborough asked.

"Too right, John," Reggie said, "but the Pooh-Bahs have been and gone. Did a few bloody speeches, and then legged it off to the Commissioner's for warm Pym's and finger food. One or two may slip back in for a look at the local talent. After they've sent their wives home, of course. But no worries. Go sit with your mates." Reggie looked at Jake, then said, "We'll be with you in a bit."

Other partiers started to shift to the VIP tables when Wiggie secured one center floor. He pulled out a chair for Émile and tilted three others. Spreadborough joined them.

"It's the *ura pa'u*—drum—dance," Wiggie shouted.

Émile nodded. He'd seen island dancing on Tahiti—mostly in bars along the Pape'ete waterfront—but nothing like this. And there was something familiar about the dancer on the left.

Spreadborough leaned over and said, "That's the girl from the motorbike. The one whose wreath you're wearing."

Émile looked up. The girl gave him a big smile, pointed to her head, and nodded. Embarrassed, he looked around at the other tables. A tiny toddler stood by the next table and attempted to follow the movements on stage. Other women of all ages did the same in the aisles between the banquet tables. A shout from the crowd in Maori had people on their feet, clapping.

The tallest and oldest dancer jumped down, ran over to their table, and pulled Wiggie up on stage. He shouted over his shoulder, "When in Rome." Wiggie pranced around the stage stomping his feet and flailing his arms. The crowd loved it, and many stood and applauded. With his hands behind his head, he wiggled and thrust his hips forward and back in an obscene manner, which brought howls from the audience. He then jumped off the stage and returned to the table. Reggie and Jake had joined them.

Wiggie took a long drink from his pint. Sweat poured off his brow and down the sides of his face. "You're next in the queue, *mon ami.*"

Émile was afraid that might happen, and squirmed in his chair. He was rescued by the arrival of the rugby players through the side doors. The crowd cheered or moaned when the word spread of the match's result—Titikaveka fifteen, Arorangi eight.

The music and dancing stopped while the players and fans poured into the building—most aimed for the bar. Already crowded, the RSA was now like a can of sardines.

"Fifteen to eight. That's a bit lopsided, is it not?" Reggie said.

"Not to be surprised, mate," Jake said. "Titikaveka did have a ringer, did they not? Your partner's cousin, Talfai Marsten? Didn't he play half back for the All Blacks?"

"Right you are." Reggie looked around at the crowd. "Be best to secure something to eat, mates. This mob will clear the decks in no time."

"Do the Swiss know rugby, Jean?" Jake asked as they stood from the table.

"Oh, *oui*, Monsieur, but I prefer the football." Émile wanted to steer the conversation away from Swiss rugby. He remembered the jubilation when France finally won against the New Zealand All Blacks five years earlier when he was in Indochina.

The men went out through a door on the lagoon side of the building and joined the queue at the buffet, which had been set up on tables under a marquee next to the building. Island mamas, wearing multi-colored muumuus, and floral wreaths on their heads, piled food on the plates—half chickens, roasted pig, *kumara,* taro, wahoo, mangos, and bananas.

"Not like the fare on the *Dorado,* is it, Jean?" Wiggie said.

Émile was impressed by the variety of foods, and the aromas. "Is there not any bread? Or cheese?" he asked.

"No, *mon ami,* no wheat grown on the islands," Wiggie said. "*Kumara*—a bit like a sweet potato—fills that gap. Most folks, like the hotel, do their own baking with imported flour."

They sat at a table near the lagoon. When Reggie had half-finished his meal, he walked to the water's edge and lit a cigarette. The *Dorado* remained anchored outside the reef. A thin column of smoke rose from her stack.

"Monsieur Cartwright, I have a question, *s'il vous plaît.*"

Jake, who was watching Reggie, turned to Émile. "Fire away."

"This wonderful festival. How is everything free? The beer, the food, everything."

"Well, Jean . . . may I call you Jean?"

"*Oui, bien sûr,* of course. May I call you Jake?"

"Right you are, mate. To answer your question, this whole brouhaha is paid for by Reggie and some others. He put up most of the dosh. And strong-armed the local bureaucrats and businesses for the rest . . . especially those who never served in the forces."

I don't know this word, dosh. Maybe slang for money. I must make a good impression on Reggie. He may be able help me find a position here.

"Monsieur Reggie served in the forces?" Émile asked.

"Right you are, Jean. He was a tail gunner in a 'Wimpy'. That's a British Wellington bomber . . . 75 Squadron, Royal New Zealand Air Force. Shot down over France in '41, I think. Spent three years in the *stalag.* But that's all before your time isn't it. Anyway, you're Swiss, so you were on the sidelines of that one. Just like the first war." He took a drink from his beer.

Spreadborough had his notebook out, writing furiously.

I so want to tell them that I've also fought in a war, an ugly war that Jake would understand, having served in Malaya against the Communists. If I tell them the truth— that I'd been with the Légion in Algeria and Indochina—my stature in their eyes would increase. But then, the questions. Too many questions. I'm not Émile Plude, ex-légionnaire anymore. I'm just Jean-Philippe, sous-chef off the Dorado. I'll stay in this role for now.

Reggie didn't return to the table but walked around to the east side of the RSA building where there was a small cemetery.

"Where's he off to now?" Wiggie said.

"Most likely to have a chat with Alberti," Jake said.

"Who's Alberti?" Spreadborough asked.

Jake didn't answer straight away, and then took a drink from his pint. "Albert Freshour—a Yank—was a writer and trader, who wandered across the southern ocean for many years. Reggie met him on Pukapuka during the typhoid scare in '38. Alberti, as he was known, gave Reggie some advice about to how to deal with folks. He's never forgotten that. He warrants it for his success, and visits Alberti's grave site often, especially on Anzac Day."

"How does this Freshour rate a headstone in the RSA cemetery?" Spreadborough said, pen poised over his notebook.

"Not at all sure of the whole of it, but he served in the American forces in the first war, so when he died of TB here on Raro, that honor was arranged. You'll have to ask Reggie for more details. But *not* today, mate," Jake said.

Wiggie stood to go to the bar and get another round, but paused when he saw Henri, the *Dorado's* first mate filling a doorway, his eyes searching the crowd, a sheaf of papers in his hand. Wiggie knew who he was looking for and spotted the harbormaster at a distant table.

"Jean, your turn to make a run at the scrum . . . the bar," Wiggie said. "No hurry. We've enough for a bit. Off you go, *mon ami.*"

Émile wondered why he was sent to get the drinks, but didn't question it—only too happy to please his new friends. He made his way toward the door nearest the bar.

Wiggie watched Henri steer his bulk around the people between the tables and hand the ship's manifest to the harbormaster. Berrynabor didn't bother to look at the papers—laid them on the table—but by his actions Wiggie could tell he'd invited the mate to sit and have a drink. Henri shook his head, gave a perfunctory salute and went back through the crowd into the building.

"That's sorted then," Wiggie said.

Émile returned to the table with a tray of drinks. He stood for a moment looking out to sea. The ocean waves pounded on the barrier reef sending sheets of foam skyward. Clouds began to congregate on the western horizon, arriving in time to create a glorious sunset. Out beyond the reef, the *Dorado* had raised her anchor and thick black smoke poured from her funnel. He wondered if anyone else noticed.

They had.

"Marooned you are now, Jean-Philippe," Spreadborough said, "Marooned in paradise." He raised his pint in salute and lit a cigarette.

Émile smiled and placed the tray on the table. He started to clear away the empty glasses and plates.

"None of that, mate," Jake said, "You're our guest. There're others to sort that out."

Émile nodded and sat. "*Pardon,* Jake. A habit, *n'est-ce pas?*"

"Did some restaurant work, did you not then?"

" Oh, *oui,* In . . . Martigny. That's a small city in Switzerland near the border with France." He almost said Paris, but stopped himself in time. "I worked for a while at a small inn. And I was a cook in the Swiss Army."

Jake took a drink from his pint and nodded toward Wiggie. "This *pommy* said you worked at some posh bistros in Pape'ete. Not that I ever found a posh bistro in that Frog sewer."

What do I answer now? I don't want to insult Wiggie. He's done so much for me. "I did pass some time as *sous-chef* in a wharf-front bar. Quinn's. Do you know it?"

"Quinn's? Damn right I know it. I plan to be its competitor in this part of the southern ocean. But without the 'Suzie No-pants', thank you very much." He laughed and took another drink. "Jean, my man, if you can hold your own with the crowd at Quinn's, I think I may have something for you at my new place. That's, of course, if you're planning to stay on Raro for a bit."

Émile nodded. "*Merci beaucoup,* Monsieur . . . I mean Jake." *I wonder why he doesn't like the French?* "I have been all the positions in a restaurant from *plongeur*—dishwasher—waiter, and *sous-chef.*"

"Nothing exotic to start with," Jake continued. "No fancy Frog *haute cuisine,* but maybe something past the usual fish'n chips and hamburgers."

"I'd like to have your impressions of Quinn's at a later date, Jean-Philippe," Spreadborough said. "It *is* a notoriously famous spot in the islands." He continued to write in his notebook.

Will they discover that I never worked at Quinn's, just drank there? Maybe that was one lie too many? Why didn't I say Madame Flynn's pension? It's not as well known. And the truth.

"Waste of time, I'd say," Wiggie said. "You've been there, John." He turned in his chair and said, "Now, look at this, will you."

Reggie returned to the table with a dancer on his arm—the dancer who owned Émile's hat wreath. Spreadborough stood. Émile followed his example. The other two remained seated.

"This lass says you have something that belongs to her, Jean-Philippe." Reggie said smiling. He pulled a chair from another table and placed it next to Émile.

The dancer sat and said, "*Kia orāna.* My name is Nga . . . Ngatokorua, but you can call me 'Bobbie'. Please don't stand." Émile and the writer took their seats. She smiled and placed a hand on Émile's thigh. "And what is your name?"

Émile, lost in the dark beauty of her eyes, stumbled to answer. "*Je suis... Oh, pardon* . . . Oh, I'm sorry . . . Jean . . . Jean-Philippe . . . Jean-Philippe ." He almost knocked over a pint of beer as he reached to shake her hand.

She laughed and said, "Jean-Philippe. What a pretty name. Are you French?" She lightly touched his offered hand.

"*Ah, oui, mais non.* I'm Swiss from a French-speaking canton." *Damn. I about did it again.*

"I remember learning about Swiss . . . er . . . Switzerland in school. A little country in Europe with many mountains. Lots of snow. I've never seen snow. Looks very cold." She took a drink from someone's pint. "What's a canton?"

Too many questions. And the others are watching. Must change the conversation. Why are my palms wet? God, I love the sound of her voice. "Do you live here on Rarotonga?"

"No, Jean-Philippe from Switzerland, I'm from Raka . . . Rakahanga."

"Where is that? Is that another island?" he asked. *So beautiful. I wonder how old she is.*

Bobbie laughed. "Yes, Jean-Philippe, it is a very small island many days from here."

Her laugh. There's something about her laugh that reminds me of Musette. Musette. I haven't thought about her for so long. "How did you come here?" *What else can I ask her?*

She laughed again and said, "On Uncle Reggie's beautiful schooner, the *Moana Tama*—the *most* beautiful ship in the South Pacific." She smiled and nodded toward the ship's owner.

"Thank you, Bobbie," Reggie said. "Toa, Bobbie's real uncle, worked for me here on Raro before he became *ariki*—chief—on Raka. I've known her since she was knee-high to a coconut crab."

"Will you be returning to Rakahanga, Bobbie?" Spreadborough asked. "I'd like very much to spend some time on that atoll. Haven't been to that one. Understand it has a quite tragic history. Would enjoy hearing the stories from the descendents of those who were blackbirded."

Bobbie frowned. She looked taken aback by this abrupt question about the island's past. She took another drink from someone's pint. "It's not a part of our story that we enjoy talking about. And *who* are you?"

Wiggie, who seemed to have dozed off, jumped in. "Don't mind him, Bobbie. He's a writer, and they always ask rude questions."

Bobbie looked at Wiggie, shook her head with a puzzled expression, and said, "And who are *you?*"

I love the way she's handling these two. She's obviously never met them and isn't intimidated. Wish they would go to the bar. Or jump in the lagoon.

Wiggie stood, bowed and said, "Malfrey Pichot-Wiggins. At your service. But my friends call me 'Wiggie'." He nodded toward the writer. "And this is John Spreadborough, another *pommy*, as these colonials call us. He's a chronicler of life on the islands. And not a bad chap." Wiggie sat.

Spreadborough reached across the table to shake her hand. "My extreme pleasure, Miss Bobbie."

The girl laughed again. "You have some interesting friends, Uncle Reggie." She looked up as a giant of a man approached their table. "Here's our hero."

Talfai Marsten reminded Émile of Henri Fauré—tall, wide, and solid.

The former All Blacks half-back nodded to Reggie and said, "*Kia orāna,* Uncle. My cousin still on North Island?"

"Right you are, son. Tooks radioed last evening. The *Suwarrow* passed inspection, so he'll be on his way soon as he's finished uploading cargo. Not much doin' today, being Anzac Day and all." Reggie looked around for another empty chair. "Fancy joinin' us?"

Talfai shook his head. "Sorry, Uncle, Must go celebrate with my mates. Came to pay my respects. Good to see you again. *Aere ra.* Good bye." He turned and walked toward the bar.

"Tooks best have my new reefer on board," Jake said. "Be filling it with top quality New Zealand beef and lamb for the punters."

"He does for sure, mate," Reggie said. "He be knowin' it's a priority. Be ashore before you open."

"When's opening day, Jake?" Wiggie asked.

"Most likely in a fortnight or two," Jake said. "Looking for a few free drinks, are you, mate?"

Wiggie, put off by that remark, turned his attention to Bobbie. "What brought you this far south? Not Anzac Day surely?"

"No . . . Wiggie. I came for a wedding. Another cousin from Rakahanga has married a man from North Island and will return with him . . . to Auckland. I'd never leave my island forever. I love my island."

I love the sound of her voice, her smile, her laugh, everything. How long will she be on Raro? How can I see her again? Where is Rakahanga? How can I get there? John asked earlier about going there. Is it my bolt-hole—where I want to hide from my past? What would I do? I have no money.

Bobbie stood. "I must find my cousins, the other dancers," she said. "We're invited to the Commissioner's for a performance." She turned and smiled at Émile. "I hope we meet again, Jean-Philippe from Switzerland. Keep the wreath. It's a gift. Come to Rakahanga someday. It's a beautiful island. No mountains. No snow, but beautiful." She gave Reggie a peck on his cheek and a rub on his nose, and then wove her way through the tables toward the building.

"Where do you look when you're looking at something like that?" Wiggie said.

Émile felt a twinge of jealousy. *She's not for you, mon ami.*

* * *

The sun set with a glorious display of colors. The running lights of the *Dorado* faded over the horizon. A soft breeze flowed through the outdoor tables. The surf had stopped pounding the reef, and a small boat went out from the harbor.

"Should organize some fireworks." Jake said. He nodded toward the lagoon.

"Fireworks?" Émile asked. "What are fireworks?"

"You don't know fireworks, Jean? Rockets, Roman candles, starbursts—pyrotechnics." Jake looked confused. "I'm sure they have them in . . . Switzerland."

Of course. How stupid of me to ask. How do I get out of this? "*Bien sûr.* I'm sorry, Jake, it was a word I didn't know. *Oui* . . .Yes. *Feux d'artifice*—pyrotechnics. We have them at home."

"Right, Jake. We could set them up on the reef. A bit like the Yanks do on their Fourth of July Independence Day. Rockets' red glare and all that rubbish." He took a drink from his pint and lit a cigarette. "Been giving some thought about a proper show in my place next year. Might be good for business. Got a feel from a Chinaman in Shanghai who said he'd fix me up with whatever I need." Jake looked at Reggie. "If I can get a mate to make a run to the Commie mainland."

"You must be on the razzle, mate." Reggie said. The smile left his face.

"Not about to talk business here. Save it for another day." He finished his pint and stood. "And I must be off. Have to present myself at the Commissioner's do. Needs must." Before leaving he turned to Émile and said, "Come by the store tomorrow, Jean-Philippe. I know you've been there since you're wearing one of my shirts and the knife. We'll have a chat about your prospects."

* * *

Émile wasn't sure where he was when he woke the next morning. Before he opened his eyes, he knew he wasn't on the *Dorado*—no engine noises. It felt like he was on a cot, and the room was full of light and a new sound— palms rattling in the wind. It can't be the hospital in Saigon, he thought. That was years ago.

He opened his eyes and saw the two empty singles. *Where'd they go? What time is it? Oh, breakfast. Have I missed it?* Émile threw on his shirt and shorts. *Where's the breakfast room?* He never thought to ask that question of the smiling islander at the desk who welcomed him and his mates back to the hotel at some dark hour.

He went to the basin and splashed cold water on his face. *Damn, this beard is starting to itch. Maybe I'll shave under my chin.* In the mirror, bloodshot eyes peered back at him. *When did we get back? Does it matter? Non, not any more. There was more dancing. Everyone came out of the building for the fireworks. Wiggie almost fell into the lagoon. The mamas brought us a platter of chickens and wahoo— didn't want any goin' to waste. Said we needed some food. The ukulele band played . . . and the drummers. I barely remember returning to the hotel.*

Wearing jandles, unshaven, and a bit wobbly on his pins, Émile made his way down the hall searching for the hotel's breakfast room. A strong aroma of fried food made his stomach churn. *I hope I don't get sick.* His friends sat at a verandah-side table and were deep into their meals. Émile stared at their plates. *How can they eat that this early in the day?*

Wiggie was first to look up. "Jean, well done, mate. Dig in. They're about to finish it." He lifted a spoonful of baked beans. "Nothing like a full English breakfast to get you goin' in the morning. The bacon is good, but I prefer the bangers. If 'n you're hungry, get 'em both."

Thank God, Kwan insisted on frying the breakfast eggs and meats in the Dorado's galley for the British passengers. Then I could concentrate on baking the croissants and pastries.

A Maori girl with a big smile said, "Good morning, sir. Would you like what your friends are having?"

"*Non, pardon.* Just some coffee and a . . . Have you any bread?"

"Oh, yes, sir. We've toast and fried bread. Which would you prefer?"

"Nothing . . . ah . . . cooked or fried, please. Is there anything like a croissant, perhaps?"

"Oh, yes, sir. We have some dinner rolls from last evening. I can warm one up for you, if you like."

"*Bon.* That would be wonderful, Mademoiselle. Two, *s'il vous plaît,* please."

"Not keen on our morning repast, are you, Jean-Philippe?"

Spreadborough said as he waded into his plate of fried eggs, cooked tomatoes and mushrooms. "Same here as in Singapore, Hong Kong, Rangoon, Calcutta, Durban, and . . . Whitby. That's what made the Empire the Empire—British traditions, including food. Ask for an English breakfast, and you'll know what you'll get. Doesn't matter if you're in Apia or Adelaide." He pointed to an empty chair at their table. "Sit yourself, *mon ami.*"

Wiggie wiped up the last of his egg yolks and sausage drippings with a half slice of burnt toast. "He's spot on, this fella. But it won't be for long. Not if they run Winnie out of Number Ten. The whole world goin' up the spout." He took a drink from his cup.

Émile assumed it was coffee or maybe tea, but wasn't sure. The girl brought him a large mug of coffee and a plate with three warm rolls. Even in his mild state of morning-after inebriation, he enjoyed watching her walk back toward the kitchen. *She has the same movements that Bobbie has— natural, almost primitive. There's a flow—maybe it's the island culture. So lovely.* He broke open a roll and spread some butter from a dish on the table. The coffee was strong, but he didn't add anything to it. Not this morning.

"That's all you're having for breakfast, is it?" Wiggie asked.

To Émile, his friend looked like he was still half-in-the-bag. *Is there something else in his tea cup?* He nodded.

"Not to wonder Boney lost his empire." Wiggie said.

"*Pardon, mon ami,* Wiggie, *mais,* but what does that to do with me? And who is this 'Boney'?" *He might be talking about Napoleon. But I must play stupid, even with these two. For now.*

"Boney-part, Jean. Napoleon Boney-part." Wiggie said. "I know you've heard of him." He paused for a moment. "Didn't that pompous twit, Major Martingale, say Ol' Boney passed through your town on the way to Italy?"

"*Ah oui.* Napoleon did do that. I didn't know he was called 'Boney'." *Must be more careful with my lies. What else have I said that may come back to haunt me? Have to think. Have to remember.*

Spreadborough had a puzzled look on his face. "Off to see Captain Pobjoy about a position, are you, Jean-Philippe?"

Émile nodded and took a sip of coffee.

"Well, if anyone can organize a place for you in these islands, it'll be him. Right, Wiggie?"

"Right you are, mate. He'll get you sorted, if anyone can." Wiggie pushed his plate away and finished his tea. "I'd wait a bit before knocking him up, if I were you. He most likely had a longish evening with the Pooh-Bahs." Wiggie stood and pulled up his shorts. "Methnks, I'll take a stroll along the High Street and look in on Jake's new establishment." He turned to the writer. "Fancy joining me, John?"

"As far as the harbor. Need to chat with Berrynabor about passage to Rakahanga."

"Ha! Be surprised if he joins the living before luncheon. Let's all meet here in the hotel bar for tea."

The two Englishmen left the breakfast room and went down the hall toward the hotel lobby. Émile finished his rolls and coffee, and decided to shave his neck before going to meet Reggie.

Émile used John's shaving mug, brush, and razor. Careful not to cut himself, he cleaned his neck below the jaw line. A bottle of cologne rested on a shelf above the basin, but after a sniff, he decided not to use it—too feminine for his likes. He laid his sheath knife on the cot, placed his soiled clothes over it, and put on a clean pair of khaki shorts and white *pommy* shirt, as Ned had called it. Émile traded the jandles for his new canvas loafers. He looked in the mirror again. Better, he thought—felt good to get rid of the week's scraggly growth under his chin.

What story do I tell Captain Pobjoy? John and Wiggie told him, and Jake, that the Dorado had rescued me east of Penrhyn Island. That I was sailing to Bora Bora. They said nothing about any trouble with the gendarmerie on Tahiti. What will he ask me? Wish I had a cigarette.

32

Émile left the hotel, wearing the hat with the floral wreath, and walked along the road to the Southern Cross Trading Company's store. He paused before going in.

The doors are open. Someone's in there. Maybe it's Ned from yesterday. He'll know if Captain Pob . . . Reggie is about. Wish my stomach would settle. Throat is so dry. My hands are shaking. Take deep breaths. What was it Wiggie said? Into the breach.

He removed his hat and stepped up onto the verandah.

Ned was behind the counter, his back to the door, but turned when the floorboards creaked. An ear-to-ear grin and a cheerful *"Kia orāna,* guv," calmed Émile.

"You're lookin' quite chipper this mornin', guv. Enjoyed the Anzac scrum at the RSA, did you then? Wiggie take good care of you, did he?"

"Oui . . . I mean yes, Monsieur Ned. A most entertaining *soirée . . .* party." *How do I ask him if Reggie is here?*

"Monsieur? Haven't been called that since my last berth to Nouméa. Come to see the captain, have you? He said you might be along." Ned went to one end of the counter and pointed toward the back of the room. "Through that door, guv. You'll see a gangway leading up to the loft." He pointed over his head. "That's where his nibs' office is."

Émile passed by racks of hats, shirts and *pareus,* and shelves of shorts, trousers, shoes, and jandles. He opened the door and looked into a massive storeroom—boxes and crates stacked from floor to ceiling; coils of rope, plastic and foam floats, and fish nets lay scattered around on the floor, and sheets of plywood, tin, and lengths of lumber piled along one wall. Bicycles, maybe twenty, rested in a rack by the rear door. The stairs to the loft rose on his left. Outside he'd noticed a dormer with two large windows in the building's roof. Émile took another deep breath and started up the stairs.

The walled-in loft's door was open. He stopped at the top of the stairs before entering. Inside, a large desk faced the windows; a tripod-mounted brass telescope stood nearby. Reggie Pobjoy sat at the desk, his back to the door. He waved a hand over his head.

"Come in, Jean-Philippe. Take a pew." He pointed at a pair of chairs to his right. "I'm about finished here."

He must have seen me waiting outside.

Émile sat in the chair nearest the desk. He watched the New Zealander shuffle through paper after paper; some he made notes on, some he set aside, some he tore up and threw in a wicker wastebasket. He saw a filled ashtray and the carved pot-bellied tiki with an exaggerated manhood on the desk. Along the front edge was a ship in a bottle. He couldn't read its name. A small wooden plaque with four coins embedded in it and protected by a plexiglass cover sat next to the bottle. Émile leaned forward. *Those are old French francs.* Opposite the bottle were a framed photograph of a young island woman and a child, and another of a teenager. *His family?* Photos of ships; one he recognized as the schooner moored in the harbor, hung on the wall. *What was its name? Bobbie had talked about it. Ah, oui, Moana Tama. Bobbie. I hadn't thought about her until just now. When will she return to her island? Raka . . . Rakahanga. John was going to ask the harbormaster about going there. Not too soon I hope.*

"Well, that's done and dusted." Reggie leaned back in his chair and lit a cigarette. He turned. "Good morning, Jean-Philippe, or should I say *Bonjour?*" Wearing only a sleeveless shirt, canvas shorts, and jandles, he looked to Émile more like a beachcomber than a shipping magnate.

Émile made to stand, but Reggie waved him down. "No ceremony, lad. Fancy a fag?" He offered his cigarettes. "Have a proper do at the RSA, did you not?" Reggie looked closely at Émile's face. "No worse for wear, it seems."

Émile took a cigarette. Reggie lit it for him.

Glad I shaved and changed clothes. "*Oui* . . . Yes. *Pardon* . . . I am sorry, I mean. Monsieur Reggie."

Reggie laughed. "A bit nervous, are you, mate? No worries." He stubbed out his cigarette. "But no more 'Monsieur', *s'il vous plaît*, Jean-Philippe. Just Reggie. I like the French. Not like my mate, Jake. Don't know what his problem is. They did well for me during the war. Fancy a cuppa, or something stronger?"

"Cuppa? Coffee? Yes. I would like a cuppa." *Does he think I'm French?*

Reggie laughed again. "Cuppa is usually tea, but coffee is on offer as well, mate." Reggie stomped his foot twice. And then again. "Two bashes for tea, three's coffee."

Reggie got up from his desk and walked around to the telescope. He took a quick look through the lens and returned to his chair. "Right, Jean-Philippe, let's hear your story."

Émile retold the tale about a job offer on Bora Bora, his ordeal at sea, and his rescue. Reggie listened with half-closed eyes, and then lit another cigarette. He moved the ashtray to the desk edge nearest Émile.

"So why'd you jump ship on Raro? If you wanted to go to Bora Bora, your best chance would've been to remain aboard the *Dorado* until she returned to Tahiti and found passage from there. Most likely Marlow Drayton would've dropped you off on Bora Bora as she passed. He's not a bad sort."

What lie do I tell now? Do they know about crime on Pape'ete here in the Cooks? Do they care? "I am tired of people, Reggie. Not all people. Not a few people, but crowds, masses of people. My village, Martigny on the frontier with France, was overrun with refugees at the end of the war. All of Europe was . . . *une fosse d'aisance* . . . a cesspool. I could have gone up into the Alps and become a hermit, but I wanted to travel. *Padre* Claude took me to Puluwat. From there, I was sent to Pape'ete." He put out his cigarette. "I thought Tahiti might have been the answer, but it is being overrun by foreigners. And I don't care for the French government and their wars in Indochina and Algeria. John . . . John Spreadborough told me they plan to destroy atolls with their atomic bombs. I want no part of that."

Footsteps on the stairs paused the history. A woman—about forty and quite attractive, Émile thought—wearing a flowered *pareu* entered the office with a tray.

"*Kia orāna*, Elaine," Reggie said as he stood. "Elaine, this is Jean-Philippe."

Émile stood. Reggie laid his cigarette in the ashtray.

"*Kia orāna*, Jean-Philippe." She placed the tray on a side table. "Milk and sugar, of course, and some biscuits."

"Elaine's our seamstress, tailor, and sometimes sail maker. Absolutely wicked with a needle and thread and her sewing machine, she is. The *Moana Tama* blew out a jib in a bad one a bit ago, and Elaine organized her brigade of mamas and knocked out a new one in no time at all."

She lowered her head, shaking it slightly as if embarrassed. "You're too kind, Reggie." Elaine turned to Émile. "Ned mentioned you may want a fitting for trousers."

Émile was a bit irritated by all this trivial chatter that interrupted his attempt to impress his future patron. "Ah, yes, Elaine. Sometime later, perhaps."

"Not to worry, Jean-Philippe, she wasn't going to measure your particulars here." Reggie laughed. Elaine went downstairs. "Milk and sugar?"

"Just coffee, *s'il vous plaît*, Reggie. I am sorry again for speaking French. But—"

Reggie raised a hand. "No apologies, Jean-Philippe." He poured a cup and handed it to Émile. "One should be proud to speak other languages. Wish I did. Picked a few words of *Deutsch* in the *stalag*, but nothing's stuck. Still can't deal with the Maori decently in their lingo. Bit embarrassed about that. But let's sort out the business at hand." Reggie poured himself a cup after adding milk and sugar. He stirred his coffee.

"So, you didn't like the Frog islands? Thought the Cooks may be more to your pleasure? We've had our fill of worthless white driftwood." Reggie snubbed out his cigarette. "What's your education level? Can you read and write the Queen's English?"

Émile sipped the coffee and nodded. *I hope he won't test me. I'm not that competent. Did I go too far criticizing the French? That was stupid. What are worthless white driftwood?*

"How about sums? Good with them, are you?"

"Yes, Reggie. I finished top of my class in arithmetic." *That's a lie he can't verify. I didn't learn much past how to add and subtract until I was in the army—the French Army.*

Reggie looked down at Émile's shirt. "Not wearing your knife today?"

Émile glanced at his waist. "No. I did not think it was, how you say, *apropos*, for this meeting with you."

"Usually carry it, do you?" Reggie leaned back in his chair.

"*Oui*, I mean yes. *Mon pére*, my father, said a man should always carry fire and steel."

Reggie thought for a moment, finished his coffee, and lit another cigarette. "Fine advice. What sort of work was your father in?"

Merde! What lie now? I can't tell him my father was a sailor in the French Navy and killed when the British sank the French Fleet at Oran. "A ferryman on *Lac Léman* . . . Lake Geneva."

"Still at it, is he, or on a pension now?"

"He drowned during a storm when I was very young."

'Well, stone the crows! That's sad, that is." Reggie offered him another cigarette. "Right. Here's my offer, Jean-Philippe. Ol'Ned—below—will be leaving us in a few months. Going back to his island. Fancy working with him and learning the trade? Lots of time for you to practice your English and pick up some Maori. It'll be fifteen pounds a week, paid each Friday." He lit Émile's cigarette.

Is fifteen New Zealand pounds a fair wage? Or is it British pounds? Is he taking advantage of my situation? I'll ask Wiggie and John.

"*Merci beaucoup*, Reggie. Sorry. Thank you very much. I am a good worker. And would enjoy remaining on Rarotonga . . . Raro . . . for a while. Everyone is most friendly. May I ask a few questions?"

"Of course, mate. Let's have 'em."

"What hours would I work? Is there an inexpensive *pension* where I could live? And what about my status as a foreigner?"

"Good questions, Jean-Philippe. As to hours, the store opens when Ned gets here in the morning. He's not an early riser, so it's usually by eight or nine. More often earlier. Whenever he gets here, he opens the door, and it's open. A break for luncheon—might last to half one or two. Finished about half five, unless there's a crowd, or it's a fine day to stay open. Shut today at midday, and all day tomorrow—Sunday. We're on island time here, mate. You'll get used to it."

Reggie rose from his chair and again went around the desk to the telescope. "A bit of smoke to the northwest. Most likely the *Pacifica Maru* from Suva. Due in port today she is. Get most of our fuel and other major bits from there. Fancy she may have my new lorry aboard." He turned back to Émile. "Accommodations? You're in the Banana Court, right? A bit dear that. There's a bedsit at the back of the storeroom. Ned stayed there until he got wed. Nothing fancy, but there's a cooker and a smallish fridge and a loo with a shower. It's yours until you find something more to your needs. Or as long as you like. No charge."

Why is he making this generous offer?

Reggie walked over to Émile and held out a hand. "Let's take a look at your papers."

Émile pulled the pouch from inside his shirt, extracted his passport, and handed it to Reggie.

"Bloody awful photo, mate. You look like a refugee from some camp. Hair's different, but the eyes are the same. Well done. Not to worry. The harbormaster, Ol' Ben Berrynabor—you met him—only cares about cargo. The immigration-*wallah* is an ex-Royal Air Force mate, so there's no difficulty there." He handed the passport back to Émile.

"Do I have to speak with these people, Reggie?" *He didn't say anything about the visa stamps. Did he even read them?*

"No, Jean-Philippe. You were left behind by your ship through no fault of your own." Reggie smiled. "It's better that you find employment here than become a drain on the social services of the government."

The shortwave radio on a table behind Émile came to life. "Avatiu Harbor, this is the Motor Vessel *Pacifica Maru*, over." This repeated twice more with no response from the harbormaster.

Reggie laughed. "Ol' Ben's most assuredly still on the razzle." He stood, walked to the telescope, took a longer look through the lens, and nodded. "That's her all right. Not brilliant arriving the day after Anzac. Be a bit of a bother organizing the lighter crews today. Nothing doin' tomorrow, being Sunday and all."

"What will they do?" Émile asked.

"Send a boat ashore after they drop their hook. Not my concern. Waited six months for my new lorry. Another day or two makes little difference." Reggie came around the desk and extended his hand. "Have we a deal, mate?"

Émile stood. They shook hands.

"Right," Reggie said, "That's done and dusted." He offered Émile another cigarette. He lit both. And then he bent down and pulled open a lower desk drawer. From it he lifted two small glasses and a square, bluish bottle. "A toast to our new contract is in order, is it not? Fancy gin, do you, Jean-Philippe?" He held up the bottle.

"*Oui* . . . I mean yes, Reggie. Thank you."

Reggie poured two fingers in each glass and handed one to Émile. They touched glasses.

"Isn't that the same as the bottle on your desk?" Émile pointed with his glass.

"Well spotted, mate. Special brand this. A story for another time perhaps." Reggie threw down his gin. "Have a chat with Ned. He'll get you sorted with the bedsit." He returned the gin bottle to the desk drawer. "Think I fancy a stroll down to the jetty to see how they'll organize the *Pacifica's* arrival." He grabbed an American-style baseball cap off a rack and nodded toward the stairs. "After you, *mon ami.*"

Down in the store, Ned was bagging items for two women. "*Meitaka ma'ata,*" he said as they left the store. On the other side of the store, Émile heard the sound of a sewing machine and soft singing.

"Right, Ned," Reggie said. "We'll give this chap a go. Sort out the bedsit for him, and a quick walkabout. Leave the rest for Monday. Get yourself to the market before it's shut, mate." He turned to leave. "I'm off to the harbormaster's office, and then over to Jake's for a pint. Cheers." Reggie stopped at the door. He came back to the counter. "How you fixed for the readies?"

"*Pardon.* Sorry, Reggie, I do not understand," Émile said.

"No worries, mate. Need some cash do you?" Reggie pulled out his wallet and gave Émile a banknote. "A tenner should see you through the weekend. Against your first week's wages."

* * *

Émile and Ned walked through the storeroom. Near the back door was a small apartment. Ned took a key from a ring on his belt and unlocked the door. L-shaped, the room's long axis had a single bed, wardrobe, chest of drawers, writing desk and chair.

"Put many hours on that desk," Ned said. "Working on my book."

At right angles to the left at the end of the room was the galley kitchen. Another door past a small pantry hid the loo. Windows on the two outer walls gave light to the apartment. Ned opened and shut some cabinet doors over the single-burner gas stove and refrigerator.

"Left a few bits and pieces behind when I moved out, cutlery and all. Anything you need you can get from the store. Be doing much cooking will you?"

"*Oui* . . . Yes, I do enjoy cooking for myself."

"Right, guv . . . mate. Just be writing it all down in the ledger . . . We'll sort that bit out on Monday. The captain will decide on the cost, if any. He's a most generous chap, the captain is. Too generous sometimes for my liking, he is."

"*C'est vrais* . . . That's a truth, Ned. He's most generous with this offer of employment. I am most grateful." *Ned doesn't seem surprised or put off by my hire. Wonder what he's thinking?*

"Well, mate, must've been sommat about you or your story that he fancied. He has a keen sense about folks. Most surely from his war experiences and organizing this company."

"*Mais* . . . but there must be others who want a position."

"Right you are, mate, but the islanders he's hired—and the captain loves these people—have a nasty habit of offering . . . how would you say... family discounts to their relatives."

"*Ah oui, je comprend.* I'm sorry, Ned. I keep . . . How you say . . . slipping into my French."

Ned laughed. "That slipping may be the reason he decided to give you a go." He handed the key to the bedsit to Émile, and took another off his key ring. "This is to the backdoor, so you can come and go as you please." He turned and opened the backdoor to the building. Four large pole sheds stood behind in an open yard. "We'll have a chat about this kit on Monday. Let's go lock up for the day."

What did he mean about my slipping into French being the reason for hiring me?

As they walked back through the storeroom, Émile asked, "Reggie said something about a market?"

Elaine was at the door putting on her hat as they came to the front of the store. She had a large woven shopping bag in one hand.

"Right you are, mate. The *Punanga Nui* market is just down the road. We'll all go together."

* * *

The market spread throughout a large, palm-tree-bordered, open area between the road and the lagoon's edge. Fresh fruits, vegetables, and fish, along with hand-carved items and woven goods filled the open sided tent-like kiosks. In the center small lorries and cars were parked with goods displayed on the tailgates and in the boots. On the lagoon side of the market stood a collection of more permanent structures—colorful shacks—that housed artists' shops and studios.

"Be finished shortly," Ned said. "Six to twelve on Saturdays for the full Monty. Some folks about during the week in hope of making a few bob. Spot on for fresh fish. My missus should be here abouts with the brats." His eyes searched the crowd.

A ukulele and drum combo performed in the center of the market's large bandstand-like gazebo. With a wave Elaine left them to join some friends.

"Right. There she be." Ned pointed toward a Maori woman with four children in tow. "See ya Monday, mate. Enjoy your weekend. Cheers." He skirted the crowd around the gazebo to join his family.

Émile wandered through the market looking at all the wares and foods on offer. He asked a man selling fish if he was there each day. The man said yes, if he'd caught any fish that morning. But if he wasn't here, his cousin would be. Émile enjoyed fresh fish for his meals. *Meals? What about today? I'm meeting Wiggie and John for tea at the hotel. Perhaps we'll go somewhere for dinner. I must find a source for flour and yeast and sugar. Why didn't I think to ask Ned? There're no bread or pastry items sold here. I'll have to bake my own.*

Émile walked through the market from end-to-end three times hoping to see Bobbie. A few looked like her from a distance, but no luck. Beyond the market he stopped to watch a boat from the *Pacifica Maru* approach the harbor. He saw Reggie and the harbormaster standing at the end of the jetty awaiting its arrival.

Must avoid Berrynabor. Even though Reggie said the harbormaster wasn't concerned about new arrivals, I don't want to take any chances. He touched the pouch holding his forged passport.

Émile returned to the hotel. He packed up his meager belongings and paid his portion of the bill. He waited in the bar. Wiggie and John should be here shortly, he thought.

What will I do tomorrow? Everything on the island is shut on Sundays. I could spend the day getting familiar with the store. Reggie and Ned would be impressed if I knew a little about what's there. Does the hotel do meals on Sundays?

"Do you serve meals on Sundays?" he asked the young Maori woman bartender.

"Yes, but for patrons only."

"What about guests of patrons? I have nowhere else to eat."

The young woman smiled and said, "If you're a guest of Wiggie, you can always get a meal."

"Just don't put it on my ticket, thank you very much, *mon ami.*" Wiggie slipped onto the stool next to Émile. "I'll have a large Scotch, Nancy, and a bottle of Suva to wash it down."

His breath smells like he's had a drink or two already.

"What'll you be havin', Jean?" Wiggie said. He grinned and jabbed Émile in the ribs when the woman brought him his drinks. "Nancy, my love, when are you and I goin' to go down to the beach at Black Rock and watch the sunset?"

"Not in your lifetime, Wiggie. My cousin warned me about you." She winked at Émile.

"Which cousin was that, Nancy, my love? I've known so many."

Nancy laughed and asked Émile, "Would you like something to drink… Is it Jean?"

"Jean-Philippe. And yes, I'd like a beer. A Suva, *s'il vous plaît.*"

She brought his drink, and then looked past them and smiled. "Now, here's a proper gentleman. Not like some I could mention."

John took the stool on the other side of Émile. "*Kia orāna,* Nancy. My usual, if you please."

"One G 'n T it is, Mister Spreadborough." Nancy reached for a square, blue bottle of gin on the shelf behind the bar.

"That's the same gin Reggie shared with me in his office this morning," Émile said. "And the same as the one on his desk with the toy ship in it. He said there was a story about that gin."

"It's not the gin that the story's about, Jean," Wiggie said. "It's the ship in the bottle. And I wouldn't be callin' it a toy to Reggie."

John pulled out his notebook and removed the cap from his fountain pen. "I'd certainly like to hear that story, mate."

Wiggie downed his Scotch, chased it with a long pull on his beer. "Story tellin' is thirsty work, my friend." He handed his glass to Nancy.

John nodded, and she poured Wiggie another double and opened a second Suva.

Wiggie took a sip from his Scotch. "Back in '38 or maybe '39—before the war anyways— Reggie and Tooks Marsten, his business partner, were marooned on Suwarrow for some weeks when the *Wallaroo* went down in a cyclone. The only souvenir from that tragic event is the ship in the bottle on his desk." Wiggie took a drink from his beer. He offered cigarettes to his friends.

"Blimey! That's one for the books," John said. "What sort of ship was the *Wallaroo?* How many lives were lost? What was it doing at Suwarrow? There's nothing there. Did Reggie make the ship in the bottle?" His pen was poised.

"Slow down, mate. Too many questions for one day. I know a fair bit about this tale, but you best have a proper chinwag with Reggie or Tooks for the details." Wiggie turned to Émile. "Speakin' about details, how went your chat with his nibs?"

"He has offered me a position in his store."

"Well done, *mon ami.* That calls for another go. Who's at the head of the queue?" Wiggie threw down his drink.

"It would be my pleasure, *mes amis,*" Émile said. Nancy was already pouring the drinks. "But, I have a question for you both. Is fifteen pounds a week . . . New Zealand pounds I assume . . . a fair wage?"

John shrugged and shook his head. "I'm sorry, Jean-Philippe. I have no idea."

"That's about the official minimum, I believe," Wiggie said. "Not quite sure. Don't pay much attention to that business." He put out his cigarette in a shell ashtray. "Might be able to secure a self-catering shack on those wages. Food's cheap, if you stay with the local lot."

"He's offered me the bedsit at the back of his store . . . *gratis.*"

"That's a fine offer, Jean-Philippe," John said. "Doubt if you find one better. Reggie Pobjoy is an honorable man."

"So, what'll you be about as a new employee of the Southern Cross Trading Company?" Wiggie asked.

"Not sure. Ned . . . You know Ned . . . is to show me my duties on Monday."

I hadn't really thought about what I would be doing—just thrilled to have a position.

* * *

Émile left his friends at the hotel bar and said he would rejoin them for dinner. As he left the hotel he met Ned, a large folio under his arm, on the steps from the road.

"*Kia orāna,* Jean," he said. "Is Mister Spreadborough about?"

"*Oui,* I mean yes. He's at the bar with Wiggie."

"Thanks, mate. I want to show him the bit I've wrote about my time on the atoll." He looked down at the folio. "Lots of memories here, don't you know. Learned more than a bit the first time. Won't be makin' the same mistakes when I go back."

"Where are you going, Ned?"

"Suwarrow. Haven't heard of it, have you?"

"Yes, I have. Wiggie said something about it. But said no one lives there. Why are you going there? Are you taking your family?"

"Sorry, mate. No time to explain. See you tomorrow. Must chat with Spreadbourough." He hurried past Émile into the hotel.

Interesting folks these islanders. Like to keep things close. Why would a man want to go live on an uninhabited atoll? I need to find a place to hide, but not by myself.

33

Back at the store, Émile went around to the rear of the building. When he entered the bedsit, he noticed the strong odor of mildew, something that had escaped him the first time because of the excitement of having a place to live. No one's been in here for a while, he thought. He opened the windows. The small empty refrigerator was unplugged. With a wooden match from a box on a shelf over the stove, he lit the pilot light and fired up the two burners. A quick search through the cupboards showed what was needed when he prepared his own meals. The single bed had only a thin mattress and no pillow. No toilet paper in the loo. He turned on the basin taps and watched brown water turn to clear. Same with the shower and the toilet.

I need to make a list, he thought. In the small desk's drawer he found a tablet and some pencils. List in hand, he went through the warehouse into the store. Two trips to the bedsit satisfied his needs for the moment. No fresh food in the store, but plenty of canned goods and coffee. And toilet paper, and soap, and utensils for the kitchen. He plugged in the fridge. *Tomorrow, I must purchase some eggs, milk, yeast, and flour.*

He'd lost track of time. A tapping on the glass reminded him of dinner at the hotel. John Spreadborough stood outside his kitchen window.

"Get a move on, mate," the writer said. "They're going to finish shortly."

Émile and John made it back to the hotel in time for their special fish'n chips dinner—large pieces of parrot fish caught inside the reef.

Wiggie was still at the bar regaling an Australian couple about the All Blacks. John grabbed him by the collar.

"Leave off, mate. Time for some supper before they're finished." He directed Wiggie toward a table. Émile followed. They ordered the special. Nancy brought Émile and John a Suva, and Wiggie a large Scotch and a Suva.

"A bit of a brouhaha down on the pier," John said. "I went back down there after you left, Jean-Philippe, to chat with Berrynabor about passage to Rakahanga. The *Pacifica's* mate and Berrynabor were having a heated discussion about getting the cargo off before tomorrow. Bad choice arriving the day after Anzac. The poor bloke had sounded the tocsin, but the shire hadn't responded. Reggie was there and watched the entire thing with a grin. I think he went off to Jake's."

"I am sorry, John, but I do not understand. Why can they not off load the cargo tomorrow?"

"It's the bloody Bible thumpers!" Wiggie said and went back to mauling his meal.

"The LMS is not too keen about any non-essential labor on Sundays," John explained.

"What is this LMS? Is it a religious organization? Are they Catholic or Protestant?" Émile asked.

"That's a deep question, *mon ami*. The LMS is the London Missionary Society. Their preachers converted all the natives a hundred or more years ago. Sent off the old gods . . . though Tangaroa does show up from time-to-time. Banned dancing, booze, lewd behavior—their definition of it, any road—and stopped most work on Sundays."

"What is allowed?" Émile asked. *I must learn these taboos.*

"You can do a bit of fishing, if that's your livelihood, or muck about in your taro patch, but don't be putting a new thatch on your roof or repairing your canoe. Some small shops around the island are open after church to sell essentials."

"But the hotel's restaurant is open and serving food and drink. How is that different?"

"Brass, *mon ami*. The islanders, especially the New Zealand government, want their bit of brass." He rubbed three fingers together. "The few tourists who have discovered this paradise and the bureaucrats from Wellington who plague these islands, require accommodations. So, the rules are bent a bit. You can get food and drink on Sundays at the few establishments like this on the island. But only after church is finished."

The three men finished their meal, and John and Émile assisted Wiggie back to the room. He made some noises about the cook on the *Dorado* attacking him with a cleaver, but once on his bed he was asleep.

"Fancy a stroll down to the pier, Jean-Philippe? That's the only action happening here in paradise this evening."

"Yes, I would like that."

They walked along the road to the pier.

"So, Jean-Philippe, what are your plans for the future?"

Why is he so interested in my future? He says he's a writer, but seems to have many influential friends here. A government agent, perhaps?

"I am not sure. I do not think about the future that much." *That's a lie. I'm always worried about the flics finding me. How much do the New Zealand police cooperate with the gendarmerie on Tahiti?* "I would like to find an island where I can have a quiet life. Somewhere to enjoy this *beau paradis*."

"The northern group might be ideal for you, *mon ami*. Lovely islands up there—Pukapuka, Nassau, Penrhyn. Not bothered much by outsiders. Don't know about Rakahanga. Haven't been there yet. Heard the trading station had closed. Next on my itinerary though." John offered Émile a cigarette and lit both.

Rakahanga. That's where Bobbie's from. Bobbie. I hadn't thought about her all day. She should still be on Raro. Wonder where she's staying? Who would know? Reggie. Can't ask him. He may think badly of me. Who else? I hope to see her before she leaves the island. Maybe Ned. He seems to know many people. But he wasn't at the RSA. Wiggie and John didn't know her. Who else? Jake. Yes! And he wanted me to talk to him about some work in his kitchen.

"Would it be possible to get a drink at Jake's this evening?"

"*Bien sûr, mon ami.* Going to give that venue a flutter?"

"*Pardon,* I do not understand 'flutter.'"

"Sorry, mate. Brit term for a chance, a try."

"*Ah, oui.* I understand. I enjoy learning the British expressions." *To survive here I must learn as many as I can.* "Yes, I will talk to him about that offer of a position."

* * *

The sun sat low in the west as they walked out onto the jetty, where a crowd had gathered. Émile saw Reggie and Jake standing in the back. The attraction was a new lorry. Two harbor lighters approached the pier. Lashed together, a plank platform extended past both outer gunwales. On this platform rested a pale-green Datsun 124. A crane on the jetty swung out, and its cables were attached to straps wrapped around the lorry. Reggie and Jake moved to the front of the spectators, joined by John and Émile.

"Organized enough lads to sort this out, did you, Reggie?" John said.

"Too right, mate. Tooks's cousins are always on hand when needs must."

"Helps to be related to half the island," Jake said with a laugh. "Jean, getting settled in, are you now?"

"Yes, *merci.* I will be most comfortable thanks to Reggie."

They watched as the crane sat Reggie's new lorry down on the pier. Berrynabor, the harbormaster, approached. "A stack of paperwork to fill out, Reggie."

"In a bit, Ben. Need to see if it runs," he said as he inspected the vehicle. "Wonder how much petrol the Nips left in it?" Reggie opened the driver's side door, sat, and started the motor. He smiled. "Time for a bit of a test run. Climb aboard, lads."

Jake slid in on the passenger side; John and Émile climbed into the back.

"The customs forms, Reggie," the harbormaster said.

"Don't be a prat, Ben. Be back directly." Reggie drove along the pier and turned right onto the road. "Everyone up for a quick island tour?" he shouted. "We'll give Jean a chance to see the sights."

They went through the town and past the airfield. The western sky was ablaze with color. Circling the island on its twenty-mile, single-lane road, Reggie honked and waved often to the islanders. He skillfully dodged many dogs, chickens, and long-legged cats. As they passed through the village of Titikaveka, Émile thought he saw Bobbie working in a taro patch with other women. When they entered Avarua again, it was almost dark. Reggie pulled into the parking lot by Jake's restaurant.

"Time for a celebratory brew, lads," he said, "if we can get the publican to open the bar."

"Bit of a mess, but there's a few cool ones in the fridge," Jake said.

They sat at a wooden picnic table on the deck. Jake went into the restaurant and returned with four beers. He pointed out the details of his new establishment.

"Half a dozen tables like this out here, the open-air bar just there for the boozer crowd, and a posh bar and restaurant up those stairs for diners. Should be all sorted in a fortnight."

"This is a most lovely view of the reef, Jake," John said. Ocean rollers smashing against the coral barrier sent up sheets of spray.

"Had a chat with the village *arikis* about organizing canoe races in the lagoon from here." Jake nodded toward the small inlet next to the deck. "Should be a good draw."

Reggie finished his beer and said, "Must go deal with the bureaucrats. Cheers, mates."

After Reggie drove away, Émile said, "Jake . . . I still feel uncomfortable using your Christian name . . . you mentioned something about working in the restaurant's kitchen."

Jake laughed. "No worries there, mate. We're quite informal here in the islands. About the kitchen, it's a bit of mess right now. Not worth a look. Thought it might be a bit posh telling the punters I had a French chef, even if you are Swiss. Who'd know the difference? Right? I haven't organized a menu as yet and would like some help with that, if you please."

A French chef on Rarotonga? I don't want to be noticed. I want to hide somewhere. This may not be a good idea. "Ah oui . . . I mean yes . . . I could help with that. *Mais,* but I don't know what is available here on Raro."

"Not much on offer except the fish, lots of different fish. And chicken. We get all our lamb and beef from New Zealand. I'm sure you can do interesting things with those."

"Thank you for the confidence, but I was only a *sous-chef.* And Reggie may have problems with it, *n'est-ce pas?*"

"No worries there, Jean. We had a bit of chat about your situation. He said you'll finish at the store by half five, and I don't plan to start the dinner menu until seven. And, of course, your Saturday afternoons and Sundays are free. Lots of time to sort things out before the crowds arrive." He laughed.

"Seems to me to be an excellent situation for you, Jean-Philippe," John said. His notebook was on the table. He'd been writing since they arrived.

I have no choice now. These men have been more than helpful. What is John writing?

"Jake, I must be honest with you. I don't plan to stay here on Rarotonga forever. Only as long as it takes me to decide where to go next. I'd like very much to stay in the Cooks, but somewhere more remote, away from civilization."

Jake didn't respond, finished his beer and asked, "Fancy another round? On the house, of course." He didn't wait for an answer and went up to bar.

"John, may I ask a question?"

The writer looked up from his notebook. "Of course, Jean-Philippe."

"What are you writing?"

"Ah, this? Just notes and color, mate. A description of today's activities. The sunset. The tour around the island. A bit about the lorry's offloading.

Wish I'd had a camera for that. Bits and bobs about Jake's place, and anything else that catches my attention. That's what writers do, mate. Nothing personal."

What was it that Jake said to John at the RSA about writing something about the new restaurant? Would he mention the "French chef?" Would my name be mentioned? How can I tell him not to?

Jake returned with the beers. A single light above the almost-finished open bar cast long shadows across the deck. "One for the road, mates," he said. "Won't get any outside work done tomorrow with the LMS preachers snooping around. Lots to do inside, though. Stop by if you get thirsty."

Émile and John walked back to the hotel. The Southern Cross rested just above the horizon.

"Come by for a coffee at breakfast, Jean-Philippe. They know you're a mate, so there'll be no bother. Sleep well." He went into the hotel.

34

Émile didn't sleep well that night. Reccurring images of Musettes's death, the night drop into Dien Bien Phu, and his fight with Vater swept through his head. And Bobbie's smile and laughter. He woke early, before the sun was up. After a shower and a shave under his chin, he dressed and walked to the jetty. The *Pacific Maru's* lights blended with the Milky Way on the northern sky. He sat at the end of the pier and smoked a cigarette.

What a beautiful part of the world. I must find a place to enjoy it. Maybe Reggie will have a position for me at one of his stations on the outer islands. Must do my best to gain his trust here in the store. Merde! Forgot to ask Jake about Bobbie. I'll walk over to his place later today.

Émile remained there until the sun brightened the eastern sky with a display of color to match yesterday evening's sunset. He stood, stretched and walked back toward the hotel. To his surprise, Wiggie and John sat outside on the Banana Court's porch. They're up early, he thought.

Wiggie waved and shouted, "G'day, mate. Out for a morning stroll, are you now?"

John looked up from a sheaf of papers on his lap. He smiled and said, "*Bonjour,* Jean-Philippe. Join us. Coffee not quite sorted yet. Be done shortly."

Émile sat in a chair next to his friends. He wondered what John was reading.

"Been giving Ned's manuscript a look through. Fine piece of writing this," John said. "Should be able to secure a publisher in Auckland, any road."

"A bit of a nutter if you ask me," Wiggie said. "Goin' back to that cursed atoll on his own, leaving his family behind an' all." He lit a cigarette. "He'd been coconut crab grub last time if'n those Yank yachties hadn't happened by. Crazy old coot."

"Not as crazy as some I could mention," John said with a laugh. "Right, lads, let's see if the coffee's been sorted." They went inside.

"Any plans for the rest of the morning, Jean-Philippe?" John asked after he and Wiggie consumed another full English breakfast—Émile only had his usual coffee and a warmed up stale dinner roll.

"No plans. Thought about a long walk along the coast."

"Don't know how religious you may be, but the LMS church service here in Avarua is worth a go. The singing is wonderful. All in Maori, of course. There is a Papist church hereabouts somewhere, but the local is better. Best is down the road in Titikaveka."

Titikaveka? That's where I thought I saw Bobbie. Maybe she'll be there.

"How far is that village? Didn't we pass through it yesterday?"

"Right you are, mate. About an hour or more. Depends on how quick a foot you are."

"What time does the service begin?" *I must purchase a watch.*

"Ten . . . half ten, perhaps. Not sure," John said. "The local mamas will have a buffet lunch organized in the community hall across the road from the church. Not as fancy as the RSA do—lots of fruit and cut sandwiches. And visitors are most welcome."

"What *is* the time, *s'il vous plaît,* John?"

The writer reached into his jacket and brought out a gold pocket watch. "Just a few past eight, *mon ami.*" He held up the watch for the others to admire. "Lovely mechanism this has. Never loses a minute. Swiss, just like you, Jean-Philippe. Gift from the King of Tonga . . . but that's another story."

"Ha! You and your stories. Most likely a Jap knockoff, "Wiggie said. "Best be on your bike, mate, if'n you're going to make the prayer meetin' in time. And don't forget your fancy hat. She'll be recognizing it sure enough."

Émile hurried back to his room in the store. He looked at the hat. The flowers on the wreath had wilted. No matter, he thought. In the store, he took a cheap wrist watch from a display case. He'd mark it on his list later. Wiggie and John were back on the hotel's porch as he walked past. Wiggie gave him a thumbs up; the writer shouted, *"Bonne chance!"*

Do they wonder why I'm hurrying to get to the church service? Did they also see Bobbie in that taro field? Strange pair, those two. Complete opposites, but close mates. Wiggie is most rough around the edges. John is well-educated, but, as he said on the Dorado, his best stories come from the lower decks. Strange pair.

Émile passed Avarua Harbor. He saw two men sitting at a table out on Jake's deck, but their backs were to him. Reggie's new lorry was parked by the restaurant.

Leaving Avarua proper, he walked along the grass verge of the ring road as fast as he could. No traffic to dodge, but he did have close encounters with an aggressive dog or two—some kind of a pit bull or other mongrel type. Many of the dwellings sat back from the road surrounded with fruit trees and large gardens. Not fancy, most were single-story, cinder block boxes with tin roofs and covered porches. One thing that surprised him was the graves. Almost every house had a grave or graves like cemetery plots in front of or alongside the building. Bordered in white, the plots and their headstones were adorned with flowers. Some looked to be plastic, but maybe they were real.

He passed a couple of small hotels, mostly thatched-roofed cottages, with fancy signs saying they were "resorts." The lagoon was a hundred meters or more off to his left but always visible through the palms. The road curved south, and soon the lagoon was alongside the road. A trio of small islands floated in the calm water just offshore inside the barrier reef. *How far have I gone? Will I get there in time? Will she be there? What time is it?* He looked at his new watch. *Damn. I forgot to set and wind it.*

Few vehicles, except bicycles and motor scooters, passed him on the road. Is there a bus service on Sundays, he wondered. I don't know if there's even a bus service on Raro. He jumped to the left when a horn honked at him from behind. The vehicle stopped alongside.

"G'day to you, Jean-Philippe, or should I say *Bonjour?*" Reggie grinned at Émile from across the front seat of his new lorry. "Out for a morning constitutional, are you?"

"Oh, good morning, Monsieur Reggie. I'm attempting to get to the church in Titikaveka for the singing. John Spreadborough said it was worth the trek."

Reggie glanced at his watch, reached over and opened the passenger side door. "Best climb aboard, mate. You'll not make it in time on foot. I'm going right past it on my way to look at some properties farther along the lagoon."

Émile got in the lorry and Reggie offered him a cigarette. They drove off, but not fast. He's driving quite slow, Émile thought. Not like us French. We'd be flying down this empty road as fast as we could go.

"That's Muri Lagoon on your left, Jean-Philippe. Quite popular with the tourists. Some say the first Maoris to arrive on Raro landed just back there by that pier." He pointed over his shoulder with his left thumb. "Big ceremony there each year on the anniversary date. All rubbish for the tourists, don't you know. No one really knows when or where they came ashore, or what happened. What's the matter, Jean-Philippe? You look a bit worried." Émile squirmed around in his seat and tapped his feet.

"How far is the church, Monsieur Reggie?"

Reggie laughed. "No worries, mate. Be there in plenty of time. Not breaking any speed records here, am I?" Émile shook his head. "Well, son. We take things a little slower here on Raro. I've seen how the Frogs drive on Pape'ete. Bloody insane and uncivilized. No more than thirty, usually less. Too many folks and dogs and chickens on the road. Local coppers strict on that, but none about today, being Sunday and all."

Past Muri Lagoon, the road curved around to the west. The tide had ebbed and more of the barrier reef was exposed. Émile saw people walking on the reef. He wondered what they were doing. Reggie noticed his gaze.

"Gathering good grub from the reef, they are," he said. "Hard to go hungry on these islands. If you know what to look for, that is. Can tell you a bit about that sometime, if you're interested, mate."

"*Ah oui,* I mean yes, Monsieur Reggie."

His boss laughed. "You can drop the 'Monsieur', Jean-Philippe. Makes me feel too posh." Reggie lit a cigarette. "There's an interesting history to this church. All built from local materials. Gigantic blocks of coral were dynamited out of the reef and hauled up for the making. Almost a hundred years ago. Long before cranes and tractors and such. All the inside structure is made from trees found here. Most hand-carved from solid pieces with no joints. Used to have a thatched roof, but that's been replaced with metal." He pointed ahead. "There it be."

A large, white-washed building with a blue roof emerged from the palms along the right side of the road. It sat back in its own grounds, which were surrounded by a low white wall. Graves filled the space between the church and the road. Reggie stopped at a wide gap in the wall.

"There you be, mate." Reggie then pointed across the road to a long, low building with a covered porch on three sides."There'll be a bit of a social do just there once the service is finished. You may have a bit of luck and find your girlfriend." He grinned.

How did he know I was looking for Bobbie? Émile got out of the lorry. "Thank you, Mon . . . Reggie." *What have I done or said that makes them all know I'm trying to see her again? I must be more careful in expressing my emotions and interests. Something out of my past may slip out before I want it to.*

"Right, mate. I'll be coming back this way later in the day. I'll keep a lookout for you. Cheers and *bonne chance.*" With a wave of his hand, Émile's new boss drove off. He seemed to be chuckling to himself.

The church doors were open and Émile heard singing as he walked along the crushed coral path to the porch. *Maybe this isn't such a good idea.*

He removed his hat, entered the church, and stepped to one side. The interior walls of the church were white washed and bare. The singing by the choir and congregation was nothing like he had heard before in churches in France. But, he wasn't paying much attention to the music. His eyes searched the room for Bobbie. All the women in the church wore broad-brimmed, white or cream-colored hats woven from some local material, which were adorned with colorful bands and other ornaments. The twenty or so rows of pews on either side of the center aisle were mostly full. The choir, men and women—a dozen or more of all ages—sat in chairs left of the raised center podium where the preacher stood behind a small pulpit. Émile looked up at the vast array of blue-painted wooden rafters. The six arched, plain glass windows that pierced each side wall let in abundant sunlight. Except for two couples who sat the back row, probably European or American, he thought, the congregation was all islanders.

I don't belong here. This is not the place to meet her. Maybe I'll find her at the Saturday market. Émile turned, went out through the door, and froze.

"*Kia orāna,* Jean-Philippe from Switzerland." Bobbie and two other young women, wearing plain white blouses, black skirts, and *rito* hats, blocked his exit.

"Oh, *Bonjour* . . . I mean *kia orāna,* Mademoiselle Bobbie."

One of Bobbie's friends laughed and said, "He's a posh one, isn't he, *Mademoiselle* Bobbie. Where'd you find him? *Kia orāna,* Jean-Philippe. I'm Rhonda. And this is Mary, my sister."

Bobbie looked down at his hat and shook her head.

"Can't have a Swiss chef going about our island with such a poor looking lei on his head." She took his hat and handed it to Mary.

Inside the church the noise of people standing, talking, and shuffling about told them that the service was over.

"Come, Jean-Philippe from Switzerland. We'll go and sit and have some *kaikai,* and fix your hat." Bobbie took him by one arm, and Rhonda softly grasped the other. They led Émile across the road to the church's community hall. Bobbie said something in Maori to Mary, who crossed the road and started collecting blossoms from shrubs and hanging vines around the hall.

A cold buffet of finger sandwiches, fruit, and desserts lay on banquet tables in the hall. Only pitchers of green or orange fruit juices, or water were on offer.

Émile chuckled to himself. *A French church buffet would not be without its selection of the local wines.*

Bobbie filled a paper plate with a half-dozen sandwiches, orange slices, diced papaya and two cookies, and handed it to Émile. The mama behind the table and Bobbie had a good laugh about something in Maori.

What's so funny? Am I the butt of some joke?

Bobbie smiled and nodded toward the tables behind the buffet. "We'll sit there, Jean-Philippe. The deacon will give the blessing and a little talk while we eat."

Émile took a plastic tumbler of water and waited for her to fill her plate. They sat at a table with the two European couples. One of the men extended his hand to Émile.

"Hi, I'm Sid Ketrow from Forest Park, Oregon. That's near Salem, the state capitol. This is my wife, Cheri, and our friends, Phil and Darlene Griffin. Where ya from?" Phil Griffin stood to shake Émile's hand.

Americans. Time for more lies. Think I'll act the islander. "Kia orāna, Sid, Phil. Jean-Philippe from Avarua." He half-rose to acknowledge the wives. Bobbie and her friend, Rhonda laughed.

Sid had a puzzled look. "Your accent doesn't sound New Zealand. More European, perhaps?"

"Well done, Monsieur." *I'll play along.* "Originally from the Alps. Little country called Switzerland. Been there, have you?"

The Americans looked surprised. "Switzerland? What are you doing here?"

"I'm employed by the Southern Cross Trading Company here on Raro. I work for Captain Pobjoy. You've heard of him, *n'est-ce pas?*"

Both Bobbie and Rhonda stared at Émile in stunned silence. Rhonda whispered something in Bobbie's ear, who shook her head and shrugged.

"No. I don't know the name," Sid said. "What do you do?"

"Inventory mostly, sorting and counting."

"Pay well, does it?" Sid asked.

Before Émile could answer, a short elderly man, dressed quite nattily in a white flannel suit, pale blue shirt complete with vest and colorful tie, walked to the open space between the tables and asked for their attention. He introduced himself as a deacon of the church, gave the blessing, and then proceeded to talk a bit about the history of the London Missionary Society's work in the Cook Islands and its first missionary, John Williams. When he finished, one of the Americans raised his hand. The deacon nodded toward him. "You have a question, sir?"

"Didn't this Williams guy get killed and eaten by the islanders?" Sid asked.

A soft murmur of discord spread among the assembled Cook Islanders. The deacon paused before answering.

"Yes, Reverend John Williams did die in unfortunate circumstances, but not here in the Cooks. His demise took place later, and farther west in the New Hebrides. May God rest his soul."

"Well, so much for the tourist brochures," Sid said. "How long you been here, Jean?"

"I've been in the islands for some years." *That's not a complete lie.*

Bobbie and Rhonda stared at Émile, but didn't say anything. Rhonda went back to the buffet to get a plate for Mary.

"Ever been to Tahiti?" Phil asked.

"Yes. Some time ago." *Have to stay be alert about what I say with Bobbie listening.*

"Well, that's our next stop. Much different from here . . . The Cooks. I mean?"

"I think you will find many differences in the culture." *Need to be careful here.*

"What kind of differences?" Sid's wife asked.

"Tahiti, especially Pape'ete is, how you say, quite modern, and very French."

"Yes, we've heard that. I would think, as a European, you'd prefer that sort of environment, Jean," Phil said.

Careful, Émile. "Yes, it has its amenities, but I prefer the more relaxed life here in the Cooks." He saw a smile from Bobbie.

"So, what brought you to Rarotonga, Jean?" Sid asked.

Afraid this question would rear its ugly head. Think, think. The old story works.

"*Ah oui.* That's a long story. I was working for a Catholic mission on Puluwat. You know where that is, of course. In the Carolines." Émile saw the confusion he wanted in the eyes of the Americans. *Maybe I can change the subject.*

"No, I don't think so. It's not on our itinerary. Are they in Polynesia?"

"No. Much farther north and west. You've been to Switzerland then?" *Hope this works.*

"No, but it's on our list." Sid said.

"It's a beautiful country, but I tired of the cold winters. No snow here. You should visit it someday."

"The folks here sure are friendly," Sid's wife said. "Never met such happy people."

Mary came to the table and showed her handy work to Bobbie and Rhonda. Émile's hat was adorned with a lei of fresh red and yellow flowers. Bobbie nodded toward Émile. Mary handed him his hat.

Emile stood and placed the hat on his head. The other islanders around the tables applauded.

"Something special about your hat, Jean?" Sid asked.

Émile laughed and said, "Yes, but it's a private matter. *Merci beaucoup,* Mary."

"I'd like to get a hat like that," Phil said.

Careful how you answer, Émile. "Lots of hats at the company store, Monsieur. There may be more like this." *Reggie and Ned should be pleased that I'm bringing some business their way.* He sat. "But the flowers are not included.

Perhaps you could find someone at the Saturday market to make a lei."

"Afraid we'll be gone before next Saturday. Got a flight out to Pape'ete on Thursday," Sid said.

"Did get one of those wooden tiki things yesterday," Phil said. "You know the one. That well-hung fertility god . . . *Tanga* . . . something. That'll be a big hit with the guys back at Dottie's place in Forest Park." Bobbie and her friends laughed.

What's he talking about? Don't know this term "well-hung." Émile smiled and asked, "How long will you be in Tahiti?"

"Just for a week, then up to Honolulu for another week, then home to the rain," Sid said.

"Rain?" Émile asked. *Get them talking about home.*

"That's right, Jean. Where we live in Oregon, we have two seasons: rain and road construction." The other Americans laughed. "We are enjoying the South Pacific sunshine, and when it does rain, it's warm."

"Can you recommend any places in Pape'ete, Jean?" Cheri, Sid's wife asked. "Some local night life, perhaps?"

Can I recommend a night spot? This'll be fun. "Bien sûr, of course, Madame. You must surely visit Quinn's Bar on the wharf front. It is quite well-known and very popular."

"Food any good?" Phil asked.

I hate doing this. "Bien sûr. Best in the islands—*cordon bleu.*" *The meals at Quinn's are rubbish. The attraction is the entertainment. And the booze. They'll have an unforgettable experience.*

"Are these your girlfriends?" asked Darlene, trying to enter the conversation. She nodded towards Bobbie and her mates, who looked at Émile with "How're you going to answer this?" expressions.

Why not? No guts nor glory, as we said in the Légion. "Ah oui, Madame. All island men have several." *Hope this doesn't backfire on me.*

The three girls laughed and shook their heads.

"No more than three," Rhonda said. "They can't keep more than that happy."

Émile was thrilled they went along with his joke. *I do like this people.*

The four Americans paused before joining in the laughter. "That's a good one, Jean," Phil said. "Finish your lunch, gang. Time to be moving on. Lots more to see." They cleaned their plates and rose to leave. "Nice meeting you, Jean. And your friends." Phil winked at Émile. "I see why island life agrees with you."

"Enjoy the remainder of your time on Raro and on Tahiti," Émile said.

The Americans shook hands with the deacon and left the hall.

"We must go also," Rhonda said to Bobbie and Mary. The three women got up.

"I'll take this," Bobbie said as she took Émile's plate. "We have to get out to the reef before the tide comes in."

"What's on the reef?" Émile asked.

"Wonderful things to eat," Bobbie said. "Do you like urchins and *trepang*—sea slugs?"

That must be what Reggie was talking about. If I ask to go with them I still won't be alone with her. "Do you cook them or eat them raw?" *I should know this since I've told them I've lived in the islands for some time. Maybe one lie too many.*

Rhonda gave Émile a puzzled look as Bobbie walked away with the plates. "Don't they eat food from the reef in the Carolines?" she asked.

Think fast. "Oh, *oui.* I expect so, but I did not know what they were called." *That's weak.* "We ate all the native dishes."

"You should come with us sometime, but you'll need proper reef shoes." She pointed at his canvas loafers. "Not those." Bobbie returned.

"There will be something appropriate at the store, I'm sure," he said.

"Ask ol' Ned, or even Reggie. They're both expert reef hunters," Rhonda said.

"Hope to see you again soon, Jean-Philippe from Switzerland. Thank you for coming to Titikaveka today," Bobbie said. "We may go into Avarua this week. *'Aere ra,* Good bye." The three young women left the hall.

Émile sat alone for a time. One of the mamas asked him if he wanted something more to eat. He declined. *Hope I didn't make a fool of myself. Bobbie's much younger. This is crazy. I've only been here three days. Only spoken to her twice. But I haven't felt like this since Musette. I'm too old to believe in that "love-at-first-sight" nonsense.*

The parishioners started to leave the hall. Émile joined them. The deacon, who stood on the porch extending a farewell to all in Maori, held Émile's hand for a moment. "Thank you for joining us, young man. Do come again."

Émile had walked about a mile up the road toward Avarua when Reggie stopped to pick him up.

"Well, mate, enjoy the singing, did you then?" Reggie asked.

"Ah, *oui,* I mean yes. But I only heard the last bit of it."

"And was she there?"

"Yes, but with other friends. Did not have the chance to talk."

"Righto, mate. There'll be other times. She's not going back to Rakahanga for a bit."

"When could she leave Raro?"

"Not at all sure of that. Depends on what comes on the *Suwarrow.*"

"The *Suwarrow?*"

"Our flagship, mate. Should drop anchor in a day or two. Be lots of bits on board for the outer islands. You'll get the gist of all this as the days go by. Fancy a pint? Jake'll be messing about." As they entered Avarua, Reggie pulled into the parking lot next to the restaurant.

35

Émile spent the next two days following Ned around in the store. He learned the inventory, where the overstock sat in the storeroom, and waited on customers. All transactions were recorded in a ledger. Émile remembered to add his new wrist watch to the employee section. Out back, behind the store in the open-sided pole sheds, Ned showed him the gear he was collecting for his next sojourn to Suwarrow atoll: sheets of tin, plywood, two small canoes, jerry cans of kerosene, and a twenty-foot cutter.

"Where's Suwarrow?" Émile asked.

"Some days from here, mate. In the northern group."

"Why are you going there?"

Ned stood silent for a moment like he was thinking about his answer. "Just something I need to do. Get tired of civilization. Need to be alone."

"But what about your family? Are they going with you? Sorry if I am being too personal."

"No worries there, mate. Everyone asks the same question." Ned lit a cigarette. "I passed a few weeks on Suwarrow some time back. Fell in love with it. But didn't have the right kit. So I came back to Raro to get sorted. Next time I'll stay until the end."

"Anyone live there?" Émile asked.

"Nah. That's why I'm going back."

"But what about your family?"

"Their kin'll take care of them. No one's on the dole in the Cooks."

I can't believe he's going to abandon his family just to live alone on an atoll. I want to escape also, but not to be alone.

"When are you going?"

"Not all together sure of that, mate. The government has declared the atoll a nature preserve, whatever that is. Me thinks they'll be needing a caretaker, so I'll just be on my way. Less dear to have a volunteer than some Kiwi bureaucrat."

"How will you get there?"

"No worries there, mate. His nibs promised to set me and my kit ashore when I'm ready and one of his ships is making a run to the northern group."

* * *

On Monday during a tea break Émile went to a shop and purchased flour, salt, yeast, butter, and other staples he needed to cook for himself. A short walk to the *Punanga Nui* market early Tuesday morning landed him a large wahoo. The fisherman he bought it from said he should return the next day and he'd have some parrot fish, which are the local favorite for fish 'n chips. "But come early. They won't last long."

When Reggie, Elaine, and Ned arrived at the Southern Cross Trading Company's headquarters Wednesday morning, the store was filled with the wonderful aroma of baked bread. Émile stood behind the counter, and with arms spread wide greeted them, "*Kia orāna, mes amis. Bon appétit.*" A platter stacked with warm croissants sat next to a carafe of fresh-brewed coffee and, on a saucer, a slab of butter.

"Well, stone the crows!" Reggie said. "Fresh out of the box these be." He took a croissant, and poured himself a cuppa.

"Well done, mate," Ned said. He tasted one of the rolls. "Might be askin' you to show the missus how to make these." He took a second roll, broke it open and smeared some butter on the ends. "I'll be havin' an oven of sorts on Suwarrow. May take a go at these while my supplies last."

Elaine hesitated for a moment, and then raised a croissant to her nose, sniffed, smiled, and took a bite. "*Meitaka ma´ata,*" she said. "Thank you, Jean." She hummed a soft melody as she crossed the room to her sewing machine.

Reggie went up to his office. Ned took a third croissant and slid the platter under the counter before the first customers arrived. "Leave these out and we'll have half the island in here lookin' for a taste. Cook Islanders share food with everyone but don't like parting with their brass." He handed Émile the saucer. "Best put that in your fridge, mate."

When Émile returned from his apartment, Ned handed him a broom and pointed toward the door. "Front porch and steps need to be sorted. His nibs likes a clean and orderly shop. There's a bin alongside for any rubbish."

This is how I started—sweeping up at Pascal's bistro in Paris. Seems like ages ago. Wonder if it's still there. Wonder if Carlo's still looking for me. I did make a good impression on everyone here with the croissants. Hope Bobbie comes in today. How can I be alone with her? Maybe invite her to the movies.

Émile had learned there was a movie theater of sorts just down the road. He looked up when he heard Reggie talking on the shortwave radio. But, he was also told half the island crowded into a not large building whenever a film was shown. As he swept the steps, everyone who passed by greeted him with a smile and *kia orāna. What friendly people.*

Reggie came out onto the porch sporting a baseball cap and holding some papers in his hand.

"Enough of that, Jean-Philippe. The *Suwarrow's* inbound. Should tie-up in an hour or two. Head on down to the jetty. I'll bring the lorry around."

Émile returned the broom to the store and went to the apartment to get his hat. Ned was back among the aisles counting something.

"Coming to meet the ship?" Émile asked.

"Nah, mate. Someone has to mind the store."

Émile saw Elaine working away at her sewing and wondered why she couldn't mind the store. *Don't they trust the islanders in their absence? Why not just close the store for a bit?*

On the jetty, Reggie had backed his lorry to the far end, and then stood with the harbormaster at the end of the pier. Émile, surprised to see a crowd, wondered how many other shortwave radios were on the island. To the northwest, he could see the narrow silhouette of the approaching ship. Émile didn't see any islanders moving to man the lighters moored alongside. Maybe she won't drop anchor outside the harbor like the *Dorado*, he thought.

Émile waited on the opposite side of the lorry's cab, half-hidden from the harbormaster. *Reggie said there shouldn't be any problem with Berrynabor, but I don't want to be too obvious. Don't remember what he said about the immigration officer. I'll try to blend in with the crowd, but I have to help with the store's cargo.* He looked around at the growing crowd. *Maybe Bobbie'll be here.*

More people came out onto the pier. The honking of a vehicle's horn opened a path through the crowd. A flatbed lorry of dubious vintage worked its way toward the end of the jetty. On its back rode a dozen or so men armed with drums, guitars, and ukuleles. The flatbed was followed by an official-looking Land Rover. A tap on his shoulder made Émile turn—John Spreadborough and Wiggie.

"Righto, mate, how ya gettin' on?" Wiggie asked. "You look a bit off."

"*Bonjour, mes amis.*" They shook hands. "I have been working at my new position. Sorry I have not come to the hotel for a drink. Perhaps this evening, *n'est-ce pas?*" He looked from side-to-side and lowered his voice. "I am afraid of being found out. There are government officials here. I left my passport at the store. What if I am asked to produce my papers?"

Wiggie and John looked at each other, and then laughed. "You haven't got it sorted yet have you, Jean-Philippe, or whoever you are?" Wiggie said with a wink. John opened his notebook and wrote.

Émile shook his head. *Is this a joke? Why are they laughing?*

"You have no worries in the Cooks, mate." Wiggie said. "You are now an employee of the Southern Cross Trading Company. You work for Captain Reginald Pobjoy, decorated veteran of 75 Squadron, Royal New Zealand Air Force and a former prisoner of war. When Reggie vouches for you . . . which he'll do . . . that's it, done and dusted. He's one of the Grand Pooh-Bahs on these islands. Thought you might have realized that. You have no worries. Be a good lad, enjoy yourself, work hard, and stay out of trouble."

Spreadborough put away his notebook and said, "You're spot on, Wiggie. But there's another whose good graces you should cultivate, *mon ami.*" He pointed toward the inbound ship. "Tooks Marsten. Reggie's partner and brother-in-law. They started this inter-island shipping company after the war, which brought, and still brings, many benefits to the economy. Tooks is from one of the oldest mixed-blood families in the islands. You've landed in a sweet situation, Jean-Philippe. I do believe you may find your nirvana here."

Maybe they're right. Maybe I can quit looking over my shoulder. This could be what I'm searching for.

The island combo got down off the flatbed lorry and formed up along the edge of the pier. Everyone applauded when they began to play, and a few of the women joined in with an impromptu dance.

"The arrival of one of Reggie's ships always calls for a celebration of sorts," Wiggie said. "Especially one from Auckland. Be lots of relatives on board."

"And they best have my reefer." Jake Cartwright joined them.

The uniformed driver of the Land Rover walked past and stood with Reggie and the harbormaster. He turned around and nodded to Jake and the others, but then paused for a moment. Reggie noticed this hesitation and took the immigration officer aside.

Merde! Now what? Wiggie said everything was sorted. Émile's palms were wet and he his heart rate increased. He couldn't hear what Reggie was saying, but the ship owner pointed over his shoulder toward him and then out to sea, and shrugged his shoulders. The two men shook hands, and the officer turned to face Émile, smiled and nodded as if to say, "Everything's okay."

Wiggie placed a hand on Émile's shoulder. "There you go, mate. No worries here."

A blast from the *Suwarrow's* horn turned attention seaward. Émile saw the ship's railings lined with passengers. He was surprised by the size and shape of the *Suwarrow*. Not at all like the *Dorado*, the *Pacifica Maru*, or other ships he'd traveled on.

"Strange looking vessel, *n'est-ce pas?*"

"Well spotted, Jean," Jake said. "She's a Yank landing craft from the last war. Reggie and Tooks found her in Auckland. About to be stripped and scrapped, she was. Stole her for a song. Scrubbed up well, she did. Yanks took great care with their kit."

Spreadborough had his notebook out and pen poised. "I must know more about this, Jake. If you don't mind."

"She only draws about a fathom fully loaded, and has bow doors and a ramp, so she's spot on for the islands without a proper harbor. Pushes right up to the reef or beach and off loads." He lit a cigarette. "Had berth space for about two hundred soldiers, so there's lots of room for passengers. But, they've cleared more than a bit out for cargo. Not the *Queen Mary*, but the islanders don't mind being all together. Reggie said she was built on the east coast of the States, sailed through the Panama Canal, and then over here to be involved in the fighting in the Philippines at the end of the war."

Like a canoe coming in sideways to a beach, the *Suwarrow* closed on the pier at an angle, turned gently to port, and slowly slid in alongside. Its engines reversed. Members of the band caught lines thrown from the bow and stern, and tied them off. The vessel settled in to the end of the pier; a gangplank was lowered from amidships.

Reggie turned to Émile and said, "Right, Jean-Philippe. Let's go aboard."

They went up the gangplank followed by the harbormaster. Reggie raised his cap to a tall, well-built Maori standing just outside the bridge. The islander returned the salute.

"That be Tooks, my mate," he said to Émile. "Business partner, brother-in-law, and Godfather to all my children."

Islanders at the top of the gangplank greeted Reggie *and* Émile with handshakes and kisses. Reggie, with Émile in tow, politely pushed his way through the passengers to the ladder up to the bridge. Tooks stood at the top of the ladder smiling and shaking his head.

"These folks do love you, *teina*. Who's this new *Papa'ā?*" he said nodding toward Émile. Tooks stood aside as Reggie and Émile came up onto the bridge.

Émile was surprised at the physical differences of these two prosperous shipping and trading company owners: Reggie, short, wiry, and sunburned European; Tooks, tall, muscular, olive-skinned islander. *What brought them together? Wiggie said something about a cyclone and the loss of a ship. I must ask Reggie or Ned sometime.*

Before Reggie could answer, Berrynabor shouted from the bottom of the ladder, "And where be your supercargo, Mister Marsten?"

Tooks frowned and shook his head. "And *Kia orāna* to you, *Herr* Harbormaster." Tooks affected a mock Nazi salute. "Your highness'll find 'im in the aft hold hidin' the contraband."

"None of your flippant island humor, if you please, Marsten."

"That's *Captain* Marsten to you, sir, if you please." Tooks winked at Émile. "And don't be lookin' under the frozen chickens."

Frozen chickens? What's under the frozen chickens?

Berrynabor went aft.

"You never miss a chance to wind 'im up do you, mate?" Reggie said.

"He not a friend of the islands, *teina*. Too close to gov'ment folks in Wellington. Know he be a hero from the first war, but needs to finish soon."

"And soon he will, mate. End of this month or the next, me thinks. Lots of talk about his replacement."

"You should be harbormaster, *teina*," Tooks said with a big grin.

"Ha! Bit of a conflict of interest there, don't you think?" Reggie walked over to the railing around the bridge and looked down at the foredeck. "Good bit of livestock, mate," he said, pointing at the circular gun tubs below the bridge and on the foredeck that now made do as pens for chickens, pigs, and lambs. Covered with wire mesh and a canvas top, the former gun emplacements were well suited for the transport of small animals to the islands. The steel tubs, their insides layered with hay, didn't reach to the deck, so a quick slush of the insides was done by the ship's hoses after each voyage. He turned back to Tooks.

"This new *Papa'ā* is Jean-Philippe from Switzerland. He'll be learning the trade from Ned. Most likely fill in for him when he goes back to Suwarrow." Reggie lit a cigarette. "And he speaks Frog, which may be a bit handy later on."

Why is my French so important? Second time this has been mentioned.

Tooks nodded in agreement but said, "James be keen to learn the business when he finish school." He nodded over his shoulder to the young Maori standing behind him.

"James'll always have a spot in our company, *teina*." He shook the boy's hand. "A few more circuits of the stations and a trip or two more to Auckland be good for him before being stuck behind the counter counting needles and thread, don't you think?"

"You be the boss, *teina*," said the older man with a grin.

"Don't go down that road again, mate." Reggie wasn't smiling. "We're all equals here."

"Yes, *teina*, in our company, but not in the rest of the Cooks."

"Can't change the whole world, mate. Just my little bit." He took Émile by the arm. "Come, *mon ami*, I'll give you the tour while we're waiting for Berrynabor to clear the cargo." He turned to Tooks' nephew. "James, go watch what the harbormaster is about. Good learnin' for you when you run this outfit someday." Reggie smiled at Tooks, who nodded in agreement.

James slid down the ladder and scurried aft.

Reggie gave Émile a tour of the *Suwarrow*. When they returned to the bridge, another man, obviously an islander, stood with James and Tooks on the bridge. Émile saw the harbormaster walking away along the pier.

"What's the deal with chickens, Uncle? That old *pommy* made us take all the birds out of the reefers," the man said to Reggie.

Reggie laughed. "The frozen chickens was your Uncle Tooks' doin', not mine."

I must find about these frozen chickens?

"Jean-Philippe, meet William. We call him Billy. Another Marsten, of course," Reggie said.

"*Kia orāna*, Jean-Philippe," Billy said extending his hand. "Are you a visitor to our islands?"

"*Kia orāna*, Billy. No, I work for Reggie."

"I detect a bit of an accent. German or French, perhaps?"

"Jean-Philippe is Swiss," Reggie said. "Billy's the educated one in the business. Got a double first in economics and accounting from Wellington."

"Right, Uncle, and now I'm the supercargo on a family barge hauling coconuts and tomatoes between the islands." He smiled.

"Too right, nephew. And when Tooks and I decide to chuck it all in and go fishing on the reef, it's all yours . . . and your cousins, of course."

"What brings you to the Cooks, Jean-Philippe?" Billy asked.

Émile looked at Reggie. *What story do I tell?*

"He jumped ship off the *Dorado*. Didn't fancy the cuisine," Reggie said, and winked.

"Collecting more white driftwood are you, Uncle? No matter. You're the boss."

Is this Billy not pleased with me working for Reggie? What did he mean by white driftwood?

Below the bridge on the well deck, two crew members attached cargo straps around a crate. Jake Cartwright stood nearby supervising. As the ship's bow crane lifted the crate up and over the side, Jake scurried down the gangplank and waited on the pier. The crate was lowered onto the band's flatbed truck.

"That be Jake's reefer," Tooks said.

It began to rain as a passing squall came ashore. The men on the open bridge stepped back under the shelter of the canvas "China Hat."

"Sure enough he'll be havin' his grand opening soon," Reggie said. He nodded toward Émile. "Our new Swiss friend is a spot-on baker and will be addin' some European cuisine to Jake's menu at the weekend."

"So, you're a cook then, are you, Jean-Philippe?" Billy asked.

"*Oui* . . . I mean yes, Billy."

"Maybe he should take a berth on the company barge, Uncle," Billy said to Tooks and Reggie. "One-hung-low isn't such great shakes in the cuisine department."

Tooks' expression turned sour. "Wang Low not best cook in southern ocean. Reggie and I owe him a chance. His father was cook on the *Wallaroo*." Tooks raised a finger. "Nephew, not say more about this."

Billy lowered his head and nodded. "Yes, Uncle."

"Steady on, lads." Reggie said. "Jean-Philippe can have a chat with Wang Low and discuss possible culinary improvements to his menu." He grinned.

Another gangplank, aft of the ship's superstructure, had been lowered to the pier and the members of the band and others—now acting as stevedores—waited to begin unloading the cargo from the aft hold.

"Best go put my eyes on that lot," Billy said. "Come along, Jean-Philippe, you can help watch for any light-fingered Larrys."

Reggie nodded, and Émile followed Billy to the rear deck.

A mob of islanders hefted the goods passed up from the hold and waited for the supercargo's okay to carry them down to the pier. Lorries from other businesses now parked next to Reggie's. Émile noticed that some vehicles parked in front of others blocking their departure. *But* no vehicle blocked Reggie's. It had a clear path up the pier. *My boss is a Grand Pooh-Bah, as Wiggie said.*

"Go ashore, Jean-Philippe, and sort each bit as it comes down the gangplank. Everything marked SCTC goes in Reggie's lorry."

"Yes, I can do that." Émile went down the gangplank and waited. Three men descended from the ship with boxes marked SCTC in large black letters, and he led them to the lorry. Then he froze. A Cook Island constable stood by the lorry.

"*Kia orāna,*" he said.

"*Kia orāna,*" Émile replied. *Now what? Why are the police interested in what I'm doing?* "I work for Captain Pobjoy." *Maybe that will have influence.*

"Yes, I know. I'm Tupuri Marsten. Welcome to the Cooks." He extended his hand.

Émile took his hand. "Jean-Philippe . . . Marsten? A relative of Captain Tooks?"

"Yes. He's my uncle. Do go back to the gangplank, Jean-Philippe. No worries here. I'll keep an eye on the lorry."

Mon Dieu! Another one. Maybe Reggie is related to half the island, as Jake said.

Soon, when his lorry was loaded to capacity, Reggie joined Émile on the pier. "Be knowin' how to drive me beauty, do you now?"

"*Oui* . . . I mean yes, Reggie." *Do I need a license to drive on Rarotonga?*

"Right you are then. Off you go. Take the goods to the store. Around back. Ned and Elaine will help you off load, and make speed back. Lots more to be sorted."

As Émile drove off the pier, he thought he saw Bobbie in the crowd. *Maybe, she'll still be there when I return.*

Ned and Elaine were waiting for him when he backed into the parking space behind the company store. *How'd they know I'd be arriving?*

Elaine offered Émile a cup of tea as they unloaded the goods into the warehouse.

"*Pardon* . . . I mean excuse me, Elaine, are you a member of the Marsten family?"

She smiled. "Of course. This is a family business. Ned is married to a Marsten. Reggie married Tooks' sister—she died in childbirth." She turned to see if Ned could hear her, and lowered her voice. "Not the best of husbands, that one. Always going off by himself to that empty atoll." She shrugged and lifted another box from the lorry.

When Émile returned to the pier, the space for Reggie's lorry was still vacant. Constable Tupuri stood next to a pile of boxes and cartons. *No need to watch for light-fingered Larrys today.*

A voice he recognized interrupted Émile's loading of the lorry. He almost dropped the case of Suva beer.

"*Kia orāna*, Jean-Philippe from Switzerland."

Émile put the case of beer in the lorry and turned to see Bobbie with her friends from Titikaveka, who echoed the greeting, all three grinning at him.

"*Kia orāna*, Bobbie. And Rhonda, isn't it? And Mary."

"Well done, Jean-Philippe," Rhonda said and laughed. "A surprise that you remember *our* names."

"I'm *très bon*, very good with names, Rhonda. Especially with those whom I have shared humorous times."

"You sure wound up those Yank tourists, Jean-Philippe," Rhonda said.

He didn't have the opportunity to answer. A large, sunburned *Papa'ā* injected himself between the island lovelies and Émile.

"You work for Pobjoy, do you? I'm Tipsord." He didn't take Émile's hand.

Émile nodded. *This one's accent is different. Australian maybe?*

"Right. Well, get his rig sorted and push off. I've three lorries waiting. It's not done—hogging the pier." He turned and stomped away.

Émile right hand instinctively caressed the hilt of his sheath knife.

Bobbie and her friends wandered off into the crowd. *Where'd they go? When will I see her again? Damn Aussie! Everyone of them I've met has been a loud-mouthed ass . . . even in the Légion.*

Émile continued to load the lorry. Tipsord waited up the pier by his line of lorries.

Billy came down the gangplank and joined Émile. He lit a cigarette. "A bit more to go, mate. This and another should do it." He offered Émile a cigarette.

"That man," Émile said, "wants us off the pier." He pointed toward Tipsord.

"No worries there, mate." He smiled as Constable Tupurai joined them. "Cousin, perhaps there might be some vehicle safety violations on Tipsord's convoy. As a concerned citizen, I'd appreciate a close inspection."

"Right you are, Cousin," Tupurai said. He pulled a notebook from the rear pocket of his dark blue shorts and walked back along the line of vehicles.

Billy laughed and went back up the gangplank. Reggie and Tooks had been watching from the bridge and gave him a thumbs-up. Billy returned the salute.

Émile finished loading the lorry and drove back to the store. *I think I will enjoy working for this family.*

After two more trips to the store, Émile returned to the pier. The aft gangplank had been raised, and Reggie and Tooks stood waiting. They loaded several cases of beer, wine, soft drinks, large cans of cooking oil, and other condiments into the lorry.

"In the back, Jean-Philippe," Reggie said. "We'll see if my *teina* can operate me beauty without causin' us bodily harm."

Émile climbed into the back of the lorry, and Tooks slid into the driver's seat.

"Billy, James, and Mariku, the mate will join us at Jake's," Reggie said. "Right you are, Captain Tooks, onward to the christening."

With a few jerks and lurches until he got familiar with the clutch, Tooks drove off the pier and turned left onto *Ara Tapu,* the coast road that circled the island. Reggie slid open the cab rear window and laughed, "My brother can master and navigate any vessel into any port in the southern ocean, but sorting out the clutch pedal is a mystery to him."

When they pulled into the parking area behind Jake's restaurant, they saw the band's lorry backed up to open double doors at the back of the building. Two metal ramps extended to the ground from the rear of the vehicle. Jake stood there with the driver. They laughed when Tooks forgot to engage the clutch and the engine died with a jerk.

"What time do you call this, you lot?" Jake said. "Heavy lifting needs doing. Where's the rest of the band?"

"Still off loading cargo for my competitors," Reggie said. "They'll be along directly . . . or not gaining any brass."

"Right. Me thinks the five of us can sort this . . . off the lorry anyways. Let's give it a go."

They manhandled the reefer down the ramps. Jake sent the driver back to the pier to collect the rest of his crew.

"A cool brew is in order. What say you?" Jake said. "We'll have a sit on the deck." He turned to Émile. "Jean, there's a frig behind the bar. Collect us each one, if you please."

Émile looked to Reggie, who nodded. *I do work for these two. Best get used to taking orders from both of them.*

Émile returned from the bar with a dozen bottles of beer on a tray. He'd found a bottle opener on top of the frig but didn't remove the caps. The other men sat under a palm frond umbrella at one of the tables. Ocean rollers pounded against the barrier reef outside Avarua Harbor; rain squalls passed by off shore. He laid the tray on the table.

Jake guffawed and said, "This man be knowing we'll want more than one. Goodo, Jean." He opened beers for Reggie and Tooks.

"I thought others were arriving, *non?*"

"Right you are, mate," Jake said and handed Émile a beer.

Émile moved to take a seat at an adjacent table.

"None of that, lad," Reggie said. "You'll sit with us."

"Oh, thank you, Monsieur . . . I mean Reggie." *They're treating me like one of the family. I must do nothing to destroy this trust. I do feel at home here. It's like the comradeship in the Légion.*

Reggie turned to Tooks. "And how went the voyage, *teina?* Any problems I should know about?"

Tooks finished his beer and lit a cigarette. "No worries, *teina.* We made stop at Raoul. Off loaded supplies. And our money mate, Dee-Dee. Sorting out some scheme with naturalists, he was. Sends his regards."

"Declan . . . Dee-Dee . . . Dearlove," Reggie explained to Émile, "is our banker in Auckland. He, also, was in the RAF, and we were together behind the barbed wire for some time. I met him during my first days on the *Wallaroo.* He was most helpful in getting us started in this business." He winked at Tooks.

"Right proper chap, your Dearlove," Jake said. "Couldn't have sorted this new scheme without his help and advice. Take that flat. Not like some *tack-wallahs* I could mention." He raised his glass. "More thanks to you, Reggie."

The band's lorry drove into parking area. A dozen islanders jumped off and headed for the deck. Jake intercepted them; he gestured toward the reefer.

"Right. You lot be putting your backs to that rig. Beers all around when it's sorted."

Reggie asked Tooks, "And how is young Malcolm? He's not a great writer of letters."

"Only fifteen, *teina.* What you expect? He's a teenager. Your father and he came down to Auckland. Had a fine time. Showed them the *Suwarrow.*"

"How's he getting along in school?"

"Your *pāpā* said he is doin' well."

"A visit is in order. Perhaps in a week or two." Reggie faced Émile. "My son, Tokerau, but we call him by his middle name, Malcolm, is on North Island, along with my daughter Nga. They spend the school year there with their grandparents. Malcolm is fifteen and Nga is thirteen. My folks have a sheep farm outside of Whangerai. I go for a visit two or three times during the school year and, of course, they return to Raro for Christmas and the summer holidays."

A great deal of shouting in English and Maori came from the back of the building. After a loud crash, the "stevedores" strolled out onto the deck. Jake followed.

"That's done and dusted," he said. "Plugged in and taking juice."

Spreading out among the deck tables, the combo members fingered their instruments.

These islanders never miss a chance for a party.

"Jean, a brew for all, thank you very much." Jake looked back to the coast road. "Here's help, mate. My new waitresses." He pointed with a bottle at three young women walking toward the restaurant.

Émile almost dropped the tray of empty bottles he'd collected off the table.

Mon Dieu, it's Bobbie and her friends!

He stood there like he was frozen in time until Jake said, "On your bike, mate. The lads are thirsty."

"*Oui* . . . yes sir. *Pardon* . . . sorry." Émile went up the stairs to the restaurant level and collected another tray of beers. *Bobbie working for Jake. Merveilleux! Now I'll see her each weekend, at least.*

"May I help, Jean-Philippe?" Rhonda had come up behind him. "You'll be needing more than one tray for this lot." She took a second tray from the stack on the counter.

"*Merci beaucoup* . . . I mean thank you, Rhonda." Émile was surprised by the amount of body contact with her as they moved about behind the bar. Their buttocks touched more than once, and Rhonda pressed her large breasts against his back while reaching past him to take beers from the cooler.

Was that intentional? She could have waited until I moved out of her way.

"Don't apologize, Jean-Philippe." She smiled. "I enjoy hearing French. Perhaps you could teach me some words. It might impress the foreign tourists."

"*Bien sûr* . . . of course. It would be my pleasure."

They walked back down to the deck. Bobbie sat between Reggie and Jake while Mary joined the men at another table. Émile and Rhonda passed out beers to everyone, then Rhonda sat with the rest of the band. Émile returned to Reggie's table and, with a bar towel he'd brought from the restaurant draped over his arm, he affected a waiter-like pose.

"Will there be anything else, Messieurs?"

There was moment of silence, and then they all burst into laughter, including Bobbie.

"Maybe I should be hiring him as a waiter, not a chef," Jake said.

"Well done, Jean-Philippe," Reggie said. "Now take a chair and join us."

Émile sat opposite Bobbie and said, "*Kia orāna.*" *I must not stare.*

She smiled and said, "Uncle Reggie told me we'll be working together here. That'll be fun."

"Yes, I believe that's right." *What a stupid answer. When may I be alone with her?*

Everyone turned when the horn of a faded green Morris Minor sedan announced its arrival. Billy, James, Mariku, and Constable Tupurai joined them on the deck. Émile stood to get more drinks, but Bobbie said, "No bother, Jean-Philippe. I'll go."

During the greetings and handshakes all around, Émile enjoyed watching Bobbie climb the stairs to the restaurant. *I must find the time to be alone with her. Tell her how I feel about her.*

"Here's the manifest, Uncles," Billy said to Reggie and Tooks. "Sort it out now or tomorrow?"

"We can take a look now, nephew," Reggie said. "Jake, my friend, may we have this table to sort out some company business?"

"Too right, mate. I'll take the constable to arrest some of these ne'er-do-wells." Jake led Tupurai to another table as the combo began to play. Émile stood to leave, but Reggie motioned for him to sit.

"You're part of this now, mate. Sit and listen. Lots to be learned."

Billy handed Reggie a sheaf of papers and said, "Priority, Uncles, should be to Manihiki. New generators for the resident agent and the clinic. Wellington was most emphatic about that. A stop at Rakahanga would be in order. Both should have copra for us. Not sure about the others in the northern group. That's your decision, Uncles."

Rakahanga! That's where Bobbie is from. She'll be leaving Raro!

Reggie passed the paper to Tooks. "Rakahanga and Manihiki for sure. We'll have to see if Penrhyn and Pukapuka need a visit. Most likely. Haven't dropped anchor there in a few months."

"Yes, *teina*. A stop at Suwarrow?" Tooks asked.

"Not sure Ned has all his kit sorted yet. Perhaps next time."

When will the ship leave? I must tell Bobbie how I feel. Maybe she isn't interested in me—so many years older. Must find a way to be alone with her before she goes away.

36

During the next two weeks Émile absorbed the store's inventory, assisted customers, and kept the place spotless. He continued to bake croissants each Monday morning. After work, he often helped Ned pack and prepare the supplies for his return to Suwarrow. A small cutter and two rowing canoes were added to the growing collection of kit under cover behind the building. One evening Constable Tupurai stopped by for a chat. Émile had noticed the lack of a fence protecting Ned's gear and other items from passersby. He also noticed the frequent police patrols past the rear of the building.

"*Kia orāna*. When's the big day, Ned? Soon?"

"No such luck, mate. Maybe after Christmas. Still some bureaucratic crap to sort with the Commissioner. He wasn't well pleased with my idea to take the position as warden." Ned shifted a pair of oars into the cutter. "Told the twit I didn't want any pay, just be left alone. Said he was concerned about rescuing me during cyclone season. Ha! Been through two of them before. Haven't had to be rescued yet." He offered cigarettes to Émile and Tupurai. "The captain said he will sort out the Commissioner and to keep collecting my kit. Fine man, the captain. Survived one himself, he did."

"Survived what?" Émile asked.

"A cyclone. On Suwarrow. Back in '38. Saved your uncle's life, he did, Tupurai."

"Right you are there, Ned. The captain's a legend in the islands."

"I'd enjoy hearing that story," Émile said.

Tupurai and Ned looked at each other. "Best hear it from the captain," Ned said.

"That would be well good," Tupurai said, "Others have embellished it somewhat."

* * *

On the next Saturday, Jake planned to have a grand opening of his new restaurant. Émile spent some hours helping the New Zealander organize his kitchen. Jake wanted a special European dish to offer to the diners. Émile suggested a traditional Parisian *cassoulet* made with local ingredients. He called it a Swiss-style favorite from the French cantons. In the evenings, if he wasn't at Skipper Jake's, he would eat a light dinner, usually fresh fish from the market, and then stroll over to the hotel for a glass of wine with Wiggie and John. Wiggie ragged him about not being more aggressive with his attempts to meet Bobbie again. Émile took these jabs in good humor and knew he'd see more of Bobbie once the restaurant opened. In fact, Bobbie and Rhonda spent all day prior to the big event helping Jake sort out the table settings for the dining area on the upper level.

Émile was shocked when he learned the *Suwarrow* would depart for a run to Rakahanga and other islands in the northern group the week after Jake's opening. He regretted not having made the trip to Titikaveka to see her again.

"When will you return to Rarotonga?" he asked Bobbie. She and Rhonda were laying out the table settings in the restaurant. He made some suggestions about the placement of the flatware and glasses.

"I don't know, Jean-Philippe. I don't think about that. I only want to go home."

"She's only been here once before," Rhonda said. "And then as a small child. I will miss her." She smiled at Émile and raised an eyebrow. "Perhaps you will visit her on Rakahanga someday."

"Perhaps." *How could I manage that? She'd probably be married to some islander by then.*

The grand opening of Skipper Jake's was a resounding success. Wiggie and John Spreadborough were first in the queue when Jake cut a green ribbon at the top of the steps leading to the open-well bar on the lower level; Reggie sat at the bar on the restaurant level. The bars, the tables on the pier, and the restaurant soon filled to capacity. A six-piece combo provided entertainment. The Resident Commissioner had reserved a large table for a party of VIPs. These included Toa Mahuta, the visiting *ariki* from Rakahanga. Émile watched from the kitchen serving window behind the bar. He and the other islander assistant cooks furiously worked to keep orders for fish'n chips and burgers flowing out to the waitresses. There seemed to be a special affinity between Reggie and the chief from Rakahanga; a vigorous handshake and hugs were exchanged. Toa, Émile learned later, had been a crew member on the copra schooner *Wallaroo* when Reggie first went to sea. He left the ship on Rarotonga before it made the dash to Pukapuka in '38.

Tooks and his nephews joined the rush of customers, sat at the restaurant bar and waved to Émile. He said something to the bartender in Maori, and Émile was handed a glass of chilled wine. "Quench your thirst, mate. It looks warm back there."

Jake Cartwright circulated throughout his new establishment greeting everyone and buying drinks for many patrons. Émile saw Berrynabor, the harbor master, and the immigration officer join the VIP table. But he was no longer concerned with their presence—he worked for Captain Pobjoy and Jake Cartwright.

Wiggie volunteered to help in the kitchen, but Émile could tell he'd had several pints and declined the offer. His *cassoulet* was well received by everyone—finished long before the mandatory closing at midnight.

"Was Ned here?" Émile asked Reggie. "I didn't see him." The three of them—Jake, Reggie, and Émile—sat at the restaurant bar while Bobbie, Rhonda, and two other waitresses cleared the tables. The *sous-chefs* sorted out the kitchen.

"Ned? No, Jean-Philippe. Ned's a bit of a recluse. Doesn't fancy crowds."

"Too right you are, mate," Jake said as he filled their glasses again. "When's he running back to that atoll of his?"

"Most likely in a month or so," Reggie said. "We may make a run up there when he gets all his kit collected." He took a drink. "Wouldn't mind seeing the old place myself." Turning on the bar stool, he looked at the surf breaking on the reef in the moonlight. "Hope our tribute to Tangaroa is still standing."

"Cheers to you, Jean," Jake said and raised his glass. "That Frog thing you created was the main event. Must make it a staple on the ticket."

37

Émile joined the crowd on the pier in time to watch the sailing of the *Suwarrow*. He hadn't found the courage or made the effort to be alone with Bobbie. When she came into the store or he saw her at the market, she was always with Rhonda and other girls. This infatuation with a much younger woman is silly, he thought. But he was disappointed he didn't get a chance to say goodbye; she was already on the ship standing at the rail when he arrived. John Spreadborough stood next to her. Émile moved to the front of the crowd, caught her eye and waved. She smiled and waved back.

The ship's gangplanks were drawn up, and with a blast on its horn the *Suwarrow* slid away from the pier. An impromptu band and dancers performed until the ship passed the breakwater. Many islanders, including Émile, stayed on the end of the pier until the *Suwarrow* was almost out of sight.

"*Kia orāna*, Jean-Philippe." Rhonda stood next to him. "Bobbie wanted to say ´*aere ra*, goodbye, to you, but she had to get on the boat." She leaned close and gave him a kiss on the cheek. "That's from Bobbie. She said the French kiss on the cheeks."

Émile smiled and said, "I'm Swiss not French. I just speak French. But thank you."

"I would like to learn how to speak French. Would you give me lessons?"

"*Bien sûr*. That means, of course. When?"

"Soon, Jean-Philippe . . . soon." She gave him a kiss on the other cheek, turned and joined the people leaving the pier.

* * *

During the weeks before the *Suwarrow* returned, Ned collected the last bits of equipment he would need on the atoll. Rhonda came by in the evenings, once or twice a week, for French lessons. After the first week, she usually spent the night. There was no talk of commitment or love, they just enjoyed each other.

Busy days. Émile helped Ned and a mob of Tooks's relatives transfer his island cargo from the store's storage shed to the *Suwarrow*. The harbormaster, Berrynabor, watched all of this in disbelief. He would shake his head and mutter, "Bloody waste of time and good kit, this is."

When Émile wasn't assisting Ned, he was teaching James, Tooks's nephew, the store business. James had returned on the *Suwarrow,* and Reggie and his uncle said it was time for him to learn the store business. James hoped to make a few more voyages to Auckland or elsewhere, but one didn't argue with Reggie and Tooks.

Émile knew he would miss Ned. He had taught Émile how to night fish on the reef at low tide, how to find snails, which Émile included in special dishes at Skipper Jake's, and best of all, he told Émile about Reggie and

Tooks being marooned on Suwarrow in '38. Reggie planned to go on this visit to Suwarrow, which surprised no one except Émile.

"Most likely gone about three weeks, mate," Reggie said while briefing Émile on what needed done. "Surely make a run up to Pukapuka, and maybe over to Rakahanga. Stay on the wireless and we'll check in frequenty."

Rakahanga! He'll see Bobbie. Should I ask him to find out if she's married yet? "Should I sleep in your office, Reggie?"

"Nah, don't be daft. Just have someone keep an ear open during the day. If'n there's any problem, we'll contact Suva. They monitor 'round the clock."

"Do give my best to Bobbie, if you see her, *s'il vous plait.* And John Spreadborough."

"Right you are, mate. Not many folks on Raka. I usually be havin' a chat with most of them."

Ned came out of the back room carrying two long canvas bags. "That's all done and dusted, Captain." He patted the bags. "Got meself an Enfield for sharks and a 20-bore for birds."

"Ever do any shooting?" Reggie asked Émile.

"*Oui.* During my military service." *They'll never know about my weapons training and combat patrols in the Légion. Yes, I know how to shoot.* "Only basic marksmanship procedures."

"Swiss Army, was it?" Reggie asked.

"I thought you said you were a cook," Ned interrupted.

"*Oui, mais* everyone is required to qualify—is that the correct word?—with a rifle."

"Makes sense to me. Right, Ned, let's be off. The store is in your hands, Jean-Philippe. Don't hesitate to seek help and advice from Elaine. She's been with us forever and can sort out any problems with the locals."

Once again Émile stood at the end of the pier and watched the *Suwarrow* leave for Rakahanga. *Will I ever see Bobbie again? Maybe that's not my fate. Should be happy with what I have here on Rarotonga.*

"*Bonjour, mon chéri. Comment allez-vous?*" Rhonda took his arm and pressed her breasts against him. "Another French lesson tonight?"

"*Bien sûr.*"

* * *

With Reggie and the *Suwarrow* away, Émile's routine became routine: the store six and a half days a week, market visits on Saturday, and cooking at Jake's Saturday evenings and Sunday. And frequent French lessons. Jake advertised Saturday as "Chef's Special Night," and Émile prepared an appropriate dish. Concerned when Jake showed him the article in an Auckland newspaper lauding his expertise, Émile thought he might have to leave Rarotonga and find a more secluded place to hide. Maybe on one of the outer islands.

Two other incidents rattled his routine. A French Navy frigate on a courtesy visit from Tahiti was in the harbor for a few days. When members of the crew came to the store to buy souvenirs, they were pleased to meet someone who spoke French.

Jake asked Émile to prepare his Parisian *cassoulet*. The French officers reserved a table and were most impressed by the meal—not what they expected from a British, albeit New Zealander run, restaurant in the South Pacific. They insisted on complementing the chef in person. Émile wiped his hands on his apron as he came out of the kitchen. The officers stood; one handed Émile a glass of wine and proposed a toast to his culinary expertise and a continued Anglo-French friendship.

On the following Monday, a French officer came to the store and handed Émile a stack of month-old copies of newspapers and magazines from Paris. He knew Émile was from Switzerland but thought he might be interested in what was happening, or had happened, in that part of the world. Émile thanked him and returned the favor, giving the officer a colorful island shirt printed with an image of Tangaroa in all his glory. Later that evening, while perusing the newspapers, he felt a chill when he read an article lauding the opening of a new apartment complex in Paris—a complex owned by the well-known property magnate, Carlo Pioletti. *Merde! Thought he might be dead by now—hoped anyway.*

The second incident occurred one Saturday evening near closing time. Rhonda was handling the cash register and Jake had gone back to the office or the Gents. A large and loud Australian who was there with Tipsord insisted on paying the bill in Australian pounds.

"I'm sorry, sir. We only accept New Zealand pounds or American dollars," Rhonda said.

Émile, watching and listening to all this from the kitchen window, knew that wasn't completely true—Jake took *Polynesie Francaise* francs from the French sailors.

"No worries, mate," Tipsord said. "I'll cover it."

"No, mate. I'll sort this. Where's the head man? I'll have a word with him." He started to come behind the bar. Rhonda put up a hand to stop him. "Please, sir. Wait."

"No Sheila darkie touches me." He pushed her aside.

Émile burst out of the kitchen and went face-to-face with the man. "Do not touch her again, you pig." His right hand grasped the handle of his sheath knife.

Inches taller and heavier than Émile, the Aussie laughed. "You're about to be hurt, you little Frog."

Émile's knife was out of its sheath when Jake, now behind the bar, yelled, "Talfai!" The former All Blacks half back and two of his rugby teammates rushed up from the lower level bar and grabbed the Australians. "Do they need a swim, Jake?" Talfai asked.

"Nah. Just send them on their way, not too gently."

Everything happened so fast, Émile seemed frozen standing there in front of the bar with his knife in his hand. The few other customers in the restaurant stared at him.

"Nothing to get excited about, folks," Jake said. "Just an impromptu floor show." He nodded toward Émile. "Who hasn't seen a gourmet chef without his cutlery?" He poured a shot of whiskey and handed it to Émile. "Sit yourself, mate, and take this."

"I'm sorry, Monsieur Jake." He downed the shot. "A beer, *s'il vous plait,*" he said to the bartender. "Never cared much for whiskey." He took a drink of beer. "Perhaps I over reacted, but he pushed Rhonda and . . . *Alors,* you saw."

"Not afraid to mix it up when the time's right, are you?"

"Some things are worth fighting about."

"I think there's more to you than just a Swiss chef, mate. Perhaps we can have a long chat over a few beers sometime."

"Jake, my past is in the past, and I prefer to keep it that way. Nothing against you . . . and Reggie, of course. You both have been more than generous to me. That I'll never forget. But I prefer to live in the present . . . for now."

"Right you are, mate. No more questions. And, by the way, I always have Talfai or other of his rugby mates hangin' about in case of trouble. If'n there's a problem in the future, just yell 'All Blacks', and the cavalry will arrive."

That night's French lesson lasted into the early morning hours. Fortunately it was Sunday, and Émile didn't have to be at Jake's until mid afternoon.

* * *

Ten thousand miles away and a month earlier, Constance Renaud read the same article about Carlo Pioletti in the same Paris newspaper. She cut out the article and placed it a large manila envelope with other clippings. The piece that rested on top of the collection—dated December, 15, 1922—described the discovery of the body of a prostitute and part-time waitress, Marla Carette, in the Seine south of *Ile aux Cygnes.* Her naked body, which had been in the water for several days, was spotted by a river barge pilot. It was wedged in some debris against the supports of the *Pont Mirabeau.*

Police believed she was the victim of a sex crime or dispute between pimps. Her throat was cut, and there were multiple cigarette burns on her breasts and other areas of her body. Was she tortured or was that part of her sex play, the newspaper asked?

Marla, dear Marla, you never told Carlo's thugs where I was from—did she even know? I don't remember—and died for it. It's been so many years. Time to do something, something to bring this creature to justice. Time to find former members of the résistance.

She returned the envelope to the drawer of her desk and locked it. She opened the telephone directory and reached for the telephone.

Constance Renaud was now proprietor of the Hotel Gaultier in Argenteuil, which had been in the family since before the Franco-Prussian War. When she returned to the inn from Paris after the first war, she had married a local butcher, Pierre Renaud.

38

When the *Suwarrow* returned from its swing through the northern group, Reggie and Tooks were the first ones down the gangplank. After a quick word with the immigration officer, they borrowed his Land Rover and drove off. Émile stood by the store's truck and shook his head. *What's going on? Never seen Reggie and Tooks this upset.*

James and Constable Tupurai supervised the off loading while Émile went onboard to talk to Billy.

"*Kia orāna*, Billy," he said to the supercargo. "Reggie and Tooks seemed a bit huffed."

"*Kia orāna*, Jean. Yes. There's a problem on Rakahanga, which will require the Commissioner's authority. They've gone to stand on his desk."

"What was . . . is the problem?"

"Bloody Frogs. But let's wait until my uncles sort this out. Back to work." Billy went down to chat with the harbormaster, and Émile returned to the pier.

An ancient moped sputtered down the pier tailing a stinky blue cloud. Jake Cartwright dismounted. "*Kia orāna*, lads. Where's my mate, the captain?"

"*Kia orāna*, Jake. He's off to see the Grand Pooh-Bah with Uncle Tooks," James said.

"Problems?"

"Yes, but you'd best hear it from them," James said. Jake sputtered away.

After several trips to the store, Émile was joined by Billy on the pier.

"Your friend, that *pommy* writer Spreadborough, sends his regards . . . and a sweet young thing named Bobbie asked when you're coming to Rakahanga." He smiled.

Reggie and Tooks returned and thanked the officer for the use of his vehicle.

"A little conference is in order this evening when the shop closes. In my office," Reggie said. "You also, Jean-Philippe."

Seated in the office were Tooks, Billy, James, and Émile, while Elaine provided a tray of coffee and stood off to the side. Reggie sat at his desk and held the case with the old French coins in his hands. As he placed the case back next to his family's picture he said, "Here's the situation, mates. We're going to open a station on Rakahanga. Reopen it, to be exact. The building is there . . . just needs a bit of fixin' up."

"What's this in need of, Uncle?" James asked. Émile knew James wanted to run a station—he'd mentioned it many times while they worked together in the store.

"The folks on Manihiki and Rakahanga are being cheated by our competitor's trader on Manihiki and the ships that call there, mostly from

Tahiti or Taiwan. They're offering a ridiculously low price for their copra and trying to sweeten the deal with cheap Flipo rum. Toa, the *ariki* on Rakahanga has refused to deal with the foreigners and placed a *tabu* on trading with the station on Manihiki." He held up a piece of paper. "Toa has signed a contract giving the Southern Cross Trading Company exclusive trading rights on his atoll." He laid the paper on his desk and lit a cigarette. "The Commissioner has approved our request." He grinned. "*And* will replace the RA on Manihiki. He was nearing retirement age anyway, and there were rumors about him taking kickbacks from the trader and ship captains. We understand from our sources that he was well-supplied with good English gin."

Reggie stood and looked out the window, then through the telescope. "I believe that's the *Dorado* inbound." The others stood and looked out to sea. The smoke and superstructure of a freighter was on the horizon. "Be a pleasure to visit with Marlow Drayton again. He left without coming ashore last time."

The Dorado! Captain Drayton. What will he tell Reggie? Maybe the subject—me—won't come up. I must try to avoid him on the pier. But what if he goes to Jake's while I'm working?

"Who's going to run the station on Rakahanga, Uncle?" James asked.

Reggie turned to Tooks. "Your turn, *teina.*"

"James, favored nephew, we all know you be wantin' to run a station, but we've decided to offer the position to Jean-Philippe." James seemed to take this stoically. He lowered his eyes, took a deep breath, looked up, and nodded.

Rakahanga! A station on Rakahanga. Me . . . Me running the station? There must be a god. Must make an offering to Tangaroa. He's as good as any other. When?

"Because of the visits from the Frogs we need someone who speaks the lingo, and someone who isn't afraid to face 'em down if the situation arises," Reggie said and turned to Émile. "We stopped at Jake's for a cold one after our chat with the Commissioner. He told us about you taking on two very large Aussies. Not much frightens you, does it, mate?"

* * *

The *Dorado's* visit to Rarotonga was uneventful, with one exception. Wiggie hired on again as purser. At a rousing farewell on Jake's deck, Wiggie proclaimed undying love for Rarotonga, but needed to get away for a while. He missed the open ocean, he said. There were rumors that one or two island girls may be in a certain "condition." With Wiggie, Captain Drayton, Jake, Reggie, Tooks, and Berrynabor sat under a palm frond umbrella-covered table at the end of the deck. Émile couldn't see that end of the deck from his kitchen window. He wondered what they were talking about. Would his name come up? His question was answered when Rhonda came back from the table.

"The captain wants you to join them, *mon chéri.*"

Merde! How do I handle this? Drayton was good to me even though he thought my passport was a poor imitation. I'll play it by ear and let the others do the talking.

Émile set his apron aside and went to the table. Captain Drayton stood as Émile approached. He held out his hand.

"Well met, lad." They shook hands. "These chaps have told me you've made quite a name for yourself on Raro."

"*Oui,* Captain Drayton. They have been most generous, but I also owe a great deal to you for your assistance. Especially my rescue and the hospitality on the *Dorado.*" Émile pulled out his wallet and handed the ship captain two ten-pound notes. "Your loan, Monsieur. I repay my debts."

"No, young man. I can't accept it. Consider it seed money for a new career. Or is it a new life?" The ship captain looked closely at Émile. "Any road, your cooking on the *Dorado* was worth more than twenty quid. We all miss it. Any time you get tired of island life, a position is waiting on my ship."

"Hold on there, Drayton," Jake said. "We're on a winner here, so you must be barkin' if'n you think you can Shanghai Jean. Besides, he's leavin' us anyway. Reggie's sendin' him out to carouse with the islanders on Rakahanga."

This is wonderful—these men arguing about me. I didn't know I was this popular.

"If you liked his cooking so much, Marlow, how come you marooned him here during the last visit?" Berrynabor asked.

Merde! I hoped that wouldn't come up. What do I say?

Drayton was quiet for a moment, then said, "A couple of your pages are stuck together, Harbormaster. If you weren't in the early stages of senility, you'd recall that we arrived, unfortunately, on Anzac Day. I understand from my mate, Henri, you were near under the table at the RSA. Any road, we didn't know that Jean had gone ashore with Wiggie until we were well over the horizon," Drayton lied and winked at Émile. "Things get forgotten sometimes when one is forced to off load cargo with one's own boats because the harbormaster and his crews were all pissed."

The others laughed, and Reggie said, "Well said, Marlow." He got up and pulled another chair to the table. "Join us, Jean-Phillipe."

The conversation wove back and forth between the shipping business and dealings with islanders and other governments in the South Pacific. Rhonda brought Émile a glass of wine.

Wonder how these wonderful men would feel about me if they knew I'd killed two men, albeit in self-defense. Those in Algeria don't count because that was war. But these men don't know about that either. Maybe I'm about to find my nirvana after all.

* * *

The *Suwarrow* made a short stop at its namesake to drop off some essentials for Ned: cigarettes, flour, sugar, matches, butter, books, and Spam. Émile went ashore with Reggie and was impressed by Ned's cabin, chicken run, and gardens on Anchorage Island. The hermit treated his friends to a batch of freshly baked croissants from Émile's recipe.

This man is the most self-sufficient and free soul I've ever met.

* * *

En route to Rakahanga, Reggie had an empty oil drum floated behind the ship on a tether. From the fantail Émile practiced shooting a few rounds with the Springfield bolt-action rifle Reggie wanted him to have at the station. He also fired a couple of shells from a 12-bore shotgun.

"Hopefully, you'll never have to use these," Reggie said. "But it's always good to have them at hand if you're forced to put a bit of stick about."

A calm sea surrounded the atoll when the *Suwarrow*, under Reggie's command, dropped anchor outside the reef at Rakahanga. Tooks remained behind on Rarotonga; he was preparing the *Moana Tama* for a trip to Fiji.

When the ship's boat grounded on the beach, Toa and a mob of islanders met them. The *ariki* placed leis over their heads. Bobbie pushed her way through the crowd, placed another lei over Émile's head and a kiss on each cheek.

"*Kia orāna* and welcome to my island, Jean-Phillipe."

Émile saw tears in her eyes.

Reggie turned to Émile. "Welcome to your new home, *mon ami*. Enjoy your new life."

* * *

Hotel Gaultier, Argenteuil, 1961.

"*Bonjour*, Constance," Paul, the postman, said as he dropped off the morning post.

"Time for a coffee, Paul?" she asked.

Paul looked outside at the rain that came down in buckets. "*Merci*, Constance. I need a break from the deluge."

Paul removed his rain coat and hat. Constance prepared two espressos and brought them to the table.

"*Merci beaucoup*, Constance." He took a sip. "Exciting news in the paper this morning. I'm glad I live out here away from that madness."

"So, what happened? More student riots?" She opened the newspaper.

"*Non*, not today." He took another sip. "A well-known property developer was gunned down near the Luxembourg. Someone named Pioletti."

"What? Where's the article?" Constance almost tore the newspaper apart looking for it.

"Shot three times, it said. Some gangster thing it looks like."

She found the article and read it. *He survived, but is crippled. Serves him right. But not enough for all the pain he's caused me. And others. Must think about this.*

39

Rarotonga, 1964.
A rain squall worked its way around the north side of the island but didn't come ashore. Even if it had, the patrons at the outdoor bar wouldn't have been disturbed.

Skipper Jake's, second only to Quinn's Bar in Pape'ete, was the place in Polynesia to rub elbows with rogues and rascals, *vahines* and wanderers, ex-pats and pirates, scribblers and scoundrels. Not internationally known, and well off major trade and tourist routes, Skipper Jake's was in a South Pacific backwater—its main attraction to those seeking a less public life.

Week's end. The usual assembly—Maori, European, and mixed blood—stood two deep at the open-well bar on the lower level.

Up a flight of steps at the long bar in the restaurant level, Jake Cartwright held court as he did every Friday afternoon before the dining room opened to the public. Two regulars sat at the bar—Reggie and Wiggie.

Reggie enjoyed his first Suva beer of the day while he watched Jake sort the lunch receipts. He lit a cigarette and turned on the bar stool to look out to sea. At high tide, ocean rollers broke on the island's barrier reef sending up sheets of white foam.

"You still serious about going back to France?" Jake said, not looking up from the pieces of paper scattered on the bar.

"Yes, mate. It's something I need to do. Things to sort out. Several reasons."

"Oh, yeah? Name two good ones."

"I want to try'n find the folks who helped me in '41. I want to see if I can find the safe house in Paris where I was hid. And, maybe—*just maybe*—who fingered me to the *Gestapo*. That enough, mate? We've had this discussion before."

"Waste of time. The *Gestapo?* It's been over twenty years. You think the Frogs are going to help you do in one of their own after all this time? Didn't they send a whole lot of French Jews—their neighbors and such—to the death camps?"

Jake raised his head from the paperwork and looked to the left. Turning back to Reggie, he lowered his voice. "Speaking of Frogs." He pointed with his pencil toward two white men—one in a linen suit, the other in a police uniform—who stood at the lower level bar talking to one of the female bartenders.

"That must be the French copper from Pape'ete who's been snooping around asking lots of questions. Bobbie's giving him the tour. Thought they might show up here sooner or later."

"Not much gets by you on Raro, does it, Jake?" Wiggie said.

Jake frowned and nodded to the Maori bartender. "Have another drink, Wiggie. On the house. And, old son, move off a bit and try to keep it shut while the coppers are about. Right, mate?"

Wiggie, with a hangdog expression, slipped down the bar away from Jake and Reggie. The bartender placed a double scotch in front of him.

The two white men walked up the steps to the restaurant level. Robert "Bobbie" Peel, a New Zealander and the Cook Islands' new assistant commissioner of police, made the introductions.

"Evening, Reggie. Jake." The policeman nodded toward Malfrey. "And Wiggie, of course. How are you?" Turning back to Jake, Peel removed his hat; the visitor did the same.

"Here's someone I'd like you to meet," Peel said. He turned to the man in the white linen suit. "Monsieur DeRemer, this is Monsieur Pobjoy, or should I say *Captain* Pobjoy. And, of course, Monsieur Cartwright, the proprietor of this fine establishment."

The newcomer shook hands with Jake and Reggie. Jake pushed his paperwork aside.

"Right. What's your poison, mates?"

"One of your fine single malts would be good," Peel said.

"A chilled glass of Chablis, if available," DeRemer said, "or a rum with cola over ice."

"Monsieur DeRemer is an inspector . . . detective . . . with the French *gendarmerie* on Pape'ete," Peel said. "He's looking for a man who killed a police officer. I told him you know most of the white men in the Cooks."

The bartender placed the drinks on the bar. DeRemer sampled the Chablis. "This is quite good, Monsieur Cartwright. Not French?"

"No. Australian, sorry to say."

Wiggie slid off his bar stool and walked toward the Gents.

"I have a photo," DeRemer said. "I would appreciate it very much if you could give it a moment of your attention."

The French policeman took a small manila envelope from the inside pocket of his coat and slipped out a photograph. He laid it on the bar. Reggie picked it up. The face in the photo was of a man—maybe thirty— with longish dark hair, wearing a floppy hat. He was sitting at a bar. There was a surprised, maybe even frightened, look in his eyes. *Reggie recognized him.* He handed the photo to Jake and winked at the two policemen. "That's you, isn't it, mate?"

"Nah. Too good looking," Jake said. "When did this all take place— the murder, I mean?"

"Seven years ago, in April, 1957."

Reggie took the photo back and held it at arm's length. "Goin' to need specs soon. Spooky lookin' fella. Who'd he kill?"

"A police sergeant and former foreign légionnaire, Heinrich Vater. A very sordid affair, I'm afraid. All over a prostitute. But to be entirely honest, his death was no great loss to France." DeRemer took a drink from his glass, and then turned to look out towards the reef. "This is an exceptionally beautiful venue." He turned back to bar.

"Vater was former German Army, probably Nazi and *SS*. He served in

Indochina and Algeria with the Légion. From my interviews, I have concluded that he was genuinely hated by everyone who knew him. He enjoyed beating up prostitutes, but no charges were ever made against him. My suspect, Jean-Phillipe DeGroote, apparently took exception to this anti-social behavior and stuck a knife in Vater's throat. DeGroote may have a Swiss passport, but we have reason to believe it is a forgery. And he may also be a deserter from the Légion."

"Why do you think he's here . . . in the Cooks?" Reggie handed the photo to the French detective. "What's his real name?"

"His real name? I'm afraid I have no idea. After the debacle in Indochina, many légionnaires took steps to avoid a return to France. Our sources in Saigon reported that a légionnaire named Émile Volantes purchased a false Swiss passport in the name of Jean-Philippe DeGroote. But the name DeGroote, or Volantes for that matter, may not be accurate. There are stories about légionnaires who exchanged identity tags with dead comrades. This entire episode is obscured by the aftermath of defeat and the fog of war. And our hurried exit from the colony seven years ago." DeRemer took a sip of wine. "When I was on Nouméa last week showing this photo to others, I interviewed a lascar seaman who said he was crew on a tramp out of Pape'ete that rescued a white man of this description adrift east of Tongareva—Penrhyn Island you call it. He left the ship here on Rarotonga." DeRemer replaced the photo in his wallet.

"What was the name? One of my ships? A tramp?" Reggie stood back from the bar.

"No, Reggie," Peel said raising his hands. "Not one of yours. No one would ever think of calling your vessels tramps."

"My apologies, Captain Pobjoy," DeRemer said, "The vessel in question was the *Dorado*. Not one of yours."

"Sorry, Monsieur DeRemer, I take special pride in my little flotilla. And no one has ever referred to any of them as a tramp." Reggie sat back on his stool. "Jake, let's have another round here for our new friend."

Jake nodded toward the bartender, who brought the same again. Wiggie, who'd returned to his stool, leaned forward with a hopeful look on his face. Jake ignored him.

"There's a lot of white driftwood floating 'round the islands," Reggie said, "Don't know them all. Could send a description of that fella out to my stations. It'd be some weeks before you hear from most of them, if at all. How long are you staying on Rarotonga, Monsieur DeRemer?"

"This is actually my . . . how do you say it . . . swan song, Captain Pobjoy. I return to France in a few weeks to begin my retirement. I am sure my superiors in Pape'ete sent me on this journey through the islands as a farewell gift. I hold no false hopes of finding this man, but the opportunity to tour *le beau paradis* is quite satisfactory."

"Where in France? I'm off to Paris myself in a month or so."

"*Très bon.* Paris is my home. How long will you be there, Captain Pobjoy?"

"Don't know for sure. Some weeks. How do you feel about collaborators, Monsieur DeRemer? Wait a minute. I can't keep calling you 'Monsieur'. What's your given name? I'm Reggie." He extended his hand again.

The French detective smiled and grasped Reggie's hand, "Theatris, but my friends call me 'Theo'."

"Monsieur DeRemer, you'll have to excuse Captain Pobjoy. Some folks tend to become somewhat informal after living in the islands for many years."

"No need to be a stuffed shirt all the time, Bobbie," Reggie said. "Collaborators, Theo. What do think about them?"

"May I ask why the interest, Cap . . . Reggie?"

Jake reached across the bar and placed a hand on Reggie's shoulder. "I can best answer that, Monsieur Theo. My mate doesn't like to talk about his war experiences. He was shot down over France in 1941, helped by the underground as far as Paris, and then got picked up by the *Gestapo*. Spent over three years in a *stalag*."

"I am most sorry to hear that," DeRemer said. "I also was a guest of the Germans for a short time. Fortunately, I was able to escape and join the Free French Forces in North Africa. Why do you ask about *collaborateurs*—collaborators?"

"I've always had the feeling that someone must've fingered me to the *Gestapo*. I've no proof that's what happened, but there was a lot of discussion about it in the *stalag*. There was some talk, rumors mostly, of a deserter, an English soldier gone bad, who was responsible for turning in Allied airmen to the Germans. Ever hear the name Paul or Harry Cole?"

"No. The name is not familiar to me." He took a notebook from the inside pocket of his coat and wrote down the name. He turned the page in his notebook, wrote again, tore out the page and handed it to Reggie. "This is my address in Paris. Please contact me when you arrive, Reggie. Perhaps I may be of some assistance. At the very least, I would be pleased to show you some of the sights of my beautiful city."

The two policemen finished their drinks and left the bar. Reggie watched them walk along the pier toward the town center, and then turned on his bar stool to look out to sea. He lit a cigarette.

"That's your man on Rakahanga . . . Jean, isn't it?" Jake said. "What're you going to do?"

"Not sure, mate. Must have a chat with DeGroote or whatever his real name is, during my next visit to northern group."

"You and Tooks serious about selling out to those fellas from Wellington?"

"Tweed and Black? Perhaps. They've made a good offer. Maybe I'll open a pub here on Raro. Could you handle the competition, mate?"

"What competition? You'd drink up all the profits. Speaking of profits, it's your go at buying a round, Wiggie."

40

Just past noon, a stiff northwest breeze flung curtains of white foam over the atoll's barrier reef. After its four-hour journey from Manihiki, the Southern Cross Trading Company's flagship, *M/V Suwarrow*, dropped anchor in deep water outside the entrance to Rakahanga's lagoon. Reggie stood on the bridge sipping tea from a white porcelain mug. Throughout this tour of the islands in the northern group, he'd thought long and hard about how to deal with this situation. What if Jean-Philippe's story—if that's his real name—sounds reasonable? How can killing a copper be reasonable? Or acceptable?

Reggie had dealt with all sorts during his almost twenty years in the islands and before, but never with someone who'd killed a policeman. After his war experiences and the years spent building the company, he thought he was a good judge of men. Jean-Philippe—or Émile—had proved to be intelligent, honest, and a dedicated employee. He didn't seem like someone who would kill for no reason. Theo did say the *gendarme* was probably an ex-Nazi. Maybe there's something to that. Killing an ex-Nazi is not a bad thing. But what's the best way to sort this out?

"James, hand me the binos, *'inē*. Please."

James Marsten handed him the binoculars.

"*Meitaki ma'ata.* Thank you." Through the surf spray Reggie saw the masts of a yacht anchored in the lagoon opposite his station.

* * *

The first shallow-draft lighter from the *Suwarrow* shot through the narrow gap in the barrier reef and motored to shore. A mob of naked children splashed around it anxious to see who and what treasures had arrived. Several adult islanders waded out, grabbed the sides of the boat, and pulled its bow up onto the crushed coral beach. Homecoming Rakas in the lighter waved and shouted to the friends and relatives who crowded the beach. The entire population of the atoll—less than two hundred—was there for the arrival of the *Suwarrow*.

With jandals in his left hand, Reggie rose from the stern seat, placed his other hand on the gunwale, and swung over the side into knee-deep water. Small fish nibbled at his legs as he waded ashore. Manihiki had sent word about his visit, and many old friends greeted him. Reggie's neck was soon festooned with shell and flower leis, his nose and forehead almost rubbed raw. Toa, the island's *ariki* and former crew member on the *Wallaroo*, said a pig was already in a pit on hot stones, and there would be a *himené* that evening in his honor. Reggie knew then he couldn't leave until the next day.

His eyes searched the crowd. The man he looked for, his station manager, emerged from the line of coconut palms above the beach. He waved and walked down to meet his boss. They shook hands.

"*Kia orāna* and welcome back to Rakahanga, Monsieur Reggie. *Très bon* to see you again."

Reggie placed a hand on the man's arm and led him away from the crowd.

"*Kia orāna* and g'day to you, Jean-Philippe. Or should I say . . . Émile?"

The trader froze for a moment facing his boss, and then looked past Reggie toward the ship.

"What has happened? How did you—?"

Reggie sensed fear in his trader's voice. He held up a hand and nodded to the right. The island's Resident Agent, a New Zealander who Reggie didn't know well, came toward them along the beach.

"Let's get the goods up to the store. Then we can talk in private." Reggie squeezed Émile's arm. He turned to greet the official. Émile walked away to supervise the unloading of the station's cargo.

"Good day, sir." The government man waved his hat in greeting. "It's Captain Pobjoy, isn't it? I'm Balmforth . . . Peter Balmforth, the Resident. We met briefly on Raro last year. What brings you out our way?"

"*Kia orāna.* Just Reggie, please." They shook hands. "Doin' a visit to the islands to have a word with my traders." *Won't mention about selling the company, unless he asks.*

Balmforth turned and looked after Émile. "Last visit is it? Heard you might be selling out. Have you then? Who would be the new owners?"

How'd he know that? "An outfit out of Wellington, Tweed and Black. We're still in the negotiation phase."

The agent took a notebook out of his breast pocket and wrote down the names.

"Surprised Avarua hasn't mentioned that detail, but they don't keep me as well informed as I would like. But I do have my sources. Can't complain. I'm only here for another year." He replaced the notebook in his pocket. "Hope Jean'll be staying on. He certainly has some interesting stories to tell, when you can get him to open up, that is. Keeps pretty much to himself most of the time.

"Well, Captain Pobjoy, stop by the office and bring me up to date on the gossip from Avarua. I'll be traveling with you back to Manihiki. Cheers." With another wave of his hat, he strode off down the beach toward Nivano village.

Pompous twit, Reggie thought. If he wants any gossip, he'll have to hunt me down. Not looking forward to the trip back to Manihiki with him. I'll have to invent some problem to sort out in the ship's engine room.

Reggie took his time strolling up the beach. Other Rakas came to him with greetings. By the time he reached the coco palms, his collar of leis almost came up to his chin. When he entered the palm forest, he was pleased to see the well-swept crushed coral path leading to his store. The company's trade store was typical colonial-style island construction: single-story, a rust-red tin roof, and a covered verandah on three sides. The building served not only as the store but the home for the trader and his family.

Everything around the building was as it should be: no debris—fallen fronds or coconut husks—or other trash on *his* property. Jean-Philippe, or is it Émile?—doesn't matter—has been a treasure and will be a great loss to the company.

A crowd mingled outside when Reggie entered the trade store. Émile stood off to the side of the counter, hands at his sides, watching Reggie. He lit a cigarette; another still smoldered in an ashtray. Reggie went behind the makeshift bar and took a couple of Hinano beers from a propane-powered refrigerator. He motioned for Émile to follow him outside.

The two men walked out and stood in the shade of the palms. Reggie handed his trader a beer.

"A French copper from Tahiti was on Raro three weeks ago looking for you. Said you killed a chap over at Pape'ete some years ago, another copper. I'd like to hear your version of what happened."

Émile took a drink; his eyes narrowed. "Vater . . . Heinrich Vater. The man was, as you English say, a swine . . . a pig. Told everyone he was at Dien Bien Phu but was really in hospital in Saigon with . . . how you say? . . . the syphilis." He took another drink. "*Oui. C'est vrai.* Yes, I killed him. And would do it again. But it was in self-defense. He had a pistol and I had only my knife. It was either him or me. And that's God's truth, Monsieur Reggie."

"Why the fight? Why'd you kill him? Why'd you sky off?"

"He had beaten a native girl and was going to rape her. I heard her screams and kicked open the door to her room. He pulled out his gun, but I was quicker with my knife." He took another drink. "Why did I run away? Who'd believe me? There were no witnesses. The girl who he'd beaten was unconscious when I knifed him. And he was a *flic,* a copper, as you say."

"Well, mate, that Frenchman's been passing your photograph and description around from Tahiti to New Caledonia. Someone in Nouméa remembered you being put ashore on Raro a while back. Jake Cartwright recognized you straight off. And that chap Balmforth . . . you've made an impression on him. He'll find out sooner or later."

Reggie placed his hands on Émile's shoulders. "Not to worry. Jake's not going to say anything, but it might be a good idea for you to think about movin' on." Reggie turned and pointed out to the lagoon. "Where's that yacht bound for?" A ketch flying an American flag rode at anchor inside the reef.

"Samoa, I think. Maybe Fiji."

Émile's thoughts jumped back to the night he'd told Bobbie that someday he may have to leave the island. He'd told her that he'd done an evil thing and men may come looking for him, that men might come to take him away. She said she could never leave the island and would wait for him to return.

"Bobbie and the children? I can't take them with me."

"No worries there, mate. Your kin have unlimited credit as long as we own the station. And I will speak to Toa. They will never want for anything. And you can send for them later if you want."

"But what about the store?"

"Got that all sorted. Always like to plan ahead. Brought Tooks' nephew, James, with me. You know 'im. He's worked for the company since he was a teenager and been itchin' to try his hand on one of the islands anyway."

"What if the Americans aren't willing to take me with them?"

"Well, mate, we'll have to sort out another scheme. Have you chatted with them?"

"Yes. They're good people."

"We'll invite them to tonight's *himené*. I'll have a word with them."

Reggie handed Émile a thick envelope.

"What's this?" Émile opened the envelope and looked at the American $100 bills.

"Your wages. And a bit extra to see you through."

Émile counted the money in the envelope. Five thousand dollars. "Why? Why me? Why now? This is too much. I'm a fugitive, and you're giving me this? Why?"

"You've done a smashing good job here. You're honest and responsible. And you're in trouble. Everyone should get a second chance. Also, you're French . . . don't try to deny it." Reggie waved a hand, dismissing any argument. "Your people helped me during the war. And you killed a Nazi." Reggie drank from his bottle. "I'd like very much to hide you out here on the stations, but independence for the Cooks is coming soon, and we old colonials may not have the influence we once had. It's probably best for you to move on."

"*Pardon*, Monsieur Reggie, but I must have time to think about this."

"Take your time, mate. We'll deal with the punters." Reggie nodded toward a young man who'd come ashore on the last lighter and waited at the edge of the palm grove until Reggie motioned for him to join them. "You remember James, don't you?" The two men shook hands. Reggie and James went into the store. Minor chaos reigned with the owner, an old friend, manning the counter—there were bargains galore.

Émile walked out through the palm grove and sat on the bench.

It's been almost four years since I had this bench placed here so I could watch the sunsets over the lagoon. Over the lagoon of my island paradise. Now it is all finished. Whose fault? Why won't my past go away? One name, one man—Pioletti. He's ruined my life. Perhaps it's time to disappear again for a while, and then return after independence. It might be easier to slip into the island life with another new identity.

Émile walked up onto verandah and waited for Reggie to join him.

"I accept your offer with many thanks and many regrets. My first concern is for my family, but your promise is most reassuring. I know you to be an honorable man. Forever in your debt I am, Monsieur Reggie. And I *will* return someday."

"I'm very glad to hear that . . . Émile. May I call you Émile?" The trader nodded. "When you return, if I can be of any help, you know where I live on Raro. Or you can always leave word at Skipper Jake's." Reggie lit a cigarette. He offered one to Émile. "I'm leaving the islands myself for a while. Don't know when I'll return."

"The word is you're going to France. Why is that?"

The island telegraph still works. "Unfinished business. Do you know Paris?"

"*Oui, bien sûr.* Of course. I lived there for many years."

"I don't recall you talking about that."

"Did you ask?"

"Right you are. I understand. You thinkin' about going back? That'd be a bit dangerous, wouldn't it? Does the reach of the *Polynesie Française gendarmerie* extend to Paris?"

"Perhaps. Probably not. And it's been many years. At the moment, I don't know what I'll do."

"By the way, who are you? What *is* your real name?"

Émile stood at attention. "Captain Pobjoy, my name is Émile Patrice Plude." He saluted.

* * *

The next morning the sea was calm. Many Rakas had paddled or swam out to the exposed reef to wave farewell. The lighters ferried back and forth through the gap taking copra and passengers to the ship. Reggie sat in the stern of the last lighter—he delayed his departure until Balmforth had gone aboard the *Suwarrow*—and saw Émile carried out to the American yacht in an outrigger canoe. He wondered if he'd done the right thing. Never would he have turned Émile over to the authorities. His conscience was clear on that. He hoped that Émile would someday walk into the bar at Skipper Jake's.

* * *

Phil Hope, the owner of the American ketch *Tailor Made*, helped the island trader up over the side of the yacht.

"Howdy, Jean. Been expecting you. Care for a beer?" He didn't wait for an answer but turned to his wife, "Hey, sweet thing, bring our guest a cold one, will ya? That was quite a bash last night, wasn't it? Didn't know anything about it until a young man, James, I think his name was, came out and invited us all. That Reggie guy must be some big shot, right? He said you might be coming out to ask a favor. Too bad we had to leave the party early, but we're heading out today. Surprised not to see you and the missus in the crowd."

"I wanted to spend the night with my family." *I can't tell him that we sat on the bench until dawn. Our baby girl slept in Bobbie's lap, and the boy on the sand by our feet—the last sunset together.*

Judy, Phil's wife, and her sister Betty were sunbathing topless on the foredeck. She stood, waved at Émile, and then bent down to retrieve her bikini top from the deck. With a playful smirk, she adjusted it over her large breasts and went below. Betty rolled over onto her back.

"Didn't know I'd married such an exhibitionist," Phil said. "It must be the tropics that does this to American women. Whatcha think, Jean? You're Swiss, a European. You know about these things." Émile didn't answer. Phil turned around and was surprised to see the islander down in the dugout lift up a large canvas bag.

"What's this? Bon voyage presents?"

"Lost my position. Sacked."

"Sacked? What do you mean sacked?" The American looked confused. Judy came back up into the cockpit and handed cold beers to the two men. She held another for the islander, but he was already heading back across the lagoon. She shrugged her shoulders and took a drink from the bottle.

"Somebody call me?" Greg Sacker, Betty's husband, came up into the cockpit. "Thought I heard my name used in vain." He extended his hand. "Hey, Jean. What's up, buddy? Come to say good-bye?"

"I've been fired, as you say in America, and have to go somewhere." Émile pointed to the ship outside the reef. "The man who I worked for has sold the store to others. They are changing everyone. The ship is going back to Rarotonga, but I'd prefer to leave the Cooks, so I hoped ...."

"Say no more, *amigo*," Phil raised his hands. "Or *mon ami*, as you would say. Sure, you can come with us. Right, Greg? You've been a great host while we were here. We'd enjoy returning the hospitality. Hey, wait a minute. What about your family? Not coming along? It'd be a little tight, but we could manage, I think."

"No. They'll remain here until I'm able to find a new position."

"Okay. We can drop you off in Pago Pago or Apia, if you like. Actually, we're planning to take a look at the Tokelau Islands before heading back to Hawaii. Ever been there?"

"Hawaii, no. The Tokelaus, are they French?"

"No. Kiwi, like the Cooks, but no one ever goes there."

"Sounds interesting."

"A cold beer would taste real good right about now." Betty Sacker sat up, topless, on the foredeck. "Or do I have to get it myself?" Judy threw back the last of the other bottle and said, "I'll get you one, Sis, and I can use another." Betty returned, went along the starboard side with two beers, and handed one to her sister. She sat on the cabin roof and removed her bikini top.

Émile had been exposed to multitudes of native breasts for years, but this display of white, albeit very tan, women's breasts stirred emotions that had become, perhaps, jaded by the daily exposure of dark brown flesh. Maybe it was the idea that these breasts were forbidden fruit. They belonged to others, not available to him.

"Okay, girls, fun in the sun's over," Hope said. "You two are on the anchor. Time to get underway. Jean, store your gear below. We'll sort things out later. I want to clear the reef before the tide turns."

The *Suwarrow* had raised its anchor and was steaming south on its return trip to Manihiki when the *Tailor Made* motored through the gap. Émile stood at the stern shielding his eyes with his hand. He could make out Bobbie and the children on the beach; Toa and James stood with them.

I must return. This is the life I want. I've never known such happiness. I hope to have the strength to deal with the future. My family will be well cared for in my absence, I know. Bobbie, I will return.

* * *

Hotel Gaultier, Argenteuil.

Constance sat alone at a table in the dining area of the hotel, as she had for almost two weeks. She opened an old edition of *Paris Match*. If she didn't get guests soon she would have to cancel her subscription. When she returned from the butcher's shop with a single chop for her dinner, she was pleased that the man who had bought her husband's business still extended her credit. He'd even hinted about wanting a new wife.

The first article she read in the newspaper announced the suicide of the Nobel Prize winner Ernest Hemingway. The article, spread over two pages, concentrated on his early career in Paris. The bit that riveted Constance was about the theft of a valise from a train on December 2, 1922. *That's the night Marcel died.* She remembered the scattering of papers in their apartment. *No. It can't be. They were all in English. What happened to them?* She searched her memory back forty years to that horrible night. She was evicted from her apartment; her belongings kept by the concierge. *I must look.*

Constance brought the green valise down from the attic to the table—the valise Klaus had left with her years ago. He'd said it held papers of literary value. She examined the bag. *Oui, it could be the same one. It's been so many years.* She undid the clasps and removed the papers. There were many typed sheets and carbon copies. Several sheets seemed to be the beginning of a novel. Constance's conversational English was excellent, but her reading skills were limited. The marking of EH on the manuscripts convinced her. *Klaus was right. These are the missing Hemingway manuscripts.*

She looked at the stack of unpaid bills on the hotel desk. *These could be worth a fortune. But what about Klaus? He knew their literary value before he left them with me. But now?*

During the past seven years she'd received a *Bonne Année* card from Klaus each winter with news about his family. They now had a daughter. The letter in the last card mentioned their desire to leave Austria someday. It also described his efforts to convince his oldest son to accompany them. But he had recently married and had a good job with a tourist bureau. Klaus always asked about his souvenirs.

The front door flew open almost knocking the bell off its wire. A man followed by a couple of young people burst into the room.

"*Bonjour*, Madame," said the older man out of breath. "Have you any rooms available?" he asked in English.

Constance stuffed the Hemingway manuscripts into the valise. "*Oui*, Monsieur, *bien sûr*. How many your party?"

"The whole bunch. Eight in all."

"Rooms, Monsieur?"

"Ah. Must think about that. Ah. Okay. The girls in three rooms, and me and the guys in two. Can we do that ?

"*Oui*, Monsieur. Just for one night?"

"Oh no, Madame. Our tour guide had us booked into a place across the river, but it is infested with rats. We were fortunate the exterminators were there when we arrived."

The other members of his party started filing into the dining area. Constance saw that some carried folded up easels and canvases.

"This is perfect," the man said, "Couldn't be better—the river, the bridge, everything.

"A week, Madame. And maybe more," the man said. "It all depends on the weather."

"*Oui*, Monsieur. That is possible. You are artists, *non?*"

"Art students, actually. We're from the Carlisle Art Institute. I'm Fred Blair, their professor and chaperone. We're on a group study tour of France this summer, visiting the places frequented by the impressionists. Just spent a week at Giverny doing Monet's garden."

"*Tres bien*, Monsieur. Would you please sign the register, and I will need to see your passports, *s'il vous plaît.*"

Blair collected the passports and signed the register.

"Will you be wanting dinner this evening, Monsieur?"

"You betcha, Madame. And breakfast, of course."

She showed him the rates and said, "I'll require a small deposit, Monsieur . . . say two nights tariff."

"Not a problem. I think I have enough francs to cover that." He reached for his wallet. "Will American Express Travelers checks be okay for the balance?"

"*Bien sûr*, Monsieur. Come, I'll show you to your rooms."

While the Americans got settled in, Constance returned the valise to the attic. She told Blair that she had to go to the shops and would return shortly. Constance hummed a tune to herself as she walked, again, to the butcher shop.

* * *

The weather was perfect. The Americans stayed for two weeks. One afternoon, as Constance prepared the final dinner for her guests, the telephone rang.

"Constance? This is Jacques. Every Thursday at 14:30, unless the weather is wretched, he goes to the Luxembourg to watch the children sail their boats. Just the three of them: Carlo, Cleo, his mistress, and a driver. Cleo wheels him into the park. No one follows them. They're gone for at least an hour, sometimes more. Robert and Pierre have followed them on a bicycle or scooter each time. All they do is stop on the rue Guynemer and enter the gardens from the west side. The driver stays with car. He never meets anyone. Just sits near the pool and watches the children. Sometimes he has Cleo give money to kids who can't afford the fee."

The bell over the front door rang. "I must go, Jacques. *Merci beaucoup.* I'll have to pay a visit to the park."

1965

Paris.

Two months later after leaving Rakahanga, Émile crossed the Alps into France. He'd taken a train from Milan to Aosta at the foot of the mountain barrier. He rode a bus to Courmayeur on the Italian side of Mont Blanc. His suitcase went into a dustbin before he bought appropriate clothing, knapsack, and snowshoes from a mountaineering shop. He shared a glass of wine with a local guide, and said he wanted to traverse the mountains using the old Roman road into France. His hike was strenuous, but he only had to use the snowshoes once. On the French side, he headed northwest to Saint-Gervaise-les-Bains. There he caught a train to Paris. He still had half the money Reggie had given him on Rakahanga.

***

Claude Rondeau—he'd retained his légion name—returned to his cousins' house after a long boring day as a docent at *Le Louvre*. Claude lived in their basement apartment, which had a separate outside entrance; an arrangement he'd found most accommodating since his return from Indochina. His elderly widowed cousins—one had lost her husband at Dunkirk, the other in North Africa—doted on him and proudly flaunted his award of the *Légion d'honneur* and service in Vietnam to all their neighbors. But they respected his privacy and never questioned the coming and goings of female guests to his apartment.

Claude always greeted them when he returned from work, told stories about the tourists, and let them know if he would be joining them for dinner. Today, Magda, the oldest cousin, handed him an envelope as he took off his coat.

"Claude, do you know a Jean-Philippe DeGroote or Andre LaLande? Strange fellow. Why would he have two names? He came by earlier today—"

Claude dropped his coat. He took the envelope and ran down to his apartment.

It can't be. Not after all these years. Mon Dieu!

He tore open the envelope.

Bonjour, old friend. I'm in Paris. You may contact me through Krakow, the concierge at the Hotel Polinaise.
Legio Patria Nostra
Jean/Andre

***

"*Bonjour,* Monsieur. Are you Krakow?" Claude looked at the elderly gentleman in tails and waistcoat standing at a large lectern across from the hotel's reception desk.

"*Oui,* Monsieur. How may I be of assistance?"

"A mutual friend referred me to you."

"*Merci,* Monsieur. I have many friends. Your friend's name would be?"

"Now that's complicated, Monsieur Krakow. Sometimes my friend is called Jean-Philippe DeGroot, and sometimes he's known as Andre LaLande."

"*Oui,* Monsieur. I understand how that could be a problem. However, for a one-arm veteran of Dien Bien Phu with a *Légion d'honneur* rosette on his lapel . . ." He shrugged. ". . . many things are possible. Perhaps, if Monsieur would wait in the bar just there," he pointed to the left, "I may be able fulfill your request."

Claude sat on a stool at the bar and ordered a *pastis.* His eyes watched the entrance in the mirror behind the bartender; he didn't notice the man with a full beard wearing a beret and dark glasses enter from a side door.

"*Bonjour, mon ami,*" Émile said, causing his friend to jump off the stool.

"Andre! *Mon Dieu!*" They hugged, and Émile grasped Claude's hand in both of his. "*Mon Dieu!* I never would have recognized you. *Mon Dieu!* You're so dark."

Émile looked at his bare arms. "The tropics, *mon ami.* Many years in the southern ocean. I've lost some of it." He nodded to the other side of the room. "Let's sit over there."

They moved to a table in the corner. Claude ordered a bottle of Champagne.

"You're looking well, Claude. Retirement agrees with you, *n'est ce- pas?*"

"Not completely retired, Andre . . . or should I call you Jean-Philippe?"

"For you, either will do." The bartender opened the Champagne and filled their glasses.

"You're working?" Émile asked.

"*Oui, mon ami.* Four days a week I shepherd tourists around *Le Louvre.* Doesn't pay much, but there are gratuities, and it supplements my disability from *la Légion.*" He raised his glass. "A toast, Andre . . . or Jean-Philippe." They touched glasses. "And it provides opportunities to meet some very attractive ladies." He smiled. "But, enough about me, comrade. Where have you been? What have you been doing? How long have been in France…Paris?" Claude withdrew a cigarette case from inside his coat and took out a cigarette, and searched for his lighter. Émile leaned forward and lit the cigarette.

"*Merci.* Sometimes I forget which pocket it is in. Not too many choices with one arm." They laughed.

For the next two hours, and well into a second bottle, Émile told his story.

* * *

After leaving the American yacht in the Tokelau Islands, he found work as a cook on various ships until finally going ashore in Brindisi on the heel of Italy. He rode trains north to the Alps. Arriving in Paris and taking a chance he wouldn't be recognized, he went to Bistro Béroud and inquired about Krakow. The elderly Polish refugee—now working at the hotel—was thrilled to see him, but chastised Émile for almost giving him a heart attack. Krakow's recommendation fixed him up with a position in the hotel's kitchen—rotten pay, but free meals and a garret room.

"*Mon Dieu!* What a story. I'm afraid mine is not as exciting. I was bored not having anything to do, but living with my cousins . . . you've met Magda . . . has been good. I attended a reunion of Dien Bien Phu veterans a few years ago and met an officer who's in charge of security at the museum. He offered me a job as night watchman. That changed to docent after a couple of years. Boring at times, but I enjoy being around all the wonderful art. I can give you a private tour, if you're interested in that sort of thing." He refilled their glasses.

Émile wondered if he should tell his friend about Vater? Claude was one of the a few people in this world he would trust with his life—he's saved it twice already. Maybe not all the details.

"Do you remember Vater . . . Sergeant Vater? We saw him at the hospital in Saigon."

"Vater . . . Vater? No, I don't think so. Wait. Yes. Wasn't he the Nazi swine who was there for the syphilis?"

"*Oui,* that's him. When I was on Tahiti I heard he was killed over some whore. He was in the *gendarmerie.*"

"Good riddance. Speaking of swine, I recall your story about that *mafioso* . . . Pioletti, was it?"

Émile's heart skipped a beat. "Still alive is he?"

"*Oh oui.* Very much so, but confined to a wheelchair now." Claude thought for a minute. "I once had his address. Or, at least, where he used to live. I'll try to find it for you, if you're still interested."

"*Merci, mon ami.* That'd be *bien.*" Émile stood. "No more Champagne for me. I begin my evening shift shortly and want to take a bath. My room is number eight. Take the elevator to the fifth floor, and then up some stairs to the attic." He offered his hand. "*Très bon* to see you again. What days are you free?"

Claude told him.

"Let's meet next Tuesday morning."

* * *

It took some searching in his apartment before Claude was successful in finding Pioletti's address. At a bar that catered to former légionnaires, he confirmed it was current from a couple of comrades whose activities were sometimes across the line.

"*Bonjour,* Monsieur Krakow. Jean-Philippe?"

"*Bonjour,* Monsieur Claude. Our friend waits for you in the Café Warsaw. Just to the left at the bottom of the street."

"*Merci,* Monsieur Krakow. Before I go, I must thank you for your service to my friend when he was a young lad here in Paris."

"*Mais,* Monsieur Claude, I know not what you refer to."

"*Bien,* Monsieur Krakow, we'll leave it at that—I know that you know that I know what happened. *Merci beaucoup* just the same."

"*Oui,* Monsieur, I know." He smiled. "And Monsieur, thank you for *your* service to our friend in Indochina." He extended his hand.

The smell of something that didn't agree with Claude's nose assaulted him when he entered the cafe. Whatever they're preparing this time of day can't be appetizing, he thought.

Émile sat at the bar and turned when Claude entered and handed him a folded piece of paper. "The address of the Italian restaurant you wanted."

Émile stuffed the paper in his pocket. "Let's take a walk."

At a small park they sat on a bench.

"My contacts are mostly reliable, and I, just for you, comrade, found a bar not too far from his front door. It's amazing how many free drinks a one-armed veteran of Dien Bien Phu with a *Légion d'Honneur* rosette in his lapel can get in a bar."

"Knowing you comrade, you've been milking that every day since you returned from Saigon." They laughed.

"*Alors. bien sûr.* And I should tell you about some patriotic ladies I've met. *Mais,* to business. Outside his apartment building are always two or three rough looking fellas. Pioletti himself is confined to a wheelchair. His car—a big Mercedes, of course—stops in front, and he and his bimbo go wherever. He has a driver. No body guard . . . sometimes. That may not be usual. I've only watched twice."

"Claude, comrade. I need . . . want a gun. Something small. Something I can hide . . . put in my pocket. I prefer an automatic, but a small revolver would do. Possible, *n'est-ce pas?*"

Won't tell him I've already asked the same of Krakow.

"What? Are you going after Pioletti . . . shoot Pioletti? That's insane, comrade. He's got armed goons around him all the time."

"I don't care. I have to do this."

"Well, think hard about what the future holds for your family if you get killed, or almost as bad, if you get arrested and the police uncover your past."

"You don't understand what this man has done to my life."

"Comrade, that's all in the past, *n'est-ce pas?* You are still young. You have a wonderful family waiting for you in a tropical paradise. Why jeopardize all that for an act of revenge, which will accomplish nothing?"

"I thought you were my friend and comrade, and would understand."

"*Ah oui, mon ami,* I understand completely, but this not the answer. Besides, he's an old man. He may die soon, or get killed by other gangsters. They've tried before. And . . . miracles do happen . . . maybe the authorities will finally finish him."

"I thank you for the concern, Claude, but will you help me or not?"

Claude lit a cigarette, looked up at the sky, and then nodded. "Of course I'll help you. It may be expensive."

"I have money."

"Next Tuesday then . . . I still think it's a stupid idea."

* * *

Parc du Luxembourg.

Francoise loved feeding the pigeons. Each afternoon she'd go to a park within a short walking distance to her apartment, a different park each day.

Thursdays it was the Luxembourg. She didn't have much to offer her feathered friends. Proudly she wore the rosette of her husband's *Légion d'Honour* on her coat lapel, but her pension as a war widow only allowed a small paper bag of dried corn, almost a gift. "Only five centimes, Madame," Etienne, the neighborhood grocer charged her. But life was good in its ninth decade.

A young woman—anyone under seventy was young to Francoise— who she often met in the Luxembourg shared a large bag of corn and nuts with her. And bread crumbs! The young woman sometimes sat on the bench with her, or on the bench opposite on the other side of the path. Some days she wasn't there, and Francoise missed her. They would feed the pigeons and talk about the weather. Did she know what time it was? The young woman had once asked that. She'd forgotten her watch. No, she didn't know. Francoise couldn't afford a watch. She'd had one for many years. It'd been her husband's, but it had quit working and she couldn't afford to get it fixed. So now she relied on the clocks on the streets and in the shops. But what did she care about what time it was? Her days were simple and always the same. She got up when she woke up, she shopped in the mornings when the markets were open, she ate when she was hungry, and she slept when she was tired.

"*Bonjour,* my child," Francoise greeted the young woman who had joined her.

"*Bonjour,* Madame. How are you today?" Constance asked. She held out a bag of bread crumbs. "We'll share again today."

"I'm well. Thank you for sharing. I'm so sorry, my child, but I don't know your name."

"It's Marie, Madame," Constance lied.

"Do you live nearby?"

"*Ah oui,* Madame. On the rue Vavin. I have a flat there."

"With your husband?"

"No, Madame. I lost him in the war." Constance fed some crumbs to the pigeons.

"Oh, I'm so sorry. I lost mine in the first war. Do you work?"

"*Oui,* Madame. I'm a waitress in a bistro on the boulevard du Montparnesse. I start in the evenings."

"That's quite close, *n'est ce-pas?*"

"*Oui,* Madame. Just a short walk from here." Constance glanced at her watch. *2:45. Where's Pioletti? He's late today. No. There he comes.*

Down the lane through the park, she saw a woman push the man in a wheelchair toward them. He tipped his hat as he passed, and they continued on to the pond.

"*Pardon moi,* Madame, but I must go." She handed Francoise the bag of crumbs. "Finish these for me. *A bientôt.*"

Constance walked away toward the south end of the park.

* * *

The train from Marseille rolled into the *Gare Montparnesse.* Reggie Pobjoy descended from his compartment and walked toward the center of the terminal. Halfway down the platform he saw the familiar face of Theatris DeRemer coming toward him. They met and shook hands.

"*Bienvenue*, welcome to Paris. I would give you a kiss on both cheeks, Reggie, but I know how reserved you Anglo-Saxons are," Theo said.

"Perhaps I should rub noses with you like our Maoris do. It's good to see you again. You got my cable then?"

"*Oui*, Reggie, both of them, from Suez and from Marseille. How was your voyage?"

"Quite comfortable. Much better than the last time. Didn't have to share the ship with four thousand returning soldiers. Missed the canal the first time in '39. Went around the Cape and up the west coast, dodging German u-boats."

"You've had an exciting life, Reggie. I would enjoy hearing about your adventures over a glass or two of wine, *n'est-ce pas?* Come. Let me carry one of your cases."

"Did you find me a good hotel, Theo?"

"The finest—*Chez* DeRemer. You must stay with us. We insist. Madame DeRemer is preparing a special meal for you. You will be our guest for as long as you like."

"That be most kind of you, my friend. So much for the tales about the unfriendly French."

They walked out of the train station to Theo's car, a Citroën 2CV. It was a short drive to an apartment building in the 7th *arrondissement*. An open cage elevator carried them to the fifth floor and Theo's flat. His wife, Bernadette, greeted them and gave Reggie a peck on each cheek.

"*Ma chérie*, the English are not that demonstrative," Theo said.

"No matter. He is our guest." They laughed.

"We New Zealanders be not as stuffy as the Brits. Kisses from a beautiful woman are always welcome to us." When she offered a hand, he kissed it.

"Theo, you didn't tell me your friend was such a charmer."

"Come, Reggie. We'll put the luggage in your room later. Some drinks in the lounge, *ma chérie*."

They went into a large room with high ceilings and large, wide windows. The room was furnished in what Reggie thought were antiques. He sat on a very comfortable divan. Mrs. DeRemer brought a tray of glasses and an assortment of aperitifs in colorful bottles.

"I know the English enjoy a class of sherry," Theo said.

"Not being English, I'll not be partial to sherry."

"Truly sorry, Reggie. We French seem to put all English in the same categories. We assume, incorrectly and regretfully, that those of you who have emigrated retained the same customs. Unfortunately, my experience has mostly been with the British nationals and ex-patriots in the southern ocean who attempt to retain those customs."

"Whatever you offer me, my friend, will be wonderful. I'm just an old copra schooner sailor and know nothing about fine wines."

"Perhaps a glass of chilled Chablis then?" He reached for a bottle in an silver ice bucket. "A somewhat better vintage than we shared at Skipper Jake's, I'm sure."

"Skipper Jake's? I'm surprised you be remembering."

"A good memory is a requirement for a policeman. Let's go into my study where we can have a view of the city."

Theo's study was a large room with floor-to-ceiling bookshelves on two sides, a large desk against the windows overlooking the street, two comfortable chairs, and in the center a banquet-size table. The table was covered with miniature terrain features—hills, streams, villages, trees, roads . . . and soldiers.

"What's all this?" Reggie asked.

"Ah. My obsession. Do you know H.G. Wells?"

"Yeah. Sure. The film *War of the Worlds.*"

"*Oui,* of course, but he also wrote a small book called *Little Wars.* It's a guide to table top war games." Theo picked up one of the 54mm figures. "Just an old man's hobby." He handed it to Reggie.

Reggie was surprised by the detail on the figures. It reminded him of Davie McCombs' ship-in-a bottle. "Did you paint this?"

"*Oui.* But not all. Many are painted by others for a small fee."

"Right, but what do you do with them? This is quite impressive."

"A few friends and I with the same passion re-fight famous battles. Mostly from the Napoleonic period . . . our favorite, *bien sûr,* of course." He pointed to the table. "This is the opening stages of Quatre Bras, 16 June, 1815. Two days before Waterloo. If Ney hadn't hesitated, Waterloo never would have taken place."

"Ney? Sorry, don't know that one. What do you be doing with these toy soldiers?"

Theo frowned, then smiled. "*Alors,* I can see where you would find them toys, but to us they are like chess pieces. We use dice to determine the outcome of actions, so it is very much like a game of chess with dice, *n'est-ce pas?* A game of chance. Like war." He picked up a mounted figure with no hat and red hair. "*Maréchal* Ney was one of the Emperor's commanders, who many believe caused the defeat at Waterloo."

Reggie went to a window. The Eiffel Tower rose above the rooftops in the distance. "That be the Eiffel Tower?" he asked.

"*Oui, Le Tour Eiffel.* Would you like to visit it . . . go up to the observation level?"

"Yes, that would be grand."

"What else would you like to see while you are here, Reggie?"

"I'm not sure, Theo. Haven't given much thought to sightseeing."

"Well, my friend, to really enjoy Paris to the fullest, one must be a *flâneur.* Indeed, the city has a centuries old tradition of solo exploration, personified by the *flâneur,* or stroller, as you might say. *Flâneurie* is, in its purest form, a goal-less pursuit, though for some it evolved into a purposeful art. Walking and observing became a method of understanding a city and its history. I would enjoy joining you on such a stroll."

During dinner, Mrs. DeRemer asked, "What brings you to our fair city, Reggie?"

"A bit of a quest, Madame. Theo, do you be knowin' anyone who was in the *résistance* during the war . . . anyone who helped Allied flyers escape to Spain?"

"*Oui,* I know a few. About those who helped you and others, I will have to make some enquiries."

"I know it may not be possible, but I'd like to find the people who hid me somewhere just outside of Paris . . . somewhere near the Seine River, and where I was captured."

"Many people were involved in that escape network, and many safe houses were used. It may not be possible, but we can try."

At breakfast the next morning, Madame DeRemer's croissants reminded him of Émile's baking skills.

"If you don't mind me asking, Theo, how'd you fare with your investigation of that killing of a *gendarme* on Pape'ete?"

"*Ah oui,* that case had a strange ending. The *prefect* in Pape'ete had a shop keeper of Algerian background arrested. He admitted knowing Vater from his time in *la Légion* in the Algeria. He also admitted the desire to kill Vater, something about a sister Vater had violated, but he found him already dead, stabbed, and shot. In his rage at not being able to exact his revenge, he took a knife to the body. Vater's whore surprised him from the next room, and he shot her with Vater's pistol. A horrible affair. I am most happy to be out of that business."

"So, what about that fella you were lookin' for?"

"DeGroote. No idea. He vanished somewhere among the islands in the southern ocean. Not unusual, *n'est-ce pas?*" Theo looked closely at Reggie.

"Case closed then, is it?"

"*Oui,* as far as the government is concerned. Not going to spend resources looking for a killer of a ex-Nazi. Why the interest, *mon ami?*"

"You said he was reported to be on Rarotonga at one time. Anything about the Cooks is important to me."

Reggie took his coffee and walked to the window. He looked down at the people passing on the streets below. *Émile. He could be down there somewhere.*

"*Bien sûr, mon ami,* I understand completely." Theo went to his study and returned with a notebook. "I did find the facts about that English traitor, Cole, you asked about." He opened the notebook. "Shot and killed by the police in 1946."

"'46? How did he survive the war? Weren't traitors and collaborators dealt with?"

"Reggie, I must be completely honest with you. It will be many years, if not decades, to bring to justice those who deserve it."

"Who protected these traitors?"

"The gray men in the tall towers." He laid the notebook on the table. "There are well-connected gangsters and politicians who made fortunes during the occupation and the war." He poured himself some coffee.

"Carlo Pioletti is a prime example. He came to Paris after the first war, established himself as a landlord of decrepit housing, and expanded his activities into the black market, prostitution, and extortion. He has many influential politicians in his pocket. Nothing has been pinned on him. He's now elderly and confined to a wheelchair—another gangster's boys put three bullets into his spine a couple of years ago. That gangster and two of his sons were later found floating in the Seine with their throats cut. There are rumors . . . only rumors, I must say . . . that he worked with the *Gestapo* and caused many escaping Allied aircrew to be captured. But unfortunately, Pioletti is one of the gray men . . . untouchable. Their towers are too tall."

* * *

On the observation level of the Eiffel Tower, Theo pointed out many of the notable sights of the city. It was raining when they descended. A visit to the Louvre, Theo suggested, would be a pleasant way to spend the afternoon. Reggie didn't care much about art but didn't want to offend his host.

After an hour of walking through several galleries, Reggie wondered if it had stopped raining. In a room full of impressionist paintings, he froze in front of one by Claude Monet. Digging in a pocket, he took out the jeton he'd found in the Suwarrow atoll horde.

"Well, stone the crows!"

"What, Reggie? You know this one? It's quite famous."

"Look at this, Theo." He handed the token to his friend.

"*Oui,* that's the same bridge . . . Argenteuil. It's on the Seine north of the city. Many artists of this period painted a similar scene." Theo examined the jeton. "Where did you come by this? Quite old . . . 1838."

How much do I tell him, Reggie thought. "Picked it up on my travels. Reminded me of that night in '41."

"I'm not positive, but I believe it is a commemorative piece given to the people involved in the building of the bridge. I'm sure the museum has others like it on display somewhere in the building." He nodded toward a one-armed docent. "Shall I ask?"

"No, Theo. That not be necessary. Let's go see if the rain has stopped."

The sun was shining when they left the building. Reggie asked if they could stop at the New Zealand embassy. Before he got out of the car, Reggie said, "Have you a city plan I may borrow? It's such a beautiful afternoon, I be thinkin' about your suggestion for a stroll."

"*Bien sûr,* Reggie." He took a map out of the glove box and marked their present location and where his apartment was. "Enjoy your *flâneurie.* Dinner is at eight."

* * *

Hotel Gaultier, Argenteuil.

Constance had completed cleaning the rooms from the previous night's guests when she heard the bell over the door and voices below. A woman's voice sounded like she was scolding a child, but it was in German. She rushed down the stairs. *Can it be them?*

A man wearing a Tyrolean hat and leaning on a cane stood with a buxom blond and four large suitcases. Two children roamed around the room looking at and touching everything. The man removed his hat exposing graying hair. He smiled.

"*Bonjour,* Madame Constance. I . . . we have returned."

"*Mon Dieu!* Klaus, it *is* you. *Bonjour.*" Constance planted kisses on his cheeks. Mattie, somewhat taken back by this display of familiarity, frowned, but this changed to a smile when Constance hugged and kissed her. "This is Mattie, *non?*"

"*Oui,* but she doesn't speak French . . . not much anyway."

Constance stepped back and said, "I received your letter. How was the journey?"

"Long, but uneventful." He pointed to his son and daughter. "They enjoyed the train ride, but weren't happy about leaving their home." The children stared at Constance. "This is Siegfried, and this is Maria. Our oldest decided to remain in Austria."

"Come, let's sit. I have a nice chilled Riesling, and some lemonade for the little ones." She brought the drinks. "Welcome back to Argenteuil, Klaus, and *Willkommen,* Mattie." She raised her glass. "*Mon Dieu,* this is so wonderful after so many years." Klaus had propped his cane against the table. "The war?" she asked.

"*Oui.* Lost the leg shortly after I left here in 1944."

"*Mon Dieu,* I'm so sorry. Does it bother you?"

"Not really. One gets used to it." He translated for Mattie.

"I have a couple of rooms vacant. You will stay here, please."

"Of course, where else? *Merci beaucoup.*"

"I know what you're wondering, Klaus, and yes, I still have it." She went into another room and returned with the valise. "*Voila!* Still intact . . . the same as when you left."

Klaus took the small green valise in his hands, but didn't open it. "Your family, Constance? How do they fare?"

"My father died fighting with the *résistance* when the *SS* tried to destroy the bridge. My husband died in the labor camp. My mother . . . she couldn't bear to live here after the war . . . left for America. We have family in California. Now, it is just me and the inn." Klaus translated for Mattie, who started to cry.

"We're so sorry for your loss." He touched her hand. Mattie gave her a hug.

"It's all in the past, *ma chère.* But let's open this."

Klaus undid the buckles on the valise and removed the manuscripts. He spread them out on the table. "I want to take some time to examine these. Spent some years studying his work."

"Of course, but first you must freshen up after your journey. I'll help take the bags up to your rooms. I'll prepare a special meal for this evening."

Constance showed them their rooms, and then said, "I must go to the butcher shop before it closes." She hurried down the stairs.

"Does she know what's in the valise?" Mattie asked.

"Oh yes. I told her when I left them here."

"I'm surprised she hasn't tried to sell them, after all she's been through."

"Not Constance. There's no avarice in her soul."

* * *

"Captain Pobjoy? Yes, I have a message for you." The clerk at the New Zealand embassy said.

"Who's it from?"

"A strange name, if you ask me," said the young man from South Island. "A Mister Rakahanga? Had a French accent. Don't think he's a Kiwi." He handed Reggie an envelope.

Reggie took the envelope and went outside. He lit a cigarette. *Émile's here! That must have taken some doing.* Reggie walked to nearest bistro, sat at a sidewalk table, and ordered a coffee. He opened the envelope.

Reggie, Welcome to Paris. You may leave messages with Krakow, the concierge at the Hotel Polinase. Only he I trust. I am in your service if you desire it. I know the city.

Kia orāna, É.

Reggie asked the waiter if he knew of the Hotel Polinaise. No, he hadn't heard of it. Now what do I do, Reggie wondered. He hailed a taxi. "Take me to the Hotel Ritz." The Ritz's concierge provided him with the address and telephone number of the hotel.

The taxi driver had difficulty finding the Hotel Polinaise. It was stuck down a narrow side street on the northern edge of the city. Reggie noticed many of the businesses had signs in two languages—French and some other. Many had Cyrillic lettering. Must be a neighborhood of eastern European refugees, he thought. He told the taxi driver not to wait.

"*Bonjour*, mate. Be you Krakow?"

The concierge looked puzzled. "*Oui*, Monsieur. *Je suis* Krakow."

"Sorry, mate. Would you be speakin' English, by any chance?"

"*Oui*, Monsieur, *bien sûr*, a little."

"I'm lookin' for a fella called Rakahanga. Would you be knowin' him?"

"*Oui*, Monsieur, I know Monsieur Rakahanga, *mais* he is not here now."

"Right. Does he live here . . . or work here?"

"Monsieur Rakahanga may return in one hour, Monsieur, *peut-être* two."

"Is the bar open?"

"*Bien sûr*, Monsieur, *et pardon*, Monsieur, what is your name?"

"Reggie Pobjoy from Rarotonga . . . Cook Islands. I'll wait in the bar. *Merci*, Monsieur Krakow."

After Reggie went into the bar, the concierge rode the elevator to the fifth floor. He walked up the stairs to the attic and tapped on Émile's door. No response. He knocked. The door opened a crack, and then fully.

"Krakow. *Ça va, mon ami?*" Émile wore only pajama bottoms.

"*Pardon*, Émile. There is a Monsieur Pobjoy . . . Is that correct? . . . waiting in the bar."

"What does he look like?"

"Below average height, quite fit, very brown. Perhaps forty." He shrugged.

"*Ah, tres bien.* That's him. I'll dress and come down. Say nothing to him, *s'il vous plaît.*"

Reggie was sipping a beer when he saw Émile enter the bar. He turned on the stool and stood. They faced each other for a moment before Reggie smiled and extended his hand.

"You're lookin' fine, Jean-Philippe or . . ." He looked at the bartender.

"Jean-Philippe. Thank you, Reggie." They shook hands. "*Un pastis,* Marcel, *s'il vous plaît.*" The bartender moved away to prepare the drink. "Do not worry about him, Reggie. He has no English."

"Well, Jean-Philippe, what brought you back to France . . . and Paris? It was an unexpected pleasure to get your message."

"I've returned, as you would say, to settle an old score. When that is finished, I hope to return to Rakahanga."

"Sounds serious to me, mate. Some danger involved?"

"*Peut-être,* perhaps."

"Well, I sorta figure you're no stranger to that, right?'

"*Oui,* Reggie. But what are you doing during your time here?"

"Glad you be askin', mate. You said in your message you could be of assistance if I needed it."

"*Oui,* that is true, *mon ami.* I have made some contacts here."

"Are you employed, or a man of leisure?"

"I work here in the hotel, but I am free every day until four o'clock, and alternate Sundays. How may I be of a help?"

Reggie told him of his visit to the Louvre and seeing Monet's painting. He took the jeton from his pocket and handed it to Émile.

"I'm most sure this is the same bridge I saw from the window where I was hidden during the war . . . the bridge at Argenteuil."

Émile examined the coin. "This is very old, *non? Oui,* I know this painting." *This is like the painting that hung in the Bistol Béroud.*

"Good . . . or *bien,* as you would say." He took back the jeton. "I've been carryin' this for years. Kinda like a good luck piece. Maybe someday I'll tell you the story of where I came to be havin' it." Reggie finished his beer. "Another?"

"Not for me, Reggie. Thank you, but I must work before long. Tomorrow I am free."

"Well then, mate, perhaps you will accompany me to this Argenteuil place? I can hire a car, or is there a the train? It would be helpful to have someone I can trust who speaks the lingo."

"*Bien sûr,* Reggie. I am at your pleasure. I will ask Krakow, the concierge, to get the train times."

"Right you are, Jean-Philippe. These Paris concierges are a wealth of information." Reggie looked around and lowered his voice even though they were alone in the bar. "You mentioned returning to Rakahanga once you've finished the other business."

"*Oui.* That is my desire, Reggie."

"A bit of good news for you then. The French police are no longer searching for you."

"*Quoi!* How did you learn this?" Reggie repeated what Theo had told him.

"*Mais,* I killed a man . . . a *gendarme.*"

"True right, mate, but no one cares anymore. You're a free man."

Maybe Claude was right. Revenge is not the answer. I no longer have to keep looking over my shoulder.

* * *

The Inn at Argenteuil.

The next morning on the train, Émile told the story about how he came to Paris. Reggie told what he remembered about his help from the *résistance* and his capture. In Argenteuil they walked from the train station to the promenade along the bank of the Seine and compared the image of the bridge on the jeton with the railroad bridge they had just crossed. East of the bridge they found an inn, Hotel Gaultier, that looked as if it had been there since the *fin de siècle.* Reggie looked up at the small window in the attic dormer.

Constance heard the bell ring over the front door. She placed the telephone back in its cradle, wiped her hands on her apron, and walked out into the dining area. Two men stood just inside the door. One looked around like he was trying to remember something or to see something familiar. The other watched her.

"*Bonjour,* Messieurs."

"*Bonjour,* Madame. I'm sorry but I don't speak French, but my friend here— "

"I speak English, Monsieur. You *are* English, *non?*"

"No, Madame. From New Zealand. But I speak a little English." The man smiled and she laughed. The other man didn't speak.

"Would you like a drink, Monsieur, or a room perhaps?" Constance felt uncomfortable. The man who spoke stared at her, moving his head from side-to-side, looking at her hair, her ears. The other looked around the room. She pushed the hair back from her forehead. "Monsieur?"

"I'm terribly sorry, Madame. Didn't mean to be starin'. May I ask a question? Were you here during the war?"

"*Oui,* Monsieur, this is my home. Why do you ask?"

"I think I was here for one night. Back in '41. Be there a small room at the top of the house? And some pigs out back."

"*Oh, oui,* Monsieur." Constance smiled. "Were you English flyers? We had many here."

"It was the bridge."

"*Comment?* The what, Monsieur?"

"That bridge out there across the river. I remember looking out the window and seeing the bridge. You told me to stay away from that window." The man laughed. "I was at the Louvre and saw a painting of that bridge, and asked where it was. Can't be believin' it was that easy."

"Monet's painting, *n'est-ce pas*, Monsieur? Many artists have painted our bridge. Many still come here and paint it. *S'il vous plaît*, Messieurs, sit and have a glass of wine." She pulled out chairs from a table. The older man sat, but the other remained standing. Constance walked behind the bar and returned with a bottle of wine and three glasses. She opened the bottle and poured each glass full to the brim.

"I'm pleased you survived the war, Messieurs. Did you return to England?"

"No, unfortunately. But just a minute. I don't know your name. My friends call me Reggie . . . Reggie Pobjoy. And this talkative fella be Jean-Philippe. He wasn't a flyer . . . just a friend."

"I am Constance Renaud."

Reggie raised his glass, "Cheers, Constance, and thank you for your help." Constance raised her glass.

"*Santé*, Reggie." She took a sip of wine. "You did not go back to England? *Pourquoi pas?* What happened?"

"*Gestapo*. Someone fingered me when I got to Paris. Spent some years in a *stalag* in Germany. Liberated in '45. I've been told that some French criminals helped the Germans for pay to capture flyers. Ever hear of a gangster named Carlo Pioletti?"

Constance almost dropped her glass. "Carlo Pioletti? How do you know this name?"

The other man sat and took a drink of wine.

"You've heard of him, have you not? I can tell by your expression . . . your face."

Constance leaned back in her chair. "*Oui*, Reggie, I know of him. He was . . . is . . . a very bad man. Many good men are dead because of him, including my first love and a dear friend."

"Your first love and a dear friend? Well, stone the crows! I'm most sorry to hear that. Why don't the police arrest him?"

"As you say, he is a gangster, a very powerful man. He . . . how do you say . . . owns many government officials. The authorities can't touch him."

"That's what my friend in the *gendarmerie* said. But there must be some way to get at him."

"Perhaps, Reggie, but he must be very old now . . . and will die soon."

"How was this Pioletti involved in the death of your first love and friend?"

"That, Reggie, is ancient history, but during the war many members of the *Maquis*, you know the *Maquis*—the *résistance, n'est-ce pas?*—were arrested and shot by the *Gestapo*. Many say that Pioletti was paid by the Germans to finger them, as you say, and some flyers."

"I'd like to make him pay for the years I spent behind the barbed wire."

How can I convince him to stay out of it so we can deal with this?

"Reggie, it's best to forget about these things. The war is in the past, and you'll only bring harm to yourself if you get involved. Pioletti has very powerful friends—other gangsters." She drank some wine. "Perhaps he'll be hit by a bus, or have a bad fall. These things happen to older people, *n'est-ce pas?*"

"*Pardon, s'il vous-plaît,* for interrupting." Émile stood. "But I *must* ask how you *both* know this man . . . Pioletti," he demanded.

A bit taken back by this abrupt question, Constance gave a short description of her time as a waitress and the death of her first lover . . . and her friend Marla.

Reggie only knew of Pioletti from Theo's comment. "Why the brouhaha, mate? What's this Pioletti character to you?"

Émile walked to the window, paused for a few minutes while draining his glass, turned and returned to the table.

"Another bottle, *s'il vous plaît,* Madame. This will take some time."

Constance brought another bottle. Reggie leaned back in his chair waiting.

Émile nodded toward Reggie. "I've trusted my life and the future of my family to this man." He leaned forward and touched Constance's hand. "I believe I've heard your story before."

She drew back with a surprised look. "*Non,* not possible. No one knows about that."

"I worked at Bistro Béroud, formerly Bistro Exquis, on rue Jean-Louis at the end of the war. Bring back any memories . . . Pascal, Francine, and the Schleins?"

"*Mon Dieu!* I haven't heard those names in so many years." She poured herself another glass. "Please, more, what happened?"

Over the next hour Émile told his story—all of it, no omissions. Reggie raised an eyebrow or two when Émile described the killing of Andre and Vater, but just nodded and shrugged.

"*Alors,* I am here. And I want to make Pioletti pay."

"Well, mate. I knew you had a rough go of it, but nothing like what you've just told us. I be havin' greater respect for you than I did before, and that was considerable."

"But, Reggie, *mon ami.* I'm a criminal; I killed two men. Killing Pioletti won't make my crimes any less. But I will rid that vermin from society."

"*Stop!* Please. This talk of Pioletti must stop." Constance got up and paced around the room. The two men could tell she was having some kind of internal argument.

She returned to the table reached out and took Émile's hand. "Émile, *mon cher,* what you've been through is worse than we had during the war. You've made many sacrifices for France. Don't throw away your future because of this man . . . this evil man." She raised his hand to her lips and kissed it gently. "I promise you on the graves of my husband and father that Carlo Pioletti was be dealt with . . . soon."

"I'll not be askin' how that'll be happenin'." Reggie said with a smile.

Constance laughed. "Best not to know," she said. Still holding Émile's hand, she kissed it again. "Go back to your island paradise and your family, *mon cher.* That's what's important."

Almost unnoticeable before, the weight of the pistol in his coat pocket felt heavier. Footsteps on the stairs leading to the upper level halted their conversation. They looked up. The man who walked with a cane and carried a small valise stopped at the bottom of the stairs.

"Oh, *pardon*, Constance. I didn't know you had guests," he said in French. "I can return later." He turned to go back up.

"No, please, Klaus. Do come and meet my friends. And speak English, if you don't mind. I don't believe Reggie has any French."

"But, of course, Constance." He walked to the table. Émile and Reggie stood. They shook hands.

"Reggie, Émile, this is Klaus von Reichenhall, from Austria. He too was here during the war and before. This is Reggie Pobjoy from New Zealand, and Émile Plude from Paris . . . the Dordogne, originally."

"Have a seat, Klaus. Most pleased to meet you." Reggie said and pulled out a chair. He pointed to Klaus's leg. "War injury, is it, mate?"

"*Oui* . . . I mean yes. Lost my leg just north of here in 1944." Klaus sat at the table. Constance brought another glass.

"I was shot down in '41 and spent the rest of the war in a *stalag*. Your *Luftwaffe* chaps took decent care of us."

"I'm most glad to hear that . . . Reggie, is it? The American doctors saved my life."

"Too right, mate. What brings you to Argenteuil, if I may be askin'?"

"This . . ." He looked at Constance, who nodded. ". . . valise." He placed it on the table." I left it here with Constance for safe keeping when we retreated from Paris."

"Another hidden treasure story. May tell you mine someday." Émile gave Reggie a puzzled look. Constance went to the kitchen.

Klaus told his story about saving the valise and its contents from being destroyed. "Hemingway became a famous American author—awarded the Noble Prize in literature. Early in his career, while living in Paris, this valise was stolen and never recovered."

"Well, stone the crows! I be hearin' that tale before in the *stalag*. So, this contains the lost Hemingway papers?"

"*Oui* . . . yes. I've examined them carefully, and I'm sure of it."

"*Pardon*, Klaus, Reggie," Émile said, "but I don't understand any of this."

Constance returned with another bottle and a platter of cold cuts, cheese, and bread.

"It'd be like finding a lost Monet, *mon ami*," Reggie said. "The value being over the moon."

"You told me the papers were important but not why," she said. "I read an article—Hemingway's obituary actually—in a newspaper some years ago about this. That's when I realized I had seen these manuscripts before." She told the story about the night Marcel died. "I never knew what happened to them or cared."

No one spoke for a few moments until Reggie broke the silence.

"Plannin' to shop it back to him, are you?" he asked Klaus.

"Unfortunately, he took his own life a few years ago. His papers are now in the possession of his fourth wife."

A commotion on the stairs announced the arrival of Mattie and the children. The youngsters ran to their father. Constance took the breakfast trays from Mattie. Klaus made the introductions, and Mattie shook hands with the two strangers.

"Mattie, *liebchen*, please take the children for a walk by the river," Klaus said in German. The daughter snatched a piece of cheese off the table as her mother herded them out the door. Everyone laughed.

"Nice kids," Reggie said. He turned to Klaus. "Are you speakin' other languages than French, English . . . and German, of course?"

"Yes, Reggie. I'm competent in several. Why do you ask?"

Reggie didn't answer but asked, "What be your plans?"

"Somewhat uncertain at present. If I can find a buyer for the manuscripts, we hope to afford the passage to America or Australia."

Reggie thought for a moment. "What sort of work would you have been doin' in Austria?"

"Teacher. I taught languages and European history at the *collegium* . . . high school, I believe you call it."

"Well, mate. I be havin' a better plan that might be to your likin'."

* * *

Parc du Luxembourg.
Carlo Pioletti maneuvered his wheelchair over to the table where Cleo had placed the afternoon post and saw the stack of letters. He looked at his watch: 2:20. Time to go to the park. "Cleo, is Louis downstairs?"

"*Bien sûr, mon chéri.* As always. You don't need to ask after all these years. He's never late. Ready to go?"

"*Oui.* It's a very calm day. I hope there's a little breeze for the boats."

Louis was waiting outside the door to the apartment and helped Cleo get Carlo's wheelchair in and out of the elevator. As they exited the building a hard-looking young man with a dark complexion opened the door to the Mercedes sedan. Carlo didn't recognize him.

"New man?"

"Charles . . . from Ajaccio," Cleo said, "Done some good things for René. Needed to get out of Marseilles for a while. He'll drive us today."

* * *

Constance and Francoise sat on their usual bench and fed the pigeons.

"Marie, my child, do you think it will rain?" Francoise asked. "It's always best to be prepared, *non?*" She laid a hand on the sleeve of Constance's cheap plastic raincoat. "Your gloves? Are your hands cold?"

"One never knows this time of year, *n'est-ce pas?* It *is* best to be prepared."

"Here he comes again, as usual," Francoise said, nodding to the right.

"Who's that, *ma chére?*" Constance pretended not to notice Carlo being wheeled toward them by his woman.

"That man in the wheelchair . . . every time I'm here. Both a bit overdressed if I say so myself. And that woman. What a floozy, too much makeup and jewelry. But it's nice that she takes him out for a stroll."

A white Citrëon type-H delivery van pulled up alongside Carlo's car, blocking Charles's view to the park. The man in the passenger seat asked him for directions to rue Davout. The van driver glanced toward the park. He disagreed with the directions and questioned Charles's knowledge of the city because of his accent. He got out of the van so Charles could show him the directions on a map.

Carlo tipped his hat, and Cleo nodded to the two women as they passed the bench. "And always polite." Francoise said. Constance put her right hand in a pocket.

A man came out of trees on the left side of the path, ran up behind Cleo, grabbed her handbag, knocked her to ground, and ran off. Constance jumped up from the bench, walked quickly over behind Carlo, and pulled the knife from her raincoat pocket. She grabbed the Corsican by the chin and forced his face up toward hers.

"Remember me? This is for Marcel." She stuck the knife in the right side of his neck and slit his throat like one of her hogs. She dropped the knife and sprinted toward the south end of the park. The blood-splattered gloves she threw among the trees. Her plastic raincoat came off and into a trashcan before she slid into the side door of a waiting car, its engine running.

Epilogue

The first snowfall of the year dusted the mountain foothills when a one-armed man with a foreign accent hand delivered a package to Mary Hemingway at her home in Ketchum, Idaho.

*

Klaus and his family arrived at Auckland on a BOAC flight from New Delhi. He would assume a position as instructor in European languages at Wellington University—a chair endowed by the Southern Cross Trading Company.

*

Reggie, Avarua's new harbormaster, waited at the airfield on Rarotonga. Constance Renaud descended from an Air New Zealand DC-3 to begin her first holiday in forty years.

*

A rusty Taiwanese-flagged trawler dropped anchor outside the reef at Rakahanga. The ship's captain hoped to acquire *bêche-le-mer* and pearl shell before returning to Singapore. A motorized life boat navigated the reef gap and slid onto the beach. Toa, the island's *ariki*, was overwhelmed with joy when he recognized the *Papa'ā* who climbed out of the boat.

fin

Acknowledgments

A conversation in the PawPaw Restaurant on Rarotonga, Cook Islands, in 2006, planted the seed for *The Inn at Argenteuil.* Over morning coffee with our hotel manager, Eileen Dashwood, she asked if I had ever thought about writing a book set in the Cook Islands. While finalizing the work on another novel, I had been mulling over the idea of something about Hemingway's lost manuscripts. I would love to write about the Cooks, but what would be the thread to tie that to anything else?

United Kingdom: I would like to thank the archive staff, William and Mark Napier, and John Larder, of the Yorkshire Air Museum, Elvington, York, for the time spent answering my questions about air gunnery and recommending other readings—a wealth of information.

New Zealand: The Whangarei Returned and Services Association has my special thanks for arranging an interview with George S. Barclay, former Royal New Zealand Air Force flying officer and prisoner-of-war.

Thanks to Keith Gordon of the New Zealand Underwater Heritage Group, Whangarei, for the details of the demise of the *Maréchal Foch.*

Thanks to the staff of the Parua Bay Hotel and Jim Heke, a local fisherman, for their knowledge of the tidal aspects of the bay.

Both the Whangarei Museum and library provided me with useful information, photos, and personal narratives.

Avarua, Cook Islands: Many thanks to the Cook Islands Museum staff, and especially to Florence "Johnny" Frisbie for details about Suwarrow atoll.

Thanks to Eileen Dashwood for putting me in contact with Don Silk, former harbormaster and shipping entrepreneur.

Thanks to Jack Cooper, owner of Trader Jack's, for his hospitality and inspiration.

Thanks to the staff of the Moana Sands Hotel for showing me how to forage on a reef.

Paris: *Shakespeare and Company, A History of the Rag & Bone Shop of the Heart,* edited by Krista Halverson, was an invaluable resource about Sylvia Beach's bookstore.

A heartfelt thanks to Ruth MacGregor, my adopted sister and long-time residence of France, for her editing skills and assistance with the *patois français*.

Portland, Oregon: Thanks to Dave McKay and other members of the Amphibious Forces Memorial Museum for the guided tour and extensive information about LCI (L) 713.

Salem, Oregon: To Genene Valleau, my formatter and editor, for making this mass of scribbling readable.

Never ending gratitude to Barbara, my first reader, editor, soul mate, and wife of forty-three years. An internationally known fiber artist and author, she "takes no prisoners" when reading my work.

About the author

Stephen John Walker was born and raised in Seattle, Washington. As a young man he explored the wharves around Elliott Bay and Lake Union gawking at and sometimes sneaking on board, the multi-masted, derelict lumber schooners awaiting their final voyage to the knacker's yard. He dreamt of running away to the South Pacific or the Caribbean to be a crew member on a copra schooner. Later in life, his work and travels fulfilled those dreams.

A writer of fiction and creative nonfiction, one of his pieces received the Zola Award in the Pacific Northwest Writers Association's literary contest and was selected for inclusion in the association's fiftieth anniversary anthology.

He spent many years living, working, and traveling around the Caribbean's southern rim. His debut novel, Hotel San Blas: A Caribbean Quest, is set in the islands along Panama's north coast.

He now lives and writes just outside of Salem in the hills of western Oregon.

Made in the USA
San Bernardino, CA
27 January 2020